The Mafioso

RENT A CAR

Gary Turcotte

This is a work of fiction. The event and characters describe herein are imaginary and are not intended to refer to specific places or living persons.

ISBN 10: 069232061X

ISBN 13: 9780692320617

Chapter One

Cargo

My name is Matt LePage. I got my first real job when I was 23, at a car rental center; actually my mother knew someone who gave me the job. I only had to mention her name and I was hired. I had a few friends; they were also young. I shared a small apartment with one of them. It worked out great since he worked second shift at a grocery store where he and his girlfriend stocked shelves, so we were rarely at the apartment together.

My job was easy — we took advantage of my easygoing boss, Jim, who we called Jimmy. He was 29, a very sharp dresser, and newly promoted. He hadn't gotten comfortable with the position yet, but he was cool-headed and had a different approach to being boss than the man I worked for in the landscaping company, who was always yelling, rushing, and frustrated with the workday and schedule. The rental center was in Orlando, Florida — a hot spot for tourists. Disney, SeaWorld, Universal, and other theme parks kept us busy, cars coming and going every day.

I'll never forget the day Jimmy asked me to take a car for a wash then check it into inventory. I found the keys in the overnight drop box that went to a Cadillac parked at the corner of the lot. It was common for a car to be dropped after hours; we would bill a credit card for any damages I could find. Some people needed to catch a bus to the airport and couldn't wait for the rent-a-car to open, and we didn't have a spot at the airport.

I was tired and walked slowly with my clipboard, stopping at the front of the car. I took the plate number and followed the checklist sheet. Windshield — OK — headlights and grille — no damage — tires — full of air, no scuffs — fenders hood and doors — no dents, dings, or scratches. I tried the clicker and the doors unlocked, and then the trunk. It lifted and I slowly walked around to see if someone might have forgotten a bag of souvenirs, or a sweatshirt. It was like a treasure hunt.

I looked in and saw a morbid sight, something from a CSI show. I didn't know if it was real. I dropped the clipboard and put my hand on my mouth. I had the key fob in my hand and I accidently pressed the alarm button. The car's lights flashed and the horn beeped. Jimmy was outside putting paper mats in an SUV. The noise got his attention, and I waved for him to come to the car.

He walked over, yelling instructions on which button to push to stop the noise. I wasn't listening, so he grabbed the key fob, and silenced the car. I pointed to the trunk and immediately began throwing up — vomit nearly hit his feet. I caught my breath.

"Is it real?" I asked.

He didn't answer, just turned, held his mouth and pinched his nose with his thumb and forefinger. He waved for Dave to come closer. The stench was thick.

"What do we do?" I asked.

Dave came closer and Jimmy spoke calmly and coolly. "Call the cops; use my office phone so no one can hear you. I don't want to scare anyone. Tell the cops no sirens or lights."

Dave wasn't close enough to see inside the trunk. "What do you want me to tell them?"

Jimmy looked at me. "Tell them we found evidence of a crime in a car trunk, and to send a detective."

"Cool, what did you find?" Dave asked.

"Don't come any closer, just do as I told you," Jimmy said. "Go, call the cops, and hurry."

I looked in the trunk, "I'd like to go home."

"Just stay put, the cops will want to talk to you. All you've touched is the key, right?"

"Yeah."

"Don't touch anything else."

Then Jimmy's phone rang. It was his wife. "Jimmy, I need to stop by and pick up the gas card," she said. "You left the car empty."

"Don't come by."

"Why not? What am I going to do for gas?"

"Use the rolled coins in the console, the coins for tolls, or just stay home. Just don't come by here, it's bad timing."

"What's the problem Jimmy? Is the big boss there?"

"No, we found a body in a car, and the cops will be here in a few minutes. They will be questioning everyone here — do you want to be questioned too?"

"What do you mean you found a body? Like someone dropped dead in a car? They drove there and had a heart attack?"

"No, someone put electrical tie wraps on a guy's wrist and neck and cut this guy's head and hands off, then threw him in the trunk. There's not much blood — I'm not sure if this guy is frozen. It's definitely a murder."

It seemed like only a few minutes had passed when a cruiser pulled into the parking lot with its lights flashing.

"Son of a bitch! I told those asswipes no lights or sirens," said Jimmy as he walked briskly to the officer who was at the glass door.

Gary Turcotte

"Hey," Jimmy yelled and curled his finger, motioning the cop to come to him.

A radio blurted out a question in a distorted voice, and the cop squeezed a black button on the handset pinned to his shoulder. "I'm at location securing the scene."

"Could you turn off the blue lights and move the cruiser? You're blocking the entrance," said Jimmy.

"No one is going anywhere, and you're closed for the day. This is a crime scene until cleared."

"Why? Nothing happened here. There's a body in the car trunk. It didn't happen here," said Jimmy, pointing to the Cadillac.

The cop walked to the car. Its trunk was open. I was ten feet away, and he was walking briskly toward me. His jaw muscle flexed as he clenched his teeth. He was a young cop and he stared me in the eye until he walked past me. I watched his face as he peered into the trunk. His expression changed, and I could see that he wanted to remain firm, but the sight had the power to make the strongest man faint. He put his hand on his forehead and rubbed his hair under the brim of his police cap. The hat moved up and down. The police radio sounded again. It was scrambled, the words distorted. He backed away from the Cadillac before he answered the dispatch.

"Affirmative on the county coroner," he said.

Then he turned to me and said, "I want all these cars opened — all the trunks."

I didn't say anything, I just looked at Jimmy. He shrugged his shoulders and we walked inside the store. Jimmy held his finger in the air. I waited while he opened the cleaning closet and pulled plastic gloves from a box, "Put these on. This cop is young and some slick detective might want to take prints from the key. I'm

4

not touching anything that I don't have to. I suggest you do the same."

"Good idea," I said.

The cop cars began arriving — seven, mostly unmarked. Then a big van and a state trooper car — some cops rode together. The lights were flashing to the point where it was blinding. Jimmy was bothered and upset. I was apprehensive, but excited — I wondered if a hit man was renting a fourth story hotel room across from the scene and was watching every move that was being made.

Two detectives took us in the building and questioned each of us, one by one. Hours passed — a wrecker came and took the Cadillac after the county coroner removed the body from the trunk. The cops took our cell phones, e-mail addresses, and passwords. I felt I had been violated but I was forced to cooperate.

Chapter Two

Happy Hour

Finally we were free to go. The cops gave us back our phones. A news team was out in front of the store. I didn't want to talk to anyone, so I walked by. A reporter stuck a microphone in Jimmy's face and rattled off four fast questions.

"Is it true that a body was found in the back of one of your rental cars? Do you think it was a drug related hit? Are there bodies in other cars? Was any of the staff arrested?"

"I didn't see anything. No one was arrested."

He walked toward me — the camera man and reporter followed. I looked into the square lens and said, "Hi Mom, I'm OK and I'll call you later."

"And who are you, young man?" the reporter asked.

"Ignore him," said Jimmy. Then Jimmy, Dave, Alice, and I walked toward our cars.

"Let's hit happy hour at O'Brian's Tavern. I could sure use a drink. My nerves are shattered," said Dave.

"Good idea," I said. "Jimmy, are you and Alice coming?"

Jimmy looked at his watch, "Yeah I think a drink will be good for me too. I'll buy the first round."

"I'll come along," said Alice.

I didn't know anyone very well — Jimmy kept us separated. I was mostly in the lot, Alice in the office, Dave delivered cars, and

Jimmy oversaw the inventory. Our shifts overlapped. There were two high school kids who worked part time — as well as four other part-time adults.

Alice led us to her car, a silver sedan with pink windshield wipers. I pulled at the door latch, but she was slow with the remote and the latch snapped out of my hand and made a loud noise. The others were patient and waited for her to click the remote a second time. I slid in the back seat next to Dave. He looked out the window. I got the feeling he didn't want to have drinks with the boss. I didn't either, but I was looking forward to a few beers, and a few menthol cigarettes. I like to smoke but most places were smoke free. I rattled my hard pack and opened the top — five cigarettes were all that remained. I took one out and bit on the cotton filter.

I looked up and saw Alice watching me in the rearview mirror.

"Don't even think about lighting one up in this car!" said Alice.

"Why not? You have an ashtray full of butts."

"There are others in the car that don't smoke, so don't light up," she said.

I saw her watch me again. I cupped my hand around the cigarette and held the lighter behind my hand and flicked the roller. It was far away from the cigarette, but Alice was convinced I was defying her orders.

"Don't push your luck, Matt, I'll stop this car and you can walk. Is that what you want? You want to walk? Don't try me," she said.

I laughed, "I was just kidding. No need to get huffy."

Dave tapped my knee with his closed fist; then he leaned close to my ear. "Can I bum a cigarette from you?"

"I didn't know you smoke," I said as I passed him the one that I was holding.

"Once I have a few drinks I like to light up. That's another reason I shouldn't drink."

Jimmy was quiet. He looked out the window at the Holiday Inn as we passed. I wondered if he dreamed of managing a big hotel. They were being erected on every corner. Then I imagined that maybe someday I might be his second in command. I didn't want to be the big boss. I would like to have some authority — respect — but I didn't like stress and responsibility. I liked to sleep at night, not turn over and over holding my stomach with knots and heartburn.

We passed a perfect parking spot; Alice slowed and then drove by it.

"What are you doing?" I asked.

"That's parallel parking — the spot is too small. I can't do it."

"Pull over and let Matt park the car. He parks cars all day," said Jimmy.

Alice pulled over and got out of the car and walked to the sidewalk. I quickly got in the front seat and checked the mirrors and the spun the car into the tight spot. "Fits like a glove," I said with a big smile.

Jimmy slapped my shoulder. "I couldn't have done better myself."

Dave was quick to get out of the car, Jimmy paid the meter, and Alice smoked a cigarette as she walked towards the bar.

Dave walked beside Alice. "Hey can I bum a cigarette? I like to smoke when I drink," he said.

"You just bummed one from Matt — I saw you," she said.

"Yeah, but he smokes menthol, that's a chick's cigarette. I like Marlboros and that's what you have."

"Oh, lucky me. Why don't you just buy a pack? They sell them next door," she said, pointing to a CVS drug store.

"I don't want to do that. If I buy a pack I'll smoke a pack and I'll have trouble kicking the habit again. Just give me one, I won't bug you again."

She reached into her small pocketbook and pulled one from the pack. The one she smoked was between her lips and a line of smoke went up her cheek into her eye. She squinted as she handed him the cigarette, then with her free hand she took hers from her lips and blew smoke near his face.

"You need to get some willpower," she said.

"Why do you say that? You smoke."

"I smoke because I want to smoke, not because I need to."

I followed them into the bar and we picked a booth near a window. Alice looked at the drink menu and pointed at fruity mixes. Jimmy was preoccupied and stared out the tinted window.

Dave tapped his fingers on the table, drumming to the song that played in the background. I could see that it annoyed Alice.

The waitress came to the table. "Not a second too soon," Alice said. "I'll have an apple martini, and a plate of nachos. I'm starved."

Dave didn't stop drumming. "Hey, Ringo Starr, what are you drinking?" the waitress asked as she touched his hand. She was dressed in black slacks that fit her form, and a tight, low-cut shirt. Dave thought she liked him and his drumming. She smiled with a mouthful of white teeth and red lipstick. Alice's eyes went up and down her body.

"I'll just have a pitcher of Budweiser," said Dave.

"You bet," she said as she turned to me.

I ordered one draft, and Jimmy did the same. I didn't want to get too buzzed in front of my boss. Dave didn't seem to care. The waitress walked off, and we sat and stared at each other.

It was awkward. I felt like I should open a conversation, but I hesitated and Dave took the lead.

"What do you figure happened to the guy in the trunk?"

"He was obviously murdered," said Alice.

"I'll bet he was a stock broker who screwed over his clients and he messed with the wrong guy. That's what I think," said Dave.

"Who knows? Maybe he was messing around with someone's wife and got caught," I said.

"What do you think, Jimmy?" Alice asked.

"I'm not good at figuring out what's happening in other people's lives," he said without taking his eyes from the tinted window.

"I'm pretty good at it," said Dave. "You see that waitress? I'll bet she's a single mom that got knocked up in high school — she got an abortion. And then a year later she got knocked up again and kept the kid. She picks up guys and they use her and that's why she flirts but she's cautious."

She approached with the drinks. I watched her carry the round tray by her ear. I wondered how she balanced the pitcher of beer and the other drinks on her small hand without dropping them. I found it difficult to carry my morning coffee without spilling it on my hand. She gracefully spun the tray from her shoulder to the table without an incident. Dave already had his hand on the handle of the pitcher. She slid Alice her drink and pushed the beers in front of Jimmy and me.

She took the pitcher and filled Dave's glass to the rim.

"Thanks," he said.

She winked at him. "The nachos will be right out. Is there anything else I can get you?"

I shook my head.

As she walked off, Dave stared at her backside. "See what I'm saying? She wants the bad boys."

Alice rolled her eyes. "Do you figure she see you as a bad boy?"

That was when I noticed that Alice answered most of her questions with a question. She had a flare of sarcasm in her delivery.

"I think so — with this day-old beard, and my tattoo, she gets warm," he said.

"What do you mean by that?" asked Alice.

"I heat her up, she's almost uneasy around me — I can sense it. It's animal magnetism."

"She just wants a tip; you're no different from any other guy that comes through that door. She planted a seed and your imagination runs wild, especially when a guy has a few drinks," said Jimmy. "My sister used to bartend at a club. She had regulars, mostly drunks who would spend all their spare money at happy hour. She led them on and made really good money. I used to sit at a table and watch her work. Some of the guys were so far out of their league they made fools of themselves."

"How did you feel about that?" asked Alice. "Did you meet your wife in a bar?"

"No, I ran into my high school history teacher, we talked for a while and got caught up. She was his daughter, and he set us up. She'd never date a guy who hangs out in bars. My sister only worked there because she was pulling in three hundred bucks a night — not bad for five hours of work."

"Damn, I should do that job," said Dave.

"What makes you think you'd make any money? You're a guy — most tips come from guys; drunk guys who think with their penises," said Alice.

"She's right," said Jimmy.

"Thanks for the confidence booster, Alice. I was going to buy you a drink, but I don't want you to get the wrong idea," said Dave.

"What makes you think I need you to buy me anything? I've got my own money and I can take care of myself. I don't need a man, and I don't need to lead one on for a lousy drink or smoke," she said.

"Oh I get it — I owe you for a cigarette. I'll get your next drink, it's settled," said Dave.

"Do you think I want to get caught drunk driving? I can't have another martini."

"Why did you come out with us, if you're going to be a wet towel? Have another drink and if you get loaded I'll get us all a cab. It's not every day you find a dead body in a car — so lighten up — let's get by this," said Dave.

Chapter Three

One Too Many

Dave ordered another pitcher of beer; he talked loudly and slurred his words. I had a second beer and so did Jimmy. Alice finished her second martini. Her nachos arrived and she was focused on them. She had a vacant look in her eyes. I watched her, but I was careful not to get caught staring. I felt awkward; it seemed like no one wanted to know anything about me. I wasn't the type to talk about myself, but I figured someone might ask basic questions about my family or schooling.

Jimmy sat and stared at his phone. His wife was texting him constantly. Dave went to the restroom and the waitress came to see if we wanted another round. Before she got to the table Alice said, "Do you guys want to see if Dave's right?"

"About what?" I asked.

Before she could answer the waitress was at the table.

"My friend Dave thinks you might be interested in dating him, since you're so friendly. Are you interested?" Alice asked her.

The waitress laughed and touched her chest just below her neck, "I'm nice to everyone. I hope he understands. I have a boyfriend. As a matter of fact, he's the bartender, right over there," she said pointing to a tall guy behind the bar — he waved.

Jimmy looked up from his phone and nodded several times, with a smirk on his face. Alice laughed into her hand.

"No harm done, Dave thinks all the women want him," I said. "Dave is the other guy; he's in the men's room."

I didn't want her thinking Alice was talking about me or Jimmy.

"Are you all set on drinks, or would you like another round?" she said as she grabbed the empty pitcher.

We looked at each other and Jimmy answered for us. "We're all set, put it on my card," he said as he handed her a debit card.

When Dave returned we were standing and pushing our chairs under the table.

"What's up? Are we out of here?"

"I have to get home, but you guys can do whatever you want," said Jimmy.

"One of you guys is going to have to drive my car; I shouldn't have had a second martini."

"I'm staying here. That waitress is melting in my hand," said Dave.

"I'm OK to drive," I said as we walked out, leaving Dave behind. Jimmy texted as we walked. The car was close by and we got in. I took the key from Alice and started the engine, then adjusted the seat and mirrors.

"Did I ask you to rearrange the car?"

"No, is it a problem?"

"It takes me a while to get that seat set where I like it — just forget it. How were you supposed to know?"

Jimmy sat in the back watching the small screen on his phone; it lit his face in the dark car. I edged the car from its parking spot. The last thing I wanted was a fender bender while I had beer on my breath. Alice was turned in her seat. Her hip was nearly against the dashboard as she watched the traffic whiz by the front fender. "Go after this car passes, you can make it."

I didn't look; I just floored the gas when the car went by. Once on the road everyone was quiet — we were tense from the day's events. A good night's sleep wasn't going to fix anything. I wondered if Jimmy would quit the job. Then I wondered if I should quit. Jobs were scarce but I didn't want stress. We arrived at the parking lot; I pulled up beside Jimmy's car — his wife had been waiting. He got out of Alice's car and took the passenger seat of his car. I could see his wife's knuckles on the steering wheel, but I couldn't see her face. I was curious to see what she looked like. I knew he didn't want to sit in the passenger seat, and not be the boss of his own car, but he was bigger than that and too smart to drink and drive. I wondered if my two beers would get me an OUI.

I parked the car next to mine and pulled the handle to get out. Alice got out too.

"What's up?" I asked.

"I'll leave my car here; you'll have to drive me home. I can't drive."

I unlocked the car and we got in. It was quiet for a few minutes then she started asking questions.

"Where did you work before this place?"

"Landscaping," she laughed, "I can top that. Me and my boyfriend couldn't get jobs. We were desperate. We were guinea pigs for a pharmaceutical company."

"What's that mean?"

"What do you think it means?" We took God knows what, and stayed in a room for eight to ten hours being observed. I got so screwed up and I didn't even know what drugs I was on. They kept it secret so the companies couldn't be sued. That was the craziest time of my life."

"How long did you do that?"

"How long do you think? Until they were afraid they were killing both of us. I think about a year. But why would you care?"

I didn't get a chance to answer. She asked questions that I couldn't answer, or ones that didn't require an answer.

"Do you know what it's like to be used as a science experiment?"

"No, of course not."

"Are you making fun of me?"

I didn't answer.

"I used to be able to drink and smoke pot before they ruined me. I'm sketched out easy and paranoid most of the time. I wish I could sue those bastards. Does it seem like I'm messed up? Not right now, but at work," she said.

"I don't know you well enough to tell the difference. What do your friends think?"

"What do you think they think? They don't say anything, but that doesn't mean they don't think it."

"Who cares what everyone thinks. I don't," I said.

"I don't really care either, but do me a favor and don't tell anyone what I just told you. I don't want everyone thinking I'm a whack job."

She looked out the side window with a blank stare. Then she turned slowly to look me in the eye.

"Do you have a secret that you can tell me? I told you mine, so tell me yours."

I was quiet for a few minutes. I thought about making up a lie. I was uncomfortable. I looked straight out the windshield, but I could feel her eyes at my temple. "I stayed back in first grade."

"That's not a good secret. You must have a better one than that."

"Okay, I was at a party a few years ago and I had to go to the bathroom, I'm talking number two. My friend drove us there and he was a dick. He wouldn't take me to a gas station, so I had to go behind some bushes on the side yard. That ass followed me and took a picture of me and my pile. How's that for a secret?"

"That's not a very good friend. Why didn't you just use their bathroom?"

"They only had one bathroom and it was right off the kitchen. The kitchen was full of good looking girls, so it was out of the question. I needed to leave and my friend wouldn't leave."

She was quiet and turned her head and looked into the dark night. "You need to turn up here on the right — the house with all the lights on," she said. "Can you do me a favor? Can you forget about what I told you?"

I stopped in front of her house. "Can you forget about everything I told you?"

She laughed, covered her mouth and nose and shook her head, no. Then she opened the car door and walked up the stairs to the front door. I waited until she unlocked the door and disappeared inside.

Chapter Four

Tight lips

The following days at work I barely talked with Alice. Jimmy was on the phone more than usual since the incident with the dead body. Dave was busy cleaning cars and putting gas in them. He worked without supervision. I checked cars in and out. I took the original write-up sheet from when a car went out and gave the car to Dave. Once Dave cleaned it I made a new sheet on the car and then compared the two sheets. If I found more damage or new damage, I made a report to Jimmy so he had final say on whether to charge the last driver's credit card. I was a quality control inspector — the last eye on the job before the car went back into service.

The next car to be checked in was a Ford Fusion, nothing special; it was silver and we rented ten of them a day. I noticed the rear door panel was loose at the bottom. I opened the door and felt the panel. I could feel the plastic clip with my finger. It was like a tack with barbs. I lined the point up with the hole and thumped it with my palm. It seemed odd that over a two month period I had found similar loose panels on four other cars that I had checked in.

Then Dave pulled around the corner of the lot in a mustang convertible. He nearly locked up the brakes — then rammed the car in reverse and put it in a tight space between two minivans. He saw me and waved. I raised my hand and flagged him to come to me. He walked briskly, causing his blue cleaning rag to fall from his back pocket. He knelt, picked it up and looked back at me. I had opened the door again and ran my hand down the bottom of the door panel to make sure it stayed fastened. He looked puzzled.

"What's going on?" he asked.

"I keep getting cars that have loose panels. What do you make of that? I've been fixing them myself, so I hadn't written them up, but if I get one more I'm going to tell Jimmy about it."

He felt the bottom of the door and pulled at the panel. Then he touched my elbow. "Don't write them up and don't tell Jimmy."

"Why not; what do you care?"

"Can you keep a secret?"

"Of course."

"About six months ago I noticed that the right rear door panel was unfastened on a Cadillac. I tried to snap it back on, but I broke the little clip. I felt my hand inside and I found a stash of cocaine. I took some of it and then put it back in the door. About twice a week I find the same thing on different cars. I watch for the same six or seven people who rent the cars. Some have money, some have drugs. I took some of the money last month, but I was afraid it might be counterfeit. This Ford has a load of cash in that door panel."

"So someone is smuggling with these cars?"

"Yeah, and they have been for a long time," he said as he crouched down and popped the bottom loose. He lay on the tar and reached inside the door and pulled out a stack of bills, all hundreds. He pulled one from the band and handed it to me. "Take it; it's for you."

I looked around the lot. We were two hundred feet from the main building, but I felt like someone could see what we were doing. I looked at the bill, to see if it looked counterfeit, but it looked perfect.

"Take it, they won't miss one. Trust me I've taken a stack of them," he said.

I thought for a few minutes. "How long ago did you take the stack of hundreds?"

"Maybe a month ago, I don't know maybe three weeks, why?"

"This is either the mob doing this or a gang, maybe a Latino gang. I'll bet they thought one of their own stole the money, and that's why we found that guy in the trunk. Oh my God! You got that guy killed. They thought it was him double crossing them. How much have you taken since then?"

"I don't know? I took a few hundred each time and if there was coke I took a few grams. No more than five grams. Have you been watching who rents the cars?"

"No, that's not my department. I don't really want to know."

"Don't you think we should tell the cops? This could be huge," I said.

"Are you stupid? Once you snitch on these guys you'll be killed. Maybe not you, but your family. Is that what you want?"

"Then why are you taking the money?" I asked.

"It's just a little bit. They won't notice, and who cares if some dirt-bag gets his ass kicked for pinching a little off the top. They won't kill each other for a few grams of coke or a couple hundred bucks. Don't worry about it, we can split the score. You get every other car. We're the only two who know. They need to pay a toll; it's the cost of doing business."

"I don't understand why there would be money in the doors. I can understand the drugs. This bill has to be a fake. It has to be. I've seen drug deals in the movies and there's always a suitcase full of money. One guy trades the drugs for the suitcase."

"Who cares, all I know is it's nice to get an extra three or four hundred a week for doing nothing. The coke is uncut and I sold half and did the other half. This time I'm going to cut it and double my money. You should do the same."

"I'm not sure I want to be involved," I said.

"It's too late, we're all involved. Like you said, there are gangsters watching our every move. We don't know who they are but they know who we are. As long as we make small hits it'll go on forever. Trust me there's honor among thieves. They're all pinching too, they'll just have to back down what they take or add a little more cut into the final product."

"What about the money though? You don't think they will miss hundred dollar bills?"

"Not a few, nothing under five hundred. Let's face it, you're probably right. This money is most likely fake and really isn't worth anything, so what are they really out then? Nothing, right? It's just paper," he said.

"It's the point; those types of guys don't like getting stolen from. That's the bottom line, and what if we get caught passing counterfeit money?"

"We won't; I use them to fill up my car, I haven't had any problem. Some of them we can trade in the register here. Then the company gets stuck with the funny money. I can get in the register can't you?"

"Yeah, but there's a camera on the register," I said.

"I know but I'll buy a candy bar or I'll get a drink and when I open the register to pay, I slide the hundred from inside my sleeve to the register tray. I put the bill under the tray and take a real hundred that's stored under there. Lately I've just bought something small like a map and paid with the hundred and took the change. As long as the drawer comes out balanced Jimmy can't say shit. Besides, we don't even know if the money is fake."

"It's either fake or someone is laundering money somehow. I don't feel good about it."

"Well what are you going to do? Are you going to reap the benefits or are you going to the cops and let the gang, or mob know you broke up their multimillion dollar drug ring? Trust me; they'll be looking for you."

"I don't know what to do," I said.

"Take your cut, even if you just put the money in your mattress, and once this blows over you might have enough to buy a new car. We're partners, we need each other. I'll take care of everything, don't worry."

"The other thing is that I don't want to sell drugs and I don't do coke or want to start another bad habit. I do like money though," I said.

"If the load is coke, I'll cut it and sell it and pay you for what I take. Like I said, I'll take care of everything, don't worry. All you have to do is keep quiet and check the cars in like normal, and don't write any reports that would call any attention to what's going on. Can you do that?"

"I guess so," I said as I slipped the one hundred dollar bill in my pocket.

"If it makes you feel better, one of the cars had both back door panels full of fifties and twenties. They pass off like nothing."

"I feel better about fake twenties."

"Remember, stay tight lipped," he said as he put his index finger across his lips. Then he walked off.

I felt the bottom of the door panel and made sure the clip was snapped. I checked the car in — no damage.

Chapter Five

Shady Characters

Inside the store, Alice had two customers. They were together — one guy was bald, fat, and wore a derby style hat. The other was younger. He looked like he could be related to the bald man. He was shorter and thinner, but his nose and chin were defined like the older man. He scratched his head and I noticed his hair was already receding.

I was suspicious when they asked for a Ford Fusion, and they insisted on silver. We had two silver ones but one was being rented. I was holding the final check sheet and the clipboard that cleared the second one. Alice smiled and handed the big man the keys and then she looked at the short man and said, "Is it a problem if I give you a black Fusion? I don't have a silver one available."

The big man walked toward the door. He put his hand on the handle, but stopped and turned to Alice. "Yes you do, I saw two silver ones when I got dropped off. It's out in the back lot. I can see it from here."

"One is rented and on the way to the airport and the other may have a problem with it. I don't have the check-in sheet," she said, going to the spot where the clipboard normally hung. "Will a black one do?" she said in an annoyed voice. "What's wrong with a black one?"

"No it won't do! A black car gets too hot and I want a silver one," said the short man.

"I have a white one, how's that?"

"I can see the friggin thing right there," the fat man said pointing out the glass door. "What can be wrong with it? It's a new car."

"Yeah, he's right, find out why we can't have that car. I'll wait!" the short man said.

Alice looked at me, "What's the status on the silver Fusion?"

"I have the clipboard in my hand. It just needs a little windshield wiper fluid, other than that it's all set," I said.

"Great, we'll take it," the short guy said. And don't worry about the fluid. We're in a hurry, so can we pick up the pace?"

"Matt would you get the silver Fusion # 332157 and bring it to the side of the building?" Alice said. Jimmy had been in the back room and was listening through the partially open door. He opened the door holding a bottle of windshield fluid. It was half full, and he shook it until I looked at him. "Top off the fluids for our fine customers, while I write them up," Jimmy said as he stood behind Alice and waited for her to move from the counter. The fat guy pulled his dark sunglasses down enough to show his eyes to Jimmy.

"How have you been, Jimmy?"

"Good, Pauly."

He turned and slid his glasses back up his nose. "We're late for a meeting — can we get that car?"

Jimmy had a serious look on his face. He looked at me — I nodded and took the fluid and handed him the check-in sheet.

"Alice, can you go in the storage room and get some paper mats and an air freshener?"

I walked out and went to the car. It seemed like Jimmy wanted to be alone with the two guys. I turned slowly and saw them laugh and then Pauly shook Jimmy's hand. I knew something was going on and I was nervous about the money that Dave and I had taken from the Fusion. These were bad guys.

Cars were parked in perfect rows and walking between them like in a maze got me to the Fusion. I pressed the key fob and the tail lights flashed. I opened the car door, popped the hood, opened the black cap to the wiper fluid, filled it, and then slammed the hood. A lump came up to my throat as I got inside and looked to the back door panels. I knew it was only a matter of an hour before they would be removed and Pauly would count the money. An image of an angry, crunched up, Italian face came into my mind. My stomach stirred as I pulled up to the glass storefront. All three were waiting for me, Jimmy had the paper mats and the air fresheners and as soon as I put the car in park he opened the passenger door and slid the mat in place and then handed me the other one for the driver's side. I tucked them under the pedals and he placed the air freshener around the rearview mirror.

"Thanks Jimmy," Pauly said as he slid into the driver's seat.

"Enjoy," Jimmy said.

I walked into the store and got out of view. I walked to the board and looked for the next check-in sheet. I noticed the sheet for the silver fusion, which the carbon copy was missing. Normally I signed them and put them in the file for the car. I figured Jimmy must have taken care of it, but to be sure I opened the file cabinet and pulled the folder. The carbon was missing. I went in Jimmy's office and the front copy was not on his desk. The shredder has fresh strips in the waste paper basket. The only active file on the Fusion was on the previous renter, it looked like they still had the car out. Something was fishy.

"What are you looking for?" asked Alice.

"The Fusion check-in sheet, I just wanted to check the box saying that I filled the wiper fluid, but the sheet went missing."

She put her arms out with her palms raised. "Do I look like I have the sheet? Where did you leave it? Did you leave it in the car?"

She had me wondering if I did leave it in the car, but I normally carried the clipboard, and the clipboard was where it belonged. It didn't make any sense.

The car drove off. Jimmy stood outside and lit a cigarette. He took a long drag and let half the smoke leave his nostrils. He was lanky. His shadow looked twenty feet tall against the side of the building. His sleeves were rolled to the elbows and his hair was parted at the side and a few strands hung across his dark sunglasses. I tried to walk by him. Jimmy didn't care; he was a calm, cool person. He even had a relaxed stance. I wanted to breathe in his coolness just like he breathed in the cigarette smoke.

"Matt why don't you see what is keeping Dave with the check-ins. I gave him three this morning. He's only done one."

"I have two on the clipboard," I said.

"Those two are from yesterday, John cleaned them."

John was a high school kid who cleaned cars after school. We had two part timers. John and Darcy, who did mostly office work, but Alice always checked whatever she did and found fault with it.

I walked to the small building where Dave cleaned the cars, both bay doors were closed. It was a nice day and most guys would have chosen to keep the door open. I had a good idea why they were shut, and I also knew why Dave was falling behind in the detail work. I knew when Jimmy asked me to check on Dave he also meant I should give him some help to get the cars back in rotation. I opened the side door quietly, but Dave was startled when he saw the daylight race across the garage floor.

"Is it just you?" he asked.

"Yeah, Jimmy wants you to get the cars done. He sent me to help you."

"Is that what he said?"

"You know him, he doesn't really say what he wants, but has a way of getting his point across."

"Yeah, he's not too direct. I'm not sure I like that."

"What's the holdup?" I asked. There was a car in each bay and two more parked beside the building.

"First of all I'm just one person, and second is that these two cars have a stash. I just got the door panels back on this one. I thought you were Jimmy and I nearly shit my pants," Dave said.

"Really? Was it money or drugs?"

"Money. Don't worry I set some aside for you. Today is going to be a good payday."

"I saw the guys that rented the Fusion, and they looked like trouble. Why don't you let me take these two cars to their spots and just clean the two waiting? Let's not press our luck."

Dave shrugged his shoulders and threw me the keys to one of the cars. He pressed the wall button and both garage doors opened. He got in one car and I got in the other and we parked them in the "done" section. I started to walk back to the garage with him.

"Where are you going?"

"I was going to help you," I said.

"I'm all set. Get the check-in sheets on those two and stock them in."

I knew he didn't want my help, and I knew he would take the other two cars apart. He was greedy, and if I hadn't found the loose door panel on the Fusion, he would have kept the secret to himself. I wondered how much money he really stole and how long it would be before he would get caught.

Chapter Six

Johnny The Bump

I did as Dave had suggested and as I walked back to the sales office I heard the two garage doors closing. I knew he wouldn't listen and he was stripping the next two cars. I went into the office to hang the check-in sheets on their hooks, but Jimmy took them from my hand. He had the wireless phone on his ear and he took the clipboards into his office and closed the door. I acted like I was getting a snack from the vending machine. I heard the shredder start and then he laughed at whoever he was talking to on the phone.

Alice was at the front counter, she looked up from the car computer log.

"Hey is the maroon Cadillac #224761, ready? That one and the dark blue Buick Lacrosse # 515564?"

"They should be ready in a half hour or so, Dave has them in the bay."

"Shouldn't they be done by now?" she asked.

"I guess, but what's the big rush? I know there are at least two more black Caddys and one more blue Buick."

"The customers are asking for specific cars, and since when do you care?"

"I don't."

"Why don't you make a pot of coffee, if you can't find anything to do? You do know how to make a pot, don't you?" said Alice.

I didn't like her tone but I knew she was right. I took the pot to the small bar sink and rinsed it. Jimmy came from the office, "Hey Matt, could you bring the two cars that you just checked in up to the front. We have a group coming to rent six cars."

"Sure, as soon as I finish making this pot of coffee."

"Never mind that — Alice can put that pot on, and as a matter of fact, she can go to Dunkin Donuts and get three dozen donuts. I'll take care of the paperwork."

Jimmy handed me a piece of post-it paper with the six cars' stock numbers. I took the keys from the key drawer and walked to the first car. I adjusted the seat and watched the store front through the windshield. The two guys in the silver Fusion were back and another car was behind them. Alice had just left in a compact car, and Jimmy waited at the counter. I was hesitant as I pulled the car up to the side of the building. I didn't make eye contact with anyone. I left the car running with the air conditioner set on low and adjusted the seat in a medium position. I didn't want one of those guys to bump their head as they got in the car.

I walked to the next car and by the time I got back the first car was gone. I dropped all the cars that were done to the side of the building. Pauly was inside with Jimmy and they looked like they were having a serious conversation. The other guys stayed in the car until Pauly waved his finger for them to take the car and drive away. I prayed that Dave would have the other cars done and to my relief one bay door opened and he moved a car out and then closed the door. I walked to the car and hoped the other car would be ready, but I knew he didn't know about the rush. I prayed the car was for a different customer. I did as I was told and pulled the fifth car to the building.

This time one guy was waiting and he didn't get in the car. He was big and thick. His hand, neck and shoulders, and even his greasy black hair was thick. Yet his teeth were small, like baby teeth, like they had been filed, each perfectly even with the one next to it. His ears and nose looked like he had been in many fights. He wasn't a pretty man. "Let's take a step inside Sonny," he said.

I was uneasy, but I walked into the store where Pauly and Jimmy were. It was quiet, the man started talking before he was completely through the door. "What does Sonny do here? What's his job?" asked the big man.

"I'm not Sonny, I'm Matt."

"No, I called you Sonny because your mom thinks you're so bright. My name is not Johnny the Bump, but that's what they call me. Now what does Sonny do here?" He looked at Jimmy.

"He looks at the cars for damage, checks the fuel and washer fluid."

"That's it? He don't take them for gas, or wash the cars?" asked Pauly.

"We have an automatic car wash on site, and most people bring the cars back full, since we charge a dollar a gallon over market price."

"I see. Who works in the garage, the one with the doors closed?" asked Pauly.

"That would be Dave, he recons the cars, vacuums, adds air to the tires, checks the spare, and runs them through the car wash," said Jimmy.

"Why don't you take the Fusion, the one we are returning to him, Johnny? Make sure you show him our appreciation for doing such a good job. He did an extra good job on cleaning that one out," Pauly said with a wink.

A sly smile came across Johnny's face, his dark eyes closed to only a slit. A shiver went down my spine and I felt the small hairs rise on my neck. I wanted to warn Dave but there was no way I could save his ass. I wondered if they would kill him and I hoped he wouldn't turn me in with his last breath.

"I can bring him the car and tell him you are pleased with his job," I said before I realized I had spoken.

"No, Johnny will make sure he gets what he has coming. Some people need to get thanked in person — one on one kinda thing. Right, Jimmy?" Pauly said.

"Whatever you say Pauly, You're the boss."

"Don't you forget it Jimmy. I'm fair though, tell Sonny I'm fair," he said.

Jimmy put his hands in his pockets and nodded.

Then the words I dreaded most: "Why don't you take Sonny with you, show him what you do to John."

Johnny smiled again and said, "Come with me Sonny, you're going to love this."

Johnny looked like a big version of Robert De Niro, he was about forty years old and slightly overweight. He looked very serious and didn't smile. He curled his finger and I followed him to the car. I got in and a second later we were at the garage. He opened the car door and waited for me to get out. I pointed to the large sign that said "authorized personnel only." He pushed my shoulder and made me enter the garage first. Dave popped his head up for a second. Johnny held the door open and didn't enter right away, Dave didn't see Johnny. He was in the backseat; the door panel was on the bench. He was caught red-handed.

Johnny held my shoulder and then slowly came around the car. He grabbed the door and slammed it on Dave with all of his massive body. It was like a lineman for a pro football team making a game-saving tackle. Dave's arm and shoulders were completely inside the car only his ribs and waist were on the outside. Johnny opened the door and again he gave a full body thrust onto the door, and Dave's body. I wondered if he broke Dave's spine. Johnny was not concerned. He grabbed Dave's leg, which was almost lifeless and dragged him across the floor.

I was scared Johnny was going to ask him if anyone else was involved, but there was no way Dave would be able to talk — he could barely breathe. Then Johnny picked Dave up. It wasn't much of a feat for the big man since Dave only weighed about 150 pounds. Johnny held him over his head and then threw him against the wall, knocking the clock down as well as a poster of a topless woman on a tool calendar. Dave landed on the bench, and curled into a fetal position.

"Where's the boss's money? You can't tell me you don't have it, the door panel is off the car, I'd kill you right here if it weren't for the fact that someone was found dead here last month. You've got two seconds to save your life. Where's the fucking money?"

Dave felt around the bench and pushed his keys on the floor.

"Get that key Sonny."

"I rushed by him and took the key, "it's a padlock key."

"No shit," he said.

Dave pointed to the locker, and then he held his chest.

"He's hurt pretty bad."

"No he's not, he looks fine," Johnny said as he looked at Dave. Dave looked at the floor and didn't dare look Johnny in the eye.

Johnny closed his big fist and I think we all knew what was coming. Dave was too weak to pull his arms from his chest and Johnny began throwing punches in his face. Dave's face rocked back at each buffet and Johnny didn't stop until his fists were red with blood. Dave's eyes were swollen shut, his lips split and his nose folded over. I tried to keep my eyes inside the locker; it was full of money and drugs. Dave was not happy skimming a small amount like he had said. He had been greedy.

"Sonny, go grab that box, put the money in it and throw it in the trunk, and get the door panel too."

I did what he told me to do; I noticed that Dave was out cold, or pretending to be. I thought I was desensitized from TV violence and special effects in movies, — but there was nothing like seeing a real beating. I was just glad I wasn't getting pounded by the big thug.

"Open the garage door. And one more thing: I want you to search this shop high and low. A rat like this usually has more than one stash. One's for drugs, one's for cash. When I come back I want the remaining shit. Are we clear Sonny? I don't care if you have to cut his fingers off. I want the stash."

Johnny washed his knuckles in the wash basin and once they were dry he wiped his fingers through his hair and looked at himself in the mirror. He had just beaten a kid who was young enough to be his son. Things like that didn't bother guys like Johnny. He got in the car and backed out.

I wet a shop rag in cold water and gave it to Dave to put on his face. He was coming around. He moaned and wiggled his front tooth. One was missing and the others were covered in blood. He wheezed, and I knew he wanted to talk, but before he could utter a word I began.

"Look before you waste your breath, he may be right outside, so let's keep this simple. He knows there's a second stash. I hope for your sake you have it here."

I pulled out my wallet and took out all the money he had given me. I was too afraid to spend it anyway since I was sure it was counterfeit. I held it in front of his face. Where did you hide the drugs?"

He pointed to the bathroom. I went inside the small room and opened anything that opened. Then I looked up and stood on the toilet, moved the ceiling tile and sure enough that's where he had stashed money, cocaine, and baggies of heroin.

"You stupid asshole, what were you thinking? You got that guy killed, I hope you know that. This is all you. How can one person be so stupid? And then you had the balls to try to put this filth on me. You are a sneaky piece of shit."

I felt like pounding him in the face. I was full of anxiety, mostly fear for what was next. I was so mad that I took a shovel that was leaning against the bench and pounded it against the bench, close to Dave's head. I couldn't help from screaming. "You better not be holding out! You're lucky I don't kill you for this shit!" I slammed the shovel a few more times until my face was beet red and my arms were sore.

I turned around and behind me stood Johnny. "That's really good kid, did he give up more stash?"

I pointed to the cash and drugs in the bathroom, some in the sink and some on the toilet tank and then I reached into Dave's back pocket and took out his wallet. Johnny opened it and it was full of one hundred dollar bills.

"You did good kid, open the door. I need to bring the car inside."

I pushed the button. The door squeaked as it rose and as soon as the hood of the car cleared the door, Pauly drove in. The trunk popped and Pauly stepped out of the car. He chewed an unlit cigar and he rolled it between his teeth.

"Sonny here found a second stash, about twenty grand and fifty grand worth of coke."

Pauly looked at me with sweat running down my temples. My red face, and messy hair, the shovel still in my hand and Dave's wallet in Johnny's hand. It looked like we had robbed Dave.

"Put everything in the back seat," he said as the back door opened and another guy got out of the car. It was the guy who looked like Pauly's son. He helped put everything in the back seat. I wondered why the trunk was open — and then Johnny and the other guy forced Dave to get in.

"Wait," I said.

"For what?" asked Pauly.

"He'll bleed all over the trunk," I said, as I pulled out a sheet of plastic.

They lifted Dave out of the car and put the plastic around him and then put him back in.

"Thanks kid," Pauly said as he handed me a small stack of hundred dollar bills. I take care of my friends. My friends call me Pauly. I like you, Sonny."

Chapter Seven

Jimmy Fund

I went back to the office, where Alice had returned with the donuts. Normally I would have been happy to stuff my face with company food, but I was worried, confused, and afraid of all that had just transpired. Alice started in with her questions.

"Where's Jimmy? Is he here? Does he know I'm back with the donuts? Do you know if I'm supposed to save him his favorite? Which one is his favorite? How was I supposed to know what ones to get?"

I couldn't think straight enough to answer her questions, but she persisted.

"Why would you know anyway?"

I went in the restroom and splashed cold water on my face. I heard the door chime and I knew it must be Jimmy, because Alice began her questions.

"Jimmy, I have the donuts, but how was I supposed to know what ones to get? Do you know how many flavors they have, and do you know how many they had run out of?"

"I heard his cool voice saying, "You did a fine job and all of them are my favorites. Where's Matt?"

I opened the door before she answered.

"Let's take a walk," he said as he pushed the glass door open and then held it until I walked through. "There's good chance we won't be seeing Dave around here anymore."

I thought about what had happened, and I didn't know what he saw, or what he knew.

"How well do you know Pauly, Petey, and Johnny? Who are these guys?" I asked him.

"I don't know, pretty good I guess; they're like family."

"What do you mean, like family, whose family?"

"Mine, mine and yours," he said with a straight face.

"They may be your family, but they sure as shit ain't my family. You don't know what they do, but it ain't good and that's all I'm saying. As a matter of fact — take that back, I'm not saying anything about those guys."

"Think back to when you got this job. Who got you the job?"

"My mom. My mom, that's who. Why?"

"Think back — what did your dad do for a living?"

"My dad's dead, so what does he have to do with it?"

He looked in my eyes and his darted from one of my eyes to the other like he couldn't pick one to focus on.

"My dad drove a tractor trailer truck for a lease company. What's that got to do with this job?"

"The same family who owned his trucking company owns this car rental center. Your dad was vested in the company pretty deep. They liked him. The family, the Italians," Jimmy said.

"Why would they like my dad, he was 50 percent French. As a matter of fact my grandfather didn't want my mom to marry him. They ran off to Niagara Falls and eloped."

"That's because your grandfather was 100 percent Italian and so was your mom. Your uncles died off and your mother was forced to turn whatever she inherited over to the family. They made a deal to take care of your family. That's why she never worked," he said, nodding his head.

"That's bullshit, my mom and dad weren't mobsters. My dad had a heart attack in the shower. Mom said he was a heavy smoker and drinker."

"I'm telling you what I'm telling you! It's for your own good. You got hired here because they want you here. Pauly told me to take you under my wing and help you out — I'll explain things as we go; that's all."

"Okay, if you are supposed to explain things then tell me what went down this morning with Dave and the thugs renting all those cars?"

"Johnny said you watched him get rough on Dave, it was for your own good. Dave was one of us, we trusted him, but he got caught stealing from the family. The good part was you found some of the missing dough and now I need someone who can be trusted to bring the cars in and out for a quick turn around. Someone who can keep their fingers out of the cookie jar, and they want you to do it."

"What if I don't want to?"

"Do you want me to tell them you quit? They know what you saw. Dave is taking a ride to the everglades. He didn't take the warning... Look what happened to the guy in the trunk of the Caddy. Dave was supposed to look in the trunk, not you. Look, you basically will have the same job; just don't go looking for cash or products in the cars. Let the family take care of you, they have been your entire life: you, your little sister, and your mom. And even your dad when he was alive."

"Do they take care of you? You turn a blind eye to everything?"

"You don't think I can make it on the manager's salary, do you? I'm one of the guys they want on the government radar. I have a clean record. That's where they want you. Do your job, mind your business, get a w-2, and pay your taxes. Pauly will give you a bonus if he's happy with you. How much did he give you today?"

I forgot about the tip he gave me. I reached in my pocket and pulled out the stack of hundred dollar bills. I fanned them. "Seven hundred."

"That's what he wants you to make every day. Seven hundred a day for being loyal, and you still get a paycheck on the books from the company. All you need to do is keep your nose clean and mind your own business. That's all I do — do I ever look worried or stressed?"

"No, you look like the coolest guy I've ever met. What are they paying you a day?"

"I can't tell you. That's going to be rule number two. Never tell anyone what you get. What if you make more than Johnny the Bump? He might not take it well."

"Shit, you're right. What was rule number one?"

"Be loyal and keep your mouth and eyes shut. You don't know nothing. And of course, rule number three."

"What's that?"

"Go back to rule number one, and that's why Dave is petting the crocodiles tonight."

"I felt better until you said that. So let me get this straight, all I have to do is get the cars vacuumed, run them through the car wash, fill the gas tank, and fill the low tires and washer fluid and check them in. Is that right?"

"That's about right; we have regular customers as well as the family, so when a car is coming in from a project, it can't be sent out for a trip to Disney. There's a method to this madness, and you'll need to get with the program," Jimmy said.

"Like the silver Fusion, Pauly insisted on that car."

"He insists on all the loaded cars."

"So I need to play dumb?"

"You need to be smart about being stupid. There's a saying — *some people are playing dumb and some people are staying dumb*. You're better off to play dumb than stay dumb."

"I'll tell you what, I've never seen a guy get an ass whooping like the one Dave got. I barely know Dave, but I feel bad about what happened to him."

"Trust me; he'd sell you out for a hundred bucks or a gram of cocaine. This was his last stop. He was no angel, so don't feel bad for him. And for the record, he had his share of warnings."

"Why do they call Johnny, Johnny the Bump?"

"Why do you think?"

"Because he gives out 'ouch bumps'?"

"He's been known to bump people off. When Johnny Bump comes to see you it's not good," Jimmy said. "I knew he was coming to see Dave."

"Why did Pauly call me Sonny?"

"It's your nickname, Johnny picked your family nickname, when people call you Matt, you'll know they are not family, but when you get known through the family it'll be as Sonny. We give each other respect, it's very important. Don't worry you'll get the hang of it, just watch out for the guys with strange names. Like Franky the Fist, Larry the Lifeguard, or Bobby Necktie."

"Larry the Lifeguard is a bodyguard I hope, and Bobby Necktie is a sharp dresser?"

"Larry drowned a guy in his pool, and Bobby choked a guy with his own necktie. He choked his wife too, but she didn't die. But the names stick once someone is labeled. Franky the Fist would slug someone in a second flat. He's a retired prizefighter."

"We should come up with a cool name for you, like Jimmy the Jackknife."

"No, then the cops would think I'm dangerous. I'm just Jimmy and you should just stay Sonny. Not Machine Gun Sonny."

"I get it, lay low, stay dumb."

"Lay low, play dumb, you'll be just fine. Never get drunk or high with these guys, and watch out for their women. You want them to like you, but not like you too much. You never want a jealous mobster on your tail. These are all good words of advice."

"How did you get involved with these guys?"

"Relatives. The wife and I are both related to the family."

"I though you met your wife at a restaurant."

"Who do you think owns the place? The family; they own everything."

"You must fit pretty well to manage your own store."

"It's taken a while, but I'm dependable and that's important to the family. I don't make problems. You should do the same, and always keep a tight lip."

"When I get home, I'm going to have a lot of questions for my mom."

"Are you sure you want to do that? The less she knows, the less she'll worry."

"She needs to know what she did to me."

"The family took care of her for a lot of years since your dad died, now it's payback time. She knew what business her family was in," said Jimmy.

"She did a damn good job of keeping it a secret."

"That's your new job — keep it a secret. Don't talk about it to your closest friends, not even your mom."

Chapter Eight

Valet Parking

Three weeks had passed. I received my pay, and just as Jimmy said I received an extra $700 each carload — cash in an envelope. Jimmy and I talk almost every day; I did whatever he asked me to do; most days it was the same. Clean the cars, check them in and out, and leave certain people off any paperwork. The only people that were on the hook were the real customers who rented the cars. In the event of a sting — the paper trail would incriminate the previous renter, a poor schmuck on vacation. It was a pretty good scam. Who would suspect a rental car agency to be a mobster smuggling ring, open to the public in the largest tourist section of the United States? It proved that the mob was everywhere.

I didn't feel that the cops were on to us. Maybe they were paid to look the other way — the world was full of corruption. Jimmy told me stories about loads of onions that my father hauled in an eighteen-wheeler. Half the truck had onions, the other half had drugs. The onions were there to throw off the dogs in the event he was pulled over. My dad hauled onions from state to state, day in, day out for years. The truck was lettered as a major shopping chain. It seemed brilliant; the mob tied in legitimate business with the smuggling business. The onions were sold to a wholesale produce business.

One day Petey pulled a rental up to the garage. I had been changing the wiper blades of a returned Cadillac. He lowered the window and yelled.

"Did Jimmy tell you that we were borrowing you for the day?"

"No, no one has said anything to me," I said with a nervous voice.

"Get in the car," said Petey. Pauly sat beside him.

We pulled up to the glass doors of the store front. Petey held down the horn and gave two annoying blasts, until Jimmy came close. The tinted car window went down on the passenger side.

"We need the kid, for the day," he said pointing his thumb to the back seat. Jimmy looked at me and saw I was concerned. He didn't answer, he only nodded.

The window slowly went up as we pulled away from the store. I watched the road signs as Petey drove down the streets. I figured I might need to retrace my path in case something doesn't go right. They didn't talk. It was awkward and the ride seemed to take forever. I started to think crazy thoughts. I wondered if there was a body in the trunk and I was going to dig a grave, or worse — forced to dismember a corpse. I got anxious — I couldn't breathe. I pressed the window button, but Petey had them locked. We pulled up to a massive hotel. There was a valet parking attendant.

When we got close, Petey lowered the window. The valet put his head near Petey's window.

"There's three hundred bucks in this envelope, how about you take a break for a half hour?"

"I can't, it's my shift and I can't afford to get fired," he said.

"Your boss, his name is Angelo, am I right?

"Yes."

"We're family, you call him and tell him that Pauly and Petey are here and I told you to take a break. It'll be all right, trust me."

The valet called someone and then he came back to the car. "He said do as you ask."

"Give me your hat and number; I'll call you when I want you to come back. Now go on, get lost!"

I was just as puzzled as the valet, but he did as Petey asked and slipped the cash in his wallet as he walked of   never looking back.

Pauly turned and spoke. His big cheeks wrinkled against his collar, his breath was foul and a small bubble of spit flew from the gap in his yellow bottom teeth.

"Sonny, take this hat and stand out front here until a silver Bentley pulls in — license plate says PD 4. It should be here within a half hour. He'll want you to park his car good and close, but you take the key and drive that car back to the store and put it inside the building. Do you understand?"

"Yes sir, Bentley vanity plate PD 4. That doesn't stand for police department 4 does it?"

"No it stands for 'paid for,' except it ain't paid for, so you are going to help us get it back. He owes the big boss a few bucks and the car is going to encourage him to pay up, but don't worry. Once you get back to the shop Jimmy will know what to do. Have him call me."

I took a few minutes to take in what Pauly had said, and then Petey turned and said, "well go on, get out there. Don't park any other cars; let the real valets do their job. You put the valet hat on when you see the Bentley pull up. This is important Sonny, don't fuck up. And you listen to Jimmy, he's a good boy."

I hesitated before I got out of the car, I didn't want to be scolded. I could see Pauly's shoulders turning against the front seat. I was out before he got his head turned. I didn't want him to lose confidence in me. It was strange, one part of me wanted to tell him I didn't want to do it and the other part of me didn't want to disappoint them. Up to this point the family had been good to me. I got an extra $700 a carload for doing the same job I always did. I knew they checked the cars after I was done with them, and they found I didn't take from the family, but that didn't mean I was up for becoming a car thief. I knew they did dirty business, but I justified smuggling with the rental car. I didn't go looking for any illegal activity and it was well hidden, so as far as I was concerned I was innocent, and just tipped well for doing a good job and minding my own business.

I stood beside a row of perfectly groomed Aphrodite bushes. They were 15 feet tall and looked like soldiers guarding the entrance of the majestic hotel. I held the hat behind my back and watched as a car pulled up to the entrance. It stopped and a valet walked to their driver's door, opened it and waited for the people to get out. The old man patted the young valet on the shoulder and then tucked some cash into his shirt pocket. He slowly drove the man's car between an opening in the tall shrubbery and out back to a large paved lot.

Another car came and was parked, and then just as Petey said, the Bentley rolled up almost to my feet. I had been quick to snap the cap on and once he stopped I was at the driver's door. I opened it and backed up a step, leaving room for the elder fat man to exit. He had a smelly cigar. I was surprised he smoked in such an expensive car, but people with his sort of money may not worry about trade-in values. He looked me in the eye. His eyes were dark, almost black, and beady. His nose was crooked and looked like it had been broken when he was young.

"Don't just stand there, get the door for the woman," he said in a voice crackly with phlegm.

I rushed to the passenger side and opened the door. A woman at least 25 years younger than him stepped out. She wore black slacks and a form fitting sweater with fancy stitching in glitter. An opening in the sweater showed her cleavage, which was spilling from the top of her push-up bra. I didn't want to get caught staring at her fake boobs. I remembered what Jimmy had said about jealous gangsters. She walked around me and I shut the door, careful not to slam it. He was at the front of the car waiting for her. He offered his elbow and she put her hand on his sleeve, and then he turned his head and looked at me. His other hand held cash. He looked me in the eye and said, "put it close and there better not be a scratch on it. Do we understand each other?"

"Yup, I mean, yes sir, no scratches and keep it close, no problem."

He turned and walked to the main entrance. I got in the car, adjusted the seat and then drove into the lot behind the tall bushes. There were many cars; all parked close together, just enough room for the drivers to get out of the cars. I rode around the lot until I saw a back entrance.

The entrance was lined by the same tall shrubbery. My heart thumped as the end of the small road approached — I was officially out of the parking lot and there was no doubt I was stealing a car. I wondered if I would be arrested as part of a set-up, or assassinated through the dark tinted windows. A small bead of sweat left my sideburns and ran to the corner of my jawbone. It was muggy and I reached for the knob on the air conditioner. Then I stopped and thought maybe I shouldn't touch anything and leave my fingerprints. What if this car was already stolen and was being tracked by the police? What if I got in an accident and the cops came? How would I explain?

I pictured a car wreck and I saw myself driving away from the scene, photographed by the intersection cameras — and then my face on the evening news. "Wanted, hit and run, man kills others in wreck and flees." I held the wheel firm at ten and two o'clock. I cussed myself for everything that happened to me in the past month and then I cussed, Jimmy, Pauly, Petey, Dave, and finally my mom for marrying a gangster. She should have moved away when my dad died and got a real job and a clean life so my sister and I didn't have to deal with this shit. There must be guys who are willing to be gangsters, so why should I be forced to be one? Just because of my family's poor choices, and their suspicions that they can't trust outside the family ... It seemed ridiculous.

One thing I knew was that I knew a little, and a little was too much. I thought about the guy and his woman. I could see their faces when they would ask for the car and realize it was stolen. His piercing eyes had studied my face, just as I had studied his. I muttered under my breath until I was at the intersection where the rental-car store was. I pulled into the lot and circled around the glass store front, looking for Jimmy. Then I saw the garage door rise and he was standing in front of the opening. He had a phone on his ear as he flagged me into the garage bay. The door went down and I shut the car off and took my shirt sleeve and wiped the steering wheel and whatever I could remember that I touched.

Jimmy stood beside the car and smiled. "Nice work Sonny."

"Yeah, it's just great. I just stole a car."

"Don't worry about it, you didn't steal it you repossessed it. It's a big difference."

"What if they call the cops?"

"They're gangsters, there's no cops. We own the cops."

"You called the cops when I found the body in the trunk."

"Yes I did, how else were we going to get publicity? That hit was a message, a mob hit, and it was no secret. The Don wanted front-page news, and he got it. That shook up a lot of people. Some people owe and they pay slow. The family doesn't run the business on love, you know."

"What are we going to do with this car? That guy saw me and I don't want anyone hunting me down. I don't like any of this shit. I don't even know how I got in this deep. What's that guy going to do when he realizes that his car is stolen? He's a mobster and I'm sure he has a temper."

"It ain't stolen, and don't worry about shit. The boss isn't going to get you killed. I used to do tasks like this until I proved I could run bigger things. I moved up from being a solider to being in management. Dave would have done your job but he couldn't be trusted. So like I told you before, just play dumb and keep your mouth shut. Let Pauly, Petey, and me do the thinking. You're family; no one is going to hurt you."

"I stole a $500,000 car, and you don't think I'll at least get an ass kicking?"

"Nope, I know you won't."

"What makes you so sure?" I asked, frantically.

"Pop the trunk."

"Don't tell me there's a body in there, don't tell me there's a body in there and you want me to dump it somewhere!"

"Pop the trunk," he said with a stern voice.

I clicked the key fob and the trunk rose. I slowly turned my head and looked inside — nothing. I walked closer; there wasn't a single thing in the trunk. I looked up to Jimmy, he was carrying a cooler — it looked heavy. I quickly took one side and helped him lower it in the trunk.

He closed the trunk lid and said, "ok, return the car to the parking lot and wait in front of the hotel until he asks for it back — get the car and be nice and don't say a word, maybe you'll get a fat tip. You didn't move the seat did you?"

"Yeah, why?"

"You never move the seat when you valet park a car. That aggravates the owner more than anything. Never do that. A real valet wouldn't do that. He's about as tall as I am," Jimmy said as he slipped into the seat and powered it into a comfortable spot and then he reset the mirrors. "All right, get going."

I got in the seat, I was shorter than Jimmy and it was uncomfortable for me to drive back. Again I hoped for a safe ride without incidents. I felt better that I wasn't stealing the car, but if the owner thought I was out joyriding in his half a million dollar car, he might get upset and beat me, maybe shoot me. I couldn't help wonder what was in the trunk. I hoped the cooler was full of either cocaine or stacks of hundred dollar bills. Maybe that was what it was and the owner would be really happy to get his car back. I convinced myself that I found the answer and all would have a happy ending. I entered the hotel at the rear entrance and picked a good spot. I locked the car, and walked to the front of the hotel entrance. I stood in front of the tall shrubbery and took the valet hat off and put it behind my back.

An hour passed and the real valet returned. He didn't know I had his hat — he hadn't seen me in the backseat of Petey's car. He had handed the hat to Petey, not me. So I did what I had been trained to do, keep quiet and mind my own business, stay on task.

Finally, I recognized the woman who was with the mobster; she stood outside the lobby and lit a cigarette. I could use one myself. All I saw was the cigarette in her hand and a huge diamond on her finger twinkling from 20 feet away. She blew out a cloud of smoke and pointed at me and then to the parking lot.

"Would you like the car ma'am?"

She had one arm across her small belly and the other pulled the cigarette to her mouth for a second drag. She nodded and pointed again to the lot. I turned and walked to get the car.

I talked to myself as I walked; I wondered if I should tell him there was a package in the trunk or open the trunk and show him what's there. I unlocked the car, got in, and drove to the woman. The man came close to the woman and was adjusting his fly. He chewed a cigar and stopped to light it. She dropped her cigarette and twisted her shiny shoe onto the remains. I got out of the car and left the driver's door open and then I opened the passenger door and waited until the lady got in. She slid on a pair of large sunglasses and looked forward. I knew she watched me. I took one more look at her, and then walked around to the front of the car and to the driver's side in time to close the door for the man. The window lowered and he passed me some cash folded in half. I could tell it was $50 — I tried not to smile.

"I can trust there's no scratch on my car, can't I?"

"No scratches sir," I said as I touched the brim of the valet cap.

As he drove off, I wondered if he could tell that I moved the seat, or when he would find the gift in the trunk.

I didn't know what to do, so I stood next to the bushes again, one of the valets came close to me. "Are you new here? I'm Steve."

"Yeah, I just started today." I went to shake his hand; I wondered what name I should use, maybe he already knew me as Sonny. "I'm Matt."

"I saw you take that guy's Bentley for a drive. Did he tell you to fill it? Sometimes they have you fill it and you get the same tip as just parking it for them, and it sucks because it takes you out of the loop for a half hour."

I didn't like how nosey Steve was but I played along. "I put some gas in and got it back as soon as I could, but he gave me a fifty, so it was worth it."

"A fifty is good; usually they give ten or twenty bucks. Some cheap bastards only throw you five."

Then Petey pulled up. Steve rushed to his window trying for the parking job. I stood behind him. He turned and discretely talked from the corner of his mouth, "hey beat it, I've got this one."

Petey heard him and said, "You beat it you punk, Sonny give this asswipe that hat."

I handed the confused valet the hat. "I quit," I said as I got in the backseat of the car. We drove off. Petey looked at me in the rearview mirror.

"You did a nice job Sonny; that was good. You didn't say a word, did you?"

"No of course not. Jimmy told me to never say a word and play dumb, so that's what I did. I acted like a dumb valet parking lot guy."

"You're a good actor, I'm proud of you Sonny," said Pauly with a big smile.

"It might be a week or two before Sal opens that trunk. I wish I could see his face when he does."

I didn't say anything else. They dropped me off and before I got out of the car Pauly handed me an envelope, "for you, and your nice work Sonny. Thanks."

I finally breathed a normal breath. "You're welcome," I said, making it seem like whatever was happening was OK. I went in the garage.

Chapter Nine

Getting A Head

I leaned against the bench and smoked the cigarette that I had been waiting for. I took in a long drag, deep into my lungs and then exhaled it through my nose, like steam from a raging bull. I puffed a few smoke rings, and then the door swung open and Alice walked in.

"Hey what's with the break time? You're smoking in here? Don't you know there's gasoline and oil in here?"

I didn't know if she wanted an answer to her stupid questions, so I answered anyway, "yes, yes, and yes," as I continued practicing smoke rings.

"What, are you getting wise? Are you almost done with that cigarette? Does Jimmy know you smoke in here?"

Again, I didn't know if I should just ignore her, but I answered, "no, yes, and yes. How does this work? Do you outrank me?"

"What do you mean?" she asked.

"Well what's with the twenty questions? Are you my boss or something?"

"I'm office help and you work out back so wouldn't you assume I'm in charge? And I've been here longer than you, so wouldn't that count for something?" She paused for a few minutes and then another question: "So are you busy right now?"

"No, no, and no."

"Well what are you doing right now?"

"I'm finishing this cigarette and then I'm going to the office. I'll tell Jimmy I'm back, and then take a piss, and then I'm getting a coffee. Are there any more questions? You know, most of your questions you can answer yourself."

"Why would I want to do that? What's the purpose?"

I didn't answer, I just walked out the door and I didn't care why she wanted to talk to me. She held a clipboard and followed ten feet behind me. When I reached the office, Jimmy was on the phone and we both stood at the counter waiting for him. He laughed at something and then hung up the line.

"What's going on?" asked Jimmy.

Before she addressed him she looked at me and asked, "Aren't you still on break?"

"Is that it, one question?"

"Do you need more questions? Isn't one question enough to get through to you?"

"OK then the answers are no, and yes."

She turned to Jimmy, "This man doesn't answer a question with a straight answer. He's complicating things."

"I answered, no and yes. It doesn't get any straighter than that," I said. "One word answers shouldn't complicate things."

"Jimmy, do you see what's happening? Do you hear him? Isn't that being insubordinate?"

Jimmy looked at me and smiled. I knew he wanted to laugh in her face. He was intelligent and knew she had an issue communicating. Before he could answer her, the phone rang and he was saved. She was frustrated.

She held the clipboard close to my face. "Did you check in this Ford Taurus?"

I saw my signature on the paper, so I didn't need to answer.

"Did you know it's missing the inspection sticker? Aren't you supposed to check for that? Did you know a customer got pulled over for not having an inspection sticker, and did you know I got my ass chewed for a half hour and had to upgrade them to a Lincoln? Did you know that, and do you know why? Maybe it's because someone is not doing what they are supposed to be doing, and you know who I think that someone is?"

"Me?"

"How did you guess that?"

"Lucky guess. I still have to pee, did you know that?"

"Do I look like I'm stopping you?"

I turned around and went to the bathroom. I wondered why the Taurus didn't have an inspection sticker. That seemed crazy — the damn car only had a few thousand miles on it. It was brand new.

Jimmy got off the phone I could hear Alice talking through the door. I could tell she was still upset that she was scolded by an irate customer, and she didn't really want to be boss, but she wanted me to cower to her. And maybe since she was a woman she wanted some errand boy kind of role play: If she needed a task done, then she should be able to snap her fingers and old Matt should have to get it done. I wasn't sure how she fit in the business, or if she was related to who knows who. Johnny the Bump was her dad for all I knew, but I was going to listen well, and find out if she outranked me at work as well as in the family.

I listened as she waited for Jimmy's attention and then grilled him with questions. "I brought the inspection sticker up to Matt. Can you see where he signed the car in for 'ready to rent?' Don't you think he should be reprimanded for missing such an important item on the checklist?"

"I'll talk to him, why don't you take a ride to Dunkin' Donuts and get a box of your favorites and an ice coffee. No one should have yelled at you, it's not your job to spot inspection stickers."

He handed her the company credit card and she walked out the door. I came out of the bathroom and laughed. "What do you make of that?"

"The Taurus had a gunshot through the front windshield that went out the back. It got replaced before the boys returned it. They must have missed the sticker, but you need to check for those things. It's really not your fault; it was when Dave was still here, but you did sign the final sheet."

"Whatever happened to Dave?"

"He's on a cruise ship."

"Really? I though he was gator food."

"He's supposed to throw someone overboard to redeem himself, and if he don't someone will throw him overboard. It's his chance to redeem himself."

"Are you kidding?"

"No, so don't fuck up, or you might have to do some real shitty things."

"What was in the trunk, in the cooler of the Bentley?"

"Remember the body with no head, or hands?"

"Yeah."

"The head was frozen in a block of ice; it's in the cooler, that's why it was so heavy. The family don't waste anything, it's like recycling."

"That's terrible, does that guy know who the head belongs to?"

"It was his partner."

"What if he thinks I put that in there?"

"He may not have checked the trunk for a few weeks, and may not for a few more. By the time he finds it he won't have any idea when or where the head came from. All he'll think is that we are everywhere and he'll be looking over his shoulder. He most likely will never leave the house. He needs to pay his bills; he's got back dues to the family. We hold his mortgage."

"Is that why his partner got killed?"

"You're starting to sound like Alice with all the questions. His partner was his brother. The brother had 75 percent of the business. We fronted the dough for their strip club. He got a few breaks and wouldn't pay our share. The Don knows Sal inherited his brother's half so he still has to pay the debt. Life's a bitch," Jimmy said.

"I'll try to do better inspecting the cars; it would have been bad if the guys would have gotten pulled over for something as stupid as an inspection sticker."

"Try to go easy on Alice too; she has trouble since she got hooked on drugs. Too bad, her boyfriend was doing good too. That shit wrecks a lot of good people."

"She was on my ass the minute I got back from the valet job, I was having a smoke and she bombarded me with questions. It was like being on a game of Jeopardy, she answers everything with a question."

"She's not that bad, she's actually pretty smart. It's her way of testing you. I don't play into it," said Jimmy.

"What does your wife think of all of this?"

"She likes the money, she can stay at home and raise a family, and she likes the respect that I get. She don't have any worries. Aren't you enjoying the extra money? I know you got a nice tip today. Pauly said to give you your regular pay also," he said as he passed me $700.

Jimmy was right. I made my rental car pay on the books, and an extra $700 cash, plus the $50 that Sal tipped me. I hadn't had time to spend the money I was making.

Chapter Ten

Little Sister

The following weeks went by without incident, cars rolled in and out. The family used a few new faces, sometimes it was hard to tell if the cars were going on a family job or the public was using them for legitimate vacations. I got so I didn't care what happened as long as I was safe and I got my extra tip money each week. I had Sunday off, and decided to pay my mom a visit; it had been a while since I last saw her.

She had moved to the west coast of Florida, Clearwater, with my little sister Marie, a freshman in high school. Mom thought the schools in Orlando had too many bad kids so they moved after I graduated. I had been on my own since. Things were beginning to make sense to me. She knew there were operations in Miami and now that business was picking up in Orlando, Mom didn't want to watch my life evolve in the world of crime. She traded me to the mob, for her financial freedom. She was a stern mother, but she had a way of making me feel like she cared. I understood since she had Marie to look out for.

I never knew my mom was on a pay plan with the family. I thought we lived off a large life insurance policy. We were middle class, well fed and happy. We went to few family gatherings. I had friends; some went off to college and others were engaged or went in the military. My mom didn't have many friends, only her sisters and one cousin who took her shopping. Some afternoons they would play cards for hours. My aunts liked wine and they would get loud after a few glasses. Their husbands would need to come get them; sometimes one aunt would spend the night. I was left alone to play video games and play on the laptop computer.

Jimmy let me take a rental car for the day. I wanted to buy a new car, but he told me to wait and not attract attention to myself. I stashed my money away. The ride to Mom's house was long overdue. I felt bad — Mom used guilt as an Italian tool; Italian, and Catholic guilt, an unbeatable force. The road was flat and straight with enough traffic to tag behind the speeders. There were a few brave travelers who pushed their luck with the radar gun. I stayed behind the fearless speeders, enough so I made good time, but far enough back so they would get a ticket and I would coast by and smile at the police car.

I drove through a sun shower; my favorite kind of rain, the sun shining through the rain, giving confidence that the day wouldn't be a loss to a storm. The wipers rubbed across the windshield, catching and letting out a squeak. I tried to adjust them, but I didn't know the car well and couldn't get the speed right.

I turned the radio up, a song played from the band U2, "New Year's Day."

> *Nothing changes on New Year's Day.*
> *And so we're told this is the golden age*
> *And gold is the reason for the war we wage*

I sang along and thought about the lyrics and what they meant. Yesterday it meant nothing, just a catchy chorus and a strong lead singer. Today it talked to me and I heard the singer tell me that the family was at war for gold — money — power. I was supposed to be living in the golden age, but gold was the reason for the war we waged. Perfectly said, and the line *Nothing changes on New Year's Day* was right. Just like nothing was going to change by going to see my mom. People, countries get in a rut and can't get out — all because of the all-mighty dollar.

I daydreamed for a few minutes and when I looked up I was at my mom's exit. I instinctively turned onto the ramp, and then turned the radio down. The traffic thickened and I had to make a couple of tricky turns. I saw my mom's road and I turned the radio back up until I turned onto her driveway. I hesitated before I got out of the car. I saw the curtains move, and my sister's small face against the window, her forehead and the tip of her nose touched the glass. Then the front door opened behind the storm door. I looked at the floor of my car and saw a new CD I had bought and not played yet, still in its cellophane. I picked it up and walked up the stairs and only then did my sister recognize me. We both had changed. I was well dressed and had cut my hair neatly, and she had grown a few inches and lightened and cut her hair.

The door opened and she hugged me as I handed her the CD. Mom stood behind her waiting for her turn to hug me. I waited for the family dog to come barking and wagging its tail, but it didn't happen. "Where's the dog?"

"He had medical problems, so we had to have him put to sleep," said Marie.

"That's too bad. How old was Dexter anyway?" I asked.

"He must have been about twelve," said Mom.

"Are you getting another dog?"

"No I'm done with pets for a while."

"Have you two eaten? Are you hungry?"

"I am," said Marie.

"Why don't we go to Renaldo's, the Italian restaurant I passed on my way here? It's my treat."

Mom smiled, she knew I had plenty of money. She reached over to my face and pinched my cheek.

"Marie, go put on a pretty dress and pull your hair back, your brother is taking us out for dinner."

Marie ran down the hallway to her room, Mom sat on the couch and patted the cushion waiting for me to take a seat. The sun shone through the curtains and the daylight revealed my mom's age. I studied her face, time was changing her too. Brown spots covered the backs of her hands; small wrinkles at her eyes and mouth were deep and nearly connected when she smiled. Most of her hair was still dark but there were white strands scattered against her natural black. She looked me with her dark eyes. I wondered if she knew I was concerned about her aging not so gracefully. I looked over her shoulder to the picture on the wall where she stood proudly holding my sister's hand at her christening. She had a youthful look then, and even her hair had a young bounce. Now it lay flat against her temples. She used to remind me of Jacqueline Kennedy, but that look was fading fast, and I hated to see it go.

My sister returned from her room. "Are we riding in your car?"

"Sure, it's one from work."

"Can I sit up front?"

"Where's Mom going to sit?"

"I can sit in the back seat, I don't mind," said Mom.

We walked to the car, I held the back door for my mom and as soon as Marie got in the seat she played with the electric seat buttons. I laughed as I started the car. The rain had stopped and the water steamed off the black road. I pulled out of the driveway and onto the street. I decided to take a few back roads that went through the neighborhoods. We didn't get far before Marie pointed to a house: "That's where Joanne lives. I hate her. She's a bitch, a fat ugly bitch."

"Hey, watch your mouth young lady," said Mom.

"Well she is."

"What did she ever do to you?" I asked.

"We ride the bus together — she calls me names."

"Just ignore her," said Mom.

"I have been, but she pushed me down, and spit on me, I hate her."

"You never told me that. When were you going to tell me?"

"I'm telling you now. She slapped me, pushed me down and spit on me."

"Holy shit, now I'm pissed. Why didn't you tell me? Why did you wait? Matthew, turn this car around and take me to that house. Nobody slaps a DiMambro and gets away with it," she said, referring to her maiden name. "If your father was alive he would kick the shit out of her father for raising a kid like that, and he would spit in her mother's face."

I turned the car around.

"Please Mom, don't stop, it'll make it worse. Please I'm begging you, don't stop. Please Matty don't stop."

I looked at my mom's furious face in the mirror; she didn't say a word as my sister cried. I decided to drive past the house. "39 Whitcher Street," I said to myself.

"These are times when I wish your father was still alive," said Mom.

"Calm down Mom, it's just kid stuff. It's not like she got in a knife fight. You heard her: The girl is fat and ugly and she's jealous of Marie for being thin and cute."

"This can't go on Matthew."

"Don't worry, it'll stop."

"What are you going to do?" asked Marie.

"I want her name, I'll call her when I get home," said Mom.

"No Mom, please don't," said Marie. "Promise me you won't."

Mom shook her head from side to side.

"I'll take care of it Mom," I said. And don't worry, Marie. I know how to handle it."

She turned and looked out the windshield until we got to the restaurant. I parked and opened the door for Mom; Marie was already at the glass door waiting for us.

We went inside and were seated next to a window. "Marie, the restroom is in that corner. I want you to go and wash your hands. I'm going to get you a root beer. Would you like a root beer?"

"No Mom, I'd rather have a Diet Coke," she said as she walked to the restroom.

"Matthew, I can't convey how mad I am that someone is bullying my sweet little Marie."

"Mom she's a freshman in high school. Maybe she's right and she can fight her own battles."

"I want to find that girl, grab her hair, and throw her down on the ground," Mom said as she clenched her fists and shook them in the air. Her teeth were clenched together as she spoke through them.

"I told you I'll take care of it, so don't worry. Try to enjoy a nice meal, order whatever you want. Look they have your favorite, seafood, Alfredo."

"Do they owe you a favor yet?"

"What do you mean?"

"You know exactly what I mean. Do they owe you a favor yet?" Mom asked with a serious face.

Still I played dumb, "like how?"

"Like you look the other way, or you had to do something risky or uncomfortable for them?" she asked in a whisper. You know I know what the fuck is going on. Have you been looking the other way?"

"Maybe."

"Good answer, well maybe they owe you one, and maybe you owe me and your sister one. Do I need to say anything more?"

"No, let's change the subject, Marie is coming back."

Chapter Eleven

Teen Trouble

It was Monday morning. I knew Jimmy worked late on Sunday and wouldn't be in until 10. I gassed up the rental — drove it into the garage bay and passed the vacuum over the carpets. The check-in sheet was on the workbench. I stocked the car in, and moved it to the lineup, ready for business, and then I went to the office.

Alice was waiting at the counter. "Where have you been?"

"Out back in the garage. Here's the check-in sheet for the white Taurus #3321121. I've been busy as a beaver this morning. What about you, where have you been?"

"What do you mean by that? Can't you see I've been right here?"

"Just checking," I said.

"Why would you be checking?"

"I don't know. Why did you check on where I was? Why do you care?"

"What makes you think I care?" she asked.

"Never mind, what did you want?"

"Jimmy's not here and we need donuts for the customers," she said.

"So."

"I need a witness — I'm taking the company credit card and making a donut run. Will you stay in the office until I get back?"

"Sure."

She left and then about ten minutes later Jimmy pulled in. His wife dropped him off. He kissed her and waved to a kid in the back seat. I didn't realize that he had a child. I turned and acted like I was looking at a clipboard as he entered the office.

"Good morning, how did your visit at your mom's go?"

"Good except for one thing. My sister is getting bullied and I'm not sure how I can help."

"Are you serious? We specialize in the bullying business. Give me some details. How old is this bully? Boy or girl?"

"Girl, about fourteen, maybe fifteen — my mom wanted to stop at her house and rip her a new ass. She actually wanted to grab the kid by the hair and throw her down. She was ripshit. I've never seen her so mad."

"What did this girl do to your sister?" he asked.

"Threw her down, slapped her, and spit in her face."

"No wonder. Your mom should be shit-house. Your mom is a fucking DiMambro. She's not used to taking shit, especially from some no-body. That family is lucky your dad's not alive. My dad told me stories about the shit he and your dad used to do. I'm sure you've heard the stories," Jimmy said.

"Actually I haven't, my dad used to come home late and when I did see him he was awkward around me and my sister. He never told stories and I had no idea he was working for the mob."

"It's the family, Matt, we call it the family. Outsiders call it the mob. Let me tell you something, your dad was a tough son of a bitch, and he didn't take any shit from anyone. My dad said he was at a nightclub with him — your dad punched a mouthy drunk in the stomach. He had four friends that saw what happened and they jumped our fathers. My dad was busy with one guy and your dad kicked the shit out of the other three guys. That's why his nose was folded over and healed crooked."

I thought it was odd that I never really noticed that my dad's nose was crooked and if it was I thought he was born that way.

"Then one night when our dads were young they hitchhiked to another state. Your dad got drunk and punched out the driver and stole his car. My father said he was unpredictable. That guy had balls, he was fearless."

"Sounds like your dad knew him well," I said.

"They went way back. They were cousins, I think second cousins."

I paused for a few seconds and shook my head. I didn't realize my father was a scrapping thug, and a car thief. I was just getting used to the fact that he was a truck driving smuggler. I thought he was an absentee father and a holiday hothead. He'd get drunk on Christmas and Thanksgiving and I had to tip-toe around the house when he was around. I didn't dare step out of line.

"So how should I handle the bully?"

"Let me call Pauly. He likes you and he'll know what to do," Jimmy said.

He poured a coffee from the pot and stirred in a packet of sugar. He stared at the Styrofoam cup as he walked slowly to the counter. I stood across from him as he waited for Pauly to pick up the phone. Pauly didn't answer, so he left a message: "Pauly, it's Jimmy; Sonny has a problem and he needs your help, stop by or give me a call when you can."

"No luck?"

"He doesn't answer the phone, he'll listen to the message and get back when he's ready. No worries."

Alice pulled up outside, parked the car, and walked to the door with three dozen donuts. I held the door open and she put the boxes on the table next to the coffee pot.

The phone rang. I thought it might be Pauly, but it was a customer looking to rent an SUV. Jimmy pulled the keys from the cabinet and tossed them to me. I opened the box of donuts and pulled one out and took a bite.

"You shouldn't have taken that one; it's covered with powdered sugar. What are you going to do if you get white powder all over the car?" Alice asked.

I didn't answer; I just walked out the door. She was right, the sugar dropped all over my pant leg as I walked and I wasn't smart enough to take a napkin. I thought about my dad and my mom, and about my life, and what my sister's life might be like. I was worried for her, but maybe she would stay away from me and the mob. That might be the best thing for everyone.

I went to the garage and finished my coffee and donut, wiped off my pants and then brought the SUV to the building. A family was waiting with a dog. I dreaded the amount of hair I would have to vacuum from the car when it returned. I stood next to the car and slowly walked around it, looking for damages and burned-out bulbs. It looked good.

A mom and her teenager came out first while her husband and daughter took a few donuts from the box while the man filled a coffee cup. The teenager jumped behind the wheel and adjusted the seat and the tilt wheel. His mom stood beside the car and read emails from her phone. The boy turned the key and started the engine. He floored the gas, and I thought he was trying to blow the engine. I tapped the glass on the side door, and said, "Hey, you can't hold the gas pedal down like that, it'll seize the engine."

He lowered the window, laughed, and refused to let up on the gas. Then I reached into the car and turned the key. He pushed at my hand.

"What are you doing?" he shouted.

"What are you trying to do, wreck the engine? Get out of that seat, you're not the driver."

"Why don't you mind your own business, lot boy," he said.

I felt my Italian temper flare; I could envision my fist on his teeth. I opened the door and grabbed his elbow.

"Get your hands off me, get your hands off me," he screamed. "Mom tell him to take his hands off me."

I let him go and he swung his foot around and kicked my knee. His mom looked up from the phone and said. "What's your problem?"

"He was holding the gas pedal to the floor. That's a good way to seize the engine," I said.

"Don't worry about it, we bought the insurance."

"That doesn't give you the right to ruin the car, you didn't buy the car, you're just renting it."

"Don't let the lot boy give you any shit mom," said the teen.

"You're right," she said as she walked into the office and wagged her head as she told her side of the story to Alice.

I opened the door and stepped inside. Alice was battering her with questions.

"Why would Matt pull at your son's arm? And what was he doing in the driver's seat? Do you think it was responsible leaving a child in a running car in the driver's seat? Weren't you watching him? Couldn't you hear the engine whining?"

Then she looked at me, "Matt why did you touch him?"

"For his safety and the safety of others... He floored the car and I was worried he would put it in gear and drive through the building."

Then she looked at the woman, "I heard the engine rev. Is this the way you treat a rental? Why didn't you stop your son from abusing the vehicle? What right did he have being behind the wheel? He didn't rent the car, did he? Don't you think it was you that should have stopped him from abusing our car and talking back to our staff?" The woman didn't expect all the questions and Alice gave her no time to answer any of them.

Alice turned to Jimmy. "Jimmy what do you think we should do?"

Jimmy looked at each of us and in his cool manner he took the rental sheet and ripped it in half. "Matt, bring me the keys."

"What are you doing?" the woman asked.

"The rental agreement states that you are not supposed to purposely damage the car, and you are to be responsible for our vehicle. Your husband is the only driver listed in the agreement and like Matt and Alice stated, your son had no right to be behind the wheel. So I'll call you a cab and you can rent a car down the street. Try Avis," Jimmy said.

I walked out to the car and the woman and her husband were right behind me. Jimmy was on the husband's heels. The teen was still sitting behind the wheel, and started the car and floored it again. I reached in the window and took the key. This time the father witnessed the situation and he opened the car door and yanked the kid from the car. The kid yelled, "get your hands off me, you're not my father. Mom, tell him to get his hands off me."

"Take your hands off him; you're ganging up on him." Then she touched the kid's elbow and he swiftly swung it away from her grip. He sat back in the car.

"Leave me alone and get away from me," he said.

"Get out of that car," said the man.

"No, you're not my father and you're not the boss of me."

"Tommy, get out of the car" his mother said. "You ruined it for everyone. Now we can't rent the car. We have to go somewhere else to get a car," she said.

"No, it's all because of the lot boy that this happened. He sucks and I wish he were dead. He ruined everything."

"Come on Tommy, get out of the car and I'll let you play a game on my phone," she said.

I could see the man was frustrated — his daughter was younger than the boy. She moved close to him and hugged his shoulder. "Are we still going to Disney today?"

"As soon as we can get a rental, Sweetie — once Tommy is done throwing his tantrum."

The woman slowly looked up to the man. It was obvious that she had been dealing with this spoiled brat since he was an infant. I was happy the man wasn't sticking up for Tommy. Jimmy was on the cordless phone. I assumed he was calling a cab. The man turned to me and said, "I'm sorry we put you through this. As soon a he gets out of the car we'll be out of your hair."

"Don't apologize to him, he started all of this commotion," said the lady.

She turned and looked at Tommy and the man looked at me and rolled his eyes. Jimmy hung up the phone and said, "Avis is bringing an SUV over in about ten minutes. It might take you ten minutes to get him out of the car." Then he waved at me and said, "come inside."

I followed him in the store I wondered if the woman thought I was getting reprimanded by Jimmy. Alice was out front smoking a cigarette.

"What an asshole kid, huh?" asked Jimmy.

"I know, he really pushed my buttons. Thanks for sticking up for me."

"Family first, when Avis gets here, don't let the guy leave without his wallet."

Jimmy pulled the man's wallet from his pocket. "Where'd that come from," I asked.

"If that guy was an asshole he wouldn't get this back, but he seems like he's in hell."

Then Avis pulled up and Tommy finally got out of the SUV and into the back seat of their car. I walked out with the wallet and yelled to the man, "Hey, you left your wallet on the counter, you might need it."

He took the wallet, opened it and fanned through his cash and credit cards. Then he handed me a twenty and shook my hand. "No hard feelings Matt, thanks for returning this."

"My pleasure and my sympathy," I said.

Chapter Twelve

Big Tony

It was almost lunchtime; the sun was beating down on the parking lot, making it unbearable to stand outside for more than ten minutes. The air was getting thick and dark clouds were rolling towards us. The earth needed a drink as badly as I did, so I went inside to get a soda. I put my dollar in the machine and it spit it out. Three times I tried. I could feel that Alice was watching me, so I looked to her to see if she could refrain from an opinion.

"Did you try to flatten it first? Maybe one corner is folded," she said.

I rubbed it against the machine and straightened each corner. I tried it again and wanted her to be wrong but the red light lit and a soda fell to the small plastic door at the bottom of the machine.

"Where'd you hear that first?" She said with a grin and a thumb up.

"You, Alice, where else could I hear it first?"

"Damn right."

Then Jimmy had the phone on his ear, he came in the store and handed it to me. "It's for you."

I took if from him. "Hello."

"Sonny, it's Petey. What's the trouble?"

I decided to go outside so Alice wouldn't hear. "I have a little sister in high school. She's small and some fat kid was pushing her around and spit in her face."

"Did she hit your sister?"

"Yeah, she said she slapped her face and shoved her to the ground, and then spit on her at the bus stop, in front of her friends."

"Oh that's bad, we need to take care of this immediately. I'll pick you up after work, what time do you get out?"

"5:30."

"Perfect that's dinnertime; most people are sitting down to a meal. Jimmy told me they live down the street from your mom, is that right?"

"Yeah, a few blocks away."

"Perfect, see you then," he said and hung up. I shrugged my shoulders and wondered what he had in store for them. Jimmy had been watching me and as soon as I lowered the phone he came outside.

"All set huh?" he asked.

"Seems like it, but I don't know what they are planning to do, and I was kind of surprised that it was Petey taking care of business instead of Pauly."

"Petey handles smaller stuff. Let's face it, a high school bully is a small matter for the family," said Jimmy, laughing.

"My sister is not laughing."

"It'll be a good thing, good for everyone, you'll learn a lot."

"Why what's coming? Tell me — I know, you know," I said.

"They're bringing Big Tony to do the dirty work and Johnny the Bump is going for the cleanup — Petey will negotiate the deed."

"What do you mean negotiate?"

"They want the seven hundred you got today for your tip, it'll cost you seven hundred for two hours for the two thugs, and trust me that's a damn good deal. They must like you."

"Shit that's a lot of money, and it's not even for me; it's for my mom and really my sister."

"Well you don't do anything for free, why should they?" said Jimmy.

"I thought I did them favors and maybe I had one coming, that's all."

"You've been compensated, but let me call Pauly and see if he can help you."

He dialed and left a message for Pauly to call him back. A few minutes passed and the phone rang.

"What do you want, Jimmy?"

"Sonny wants to do a swap for the teen bully, are you interested or does he need to use cash?"

I could hear Pauly laugh over the phone, his deep loud voice carried. "A favor for a favor, of course, he's family. He needs to learn that he doesn't need to bust his knuckles, we have guys for that, but he does need to grow some balls. He needs to be there to watch the boys in action."

They both laughed and Pauly hung up without saying anything more. Then the sprinkles started, light at first, soothing on my shirt and then the breeze picked up and the trees bent. The drops got big and I felt like I was being shot from a BB gun. We went inside and then the lightning struck. Alice looked scared.

"Shit I have my windows down," she said holding the key up. "Will you shut them for me? I forgot and left them open."

"Do it yourself," I said as a huge crack and flash went through the sky and the building seemed to tremble. "I'm not going out in this shit."

"Why don't you take the umbrella and do it? Please. I don't want my car to get moldy."

"Lightning will hit an umbrella," I said.

"There's a raincoat in the closet," said Jimmy. "I think the SUV that Tommy was in still has the window down too. You better check it and get Alice's window on the way by," he said.

I rushed to the closet. I was scared. Jimmy had the SUV key and Alice's key in his hand. The lightning crashed and the lights flickered. "Any last wishes?" Jimmy said, laughing and pointing to Alice, who was under the counter.

"Yeah I wish it was you going out there."

"Pauly said you need to grow some balls, so get out there and make him proud."

I flipped the hood of the raincoat over my head and ran for the SUV. Jimmy was right, the window was open, and then I ran to Alice's car, but hers were not open. "Stupid shit," I yelled into the rain, "makes me run over here for nothing." Then another big flash and a roll of thunder put the store's lights out. I ran to the door and hoped the metal frame wouldn't get struck by lightning. A small emergency light lit up and we stood in the semi dark office. A few minutes passed and we heard a siren that sounded like it was coming towards us.

"Maybe someone hit a telephone pole?" Alice asked.

The lights flickered and came back on, a surge of power started the ac unit and cool air dropped from the vents and pulled at the stiff muggy air that filled the store. We watched the lightning as it rolled across the flat state, moving to another city. The big storm could be seen for miles. The wind died and the rain stopped and then the sun shone again, steam rose from the hot top like someone turned on a heater below the ground.

Time flew by and my shift ended. Petey pulled up to the building and Johnny the Bump got out. I almost forgot how big he was. Then a little guy got out. He was middle aged and looked like he was about 140 pounds — he reminded me of Joe Pesci. Petey was on the phone, and he stayed in the car. The other two stayed beside the car smoking cigarettes, and watched Alice walk around the lot. The small guy was making perverted gestures when she wasn't looking.

"Who's the short, little guy?" I asked.

"That's Big Tony."

"Are you shitting me? That little shit? He's five feet tall. Why'd they send him?"

"He's got little guy, big guy syndrome. He's got balls the size of grapefruits. Don't piss him off. He's quick tempered," said Jimmy.

"I don't get it, he's doing the deed and Johnny is cleaning up if there's a problem? Why don't they do it the other way around?" I asked.

"Two reasons, first this guy is a lot smaller than you, and you don't have the balls to do what needs to be done do you? Do you know what needs to be done, by the way?"

I shrugged my shoulders.

"They are going to the house to beat the father and slap the mother and spit in her face. It should be priceless. You just have to stand behind him and make sure you say whatever needs to be said to the people, and of course stop Big Tony from killing them. Once he gets started, he's hard to stop, he's very violent."

"That little guy, are you fucking kidding me?"

I turned and I saw the little guy stare at me through the glass, it was like he heard every word. And then out of the corner of my eye I saw Jimmy point to me and then put his fist in the palm of his other hand. Tony dropped his cigarette and stepped on it as he reached for the aluminum handle on the glass door. I put my hand out to shake and he twisted his hips and fired a gut punch just below my ribs and then a swift upper cut to stop just under my nostrils. He backed up quick and bounced on his toes to see what I would do. I held my gut and waited for the air to fill my lungs.

"They call me Big Tony, glad to meet you Sonny," he said with his hand out. "Hey that was for nothing; just imagine what I can do when I'm mad."

He turned and looked out the glass and Johnny the Bump laughed. He went back outside and took another cigarette out and lit it, laughing as he smoked.

"What was that all about?"

"He took you by surprise. That's how he works, strike first, strike fast, and strike hard, and don't let the other guy hit you. It's humbling when a guy a lot smaller than you kicks your ass. Pauly wants you to see the size of the man don't matter, it's the size of the balls that do. He could have taken you out if he wanted to. When he beats that girl's father, and he sees the smallest guy in action, he won't want to see the biggest pay him a visit and that's all Johnny the Bump is there for. Tony will do the work and Johnny will scare the shit out of them. Trust me, no one will touch your sister again."

Chapter Thirteen

The Home Wreckers

A few more minutes passed — I stood up straight. I was afraid to go with these two thugs. My mom's house was a long ride to be trapped with two gorillas. What would I talk about? I walked out front and they stopped talking. Petey had his elbow out the window.

"The boys will call when they're done, we'll meet at the strip club — it's a few miles away, they know the place," he said looking over his dark sunglasses.

I stood silent.

"Well, you going to say something?" he asked.

"Thanks."

"Tell your mom I said hi," he said, and then the window went up and he slowly drove off.

Jimmy came outside and handed me a car key. "Take the white Malibu, it's low profile. Gangsters don't usually roll up in a Malibu, especially a white one."

"Thanks Jimmy," I said as I took the key and walked to get the car. Johnny and Tony didn't follow.

I pulled around the front of the store and Tony got in the front seat. I drove for about ten minutes and the air in the car got foul. I didn't dare say anything.

"Did you shit yourself?" Tony looked at me with his beady eyes.

"No, it wasn't me," I answered.

"John, did you die back there?" he asked as he put his window down.

"I should have taken a shit at the office. This job won't take long, let's just get there. Sonny, stop driving like an old lady," Johnny said.

I sped up — I didn't want to get pulled over with these two losers. There was most likely warrants out for their arrest. I counted the minutes until the exit. I drove past my mom's house and then I pointed to the house where the girl lived. We drove by slowly and then turned around. Tony read the mailbox. "Phillips. You know any Phillips, Johnny?"

"No, and that's not Italian so it's open game."

Tony turned to me and said, "let me go to the door, you stand on the bottom step behind me and stay out of the way. I don't want you to get hurt."

"What about Johnny, isn't he coming with us?"

"Maybe later, we don't need him," said the arrogant little Italian.

We got out of the car and walked up to the steps. I stayed a couple feet behind him. He pulled a pamphlet and an envelope from his inner coat pocket, then rang the door bell. The curtain moved and the door opened. We were well dressed. The man was not afraid of the small man at his door.

"What can I do for you?" the man said.

"I have a petition in this envelope; all the neighbors have signed it. I also have a pamphlet on what we propose. Could we come in for a second and get you to sign it?" said Tony.

The man backed up from the door and Tony walked in. The man towered over Tony. I didn't feel well, but I followed him inside. His wife came from the hallway. She, too, towered over Tony.

"What's this about, a neighborhood petition?" she asked.

"The bus stop. There's a bully at the bus stop and that needs to stop. People get hurt by bullies and sometimes they get killed, and a concerned neighbor brought this to our attention, so the way to stop a bully is through the parents. Would you agree?"

"Absolutely," she said.

Tony handed the envelope to the big man. He took it and used both hands to look inside. Tony's face crinkled, and swift as lightning he swung his foot up and caught the big man in the balls. The man bent over and was the same height as Tony, his mouth and eyes wide open. Tony poked two fingers into his eyeballs. The man raised his hands to touch his eyes and Tony cocked his arm and threw a punch, full force, into the man's Adams apple. He couldn't breathe. The tall woman held the side of her head. Tony slapped her face with one fast fanning of his hand. "It's your fucking daughter that's the bully — tell them Sonny!"

Tony grabbed the woman's arm and threw her to the floor.

"Your daughter picked on the wrong kid, Tony is just a messenger — this is your warning. If you don't fix the problem we will. We better not have to come back here."

I turned around and Johnny the Bump was standing at the front door, watching through the storm door. He opened the door and walked in. "I'm here to clean up this fucking dump," he said as he knocked the coffee table over and then he went to the kitchen and pushed the microwave off the counter, along with a fruit bowl and a loaf of bread. Then he grabbed the refrigerator, set his foot and pulled it over onto the floor — groceries and milk poured over the tile. The man started to get up and Johnny took two steps and kicked his ribs like he was kicking a field goal. "Stay down asshole, I have to take a shit — where's the shitter?" No one answered; he went down the hall until he found the bathroom. He used the toilet and didn't close the door. A few minutes later he came out — he didn't flush.

Then Tony put his finger in the woman's face, "Where's your fucking kid?"

She didn't answer; Johnny opened the other doors and found the girl under her bed. He pulled her by one ankle all the way into the living room, and dropped her by Tony.

"Are you going to beat this kid, or am I?" asked Tony.

The woman cried and nodded.

"I don't believe you," he said as he gave a swift kick into the kid's gut.

"Call the cops if you want, and I can assure you we'll be back," said Tony.

"If there's a next time, I'll bring gasoline and matches and your family will die in a house fire. Do we understand each other?" Johnny said as he kicked the father in the head.

The kid looked up at me. "You caused all of this," I said to her. "How do you like being bullied?" I turned to leave and then I turned back, "oh yeah, you spit on my sister. She didn't like that."

I looked at Tony; he pulled a long draw from his smoker's lungs and launched a phlegm clam onto the girl. Johnny did the same. I turned and walked out, and the men followed me. We got in the car and drove away. My heart raced, "I wonder if they'll call the cops. Do you think they got the plate?"

"Tony and Johnny laughed. "Are you shitting me? Didn't you see that big coward lay on the floor? He's what 6-foot-3? I'm 5-1 and he saw me slap his wife and kick his kid. I would use the last drop of my blood to kill someone who did that to my family. He's a lily livered fucking coward, and he's lucky that was your sister and not mine. Are you sure you're happy with the job we did? Because if you're not happy, then we should turn around and really fuck them up," Tony said as he put a finger inside his collar and turned his head from side to side.

"I would have done more damage but I had to shit, and I figured the refrigerator tipped over was a nice touch," Johnny said.

"You should have made that kid eat a turd," Tony said laughing. "The kid and that kitten of a father. Cowards piss me off. I can't help it, my dad raised me to be tough. He raised me to be a fucking man. That wasn't a man in there, that was a woman trapped in a man's body. We should go back. You guys want to turn around? I should have put a gun in their mouths," Tony said as he pulled a pistol from his inner coat pocket.

"We're not going back. They got the message, and besides Johnny stunk the house up, and didn't flush," I said.

"Another nice touch, it won't go down anyway," Johnny said. "Fuck 'em."

"You guys don't worry about the cops?"

"We've been to cop's houses and gave them the same treatment," Tony said. "And half of them are in our pocket, so what's to worry?"

"Your sister won't have any more troubles, and if that kid talks, you let us know," Johnny said.

"Will you go back and burn the house down with them in it?" I asked.

"Not right away, you have to make people squirm. There's an art to intimidating your victim. We would need to leave a subtle message, something to get the parents to beat the kid, you know, involve the entire family. That's the best way," Tony said.

"I usually take a sharpie and write the names of the victim on a bullet casing and put them in an empty whiskey bottle and throw it against the house, sometimes I throw it through their bay window — depends how I feel. They find the bottle and see the shells in it and they think the next time I get drunk, someone is getting executed, and you know, sometimes they do," Johnny said as he lit a cigarette.

Tony lit one too, and blew a relaxed breath of blue smoke against the windshield. I didn't dare tell them that there was no smoking allowed in the rental. I was surprised how much conversation we were having compared to the ride to the house. It's like the dirty deed made us closer.

"What did you think of big Tony in action?" asked Johnny.

"It was awesome, most people would have bet on the big guy. You took him down like he was a ninety-pound weakling," I said.

"That was nothing, Johnny. Tell him about the Clements job."

"Oh yeah, that was great, we were at a card game with this deadbeat, Clements — Tony was young then," Johnny laughed a low rumbling laugh, and then he continued. "He used to puff his chest up and point to whoever he was going to rough up. That was his style."

"No wait a minute, that's not fucking true. Maybe I should tell this story."

Johnny continued anyway. "Tony puffs his chest up and points to this guy Clements and says, 'Hey, needle dick how'd your wife like to sleep with a real man?' It was out of nowhere, we weren't even talking about the man's wife. He may not have even been married, but the guy laughed it off."

"Wait a minute. OK, I used to do that. I used to try to piss people off, embarrass them in front of their friends and then they would call me outside and I'd deck 'em right there. Now I don't wait, I just drop them like that guy Phillips."

"Who's telling this fucking story, me or you?" asked Johnny.

"Go ahead but get it right."

"So like I said, he's running his mouth, trying to get under the skin of this big motherfucker and his two friends, but Tony isn't exactly a gorilla so all three guys start to laugh, and instead of Clements getting mad, he moves his hand back and forth like Tony is a fucking mosquito, you know, like a pest flying around him." Johnny stops the story and starts to laugh.

"OK, fuck this. I'm taking over the story, because now you're really starting to piss me off," the hot-tempered Italian said.

"This fucking guy laughs and so does his friends, so I took the whiskey bottle that was on the table and before those fat fucks knew what was going on I smashed it over the heads of two of his friends and folded their heads over like folding laundry, and then I bashed the bottom of that bottle on the tip of Clements' nose. His nose erupted with blood. He thought I was after the money on the table, there must have been ten grand for the taking, so he puts his hands over the dough and I slammed the butt of that bottle on his finger tips. He must have had some black fingernails the next day."

Johnny interrupted.

I was uneasy listening to this psychopath, and the passion in his voice.

"So Tony smashes the bottle on Clements' other hand and the base of the bottle breaks off and Clements stands up. Tony rams the bottle on his forehead and turns it, cutting a circle in his skin." Then Johnny stopped. "You want to finish the story or do you want me to?"

"No you're doing fine, go ahead."

"Clement had two broken hands and a bleeding forehead, he stands up and grabs Tony by the collar and gives him three head butts. It sounded like two hollow logs clunking together," Johnny said laughing.

"Fuck you, I'll take the story," Tony said with spit flying from his jaggered teeth. "After the third head butt I figured that it must be hurting him as much as it's hurting me, right? His head was the size of a friggin pumpkin," Tony said, holding his hands apart about a foot. It was his hollow head that made the clunking sound, not mine. My head might be small, but it's full of fucking brains. I'm ready to make my move and The Bump here did a flying tackle across the table and hits more of me than Clements. I'm talking broken chairs, bottles, glasses, and money flew everywhere. I landed on a chair; it broke and went into my ribs. Johnny rolled over on me and squishes all my air out, so I'm fucked because he tried to help. Johnny gets up and kicks Clements in the back about twenty times, but that mother fucker has me by the collar still, and every time Johnny hits him, he hits me."

"You should have seen Tony's face bouncing off Clements big fist," Johnny said, still laughing.

Tony held his hands out and made a gap between them, "This fucking big, no shit."

"He didn't stop until Tony was out cold. I started kicking Clements in the head until he was out too. I put all the money in a bag and carried Tony out. That was one of your best fights, Tony."

"Did you get the point of the story Sonny?"

"I'm not sure."

"Clements had two broken hands and a serious head wound, but he didn't lay down like a baby — like that pussy Phillips, and I fought that big fucking lug until I got knocked out, and to this day

I think I would have kicked his fucking ass if Johnny would have waited till I needed a hand. I already had two down. I was going to reach a bottle that was on the table and crush his head in. He was right where I wanted him. You never give up in a fight. What if Phillips didn't go down so easy? We would have had a fuck of a fight on our hands, but you know what? I knew I could take him, and once your balls come in you can too. Your balls need to drop, like a dog."

"Tell him the best part of the story," Johnny said.

"Oh yeah, Clements was the wrong guy, he didn't owe money. Johnny fucked up and we rolled the wrong guy."

"What?"

"It was Clements' younger brother. No one told us he had been arrested and was in prison. The good news is that we had him fucked up on the inside," said Tony. "They never get away."

Chapter Fourteen

All For A Buck

"Hey take that turn and go down Glenwood — it'll put us in the parking lot of the strip club," said Tony.

I did as he said, it was getting dark. We got out of the car; the music thumped and could be heard out in the parking lot. As we got close to the door, Tony turned and said, "I hope you've got money, 'cause this is on you."

"What do you mean?"

"We just did you a favor and it's customary to take family out for dinner and drinks. They've got good hot wings and nachos here, and you can't beat the scenery," Tony said.

A bouncer stopped us and asked for my ID, and then I paid the cover charge for all three of us. We walked through a small crowd. I had never been to a strip club, so I was surprised to see a stage full of naked women. The waitresses were topless and wore short shorts or bikini bottoms.

"Let's sit up front in pervert alley," Tony said. "Wait here for a second; I'll get us a seat."

He went up to table that touched the big octagon stage, a man sat there lusting for the young stripper who bent over and teased him for his five dollars. Tony tapped him on the shoulder and whispered in his ear. The man got up and moved. Tony sat down and waved us over. I took a seat — I couldn't believe how perfect the girls were built. I knew their boobs were fake. They were slim and didn't have an ounce of body fat anywhere. Some danced; others strutted across the stage dropping their skimpy outfits as they walked. They were totally nude. I had never known a woman would who would get nude in front of a large crowd. There was no shame.

The waitress came by to get a drink order; her boobs were inches from my face. She smiled and waited for me to look up to her face.

"We want two pitchers of Bud, and three glasses," Tony said. "And do you have those hot wings?"

"Yes, one order of hot wings?" she asked.

"No three orders, one hot wings and one French fries, and one nacho," said Tony.

"Will that do it?" she asked.

"Do you happen to have some one dollar bills, so we can tip the fine ladies?" he asked.

"Sure, how many do you want?"

"How about a hundred?" he said. He pointed to me: "Bust out a hundred."

The waitress looked at me and winked. I twisted to get my wallet out and my head bounced off her boob, "I'm sorry."

"No problem," she said as she backed up and let me give her a hundred bucks. "I'll be right back with your ones and the beers."

I turned in my chair to face the stage, and a girl was lying on the floor, looking like she was having a baby: on her back with her knees up. Tony put a five on the stage and she took it with her toes and lifted it high in the air until she reached it with her hand.

"What do you think of that?" asked Johnny.

Before I could answer Tony said, "that's what I call an eager beaver."

I knew she heard him, but it takes a lot to embarrass a stripper. She stayed on her back, waiting for a few more guys to get their tip money out.

She rolled over and did a cat crawl to the edge of the stage, took all the remaining tip money, and then crawled to another section of the stage that another stripper had just vacated. Some of the perverts already had their tip money out, and she was lured to it like a mouse to cheese.

Another stripper soon came to our section of the octagon and she danced to the song "Night Moves" by Bob Seger. She was built and knew how to move — she liked to dance. Her Catholic school outfit was tight and when she bent over, she had no underwear. She was tall, sexy, very beautiful and young — very intimidating. She smiled at me and I knew in a second that it was her professional phony smile; she wore it for everyone — the fat, the ugly, the old, and the obnoxious college guys hooting at the table next to us.

"What do you think of that? What a woman huh?" asked Johnny.

"That's not a woman, that a vacuum," said Tony.

"What do you mean?" I asked.

"She'll suck every penny out of this crowd and the life out of the guy that loves her. Trust me I've dated woman prettier than her," said Tony.

I almost laughed at the short, leather-faced mobster, but I knew he had a temper and I held my laugh to a smile. Johnny didn't care. He laughed and said, "you can't get her she's twenty years old and she's too tall for you."

"Bullshit Johnny, I'm 38, and she's maybe 22, that's not too much of a gap, guys are with chicks twenty years younger all the time, and another thing, she ain't too tall for me, I've climbed taller trees than her."

"You can't get her," said Johnny. "I'll bet you fifty bucks."

She came close to us. I think she was offended that we weren't paying attention to her — now she was totally nude. She crouched down and wasn't bashful. "There's a naked woman up here and you guys want to talk? I don't get it," she said.

"My friend here says I can't get you. I think I can. What would it take to convince you to spend the night with me?" asked Tony.

"Do you have a thousand bucks?" she asked.

"As a matter of fact I do."

"That doesn't prove anything," said Johnny. "Hey, how much for a night with the young guy here?"

She looked me up and down and said, "he's kinda cute, I'd go with him for $750 and a bottle of champagne."

"See," Johnny said, "she don't like you. She'd fuck Sonny for a discount, and she probably don't like him either."

Tony was mad; he tipped the girl and waved his hand for her to move away. The beers arrived and the waitress rubbed the cold pitcher across her nipples. She handed me a hundred in ones and another girl stood behind her with a platter of hot wings and nachos. "That's $61," she said looking at me.

I started to peel off the pile of ones, but Tony stopped me. "She don't want ones, those are for the strippers. Sorry Toots, I got to teach him everything. By the way, are your tits real? They look real, they look nice."

"You must get that all the time, don't you?" Johnny asked.

She looked at him and smiled and said, "they're real."

I was embarrassed for the guys but she handled it well. I gave her four twenty dollar bills and she disappeared. I waited and watched for a while, and Johnny asked, "Why are you still watching that waitress, you like her?"

"I gave her eighty bucks, I was wondering if she was coming back with my change."

"I love this kid, where the fuck are you from? There ain't no change," Tony said laughing as he bit into a hot wing. I told you these women are vacuums. He poured me a beer. "Drink a few beers and lighten up. Have a hot wing, you paid for them."

I didn't want to eat messy food, but it didn't bother Tony and Johnny. They bit the hot wings and dragged the meat from the bones like two dogs. I took a few nachos from the heaping mound of chips and cheese. These guys didn't have any table manners or any regard for who was watching them. A short young stripper came and stood next to the table and asked, "would you guys like a lap dance?" She was wearing a see-through negligee that barely passed her hips.

Tony looked up from his plate and nearly spit food from his mouth, "does it look like we're not doing something?"

She paused and he lifted one hand with his palm up until she walked off.

"Don't you think that was kinda rude?" I asked.

"She can see we're eating," said Johnny in Tony's defense.

"She's not here for her brains, you know. Sometimes you need to tell these numb chicks. These ain't regular chicks, most of them are high as a kite and they don't know how to make a living except by stripping and whoring. You ain't going to meet your wife here — at least I hope not," Tony said.

"Pauly said they're just a life support system for a vagina," Johnny said, laughing.

"He's right, that's a smart man right there," Tony said.

A stripper was near us on stage, she looked at me and I could tell by her face that she heard every word. I pulled a few ones from the pile and put them up on the stage; she shook her head and didn't take the money. She moved on to the next group of guys and started her routine.

"Hey that chick heard you and she was so pissed, she wouldn't even take my tip."

"I told you they're vacuums, and even a vacuum gets clogged once in a while. Then he pointed to where she was and she took the tips from the other group of guys. "Whoop, see, the vacuum is unclogged — keep sucking honey," Tony yelled.

"You don't have any respect for them, do you?"

"They don't respect themselves. Look at that chick right there, she's maybe twenty. She don't know who's coming in here tonight, maybe her own dad or uncle or her father's boss, her school teachers. She don't give a fuck, so why should I? She shows it all for a dollar. They used to save that for their wedding night, but not no more, not these girls. I call them as I see them, and if someone doesn't like it they can go fuck themselves. I call a spade a spade and a queer a queer and a whore a whore. It's important they know that, so I kinda do them a service."

Tony was loud and someone pointed a laser pointer on us. It was aggravating. I saw where it came from. It was from a big fat black bouncer, and he was signaling us to come to him. It was too crowded near the stage to remove us and make a scene.

Tony saw him too. "Oh fuck, here we go. I ain't even done my wings yet. I already worked tonight. I took out that pussy Phillips. You're on, Johnny. I'll play back-up for you, maybe the kid can keep one of them busy till you get to them."

I saw Johnny reach in his coat pockets and slip on brass knuckles. They were painted black and didn't show up well in the dark club. Tony stood up and clapped, and said to the young stripper, "nice show honey, but tell your friend over there she should get her pussy checked, it didn't look too good. I almost couldn't finish my dinner."

I was embarrassed, but I was more afraid when I saw Johnny put on the brass knuckles. There was no doubt we were going to be in a terrible fight. The bouncers were as big as John. Tony led the way to the guy with the laser, who was close to the main bar. A few strippers and one waitress stood close to him, and slowly another bouncer came over. I figured the strippers might be the type of girls who liked to watch men fight. They must see it all the time.

We got close to the big black bouncer, and he bent down to talk with Tony. "The manager has asked us to escort you guys out."

"Oh is that right?"

"Yeah that's right, you guys are loud and disrespectful to the girls — you're disrupting the show. Let's just go, we don't want this to involve the cops."

"I came in for a blow job, and my friends want one too, and the young guy wants to get laid. You must have known that, and called us over for a blow job. Johnny do you want this guy to give you one?"

"No, but maybe his girlfriend can. Maybe he can give Sonny a blow job with his big lips."

The bouncers tightened around us and the girls moved out of the way.

Then Tony spoke. "Sorry guys, we're going, we're going. I just misread your signals. You look gay, and you must hear it all the time with that round mouth. We need to have a word with the manager, we didn't finish our meal and beers and we need that taken off our tab."

A bouncer had each of us by the elbow and it seemed like we were leaving peacefully. A well-dressed man, whom I presumed was the manager, had heard Tony and followed at a safe distance. We got to the doors and the doorman held them open — we went outside and the manager said, "walk them down the stairs, they may be drunk. I don't want anyone to fall." Once we were down the steps the big black bouncer shoved Tony. Tony brushed out the wrinkles from his coat with his hands, and backed up a few steps. "Keep your fucking hands off me, and watch your back, you fucking goon."

The big bouncer smiled at the threat from small Tony. Johnny was behind him, and before he could turn around Johnny leaned forward and punched him in the base of the neck with the brass knuckles. His knees folded and he fell at Tony's feet. Tony kicked him in the head. "I told you to get the fuck off me you stupid motherfucker."

Johnny turned, elbowed the bouncer behind him under the nose and then landed a hip twisting punch on his jaw. He was out before he hit the ground. The third bouncer had my elbow and it seemed like he was using me as a shield from Johnny. The bouncer was a foot taller than me, and Johnny fired a punch that barely cleared my head. I instinctively ducked and he caught the bouncer between the eyes, as he tried to duck the punch. He staggered and released me. I got out of the way. The bouncer shook his head from side to side and put up his fist. Johnny tucked his head down and brought his fist up. He looked like a trained boxer, and was ready to toy with the young bouncer.

Johnny fired two fast jabs and set up an uppercut to the bouncer's jaw, and he dropped instantly. The manager was in awe and held the glass door open watching the action. "Wait a second; are you the man in charge?" Tony asked.

He hesitated before answering, "yeah, I'm the manager."

"Did any of these two lightweights give you my message?"

"No they didn't, what's the message?"

"Sal owns this club, isn't that right?" Tony asked.

"Yeah, why? Make this fast, the cops are on the way."

"We came here for a good time, we were going to eat, drink, get blow jobs and get laid by the best whores that work here, but most of all we came to give Sal a message. A message from 'the top,' and I'm not talking about Petey or Pauly. I'm talking about from the fucking top. The fucking Don. Do you understand?"

"Sal's not here right now, what do you want me to do?"

"You tell him there's a payment due, with a late fee and interest, and my friend Sonny here got fucked but not the right way. He treated us to a good time and we got taken away from our beers and from our meal. He's out a hundred bucks and I want you to go back inside and fetch his money, or Johnny the Bump is going to fuck you up," Tony said. "Do you understand?"

He nodded.

I could hear a police siren in the distance. I tapped on Tony's sleeve in case he didn't hear. "It's the cops."

The manager was still at the open door. "I don't give a fuck, this man is too smart to have us arrested. Now get out here and help these bums off the sidewalk," Tony said as he kicked the closest one.

The cops got closer and shut off the siren, "you tell the cops the troublemakers ran away. This is business; don't get in the way of business. We're here to collect, and I suggest you get that hundred out pretty fucking fast, because tomorrow when we come back it's two hundred. Do we understand each other? You're the face I see. Johnny, remember that face."

Johnny slid the brass knuckles off so the manager could see him put them back in his pocket and then he opened his jacket and exposed his gun. The cops stopped and one officer came close. "What's going on?" he asked.

"All of us looked at the manager, who said, "The troublemakers are getting away. They may still be in the parking lot across the street, they looked like bikers."

The cop talked into the microphone on his sleeve. They were young cops and I didn't have any doubt that Johnny would have knocked him and his partner out. The partner stayed in the car and used the searchlight on the driver's door to look through the lot before he drove over there for a closer look. The other cop called for an ambulance and walked across the street. We didn't move.

"Sonny is still waiting for his money. What are you fucking numb?" Tony said as he kicked the bouncer again. "Today is a hundred and tomorrow is three hundred."

"I thought you said two hundred," I said.

"I did, but now he pissed me off."

The manager opened his wallet and pulled out two fifties and waved them.

"Go get them Sonny, because if I go over there I'm going to punch that motherfucker in the mouth." Then he grabbed his crotch and jiggled his balls. "Don't forget to tell Sal my message, and he owes us a blow job and a piece of ass," said Tony.

I got the money and I couldn't help but smile as I tucked it in my wallet. Johnny waved at the manager and said, "see you around fuckhead."

I smiled but Tony frowned — he was still mad. "What are you smiling about? You didn't get laid — now I'm pissed.

Chapter Fifteen

Late Payment

I rode home in a car full of smoke. I had never been around people who had no regard for their words or actions. I don't know when or how they learned to behave the way they did, but they thought alike and the smaller guy was not necessarily the weaker one. Tony threatened and stood up to the biggest men, insulted them like no one in their right mind would have the guts to do. He called their bluffs and he pushed their buttons. These guys lived a life of threats, and extortion. That night I went through all my emotions. I felt threatened, weak, scared, anxious, ashamed, and embarrassed, and yet I felt excited, safe and powerful, feared, and protected. I wondered if the guys liked me, and then I wondered if they liked anyone.

I'm still hungry, what's to say we don't stop by Dante's Costa DiPasta?" asked Tony. "Sonny, you ever eaten there?"

"No that place is expensive, I eat at Papa Gino's."

"Those days are over my friend. Johnny, tell Sonny about the gravy on the angel hair pasta. I like alfredo, but their meat sauce is exactly like my mom's except she don't think so, but that's my mom, so I can't get it when I take her there. I have to get Alfredo out of respect, but she's not here and I have a craving for it, so turn right up here and get on the highway."

"The gravy is thick and has bits of spicy sausage, and small chunks of stewed beef, the kind that breaks up into strands, like hair when your fork touches it, and they give you a chicken leg that's been broiled and then simmered in the sauce for hours . . . I love it so much, I can eat two pounds of it. I get an extra side of gravy to dip my garlic bread in and sip a nice wine," Johnny said.

"It's like a sore dink — you can't beat it," Tony said, as he laughed and blew smoke in my face.

I turned in the parking lot. There were a lot of expensive cars, and I wondered if they were all politicians and mobsters. I wasn't very hungry but I knew better than tell these two they couldn't have their spaghetti. "Do they have cheeseburgers? I feel like a cheeseburger."

"No fucking way are you getting a cheeseburger, and no, they don't have them anyway," said Tony. "Johnny do you believe this fucking guy wants a cheeseburger?"

"He's fucking with you Tony, don't you see that?"

I laughed and Tony reached over and cuffed the back of my head. "Don't you be fucking with me over Italian food. I've seen people get killed over smaller matters."

I pushed my hair back in place, and got out of the car. Tony strutted in front of us. He opened the big wooden door and didn't hold it for anyone. I opened it and held it for Johnny. Tony went up to the hostess her smile dropped when he started pointing to the table where he wanted to sit.

"There's a party of four that reserved that table," she said.

"Well they ain't here, and that's too fucking bad for them. You ever heard the expression, you snooze, you lose? That's what happened here, they lost," he said wagging his head.

She didn't know how to handle Tony, as he paced in front of her stand. "Tell Dante a party for Mancini is here for that table, see if that gets his attention." She picked up the phone and called her boss.

I whispered to Johnny, "who's Mancini?

"You don't know the boss' name? Don Mancini. Trust me, we'll get a table, and good service too," said Johnny.

The office door swung open and a tall man came to the hostess's side. He looked over his thick glasses at the board that was on her wooden stand.

"They want to sit here," she said pointing to the board. "It's reserved for the Johnson's."

"They're not even Italian, you can sit them anywhere," said Tony.

The man looked at him, "is Carmine coming in? Is he here?"

"Not yet, but get us seated, he don't like to wait."

The man moved the Johnsons on the board and then nodded to the hostess. "Get them whatever they want and bring the slip out back when they're done."

We sat at the table. It was close to a window — they watched the parking lot. Johnny sat so he could see the door and Tony sat so he could watch the crowd. The waitress came to the table with a bottle of wine and three glasses. Johnny and Tony were quick to order, and I ordered the same: angel hair pasta with gravy. Tony ordered a linguini Alfredo dinner to go, saying Carmine would eat it later. The meal came and just as Tony had said, it was the best I ever had. The portions were huge. Johnny was the only one who finished. We drank another bottle of wine. Then Tony stood up. "Well, let's get going," he said as he turned his wrist to look at his watch. Then he threw a twenty on the table.

"Aren't we going to wait for the bill?" I asked.

"There ain't no bill, the twenty is for the waitress," said Tony. I even got take home for the old lady; they think it's for Carmine," said Tony, laughing. "Whatever money you spend comes back to you, you just have to know how to get it. That's the lesson for today."

We got in the car — the radio played a song from the band, Tears for Fears, *Everybody Wants to Rule the World*. And in the company of these mobsters, each word made sense.

Welcome to your life, there's no turning back.
Even while we sleep we will find you
Acting on your best behavior
Turn your back on Mother Nature
Everybody wants to rule the world

I listened to the song but the sound of Johnny coughing broke my trance.

"What's with this guy Sal, and why is the Don after him?" I asked, apprehensively. "Pauly had me steal his Bentley and then I gave it back with a present in the trunk."

"Oh yeah, the head in the cooler, that was a nice touch," Johnny said.

"It was supposed to be the head and the hands, but Carmine fed the hands to his dog." He laughed. "We were sitting around the dining room and all of a sudden this big fucking German Shepherd comes in the room with a hand in his mouth. It was quite a sight," said Tony.

"You don't see that every day," said Johnny.

"What about Sal, is he going to kill him?"

"The Don don't usually kill anybody, he just calls in a favor. Who knows, he might want Sal to kill someone to help clear his debt. No one knows what the Don is thinking. All I know is that we brought a shitload of funny money to Sal, and he was supposed to 'wash it' and give the boss back clean money, but he's not co-operating," said Tony.

"He's taken a few big shipments of coke and he's slow to pay for that too," Johnny added. "All I know is that Sal doesn't agree with how much he owes. He's been paying something, but it's not enough."

"What about the dead guy, it was his partner, right?" I asked.

"Right, but his partner flat out told Johnny that he was giving him three million and that was that — that was the way he remembered the deal. He said he didn't give a fuck what the Don said, he didn't owe no more than that. I know because me and Johnny tried to collect and that was his exact words," said Tony.

"Them was his last words," said Johnny.

"Is that why you killed him? I mean is that why he got killed?" I asked.

"He was hard to get to and had a few goons protecting him at all times, until Pauly made him think the Don was OK with his offer. He received more drugs and funny money until he got kidnapped. The Don don't like people stealing from him so he had his hand cut off. First just one hand," Tony said.

"He got mouthy and threatened to kill everyone, including Don Mancini," Johnny said.

"'So I figured he couldn't hold a gun without no hands, so we lopped off his other one," said Tony.

"The Don said to only take off one hand, and Tony got his ass reamed for that stunt," said Johnny, laughing.

"He kept talking shit about killing everyone in the family, so I dialed the phone and let him run his mouth, I let the Don hear it for himself, and that's when he gave the order to bring his head on a platter," said Tony.

"Really? He wanted his head on a platter, like in the movies?" I asked.

"No you stupid shit, that'd be too messy. We put him in a freezer truck for two weeks. You know the rest of the story," Johnny said.

"He's the guy I found in the trunk at work. I'm the one that found him," I said.

"Good for you, that was some of Tony's best work."

Chapter Sixteen

Home Sweet Home

A week had passed, and I had a late shift on Wednesday, so I decided to drive out to my mom's and see if the bully had gotten the message. I didn't ask Jimmy for a car to use. I used my own. I felt like my life was changing too quickly and my car, as shitty as it was, made me feel like I was still the same guy. I think the sudden urge to see my mom made me feel like I was recapturing my old self. I needed family and familiar faces, people who had history with me.

I saw a guy walking his golden retriever. He stopped to tie his shoe. The dog wagged its tail and licked the man's face. I thought back to our family dog — he wasn't friendly. He was my dad's dog and only answered to him. They left in the morning together and got home late — it all made sense. It was my dad's guard dog and most likely trained to kill on command, just like Tony and Johnny. Like the dog they were rewarded with handouts and a pat on the back.

I reached my mom's house; she was coming from the car with a bag of groceries. She went in the house leaving the trunk open. She didn't see me — I parked and grabbed the rest of the bags before she came to the door to get another load. She opened the door — perfect timing — and I went into the kitchen and set the bags on the table.

"I'm making your favorite, spaghetti and meat sauce," she said.

Then she unloaded the bags and left a box of angel hair pasta beside the stove.

"That sounds terrific," I said. "Is that what's on the stove?"

"It's been simmering all morning; I'll get you a taste," she said as she took a small bowl and spooned a puddle of red sauce into it.

She brought it to the table and pulled out a chair. I sat and took the spoon from her hand and lifted a small amount of the gravy to my mouth. I blew on the spoon until I was confident I wouldn't scald my tongue. I loved my mom's sauces, but it only took one mouthful to know that Dante's was better. She didn't have enough salt or sugar, or something, or maybe she used cheap tomatoes.

"Isn't that delicious? Did you get a piece of sausage?"

"I don't think so, but it's great. Was that fresh basil I tasted?" I said with a puzzled look on my face.

"No, I used dried basil from the spice rack. Are you going to be staying for supper?"

"I have to work the late shift, so I'm afraid not."

"I'll put on some water and you can have a plate for lunch, how's that? It's been a while since you've had my homemade pasta," she said as she put the pot in the sink and filled it with water. She sprinkled in salt and a dash of oil.

"Mom, has Marie had any more problems with that fat kid at the bus stop?"

"No, she doesn't have any problems with any of the kids anymore."

"Were there more bullies?" I asked.

"I guess there were three or four of them, that little bitch had a gang — they harassed all the small pretty girls. She said it suddenly stopped." Mom had her back turned. She poured herself a coffee and stirred in some sugar. "I don't know what you said to that kid, or the family, but thank you. It had to stop."

"Marie doesn't know we went over there does she?"

"No, but I think she suspects that I made a call. She said everyone has been nice to her, doesn't need to know anything more than that. Frankly I don't either," she said, like a good mobster wife. Mom knew we beat the family, and I think Marie knew it took more than a phone call to stop the bully. I watched my mom's lips curl at the top of her coffee cup. She slurped the hot java, and I finally got the nerve to ask about my father.

"What was the story on Dad?"

"You know how your dad died, he had a heart attack in the shower at a truck stop — there wasn't anyone there that could help him. He lived a high stress life and sometimes a man's heart can't take the stress."

She stirred a portion of the box of angel hair pasta into the boiling water and then she adjusted the heat, took her coffee, and sat at the table across from me. I looked her in the eye. That story might have worked when I was younger, but knowing what I learned in the past few months, I felt there was more to the plot. She looked down at the table and I let her change the topic. Maybe she knew more and maybe not.

"So have you seen that girl Jenny lately? The girl that you were dating. That's her name right?"

"I haven't, since she said she thought we should see other people. She still calls once in a while, but I let it go to voicemail."

"Well you're too young to put up with that shit. You need a good girl, one that can settle down and give me some grandchildren.

Good women are hard to find," she said. "You should find a nice Italian girl; at least you would like the food."

"What if she can't cook?"

"Then I'll teach her, you have to find a girl that can get along with your mom. We need to spend time in the kitchen together."

"Maybe I'll find a nice French girl, I'm part French."

"You're mostly Italian – 95 percent Italian. Your dad was 75 percent Italian, he was only one quarter French, so its Italian blood running through them veins," she said, looking me straight in the eyes. "You should date an Italian girl. Maybe I can find a nice one for you, it's not good for a young man to be lonely."

"Mom, I need time, and besides what you think is a good looking girl I might not agree with, and I hate fix-ups, so please don't play matchmaker."

"Who knows better than your mom?"

I stood up and stirred the pasta, took a piece from the water and ate it. "It's done."

"Turn the burner off and pour it in the strainer."

I took the pan and walked to the sink. Halfway there I had wished I used pot holders. I dumped the pan and steam rose, nearly burning me.

She stood beside me holding two plates.

"Take what you want and I'll eat the rest," I said.

She lifted a few forkfuls onto her plate and then walked to the sauce pan. I took the majority of the pasta, leaving her with a second serving, and then went to the sauce pan and waited for her to spoon some on my plate.

We sat and ate, silent, then I realized she was waiting for my comments. "This is really great Ma; it might be your best."

"I want to have a serious conversation. I've been thinking about if something happens to me, there are certain things that I want, and it needs to be clear," she said.

"Like what? What's going to happen to you? You're not sick are you?"

"No, but I recently redid my will. One of the issues is Marie — if she's still in school I want her to go live with my sister. Until she turns twenty one, and then she should be able to make her own choices."

"She can come with me, I'm on my feet."

"I don't want you to be offended, that's why I'm bringing this up. You need to go on with your life and not have the responsibility of your sister. She needs a woman around her and she's gotten used to you being away, so it would be best if you let my wishes be."

"I don't want my sister forced to live with anyone else, we're family. I'm getting my own place and you can see that no one can protect her better than I can," I said.

I tried not to be offended but I was. I felt like I had been disowned by her and I knew what that felt like and I didn't want Marie to feel the same way. I'm her blood and we need to stick together, especially in the bad times. I felt like Marie had already been pulled from my life, and this was the final straw.

"The other thing is that I have some CDs and some investments that would go along with Marie. She would need it to help support herself. My sister doesn't have the money to raise another child and I wouldn't put that burden on her."

"Is that what this is about? Do you think I'd take her inheritance and blow the money? Mom, I'm responsible. I can take care of whatever comes up; trust me this is the wrong move."

"What if something happened today, God forbid?" she said, you live in a dirty apartment with some other guy. Marie can't live like that, and you're not ready to grow up and face the facts. Just do what's best for your sister and let my wishes be carried out."

I was pissed. I felt like telling her that Dante's sauce was better than hers and if she dies I'm fighting the will and taking my sister to live with me. Instead I stood in front of the sink, and ran water over my tilted dish until the red sauce disappeared against the white porcelain and made its way down the drain.

"There's enough to take some sauce home with you," she said as a peace offering.

"You know me; I only eat at drive-up windows. I don't even have dishes."

"Listen Matthew, I brought this up because I think it's important. I put a lot of work into Marie and my sister will keep her on the same path. I want it to be different for her; she should go to college, find a nice guy, and have a family. You're a single guy. It's different, Matty. Can't you see that?"

"I get it mom. I understand. You did it all for Marie and I'd ruin her. I get it."

"No, you're taking it all wrong."

"I need to leave," I said as I walked out. She stood in the window with her arms crossed watching me back out of the driveway.

Chapter Seventeen

Mommy Dearest

I was madder than a wet hornet as I drove back to Orlando. Mom broke up the family once and if she died early, she'll have done it again. I talked to myself almost the entire ride to work. When I arrived I parked and hesitated before getting out of the car. I wasn't in the mood to work. Alice was sitting in her car. We must have had the same shift, and both of us were reluctant to move. I got out and walked by her car. She looked upset. Her door swung open and she put one foot on the tar and backed out of her car, putting something in the center console.

"What's up?" I asked.

"The usual. I've been fighting with Ricky all day. He has a way of wrecking my morning off."

I assumed Ricky was her boyfriend.

"What's his problem?"

We walked side by side as we talked. "It all started when I looked at him, it's really stupid, but I was just studying his face. Sometimes I do that, doesn't everyone?" she said with a slight smile.

"Of course, what's the problem with that?"

"He got defensive and then he got mean. He says mean things when he gets defensive, but that's not normal, is it?"

"No, I don't act like that." I figured I would agree with her. She needed someone to listen, though I was surprised she picked me to open up to.

"I figured he must be hiding things and he knows damn well what he does behind my back. He's a sneaky person and one day I'll grow tired of his ways and shit-can his ass."

"Why wait? Shit-can that sneaky bastard. You can do better than him, can't you?"

"You know how it is — he's familiar and we have a cat together, and we share the car. What if he takes off with the cat and the car? What do I do then?"

"Look Alice, is he some great looking guy that dazzles you and you see stars when he walks in the room?"

"No, not hardly. But he's tall and he has big brown eyes — I like his eyes."

"Well look at you . . . nice hair, nice eyes, and perfect teeth," I said as I held her small jaw in my hand until she smiled. "You're thin and have a nice personality."

"I'm working on it, but don't you think the problem might be me? Do you think he's right? What if it is me, and he's right? I'm paranoid and all fucked up from the drug experiments we did. He says I badger him with questions and pick at him."

"You don't need his shit. That's why me and my girl are done. She wanted to date me and another guy, or guys, and she expected me to be OK with it."

"What did you do?"

"I don't take her calls and I don't care if I ever see her again, but I sure as hell am not putting up with a bunch of shit from her. The second she said that, I was done with her."

"It's not that easy for me. We've been staying with my mom, and she thinks I've been fucked up for a while. She thinks I'm suspicious too."

We were at the door to the office. Jimmy wasn't there yet. I held the door and we went to the coffee pot, and I opened the lid on the pastry box.

"Can you answer me honestly?" she said looking directly into my eyes. "Do you think I'm fucked up? I need to know: Is it me or them?"

"You're not fucked up. You have a few little quirks, but so does everyone," I said, turning my face away.

She wouldn't let up. "Like what? What quirks do I have?"

"You have this thing where you ask a lot of questions in a short conversation." She looked at me with great interest. "It's like the questions are not necessary."

"Why wouldn't they be necessary?"

"Some of them are open ended questions and they can't be answered."

She nodded her head "You know I've been working on that, and you're right, I do that. But it's only since we did the experiment, and I'm hoping it will go away soon — but I'm working on it."

"Does Ricky do the same thing?"

"No, but he has a hard time sleeping through the night. He twitches and wakes us both up."

"It sounds like he's the one that's fucked up." I poured us each a cup of coffee and stirred sugar into mine and cream into hers, and then handed it to her. "Why does your mom side with him and think you're suspicious?"

"It's because I'm on to both of them," she said as she rested her hand on my forearm. I'm almost positive that they had a fling and I'm not sure it's over. It's really fucked up to live through. It drives me nuts. It's so fucking complicated. I love them both and I hate them both. There's no other way to describe it. You probably think I'm nuts too."

"What led you to these conclusions? Did you catch them in the act?"

"No, but my mom's a cougar. She's aggressive and likes the young stuff — always teasing him, and he's the same way around her. I know they had sex, or she blew him or something. They act like the cat that ate the canary. She sits around with her night shirt on — no bra, and he wears his boxer briefs. We sit on the couch and watch TV and I wonder whose boyfriend he is. He makes playful dirty jokes and she laughs likes he's the funniest man alive."

"Maybe it's innocent and they're just close."

"Last week she came out of the bathroom totally naked except for a towel on her head. We both saw her. I was pissed and she acted like she didn't see either of us. Sometimes she kisses him on the lips. Don't you think that's odd?"

"Sounds like your mother is totally fucked. That's just wrong. I'd shit-can both of them. I've never met them but I hate them both. My mother sold me out too, so don't feel bad. She's fucked too."

Then her phone rang. "Speak of the devil. It's Satan himself calling," she said.

I could hear his voice on the phone: "Hey I forgot my wallet and I need to stop by and get it, make sure your car is unlocked, me and Joey will be by in a few minutes."

"What are you doing with Joey?"

"He's going to get some snow and we're going bar hopping, he hit a scratch ticket for 200 bucks and needs a friend to help spend it, and that friend is me."

"He's lost his license for drunk driving — what are you think-ing? Do you want to lose yours too?"

"Don't worry about it, just unlock the car. I need my wallet," he said.

"For what? You said it's his treat."

"I need my ID; I can't get in a strip club without it."

"You're going to a strip club? I thought you were going bar hopping."

"One of the stops is a strip club, I told you that."

"When? When did you mention that?"

"A few seconds ago, you need to pay attention and stop ask-ing so many questions. Joey's listening and I sound hen-pecked. Just unlock the car and we can talk about this when I get home. If I get too drunk to drive I'll stay at Joey's house."

"How will you get to Joey's?"

"Don't worry about it!" he said and hung up.

She was mad and upset. "I hate that asshole and his drunken friend Joey. He's a loser and a whore-master. How would you like your boyfriend hanging around with a whore-master?"

"Why don't you shit-can him?"

"It's not that easy. He lives with us and he won't move, and besides my mom would let him stay. She likes the attention."

She turned and fished through her pocketbook and found her keys, held them to the window and pressed the button to unlock the car. The car lights didn't flash. "Shit, it won't unlock."

"I'll walk out and unlock it," I said, opening my hand for her to drop the keys in it.

A car pulled up close to hers and one guy hopped out. "Shit he's here," she said.

"He can wait a minute. Which one of those assholes is he?"

"The one with the tattoo on his neck, tall guy with short black hair, and a scar on his cheek."

"Sounds like a real charmer," I said as I walked out the door.

I decided to meet this ass-wipe, and get a feel for what Alice was dealing with. He saw me walking and I held the key fob up so he could see and I pretended to push the unlock button. He pulled at the door latch like an impatient child. I got close and pretended my phone had a text message. I took his picture, and then clicked the remote and the door unlocked. He fished around the center console and pulled his wallet out. He smiled with deep yellow, chipped teeth.

"Hey, Alice says you guys are out on the town tonight. Where are you headed? I have a few bartender friends and they give out cheap strong drinks. I can meet up with you guys after I get out. Alice doesn't have to know. I need to blow off some steam — my friends are all hen-pecked. One of the bars is where the strippers hang out after their shifts. I know most of them. It's a sure thing — drinks and hot ass wherever you turn."

"No shit dude, I was just saying the same thing to Joey. Give me your number — we can meet up."

I shook his hand and we exchanged numbers.

"Who knows dude, you just doubled our chances of getting laid tonight," he said.

"Don't you worry, dude — I have a feeling there's going to be a lot of ass pounding tonight. Mark my words, it's going to be a night to remember," I said, laughing. He laughed too.

Chapter Eighteen

Gold-Digger

I walked in the store and gave Alice her keys. Jimmy was in his office with the door shut.

One of the part-time workers came to the front door and held it open just enough to stick his head inside. "A dog must have pissed in the minivan. It smells like piss, what do you want me to do?"

"Why don't you ask Matt? Does it look like I pick up piss for a living?" asked Alice.

"No but you were looking at me, so I asked you," he said in an annoyed voice.

"You didn't like my first answer? Didn't your mom ever teach you to either come in or stay out? You popped your head in here like a gopher. Come in or go out."

I knew she was getting heated. He was just a high school kid. So I held my hand up and walked to the door. He backed out and I went outside to join him.

"The van it smells like hot piss. She's mad because she checked it in and missed the problem. That's why I asked her," said Jay.

"Don't worry about her; she's pissed at her man. People leave their pets in the cars for long periods of time and some get pissed in. It won't be the last time it happens. Is it the seats or the rug?"

"Both," he said.

"Open all the doors and mix up a large bucket of interior cleaner and swamp the entire insides, scrub it with a broom and lather it up real nice. Then use the wet vac and suck up all the water that you can. Leave it in the garage with the doors open all night — it should be fine. It's going to be ninety tonight — it'll dry out."

He nodded and walked away. I went back in the store. Jimmy was at the desk, on the phone. He looked at me and held a finger in the air, then slid a set of keys near me. I walked out without a word, found the Cadillac and brought it to the storefront and let it run. When Jimmy came out, I lowered the window. "You need to get to the airport, and pick up these people," he said as he slid a cardboard sign on the dashboard.

I read the name on the sign. "Angeli," I said out loud.

"Go to terminal 'C' and hold the sign until someone approaches you. Be polite — they're guests of Don Carmine Mancini. When you get to whatever location they tell you — give them the keys and call me for a ride back here."

"I was going to ask you a favor."

"What's that?"

"I need Tony's number. Would you happen to have it?"

"For what?"

"I need a favor. Well it's not for me, it's for Alice, but she doesn't know what I have planned."

"I don't want or need to hear anything, but you can't just call Tony and get a favor. That's not how it works. You have to ask Pauly. He's the boss and if it's a big favor, he'll run it by Don Mancini. Those guys won't work for you without the OK from the top," said Jimmy.

"Can I have Pauly's number?"

"No, I'll have to ask him if it's OK to give you his number. It's better if I give him your number and if he calls he calls and if he don't, then that's the way it goes. Do you understand?"

"Yeah, what's not to understand? Of course I understand. He doesn't want to be pestered with the little people. I get it."

I drove away wondering what I was thinking — imagine what Jimmy thought of me. I was so stupid, thinking that he would just let out the phone number of a notorious gangster like Tony or Pauly. I'm lucky that Jimmy likes me or he might have sent Tony to rough me up for being so stupid. I was on the bottom and it would look like I was trying to jump rank. I didn't understand it at that time — I not only worked for Jimmy at the rental store, he was my boss in the family. He was so cool that it didn't appear he was in charge. He didn't look, or talk, like a gangster, but he was sewed in tight, real tight. I thought about the events of the past — the valet job and the car check-in job that he gave me. He gave me to Pauly. He had confidence that I was 'all right' for the task, and I was sure it was Jimmy who sent Tony and Johnny the Bump to fix my sister's bully problem. I wasn't sure who I was indebted to — Jimmy, Pauly, or Don Mancini.

On the road leading into the airport, a passenger jet taking off seemed to barely clear my car. I watched the wheels lift into their compartment and the doors close, leaving no trace of landing gear. I thought about the hundreds of people aboard, leaving vacationland with their mouse ears and T-shirts — every one of them dreading their return to work or school. Some may come back in a few years and others, never. I had a season's pass to most of the fun parks and couldn't imagine living in a state without such excitement — someplace where a spinning windmill or field of pumping oil wells was the focus along a familiar road. I could picture those pumps moving up and down, like mechanical horses, like the ones I used to ride at Wal-mart when I was small. My familiar roads were filled with one-of-a-kind theme build- ings, and billboards to theme parks. One building was actually built upside down, like it had been lifted and dropped by a tor- nado. Another was broken from an earthquake. Both were on "International Drive." I looked back to the sky, as soon as that jet was banking it climbed into the sun, and out of sight. Another was dropping its wheels and targeted itself for a landing. The airport was one of the busiest in the nation — people arrived happy and excited from all over the world, and returned reluctant and tired for their journey home. No one came for vacation and left having seen all that could be seen. It was impossible. I was a resident and still hadn't seen most of what was here. Every month something else opened and kept it fresh and exciting.

I pulled up to terminal 'C', parked and held the sign as I sat against the fender. A few people came through the glass doors, and were greeted by the heat. The vacationers were happy for the burst of warm against their white skin. The airport workers were bombarded by the same questions — where are the taxis, where are the buses, where's the luggage?

Finally I saw a man point to my sign. He was short and round, clean shaven and bald except for black hair above his ears and around the back of his head. He looked like George Costanza from the Seinfeld show. He stopped and waited for a woman to get her sunglasses from her pocketbook. She was taller than the man, and her teased blonde hair, nearly white, rose at least five inches above her head. She held her hand out and he took a stick of gum from her and threw the foil on the ground, folded the gum, and popped it in his mouth. He chewed like a cow and flipped his index finger at me, gesturing me to open the trunk and the back door for his woman.

They dropped their luggage ten feet from the car, I swung the door open and he slid in the back seat. She held the top of the door as she slowly lowered her bottom onto the cushion. Her big diamond ring scratched the car. I closed the door, loaded their luggage, and then got behind the wheel. I looked in the rearview mirror, and he said, "take us to Pauly's place."

"I thought we were going to Carmine Mancini's place," she said.

"We're going to Pauly's and then this kid is taking me to see Don Mancini, not you. He wants to see me," he said.

I knew I had a problem — I didn't know where Pauly lived. I texted Jimmy and within a few seconds he texted the directions.

I took the most direct route to Pauly's home. The front of his house was set back and hedges lined the road with a row of eight foot high, pointed, iron fence that showed through the thin spots. It looked like a row of spears, and of course there was a gate with a camera and a buzzer. I pressed the red button and waited until I heard Pauly on the speaker telling me to come in. The gates swung open and I drove onto a stamped concrete driveway to a circle in front of a four car garage and an open breezeway with a forty foot roof that connected the garage to the house. Tables and chairs were under the roof and Pauly sat waiting for the car to stop.

I parked and sat until he got up and walked to the car. Then I got out and opened the back door to let the woman out. An old man was waiting to take her and the bags inside the house, where a woman held the door open and smiled.

Pauly got in the back seat and shook the man's hand. They began speaking Italian, then Pauly spoke to me.

Drive to the Hilton, leave the keys with the valet and call Jimmy for a ride back. The rest of the ride they talked Italian. I understood most of the conversation. Mr. Angeli talked with a different accent than my mom, but I understood the discussion involved counterfeit money in exchange for gold that Mr. Angeli had bought wrong and was caught in a falling market. Pauly was going to give him all his money that he lost, but with funny money. I wondered if Pauly knew I spoke Italian.

Mr. Angeli was happy and laughed. That night the money, Pauly, and Angeli would be flown by a twin engine private plane that Don Mancini owned. Angeli would empty his safe and they would fly back with the gold — a half a million dollars in gold. Pauly told Angeli not to worry and that it was a small deal.

Chapter Nineteen

An Associate Returns

The next day at work, I almost fainted when a car pulled up and the driver beeped and waved me over. I knew who it was, and it was awkward. I got closer and the window went down. "Get in."

"Dave, I can't believe it's you. What happened?"

"What do you think happened? Never mind — Jimmy said you need a favor."

"It's not me that needs the favor, it's Alice."

"They ain't going to do a favor for her; it's you that asked Jimmy, not Alice."

"She has an asshole boyfriend. He cheats on her and. . ." He held his hand up and stopped me in mid-sentence.

"I don't need the details, all I need to know is are we going to kill him or break his legs?"

"Are those the only two options?" I asked.

"Pretty much."

"I guess broken legs will have to do. Did Jimmy have Pauly send you?"

"Something like that . . . look, what's the plan?"

"Tonight I'm supposed to meet with her man at a club, but a parking lot might be better."

"No, I know a skanky bar where I can wait in the bathroom stall with a baseball bat — no one will bother me. I'll break his legs and throw him in the trunk. What's this guy look like? I might know him."

I pulled my phone from my pocket and thumbed through the gallery until I found his face. I held it up. "That's him."

"I don't know him. It makes it easier, but it really doesn't matter."

"I'm sorry for what happened to you," I said.

"I'm an associate, I didn't have the right to take a cut — I'm only half Italian. Jimmy recruited me and I fucked up, end of story. I'm just happy to be alive — I'll be at the bottom — doing shit like this, for a long time until my debt is paid."

"Do you have a big debt?"

"The saying goes, borrow a dollar, pay back two — steal a dollar pay back four. Jimmy said I'm in for about twenty grand. I can't come up with that kind of money so I have to do dirty deeds. What about you — how deep are you in? They're doing you favors — trust me they want payback, don't kid yourself," said Dave.

"I already did a few favors."

"Are you a soldier? Have you been a soldier all this time and I never knew it? Why aren't you breaking this guy's legs yourself?"

"No, wouldn't you have known that?" I asked. You've been working with me all this time."

"I didn't know that Jimmy was a Capo either. You guys are all good at playing dumb, especially Jimmy. But you know what? They didn't put a fool in charge of this operation. He's smart, and who knows how many soldiers he's boss over," said Dave.

"He knew a lot about my family and especially my dad. How do you fit in this picture? Why you?"

"What do you mean?" he asked.

"You said Jimmy recruited you . . . what's that mean? Why you?"

"Tony's father had an affair with my mother; he had a kid with her — my younger sister. I got to know him and he got me the job at the rent-a-car."

"Well couldn't he get you out of this mess?"

"He did, you don't understand? If he didn't talk to Pauly, I'd be dead. You don't get caught stealing from Don Mancini and live to tell about it. He said they would consider the money I took as a loan, with interest of course, and no chance of advancing in the mob. I'll be an associate probably forever."

I began to wonder what was going to happen to me, and if Jimmy had plans for me. Would I turn up naked in a rolled up rug somewhere on the side of the road?"

"I had big plans; I was going to work my way up. Once they like you they take care of you. They must like you, Matt."

"They call me Sonny."

"Are you shitting me? That's really good."

We turned into the store and parked. He took my phone number and said "call me when the deed is set up. I'll drive, you drive, whatever. You just tell me what you want and it's done."

I walked in and Jimmy was alone in the store. "Are you all set now?" he asked.

"I guess so, but there's two of them, and I thought I might have Johnny or Tony along. I was surprised to see Dave."

"Last time Tony was there to show you that having balls is more important than almost anything. Brains are always number one, but balls are a close second, and sometimes you have to be willing to fill in the blanks yourself. In the future you wouldn't waste a favor on something so small, unless you're an old man of course and then hitting someone could break your hand. Tony is a much smaller guy than you and he would go there and kick some ass. He wouldn't need Dave."

"Yeah, but I'm a lover, not a fighter. And besides, Tony was with Johnny the Bump."

"Tony is a 'made man' and Johnny is not, he's a 'Piciotto,' a lower ranking soldier. Tony is in charge when they're together. Tony didn't have to fight; he wanted to...That's just Tony."

"I would have never guessed that. What am I?"

"After your next deed, I'm recommending you advance to a 'Piciotto' just like Johnny the Bump."

"What's my next mission?"

"I'll tell Pauly that you're a lover, not a fighter and he'll find something fitting for you."

Chapter Twenty

Batter Up

My shift flew by; we were surprisingly busy with regular customers. I actually had to do my real job. It almost appeared that Jimmy enjoyed managing the store. I wondered how long he had been in the mob. His last name was Maretti; I felt stupid never putting it together. First my father fooled me and now my boss. I waited at the store until Dave came by to get me. He looked as anxious as me. We drove for a few blocks and then he said, "why don't we drink a few beers first and then you can call that guy."

It seemed like a good idea, so we stopped at a local bar, sat at the bar, and each ordered a beer. After the first one was gone, Dave ordered another round. I drank half of mine; Dave drained his glass and held his finger up until the bartender brought another. I held my hand up to stop him from giving me another. Dave was quick to put the beer to his lips and he drew half the glass down in one swallow.

"Hey, go easy, you've got a job to do."

"Don't worry about it. I'm going to have one more beer, and then we can go."

"One more beer — you're driving; don't you think you've had enough?"

"You can drive if you're worried about it," said Dave.

"That's not the deal, you picked me up and you drive!"

"Then don't worry about it," he said as he held his finger up for another beer.

The bartender was quick to fill a glass. I peeled out some cash and placed it on the bar. "We're done," I said, pointing to the money. "Cash us out."

"What's the rush?" asked Dave.

"The rush is, if you have another beer you won't be able to fight. That's the rush, Dave."

I remembered when we had gone out that time after work, Dave ordered pitchers of beer.

He stood and guzzled the draft then said, "I have to take a leak; I have time to take a leak, don't I?"

I finished my beer and waited for him to return: I was pissed. I knew I'd have to drive. I didn't have the patience to babysit a guy who can't hold his liquor. He came out of the bathroom and we went to the car. I fished through my phone and before I could find the number my phone rang.

"Hey what's up? Did you forget about us? We're out and are looking for some women."

I knew the voice and ignorant tone: it was Alice's boyfriend.

"I'm out too."

The call had Dave's attention, and he tapped my arm. I covered the phone.

"Tell him to meet you at the Satellite club, off exit 44. He can't miss it."

I uncovered the phone. "The Satellite club, exit 44."

"We'll be there in a half hour. How's the strippers?"

"Ready and willing," I said as I hung up.

"How much time do we have?" asked Dave.

"Half an hour."

"I hid a bat in the men's room; it's in the trash can. I'll wait in there and when he comes in I'll fuck him up. What's he look like?"

"He's about the same height as you and has a tattoo on his neck, shitty teeth. You know the type," I said as I showed him the picture on my phone. "I thought I showed you this before."

It seemed like Dave had a plan after all. We drove to the club and I sat at a table close to the bathroom. I decided to check out the men's room. I figured I'd go in after Dave beat him and give him a message. It had two urinals and a toilet stall far away from the door. It smelled like piss and the floor was wet near urinals. I walked to the corner and lifted the lid on the trash can, and like Dave had said, there was a wooden bat inside. I closed the lid and came out to the table. Dave had ordered two beers.

"What are you doing? I'm supposed to be alone." I looked at my watch. "Get in the restroom; they'll be here in a few minutes."

"I will, just let me finish my beer," he said as he lifted it and drank it all down except for a few swallows. "It's liquid courage," he said, belching.

He swallowed the last of his beer and dropped the glass off at a different table as he walked by. The club was a dive and only a few people sat at the bar. It seemed like a happy hour stop, and maybe an after-hours bar, with late drinks and breakfast to sober up.

Ten minutes went by, I finished my beer and then they walked in. I waved and the two of them came to the table. A waitress came behind them and took their orders.

"We found some coke — I'm wired. I hope these strippers of yours can party all night."

"I don't remember your names," I said. "I'm Matt."

"I'm Ken, and my friend here is Troy."

"Where's the girls?" asked Troy.

I held one finger up and curled it to have Ken get close enough to whisper. "There's one in the men's room. I don't want your friend to hear, she only does one at a time, a blow for some blow — she waiting for you."

Ken smiled and stood up, just as the beers arrived. He took one draw from the glass and walked to the men's room. I listened closely and a few seconds later I heard a noise and then nothing. The men's room door opened slightly and Ken poked his head out and curled his finger for me to come in. Troy looked puzzled.

"I think he wants me, probably ran out of toilet paper," I said as I walked to the men's room.

I opened the door and Dave was out cold on the floor. "What's going on?" I asked.

"I came in and this fucking guy was all over me. I didn't want a blow job from a guy. He was pissing in the urinal and started grabbing me," he said. "What's going on? Where's the ho?"

Dave still had his fly down; I crouched down and pointed to the toilet stall far away. She must be in there, she's afraid of drunks, she's just a little chick. She must be standing on the toilet."

Ken smiled and rubbed his knuckles as he walked to the stall. I backed up and quietly lifted the lid on the trash can, and slid the bat out. Ken went inside the stall.

"No one's in here, what the fuck?"

When he came out I was waiting. I belted his ribcage with two fast swings of the bat, and then one across his back. He was out of breath, I was sure I broke his ribs. He held his chest and lowered himself to the floor.

"I'm a good friend of Alice and she doesn't have the strength to dump your two-timing, dumb ass. You're going to stay away from her, and if I hear you've called her or stopped by the house

I'll finish the job. And you better stay away from her whore mother too. Do we understand each other?"

He didn't answer, so I swung the bat and hit his shin bone. "I said, do we understand each other?" Then I rammed the bat into his stomach until he nodded. Dave was waking — I wet a paper towel and dropped it on his face.

"I told you not to drink you stupid asshole. Get up before I take this bat to you."

He stood and felt his jaw, then looked at Ken. He took the bat from my hand and hit Ken's other shin. Ken only had enough air to moan.

"Let's get out of here," I said, as I put the bat back in the trash can.

"I ought to break his skull," Dave said. "He sucker punched me."

"Let's go," I said as I opened the door. I saw Troy at the table looking at me — I acted like I was zipping up my fly. I leaned over to Dave, "Just walk out to the car and wait for me, I'll be out in a second."

I went to the table where Troy was sitting.

"There was another guy in the men's room. Ken said give him a half hour and then come get your turn with the stripper. I drank the rest of my beer and then I pretended the phone was ringing and put it to my ear.

Then I stood and said to Troy, "sorry I have to go, but tell Ken if I see him again, this was nothing and there's more where that came from."

"All right, it was great meeting you, Matt, and thanks. I'll cover your tab."

I walked to the car with the phone still on my ear. Dave was behind the wheel and I gestured for him to get in the passenger seat. I got in and started the car, and drove away. "What happened in there?" I asked.

"The guy came at me like a ninja, that's what happened. You never said I was fighting a black belt."

"That's bullshit and you know it. You were taking a piss and were too drunk to do your task. You grabbed him and he throttled you, that's what happened."

"How do you know? You weren't there."

"Ken told me. I walked in the men's room and you were out cold, on the floor. You're supposed to be doing a hit, not taking a nap. The bat was still in the trash can. I got it out and smashed his ribs. That's what you were there to do, you, not me — you!"

"Sometimes things don't go the way they're planned — you can't blame me for that," he said.

"Look, the bottom line is that you didn't take the job serious and you got drunk. That's the bottom line. That could have gone really bad if Ken would have got the bat and then I would have the broken ribs. You're lucky I came in there before he figured out there was no stripper waiting in the stall for him. I tricked him and you were lucky. Guy's like you get guys like me killed."

"What are you going to tell Jimmy?"

"I'll tell him the truth."

"And what's that? What's the truth?"

"That you can't handle a simple task — that's the truth, and I don't want nothing to do with you. Every time you're around, bad shit happens. I don't need it, so stay away from me."

"What do you mean by that?"

"You know exactly what I mean, it's twice that you got your ass beat because you can't do your job. You need to find a different line of work, you're dangerous."

Chapter Twenty-One

Quarterback

I had the next two days off, and spent them at the beach, I was still young and the beach reminded me of that. I had money, a new car whenever I wanted, and that was pretty much it. I sat in a mini folding chair about twenty feet from the incoming tide. I pulled the visor on my baseball hat down and watched girls through my mirrored sunglasses. I only moved my eyes and rarely my head. I played it cool. I thought about my family — I felt I really didn't have one; Dad was dead, and Mom might as well be, especially after she took a stand about Marie.

No girlfriend, no real friends, only an absentee roommate who stayed over his girlfriend's place most of the time. I wondered if I should try Match.com. I imagined what I could write about myself.

Lonely guy with possible Mafia ties...Interests are none.... hobbies, none....sports, none...

Occupation, turn my back on crime and drugs, occasionally beat some schmuck with a bat...

Not exactly marriage material, I thought. Then I thought, shit I'm alone right now. I don't even have a friend to go to the beach with and look at girls. When did all this happen?

Then there was a sudden pain between my shoulders and the wind was knocked out of me. I thought quick and wondered if Troy had found me and cracked me in the back with a baseball bat. I couldn't talk for a minute, and then I saw a football roll down to the water. A chunky girl in a loose-fitting bikini touched my shoulder, bent over, and said, "I'm sorry about that, I couldn't catch it. Are you all right?"

I didn't speak; I nodded and watched her get the ball as it rolled around in the surf. She walked slowly up the sand and stopped again. "That must have hurt. Why don't you come over to the cooler and grab a beer — you drink beer don't you? My friend threw it."

I could tell she wasn't going away easily, so I stood up, stretched and took a look at who threw the ball. A smoking hot girl with a perfect body, flowing golden hair blowing in the hot breeze — her bikini was small and was the same color as her tan. I held my back as I walked closer. She laughed, "I'm so sorry, I'm no quarterback."

"I was hoping you're a nurse or maybe a chiropractor." The closer I got it seemed like I got taller, but it was just the angle of the sand. She was only as tall as my nose. Her friend had the cooler open and she came up with a cold bottle of beer and twisted the cap off.

"We're not nurses, but we have medicine," she said, laughing.

She had bright white teeth; the only feature I couldn't see was her eyes. She looked like Kate Hudson, but with bigger boobs and darker hair.

"Beer is the medicine, no wonder you can't hit your receiver."

"Who says I didn't? I'm Jill, and this is my friend Bonnie. My brother and his friends are in the water," she said, pointing to three teenaged boys.

"I'm Matt. Is that how you meet guys? You hit them with a football?"

"Sometimes a rock works too. We were just trying to get rid of these beers, so we won't have a heavy cooler to carry."

"Really?"

"No but you looked like you were falling asleep and Bonnie was afraid you'd slip out into the undertow and be swept away. I hit you for your safety," said Jill.

"No thanks necessary," said Bonnie.

"It was her idea," Jill said as she threw the ball at me. I tried to catch it with one hand and not spill the beer.

"Hey I wasn't ready," I said.

"Well you better stay on your toes with Jill around," said Bonnie as she got herself a beer and sat on the blanket.

"Why don't you grab your chair and join us before that old guy with boobs takes it," Jill said as she covered her mouth and laughed, pointing at a man near my chair.

It looked like he was getting ready to sit down so I jogged to the chair, "excuse me that's my chair," I said.

He looked at me, puzzled. "Are you certain? I was just sitting here and went in the water, you must be mistaken," he said.

I looked down the beach and then I saw a chair very similar to mine and I pointed. "There's your chair, over there by the umbrella."

I couldn't help looking at his man boobs, since Jill brought them to my attention. They were cone shaped and swung when he lifted his wrinkled arm and pointed to the umbrella. "My mistake young man, you're right — I sat in front of that umbrella. I must have gone in the water and walked out sideward."

I smiled and then lifted my chair, and as I turned the football landed at my feet. I shook my head. I bet she was going to hit me in the gut when I wasn't ready. Jill was bent over laughing and slapping her knee. I might know the reason there wasn't a guy with her. I threw the ball back and carried my chair close to the blanket. Bonnie knelt down next to the radio; she tuned the small dial until she found a station that only partially came in. "Oh I like this song."

"Pick a station that comes in," said Jill.

Bonnie ignored her and grabbed a tube of suntan lotion and acted like it was a microphone and sang along with the crackling song. *"Just like the white winged dove sings a song, sounds like she's singing, say who, baby who, said who."*

Jill joined in, singing to the neck of her beer bottle

"What is this, American Idol?" I asked. Then the radio station faded and a second station overpowered their song.

"This damn radio only gets one station," said Bonnie.

"Well what do you expect? It was your ex-boyfriend's and he only shopped at K-Mart," Jill said, laughing.

"I borrowed it and never gave it back; it was like a parting gift."

"I borrowed this bikini from my ex-boyfriend's sister and never gave it back, and that towel I borrowed from my cousin and kept it. And you know what? These sunglasses — I think they're hers too," she said as she pulled them from her face and looked at them. "And what about the cooler? Bonnie, where did we get that?"

"I don't know, it was one of the ex's."

"That's why a girl needs to date a guy with good stuff — when it's over, we get it," Jill said laughing and giving Bonnie a high five.

"Are you serious, you girls actually do that?"

They laughed, "You're so gullible Matt, you must think we're terrible," said Jill.

"Well, I don't know what to think, I don't know you guys."

"The bikini is mine, the rest of the shit Bonnie took from guys," she said laughing. "That ass ain't free — right Bonnie?"

"Damn right. When a guy breaks up with this girl — he breaks up with some of his stuff too."

"What if you break up with him?" I asked.

"Same thing," they said at the same time, and they burst out laughing.

Then Jill held her small hand out. I was puzzled. "Your hat."

I gave her my hat. "See, you're learning," she said as she put my hat on her head.

"Check one baseball hat off the list," Bonnie said as she made an imaginary check mark in the air.

"You two girls don't have boyfriends? Just two single girls taking their little brothers to the beach?"

They looked at each other and Jill said, "Matt, we're lesbians — Bonnie is my lover."

My mouth dropped and I just looked at her and then at Bonnie who had a stone cold face. Then they burst out laughing. "You are so gullible Matt, we're not lesbians. Bonnie just broke up with her man, and I'm taking a break for a while."

"That's why I have the radio, remember?" Bonnie said as she tried to find a station.

"And you are taking a break?" I said pointing to Jill.

"Yeah I had a close scare, between herpes and a pregnancy. It was too much drama."

Bonnie started laughing again. "Jill you're such a liar, you should have seen his face."

"I've never met two girls with more bullshit in my life; I can't believe a word you say."

"It's her," said Bonnie.

"Oh don't let her kid you; she spins a fat lie every now and then that you can trip over," said Jill.

"What about you, Matt? No woman? Are you gay? No offence if you are, but it seems like the good looking guys are either married or gay, so which one is it?" Bonnie asked with her head tilted.

"I know, I bet you're gay and married, and that guy is your husband," Jill said pointing to a pot bellied middle aged man coming out of the water. He wore a small bikini bathing suit colored like the America flag. "The American fag, I mean flag. What do you think Bonnie? Do they make a good couple?" said Jill.

"No, you have it wrong," I said as I put my hand on my forehead.

"He's right; you're wrong Jill, that's not his husband, that's his wife," said Bonnie.

They laughed.

"I'm sorry if I offended you Matt," she said as she touched my elbow. I know you are too masculine to be his wife. You are definitely the man in the relationship. Wave him over here so we can meet him."

"Are you for real or what?" I said.

Then she put her finger between her teeth, whistled, and waved at the man. He looked up and so did ten other people, mostly kids who were at the edge of the water.

"Will you stop that?"

"OK, so you're not with that guy. Are you married and out on the prowl?" Bonnie asked.

I wasn't sure which one of the girls was interested in me or if they just got a kick out of messing with people.

"Never married, no kids, no herpes, not gay, no girlfriend. Does that cover it?" asked Bonnie.

They looked at each other and then Jill asked, "escaped convict?"

"No, sorry."

I reached in my pocket and pulled out a cigarette, and put it in my mouth. I pinched the cotton filter between my teeth as I fished for a lighter.

"Oh, a smoker — that's why he can't keep a girl. He keeps blowing smoke in her face," Jill said, pinching her nose and rolling her eyes.

"And he don't even have a radio, and he's a beer mooch too," Bonnie said.

"My mom said stay away from guys who hang around the beach smoking and drinking. Tell me, Matt are you an alcoholic?" asked Jill with a straight face.

I lit the cigarette and took a long draw, and then a swig from the beer. I laughed and then they did too.

"Give me a cigarette, you big lug," said Bonnie.

"Do you want one too?" I asked Jill.

I passed one to Bonnie and held the lighter for her until the cigarette lit.

"No, not me, it makes your boobs sag. Look at Bonnie's boobs — she's been smoking since junior high."

Bonnie gave Jill the finger. "At least I don't have an inverted nipple."

Jill took a deep inhale until it made a noise. "I don't either; don't go telling him that, he'll believe you."

"Ten minutes ago you were telling everyone I was gay and you called Captain America over.

"Well how were we supposed to know? Like Bonnie says, the good looking guys are gay or married. What happened to your girlfriend? Why did you break up?"

"You cheated on her, didn't you Matt?" asked Bonnie.

"No, it just didn't work out, that's the bottom line."

"Did you hit her? I'll bet she had it coming, huh?" asked Bonnie.

"No, I didn't hit her. What about you? What happened to your man?"

"Bonnie's man used to get fresh with me when he got drunk. I didn't want to tell Bonnie because we had been friends for so long. Stuff like that can wreck a friendship, so one afternoon at the pool, he was pawing at me and saying all perverted things he wanted to do to me."

Bonnie took over the conversation. "Jill got him on video, on her phone. I wouldn't have believed it. The next day I shit-canned his ass, and haven't talked to him since."

"Girl power," Jill said as she high fived Bonnie.

"What about you?" I asked Jill.

"I had been seeing a guy for two years and when Bonnie's man started hitting on me — I told my man about it and he wouldn't stick up for me. He thought I was leading her man on and I wanted every guy to want me. That's not who I am. I'm very shy, until you get to know me."

"That's not true, her guy is in the National Guard and he got shipped to Afghanistan," said Bonnie.

"I'm too young to wait around for him, besides all those guys are sleeping with anything that moves. We weren't going to get married, so why be tied down with a long-distance relationship?"

"Do you guys talk or write each other?"

"Just on Facebook."

Then a teenager ran up to the blanket and excitedly pointed to the water, "Eric stepped on glass and he's bleeding pretty bad."

"Get him out of the water before a shark smells the blood," Bonnie said. "Go back there and help him — you and Chuck get him up here."

The kid turned and ran for the water; a few minutes later they were at the blanket, where Bonnie wrapped the foot with a towel. The cut wasn't very deep but they decided they would pack up and leave. "I have hand sanitizer in the car. We'll clean it, and stop at a drugstore for some bandages and then take you home," said Bonnie.

It was awkward, and I didn't know whose number to ask for, until Bonnie spoke up. That's when I realized they hadn't talked between themselves and decided on who was interested in me. She was pretty smart about it, like they had come across this problem before.

"It was fun Matt, but we have to get going. Why don't we take your number and maybe we can meet up again?"

"Sounds good, and maybe I can get your numbers."

"It doesn't work like that," said Bonnie.

"We flip a coin and if it's heads, then you get called, tails no one calls. It's all up to the coin, Matt," said Jill as they walked off.

"Hey, what about my hat?"

She didn't answer. She just kept walking.

Chapter Twenty Two

The Rat Pack

I went back to my apartment; I couldn't get Jill out of my mind. She had more personality than I was used to and I was thinking about whether I would get tired of her nonsense. I had a feeling she had a way of beating a man down. Bonnie was a nice looking woman, and if Jill wasn't there I would have been interested in her. She had a good personality too, but she played off Jill's lead. I think she would be milder if Jill was not around. I saw a sensitive side to her. I wondered if I would hear from them.

My apartment was dirty. I wondered if it was me, or the excuse that I lived with another guy that enabled me to keep the place messy and cluttered. I looked around and realized a large part of the mess was mine, but I didn't have the drive to sort out where my mess started and his ended. His coat was over one chair, mine over the other. His plate was in the sink, mine on the table; his chips on the couch, my crackers on the coffee table. A pan on the stove still had last night's food in it, and a pizza box on the table had a few slices from a week ago. Then there was the mail all over the counter, some junk, some bills, and some newspapers. If I did end up dating one of the girls, I would have to either clean the place or move.

I lay on the couch, reached the remote that was under the coffee table, and clicked through the channels. I had my elbow over my forehead and watched with one eye. Then the phone rang. I was optimistic for the girls, but it was Jimmy. I thought it was odd that he called when I was not on a shift.

"Matt, Pauly called me and wants you to do a payback," said Jimmy.

"Already? That was fast. What does he want me to do?"

"Don't worry I told him you're a lover, not a fighter," Jimmy said, laughing.

"What's so funny?"

"Come down to the store. Tony is going to pick you up in a half hour."

"Great."

He hung up and I went to the bedroom and tossed around the shirts that were on the bed until I found one that only had a few wrinkles. I wet my hair and rubbed my hands across my head until it flattened, and then went out to the car and down the road. I arrived at the Rent A Car Center — Jimmy was out front smiling. I didn't like his smile, but I couldn't very well ask him to stop. I wondered if Pauly wanted me specifically, or if it was Jimmy who wanted me.

"You never told me how things went with Dave."

"OK I guess, we got the job done."

"What exactly was the job?"

"Alice's boyfriend is a piece of trash, stays out all night, cheats on her — got her on drugs and slept with her mom. So I beat him with a baseball bat and told him to stay away from her. She doesn't have the strength to dump him."

"How did Dave do?"

"He got drunk and got knocked out. I had to do the deed myself."

"He's such a fuckup; I don't think we can use him anymore. He can't get anything right," said Jimmy.

"I was hoping he could run a camera, but that's OK. I want you to know that Alice hasn't been to work since you took care of her boyfriend. You're going to have to take responsibility for your actions."

"What's her problem? I took out the trash."

"It's not that easy. I want you to take her to lunch tomorrow, it's her day off. Her mom called and said she hasn't got out bed in two days. She'll be ready tomorrow."

Then a Cadillac pulled up, with Johnny the Bump driving and Tony in the passenger seat. Tony opened the door, stood up, and waved at me over the car roof.

I started to walk to the car and Jimmy said, "hold up, you're going to need this."

He opened a drawer behind the desk and pulled out a small video camera, "charged and ready to go."

"What's going on?"

"You're filming a movie. And who knows, you might star in it."

"Am I filming a beating, a murder?"

"Better. Now get going — can't you see how anxious Tony is getting?"

I took the camera and opened the car door, and got in the back seat. Tony turned around to face me. "I'm glad we have another job together. It's good to see you Sonny."

"Thanks, it's good to see you guys too." I said.

"Jimmy said you're a good camera man, that's going to come in handy. Do you want to be behind the camera or in front of the camera?"

"What am I filming?"

"You know the strip club that we took you to?"

"Yeah."

"I said we left without getting some ass, remember that?" said Tony.

"Yeah, that didn't matter to me though," I said.

"Well it mattered to me and it mattered to Johnny, so we're collecting. Sal owns that club and he's behind on his payments, so it's time to give him another message, a personal message."

"What's his problem? Why doesn't he do what the Don wants him to?"

"There's another family fighting to control that club, he's squeezing Sal's balls. We protect Sal, but he got behind once his partner split with the money. But we found him. They can't run ... we always find them."

"But what if Sal can't pay? What if it's impossible?"

"Then he signs the club over to Don Mancini. He ain't done that yet, and this might be the last straw."

We drove to a motel and Tony fumbled with his wallet to get a card key out. "Turn the light on so I can see the room number," he said to Johnny. "Number forty seven."

I followed behind them, not knowing what to expect. They opened the door and there was a woman tied up on the bed — her mouth was taped. Johnny locked the door and closed the smallest gaps in the shades. He turned the lights on — I recognized the woman: It was Sal's fiancé. Tony took a switchblade and held it under her chin.

"Listen honey, we both know what's going to happen here. It's up to you if you want the beating of your life, or you want to leave without black eyes and a broken jaw. If you scream when I take the tape off, Johnny is going to break your jaw and maybe knock your eye out of the socket. Is that the way you want it? We know your background, and you're no virgin, so I suggest you cooperate. We're making a movie for Sal. It can either be a sex tape or a murder tape, it really don't matter to me. And for the record, dead or alive we're going to have sex with you."

He pulled the tape off her mouth and she whimpered but didn't talk.

"Now do you want to get undressed or would you like me to cut your clothes off? Last time the girl moved and she needed a few stitches."

She willfully got undressed.

"What are you waiting for? Start filming — action!" Tony said as he got undressed.

I filmed while they took turns with her, and I felt sorry for her. When they were done, he called a cab for her. Johnny took her big engagement ring. She cried more about losing the ring than being raped.

We waited with her for the cab, Tony knew the driver. Johnny told her that if she called a cop, we'd be back with twenty guys and it would be her last film ever. She nodded, confirming she understood.

We got back in the Cadillac. "You know, you should have joined in. I know it's strange, but there's honor in thieves — do you know what that means?" asked Tony.

"I guess."

"It means that if you would have done like us, it makes us tighter. It's like robbing a house and two guys are stealing stuff and one lame dick is holding the flashlight. Sure he's there but he ain't really stealing. Next time, if there is a next time, you get your dick out and I'll hold the camera. Do you understand?"

"You let us down, Sonny," said Johnny.

"Sorry, it was my first rape."

"That weren't no rape; that woman is a plastic-titted ex-stripper whore. She's twenty five years younger than Sal and he was the last trick she turned. She's been in bed with three or four guys before, the only difference was this time she didn't get paid," said Tony.

"Then why did you do it then?"

"It was to show Sal that we're everywhere and we can get anyone. Jimmy said either beat her or bang her, it was really up to her," said Johnny.

"Jimmy? I thought you answer to Pauly?"

"We do, but he had Jimmy handle it. Jimmy is under Pauly and Pauly is under Carmine Mancini. Pauly just made Under Boss, Jimmy just made Capo," said Tony.

"Tony has just been made sgarrista, a 'made man.' After this you should be a Piciotto," said Johnny. "A soldier, like me," said Johnny.

"You and forty others," said Tony. "Do you want me to tell Pauly you banged Sal's woman? It might help you get promoted," said Tony.

"No."

"Are you sure? I'll cover for you too," said Johnny.

I knew those guys would most likely want some kind of favor in return. I was learning there's no free lunch. Everything came with a price, and they kept track of anything that worked in their favor. I didn't want to be indebted to Tony or Johnny the Bump. They dropped me off and I drove home and went straight to bed. Tony kept the camera.

Chapter Twenty-Three

The Roommate

The next morning I woke early and stayed in bed — looking at the ceiling, and just thinking. I was disgusted with myself and my life. I thought about quitting my job, but there really wasn't much of a job. I couldn't punch a timecard and stamp out parts in some factory. Tony and Johnny justified what they had done by dehumanizing the woman, and calling her a whore. Maybe she was, but they weren't beyond doing the same thing to anyone, as long as Jimmy, Pauly, or the Don pulled their puppet strings.

I couldn't lie to myself: I liked the money, I liked the easy job, I liked how fearless these thugs were. I hoped something inside me would stop me from becoming them. I didn't see Jimmy as that type. He was married with kids, went to church, and sang along with the choir. He rarely swore and I never saw him steal or raise his fist to anyone. I had no idea that he bossed around a bunch of Mafia soldiers. I wasn't sure when the guys would sponsor me, and spot me in the mob. I didn't know if I could take the pledge and become Mafia. Had I come too far and no longer had a choice?

I wondered if I refused the oath and didn't ask for any more favors, would I still be called on to do dirty deeds? I wanted to talk to Jimmy, but knowing his rank in the Mafia changed the way I felt about him. I developed a new respect then, and I actually feared him. He could snap his fingers and have my neck broken. I remembered his last orders were for me to take Alice to lunch. I got up and looked at the apartment. I opened a large trash bag and started throwing away everything that didn't look important. I filled two bags with laundry, to drop off at the cleaners on the way to work. I looked in the bathroom and decided it should wait for another day.

I drove to work, but there was still no Alice. A young guy was inside with Jimmy. I wondered if he was a soldier. I went in; Jimmy was explaining some rental details. I pretended not to listen as I poured a coffee. He sent the guy out to the lot.

He looked at me and said, "things went well the other night, Pauly got his film and once Sal sees it he'll cave in," said Jimmy.

"You think so? He's been pretty stubborn."

"Not when he hears the next film will star his two daughters."

"Are you fucking kidding me?"

"Trust me he'll cave in. Pauly knows what he's doing."

Jimmy made a coffee — his attitude was like we were talking about a sports event or the weather — it didn't mean a thing to him.

Then the phone rang, and Jimmy answered. A fast talker was on the other end. Jimmy nodded his head like the other person could see him as he wrote on a small pad of paper. "Will do," he said, then he hung up and looked at me.

"I need you to get the Ford Focus and take this GPS, set this location on it, and call me when you arrive." He gave me the slip of paper.

"What's going on? This place is in North Carolina."

"You're going to have to stay overnight."

"You told me to have lunch with Alice."

"Take her with you, have lunch on the road. Just be back before the store closes tomorrow. Here's a gas card and there's an E-Z pass in the car. I told Pauly that you've come a long way and you are invited to a birthday party for Carmine's granddaughter at his mansion. Do you own a nice suit?"

"No, why?"

"You're going as a guest of mine. There are people I want you to meet, influential people. It'll be good for you. This trip is a big deal, and if you handle it right, me, Pauly, Johnny, and Tony will spot you. You may be asked to pledge to the family — to the Don, and kiss his ring. You'll officially become a Piciotto."

I didn't say anything. I figured I wouldn't ask questions, then maybe the Don wouldn't ask me to pledge. I wasn't going to worry about it. I remembered Jimmy had told me to play dumb, and that's what I needed to do. I walked outside and smoked a cigarette, and collected my thoughts. I got in the car, and drove to the gas station, filled the gas tank. My phone rang. It was Jimmy.

"Alice just called in sick. I told her I need her to go on a road trip, and you would pick her up in a half hour."

"What if she won't go?"

"I didn't give her a choice. I told her she's fired if she doesn't get in that car. So be easy on her — this job is all she has."

I took the time to get my laundry from my trunk and drop it off at the cleaners. I drove to Alice's apartment. She was already outside smoking a cigarette that she held like a joint, and I wondered if she had fallen back on to an old habit. I didn't know where she fit with Jimmy, or maybe he just cared about her. She had worked there since the store opened and maybe she had her share of secrets too. I pulled up to the curb and she crossed her arms and looked at the ground as she walked to the car.

She took a final drag from her cigarette and flipped it on the sidewalk, then opened the car door and got in.

"How's it going?" I asked.

"How's it look like it's going? Shitty that's how it's going."

"Well we have a two-day ride ahead of us so it should be enough time to get some things out that are bothering you."

"Where are we going?" she asked.

"I don't know. Somewhere in North Carolina."

"For what?"

"I don't know?'

"Why?"

"I don't know?"

"For who?"

"Again, I don't know."

"I called in sick and Jimmy said I was out of sick time. Have you ever seen me sick?"

"No, I don't remember when you stayed out."

"Why would I be out of sick leave then?"

"I don't know."

"Then if I have to go in to work, then why doesn't he have me do my job? I'm not a delivery driver."

"I don't know, but remember when you said you were going to stop asking questions — one after another so we can talk normal? Let's use this trip to break that habit."

"What makes you think it's a habit, and maybe it's something I can turn on and off? Maybe I like to ask questions and I need to know the answers. Is that so hard to understand?"

"No, but you don't have to get mad at me. I'm trying to help you here."

"Maybe you're used to hanging around with stupid people that don't need answers and you're not used to what's normal. Did you ever think that maybe it's you that isn't normal?"

"Why don't we just listen to some music? This car has a great radio; pick a station."

She touched a button and listened for a few seconds as she looked out the side window. Then she reached over and turned the radio down.

"Ken left me." Then a tear streamed down her cheek.

"So? He was a loser, you're better off without him."

She curled her hand in a loose fist and bit her two first knuckles, and bobbed her head, and started to cry.

"You were going to dump him anyway. Remember he was banging your mom? He's an actual mother fucker. What more reason do you need?"

"I know but I didn't catch them."

"You know in your heart that something happened between them. You and your mother will never be the same. What kind of mother does that, and what kind of boyfriend would do such a scarring thing to his girlfriend? It's one thing to be a cheat but that's about as low as it gets."

She cried and continued sobbing as she talked. "He just left. His friend Troy, who I hate, came by and got his stuff. He didn't even say goodbye to me or my mom."

"How's she taking it?"

"She's all messed up, crying and calling his phone. She doesn't know why he left us. I called a thousand times."

"He probably met another girl and she had a younger mother that he could bang."

"That's what my mother thinks."

"Are you serious?"

"She thinks he met someone else, with a nicer apartment and maybe a nicer car to borrow, and who knows, maybe she likes to do coke."

"Are you listening to yourself? This guy is a loser, a fucking loser. They don't make losers any bigger than that shithead. You're a pretty young woman, what are you doing with a shithead?"

"I know but it still hurts, I wasn't ready. I wanted to tell him off, tell him what a piece of shit he is. I wanted him to tell me he was sorry and he wouldn't do it again, maybe he'd make it up to me. I know he's a loser, but he was my loser, and maybe that's all I deserve. I waited for him to come home, and when he didn't I began to worry — my mom worried. I thought he got into an accident or maybe overdosed. I thought all kinds of things."

"Are you listening to yourself? You're just insecure right now, it's perfectly normal. Today is better than yesterday, and tomorrow will be better than today. Be strong Alice, you can do better than Ken. I think you should get away from your mother too. She's no good for you. You work and have your own money. You need to start fresh, get out, be independent, get on a dating site. Girls like you are hard to find."

She looked away from the window and I could see a slight smile as she nodded her head. I pulled into a small diner.

"How about a coffee and danish? I haven't eaten breakfast."

"I can go for a coffee."

We walked inside and sat at a booth next to a big window. The diner was almost full, a waitress walked around with a full pot of coffee filling cups that were running low. She was about fifty years old, with reddish, brown hair pulled back in a ponytail. She was almost too old for a ponytail. I took my cup that was already on the table and slid it to the edge, Alice did the same. The waitress came to the table and poured our coffee, and then took a notepad and pencil from her apron. She looked at Alice with all her attention, and had her pencil firm on the paper.

"What will you have, Darling?"

"I'll have a cinnamon roll," said Alice.

"I'll have the big breakfast," I said with my finger still on the menu.

I looked out the window and the lot disappeared down a sharp bank. A squirrel stood on his hind legs and bobbed up and down before taking a few short steps, Alice pointed to him.

"I love squirrels, those and chipmunks," she said.

"What's so great about them?"

"They're savers, like me. Maybe I used to be a chipmunk in a past life. I like how they find food and put it away for later, like money in the bank. They only live on what they need for today and they save the rest. I think it's neat that a little animal does that and most people aren't smart enough to copy a squirrel."

"I never thought of it like that, but it's true. So you have money squirreled away?"

"I have some, but most of it I had to lend to my mom, and of course Ken needed money every time I turned around."

"The more you tell me about your mother and Ken the less I like them. Don't you see that they both played you for a sucker? You need to move. As a matter of fact, I'm getting a new place and you can take my apartment until you find a better one."

"Don't you have a roommate?"

"I do, but he's never there, and besides it doesn't work with two guys, we're too messy. I have to get out of there and see if it's me, or him that's the slob. Either way, I'm moving ASAP."

Chapter Twenty-Four

No Turning Back

The road trip was good for Alice; I noticed her conversations had fewer questions. She finally dropped her guard and realized I was a friend and not looking to use her for anything. We drove for hours, we had lunch and she ate more than she had for breakfast. I told her about how my mom had all but disowned me and what she was doing with my sister. She said she despised my mother and her cruel ways. I reminded her of her mother and her life-style, and we had one thing in common, we would turn our backs on them. We made a pact. Alice was going to help me clean my apartment and I would move her in after her mother had gone to work. I would stay with her until I found a place, and I'd make sure she got along with Brad, my roommate. I didn't see a problem.

By suppertime, I felt like I had talked some sense into her — she smiled a lot more. We sped along the highway, I pointed to a billboard featuring a large hotel with a restaurant, HBO, a lounge, and twin double beds.

"We need to stop for the night. This place has everything. Do you want your own room, or are you comfortable sharing, I mean they have two beds in the room, so it's not like we'd be in the same bed," I said.

"I'm OK with sharing the room; as a matter of fact I'd be scared staying in my own room, all alone."

"Good, me too."

She tapped my elbow "No you wouldn't. We can watch HBO until one of us falls asleep."

"It's been a while since I've watched a movie."

We pulled into the parking lot of the restaurant, which was almost full. "It must be good food, the place is packed," I said.

"I could go for a chef salad."

"Not me, I'm getting steak. Unless you'd rather go in the lounge and get appetizers — I like nachos, and hot wings."

"That sounds good, let's do that," she said.

We went in the lobby, booked a room, and moved the car in front of the unit. It was getting late fast. We went in the lounge and took a seat at a table close to the bar. There was a drink special, which Alice couldn't resist. I ordered a draft beer, nachos, and hot wings. There was a DJ who sang karaoke songs who was quite good.

"Have you ever done that?" she asked.

"No, I can't say that I have."

"I have, but I need another drink before I dare."

"Well go ahead, you're not driving."

"OK I'll have two drinks, but don't let me have three. It goes to my head and I don't want to be sick tomorrow. It's been a while since I sang karaoke. Me and one of my friends from high school used to sing at the Elks club every Saturday night, until she started having kids and that party was over."

"You haven't asked me any questions, did you notice?"

"Why haven't I?" she said as she hit my arm and laughed. "Shit I was on a good run before that."

"It must be your mom and Ken, they must make you defensive and they're not around now. See, them being out of the picture is good for you."

"Yeah, you might be on to something. They tense me up inside; get me on edge, suspicious, and insecure. I'm anxious to start my new life, but you have to promise me that you won't let me get weak and take him back or let my mom run me into the ground again. I know it's only been a few days, but with you at work and there in the apartment, you might be the person I can lean on until I get it together. You know, Matt, yesterday I prayed. I didn't even know why or who I was praying to. It was the first time I ever tried praying, but I prayed to either let me die in my sleep or to please send someone to help me. I was so down and I wanted to crawl under a rock and die," she said.

I smiled, and pointed to the girl getting ready to sing a country song.

"I'm going to get you that little book with the songs so we can pick one together," I said.

"We can sing a duet," she said with a bright smile.

"The crowd isn't ready for that."

The booklets were on a nearby table, and I handed one to her while I looked at another. I recognized some of the older songs my mom used to play in the car. I grabbed the salt shaker and acted like I was singing the chorus. *"Girls just wanna have fun, girls they wanna to have fun, that's all they really want,"* I put the shaker down and we laughed.

"It's been a while since I had fun."

The food came and we forgot about picking a song as we pulled at the mound of nachos, while the wings cooled. I ordered two more drinks — we listened to a young man sing a Garth Brooks song, *"I've got friends in low places."*

"That guy has a nice voice," she said as she turned her chair to watch him.

"If I could sing like that, I'd be up there all night."

He finished the song. The crowd loved him. He seemed polite and genuine. He went back to his table and sat with a guy who looked like it could be his younger brother. A heavy woman was next and her voice was not well suited for the song she had chosen. The high notes were painful to listen to and the low notes were out of sync with the music and seemed like she talked through most of the song instead of singing it. Still the crowd clapped and one of her friends whistled through her fingers.

The Garth Brooks singer got up and went to the bathroom. I decided I needed to go too. It was just the two of us inside the men's room, and I decided to ask him a favor.

"You did Garth proud up there."

"Thanks, I get a little shaky until I get a few beers in me, but it's fun."

"The girl I'm sitting with is dying to sing a duet, and I'm not the guy for it. Maybe you could do a song with her. I'll buy you and your friend a drink. She recently broke up with a guy and needs to blow off some steam. We work together and this is her first time out in a long time — karaoke is her thing."

We washed in the sinks side by side and as soon as his hands were dry he held one out to shake. "You have a deal, buddy. I'll pick a nice duet and then come get her. What's her name?"

"Alice, I'm Matt."

"Alice in wonderland," he said, laughing. My name is Steve."

We walked out and I took my seat. Alice had half of her second drink down and she was more interested in the singers than the food. I was the opposite. I wanted to eat before the nachos got soggy. I watched the guys. Steve pointed to our table and then he looked at the music booklet. He stood and brought a slip of paper to the DJ. Then he slowly walked to our table and knelt down beside Alice. She wondered what was going on.

"I requested a song, by Kenny Rogers and Dolly Parton — would you do me the honor of singing with me?"

"Oh, I don't know, let me think about it for a minute."

Then the DJ read their names and the song. She was on the spot. "Let's go, Darling," said Steve as he offered his hand.

She put her hand in his and smiled at me. "Did you do this?"

"No, get up there, and don't forget to put your chest out like Dolly," I said.

They walked quickly to the stage and took the microphones. Steve picked a good song — when Alice sang her part she didn't need the prompter. She tilted her head back and a surprising, crisp, pleasant voice came from her small body. He put his hand on her shoulder and they huddled together like they were a couple, almost sharing the same mic.

Islands in the stream
That is what we are
No one in between
How can we be wrong?
Sail away with me
To another world

It was beautiful; they had timing, pitch, and harmony. They were happy and looked good together. I signaled the waitress. She came close and bent down until her ear was close to my mouth. "I want to send a round of drinks to the table that Steve is sitting at, he's a friend of mine."

"Steve?"

"Yeah, the guy singing   that's Steve."

"Do you want me to tell him you sent the drinks?"

"No, he'll know."

The song ended and Alice hugged Steve. I don't think he expected her to be as good as she was. As the crowd cheered, he held his palms up and pointed to her. She took a bow. It was the happiest I had seen Alice since I met her. She came back to the table and sat down.

"That was unbelievable Alice, you should go to Nashville. You made Steve sound like a back-up singer."

"No, he's really good," she said. My hands were on the table and she reached out and touched one of them. "Thanks a lot."

"For what?"

"For this, it's been so long since I had some fun."

"See what can happen when you hang out with normal people? Steve isn't out looking for a stripper whore, he's out here with his friend, having a beer and singing a few tunes."

"He said he'll pick another song for us, or I can pick the next one. Can you help me pick one?"

The waitress came back. I nodded that I'd have another beer and offered Alice another drink. She looked at me, and shook her head no. "I've seen my share of drunks and I'm not one of them," she said.

"I wanted to offer but I wouldn't have let you drink it. I want you to sing and have fun."

"Thanks for keeping me on track. I could feel sorry for myself and get shitfaced, but that would only make it worse," she said.

"You're right, there are no answers at the bottom of a beer bottle."

We ate a few hot wings and she scanned the song chart. I didn't see many duets, and then I looked up from the list and Steve was at the table.

"Did you have any luck?"

"Not yet," I said as I looked to his friend at their table and waved for him to join us. "Steve, have a seat. We can't finish these nachos and it's a sin to waste them. Call your friend over here."

Steve signaled his friend to come over as he sat down, he ordered a beer and looked at the song booklet.

"That's my brother Trapper," Steve said as Trapper got to the table.

I shook his hand and he introduced himself again.

"Is your name Trapper because you're a hunter?" I asked.

"No my name is Terrence, but Steve has been calling me Trapper since I was about five years old. I know a song that you might like," he said pointing to a line in the booklet.

She nodded and then showed it to Steve. He had his face innocently close to hers. He didn't strike me as a player. "I know you'll do a nice job, and I think I can hold my own, but Trapper has a higher voice and he'd like to sing with you too."

Alice covered her mouth. She wasn't used to being the center of attention. "I'm flattered that you guys want to sing with me. You guys pick whatever you want and I'll sing with you, but we need to find one that all of us can sing, and that means you too Matt."

Trapper brought the note to the DJ and he announced the song, 'You Don't Bring Me Flowers Anymore' a Neil Diamond and Barbra Streisand song. Trapper was a gentleman and waited for Alice to walk to the stage first and pick a mic — then the music started. They looked in each other's eyes and sang as if they'd been friends for years.

"You seem like nice people. I've never seen you here before," said Steve.

"We're from Orlando, and doing a delivery for the company we work for."

"She's really talented — too bad you're not locals. We're here every Friday night. We sing a few songs, have a few beers, and that's about it. I get up early for work and can't stay out late. I have an odd shift and it's hard to meet people. My brother is married and she lets him out for a few hours. Sometimes she comes with us when they get a sitter. It's just good clean fun, with family. I can only stay for one more song. It would make Alice happy if we could all sing one. What about 'Love Shack?'"

"No way, anything but that one."

"'The Piano Man,' everyone likes Billy Joel," he suggested.

"OK, I'll do it. But I'm only singing the chorus."

Steve laughed and wrote down the song on the little paper and brought it to the DJ. Trapper and Alice came back to the table and sat down.

"Matt is singing one with us and then we have to get home. Trapper's wife is waiting and I've got to turn in early. I have to work tomorrow, I was telling Matt we're here every Friday night for a few hours," said Steve.

"Usually 8:30 to 10:30. I drink my three beers a week and go home," said Trapper.

"We might be back here next weekend," I said. "It's not that far. Why don't we exchange numbers, so we don't miss you guys."

"No offense, but I can't give out my number or take a woman's number. I'm married and I don't cross the line. But Steve might take it," said Trapper.

Alice tipped her head, admiring his sincerity, this stand-up husband.

"I'll exchange numbers," said Steve. "I get down to Orlando about once a month. I don't know anyone in the town — maybe you guys could come out for a bite to eat, or a coffee, my treat," said Steve.

I gave him my number.

Alice tipped her head again.

The DJ announced our song. Steve led the beginning and then we joined in. It wasn't long before the crowd sang the rest. The guys left after the song was finished.

Alice and I went back to the room. She was floating on air. She had a good time, and it was too bad the club was so far from home. New town, new people, and her dark cloud was gone.

"Do you think we'll be back here next weekend? Next Friday night?" she asked.

"It's possible, but we'd have to leave work by noontime. We need to stick to a plan. You better get a new phone number too, so your mom won't be bugging you. You need to flush your entire life — everything but your job."

"I'd like to come back here and recreate tonight if it's possible. It gave me hope. I feel like moving up here."

"Don't go crazy after one night of singing the oldies, but if it will get you on the right track, I'll talk to Jimmy and see if we can get up here next week. But you have to be strong."

Chapter Twenty-Five

Mission Accomplished

Both of us were exhausted and slept until the sun shone through the blinds. I wanted to get dressed and get on the road. My stomach growled — I waited for Alice to get out of the shower. I made the small pot of coffee that was provided in the room and turned on the TV. I liked to watch the news, especially these days, since I figured it was a matter of time before Tony and Johnny the Bump would be caught for something.

Alice dressed in the bathroom, and came out refreshed.

"What are we doing out here?"

"I don't know, I'm supposed to call Jimmy once we get to the job site. I don't know if we're driving a different car back, or giving someone a ride. He didn't say — all he told me was to call."

"I just want you to know — I'm going to do what you said, and cut my mom, and Ken from my life — I'll never talk to him as long as I live. I have a new outlook on life. I'm getting a new phone, new number, and new life."

"What if Steve tries to call? He won't have your new number."

"Then he'll call you if he wants to get in touch with me. "I'm not going to chase him, I'm all done with that."

Then she took her phone and put it in the sink, ran water over it, and threw it in the trash.

"Good for you," I said.

"The last straw was when I got up this morning and no one tried to call me — not Ken, and not my mother. She doesn't know where I am or who I'm with. She doesn't know if I committed suicide. It's been over 24 hours and legally I'm a missing person, but she doesn't care. But when Ken wasn't home she was calling him and making me call his phone. It's a shitty feeling. So fuck her, and fuck him too. They're dead to me. This is what it took for me to see the truth."

"Have a cup of coffee so we can get on the road. How do you feel about a drive-up window for breakfast? We need to make some time."

"I don't care, I'm not fussy."

We checked out of the hotel and got on the road. I stopped at the first Burger King and ordered breakfast sandwiches, hash browns, and coffee. We ate while I drove. Three hours had passed and we were closing in on our destination. The GPS brought us to a side road and a house with a long driveway. I called Jimmy.

"We're here at a long driveway with a big house and barn."

"That's the place. I'll call the house, he's expecting you. Just stay in the car. I stopped the car and a few minutes later a strange guy walked out. He was on the phone but he flagged us to the garage as he pushed the keypad beside the garage door. I pulled up to the door as it rose. He walked close to the car and said, "open the trunk."

I stayed in the car, touched a button and the trunk lifted. He carried paintings and other artwork, and he put them between blankets. I wondered if they were forgeries. Then he opened the rear doors and put four more paintings on the backseat and a vase on the car floor. He shut the door and shut the garage door.

He came to my window. "I took a picture of everything that's in the car. I'm sure Jimmy trusts you, but I don't trust anyone," he said.

"I understand."

"What's going on?" asked Alice.

"I'm not sure, but we should take shifts driving and get back home tonight."

She agreed and we headed onto the turnpike. I drove until lunchtime, when we stopped for gas and sandwiches and then she drove until dark. It was my turn again and I knew I could be back before midnight. I called Jimmy; he wanted us to meet him back at the store as soon as we reached town. I drove until my eyelids were so heavy I could feel them flutter each time I blinked. I looked to Alice — she was asleep and emitted a faint snort. I wanted to wake her but I figured she had been through a lot and needed the sleep. She was emotionally tired.

I saw a coffee shop, and figured a cup of Joe might keep me on my toes. I pulled up to the speaker board and the distorted voice startled Alice. She relaxed when she saw where we were, and fell back asleep. The coffee was just what I needed to finish the drive to the car rental store.

The lights were on and Jimmy stood at the desk. He was on the phone — another guy was standing with him. I reached over to Alice's shoulder and shook her. She moaned.

"Alice we're back. You should get your car started and follow me back to my apartment."

"OK," she said.

We got out of the car. She went to her car and I went in the store. "That wasn't so bad, was it?" asked Jimmy.

"No, not bad at all. What's next?"

"Donavan will take the keys. You'll take a different car home."

Donavan took the keys and walked out to the car and drove away. "What's with the paintings?" I asked Jimmy.

"They were Sal's, he's starting to cooperate. Those paintings are worth a lot of money. Don Mancini is very happy, as a matter of fact. Pauly has invited us to a birthday party for his daughter. Everyone will be there, it's an honor, so you better be there — and dress sharp, it's formal."

"How old is she? Should I bring a present?"

"No, just come along, there's going to be fine food and music," he said.

Alice was waiting next to my car.

"I'm going, it's been a long day," I said to Jimmy. "I'll get the details tomorrow."

I walked out to my car, I wondered if the paintings were stolen. Alice followed me home. Once I unlocked the door and turned on the light, I turned to her.

"It's a little messy. Check out the room on the left; you can sleep in there or on the couch."

I could tell she was uncomfortable, but she took a deep breath and said, "the couch is fine. I'll need to get my stuff from my mom's house. She works tomorrow and I can fill my car and I'll be out of there forever."

"We'll both go — you'll need help."

"Thanks for being there for me," she said in a low voice as she lay on the couch and put her head on the arm. I went to my room and grabbed a pillow and the covers from the bed. I handed her the pillow and draped the thin blanket over her.

"Get some sleep, Roomy," I said as I put the light out and went into my room.

The next morning I woke to the smell of bacon and coffee. I got up and remembered that Alice was in the house. I walked to the small kitchen, where she was sitting at the table. A plate of eggs, with two slices of toast sat on a plate across from her. She sipped a coffee and pointed to a paper towel with bacon on it. "There's a pot of coffee. I was thinking, if we went grocery shopping, I could make suppers, it would keep me busy. I like to cook; I just need someone that likes to eat."

"Well you're in luck, because I'm a good eater. I'm not good at cleaning though."

"I have the next few days off and I'll whip this place into shape, it's the least I can do."

After we ate we went to her mom's place and took all of her belongings. She was angry, but focused. She left a note on the refrigerator: *"Mom, I'm moving out, I don't have a phone. I hope you and Ken have a good life; it got too crowded for me..."* I helped her move her things into my apartment. I decided to let her have my room. She hung her clothes in the closet and stripped the sheets from the bed. She protested but I told her I was moving anyway and it was nice to find my roommate someone to replace me.

Chapter Twenty-Six

The Movers

Most of the week I worked a different schedule than Alice, our shifts overlapped only by a few hours. It seemed living together might work out. When I got to the apartment I found it neat and clean; one night there was a note on a plate of food wrapped in wax paper on the counter. Another night she had dinner simmering all day in a crock pot. It was nice; the house smelled wonderful. I felt I was filling a void. She liked to cook, and care for someone; she liked to feel needed. I noticed she had paid the cable bill — the discarded bill was in the trash. She had a positive effect on me. I did the man chores that I had been reluctant to tackle in the past, and was conscious of where I let my clothes fall when I changed. The mail was organized, fliers and junk mail were discarded; normally it had a way of piling up on me. I'm not sure why, because I had money to pay my bills and I didn't bargain shop, so the fliers had no value to me. I hated sitting at the table and dealing with the mail.

It was Thursday, and Jimmy was happy. I figured maybe one painting sold and he got his cut, or maybe a monthly bonus. I didn't care, as long as I got my extra cash and he didn't ask me to kill anyone. I had gotten used to the money and it was twisting my moral compass. I couldn't imagine working for my old salary.

I was under the hood of a car, adding washer fluid when I saw Jimmy's shadow.

"I told Pauly you were going to be at the party. I just wanted to remind you to dress nice — and here's the time and place," he said as he passed me a piece of paper.

I took the paper and just as I opened it and looked at the address, my phone rang. I didn't want to answer it in front of him; after all he was my boss, in more ways than one.

"Go ahead and get it."

I pulled the phone from my pocket and looked at the small plastic screen. "I don't recognize the number, so they can leave a message," I said as I put the phone back in my pocket.

"This party will be important for you; it's not just for a birthday."

"What do you mean?"

"You, me, and Pauly will go into chambers with Don Carmine Mancini, and you will be asked to pledge to the family. It's your family too, so it's not like you are pledging to some crazy fad religion. You're moving up from being an associate to being a Piciotto."

"Isn't that a soldier?"

"It's one level higher than an associate. We call it a button man, but yes they refer to the spot as a soldier, but you're still one of my hand-picked crew. Congratulations, you've done well."

I didn't know what to say. "Thanks," seemed to be the right word. He held his hand out and I shook it.

"I'm leaving town for a few days. Sal has a large collection of exotic antique cars. We're taking them for back payment. I have to go to where they're stored — I'm bringing back a Lamborghini for the party. It's Don Mancini's gift to Pauly's daughter. I was asked to do it myself, or I would have sent you down to get it cleaned and bring it back here," said Jimmy.

He walked away. Now I knew why he was happy, he had the best job. I pulled the phone from my pocket and redialed the number. I suspected that it may be Alice with her new phone.

"Hello."

"Hey Matt, it's me Bonnie. Remember, me?

"Yeah I do. Bonnie and the quarterback at the beach."

"Jill's the quarterback."

"I'm surprised to hear from you. What's going on?"

"Jill and I are moving this weekend and we are fresh out of guys with big arms and strong backs. I didn't know if your back healed from getting hit with the football, but if it has we're having a moving party and you're invited. There's free beer, Matt ... I know you like free beer."

"Sounds like fun, what day?"

"Sunday, it's the first of the month and we have to be out by the first. We're calling everyone we know. You don't happen to have a truck, do you?"

"No sorry, fresh out of trucks."

"Can we count on you for Sunday?"

"Sunday, I'm in church, and it's supposed to be a day of rest."

It was silent for a few seconds and then she asked, "Are you serious?"

"Do you want me to go to hell?" I said laughing.

Why don't I text you the address and if you can make it, it would be good to see you — Jill says hi."

"That sounds like a plan. I have a big party to go to Saturday night, so it might be later in the day."

"That's fine," she said, and hung up.

I thought about what Tony said about women, that a good one is hard to find and the bad ones are like vacuums, sucking up all your time, money, emotions, favors, cars, trucks and whatever they can get. I'm sure Jill and Bonnie had a few suckers on their call list, and I wasn't impressed that the first time they called me it was for a shitty moving party. Probably some dump apartment that they were being evicted from, on the third floor with heavy furniture, sofas with sleeper beds, and big women's dressers.

Then my phone rang again. I thought it might be Jill, but when I got the phone out of my pocket I saw that it was Brad, my roommate.

"What's up?" he asked.

"What's up with you?"

"What's up with the chick staying at the house? You didn't mention you have a girl living there."

"She needs a place for a while, and you're never there, so I let her have my room and I took the sofa. What's the problem?"

"Are we splitting the rent two ways or three ways?"

"Whatever you want, I don't care. As a matter of fact I was thinking about getting a different place, maybe closer to work," I said.

"The place was nice and clean, and you're right I don't stay there often. I'd like a place closer to work too. Me and my girl are thinking about splitting her rent. If you think this girl is staying, I can give up my room and when I'm in need I can flop on the couch. I just don't want to pay for a place for your girl to live, especially since I'm never there."

"I hear ya. Take whatever you own and I'll cover the rent. I can handle it alone, and you're always welcome to come and go as you please. I just figured I'd be the one that would move, but either way is OK with me."

"Why don't you just give me five hundred bucks and I'll leave the bed and TV. I'll throw in the nightstands and the coffee table."

"Sounds like a plan," I said.

"I'll be by in a few days and get my clothes and a few other things."

"Good, I'll leave the cash in an envelope on the counter."

I didn't know if Alice was truly going to stay, but I liked having a cleaner house, and living with him and his mess was getting on my nerves. I did want a new place but staying there was easy. I wondered if I invited Jill and Bonnie to a moving party if they would show up. I doubted it.

My shift was nearing the end. Jimmy was in the office and Alice had pulled into the parking lot. She was nice now that she was staying at my place. I walked to her car; she was fifteen minutes early for her shift.

She got out of her car and pulled her small lunch box from the seat.

"I made American chop suey. I put some on a plate for you; just microwave it for a minute."

"Thanks. I talked with Brad, he shares the apartment; he said he knew you were there."

"There's no problem is there?"

"No, he was moving in with his girlfriend anyway, so he's just going to take his clothes and you can have his room for as long as you want it."

She smiled, "I was afraid you wanted me out, I don't know where I would go, so that's good news. I'll go to Wal-Mart after work and get new bedding, and some towels. I'd like to stay for a while; I can help with the bills too. I paid the cable bill."

"I know, I saw it in the trash. Thank you. We can work out the details later. You need to get a phone, and you need to stay strong."

Then she reached into her pocketbook and pulled out a new phone. "I got this today. It's strange since I don't have anyone to call ... look, no contacts," she said as she showed me a blank screen.

I took her phone and I put my phone number in it and then called my phone. "There, now you have one, and call me whenever you need something, or if you get weak."

"Living at the apartment has really kept me busy, with all the cleaning and cooking, grocery shopping and I organized the cabinets and the refrigerator. I get into cleaning when I have a broken heart."

"Not me. I get into drinking when I get shit on."

Chapter Twenty-Seven

Kiss The Ring

I stayed home the next few nights; it was just me and Alice and a big bowl of popcorn. We sat on the couch and watched some of her collection of DVDs. I liked the same type of movies, action comedies with a hint of romance. It was good to hear her laugh. The following night was Don Mancini's party. Alice had to work until 11, so I didn't feel bad about leaving her alone. I figured we would get back at about the same time.

The party was to start at 7; I was dressed in a new suit I bought for the occasion, and after three tries I mastered my necktie. I stopped at the local CVS and picked up a birthday card and put a fresh one hundred dollar bill inside, signed my name "Sonny," and sealed it.

I drove for a half hour; I knew I had the right place when I saw Johnny at the front gate, checking cars, and familiar faces. He stopped me and then patted my shoulder through the open window.

"Congratulations Sonny. Don't over celebrate," he said. "Just words of advice."

"Sure, thanks," I said as I drove up the driveway to where Joey was parking the cars. I walked in the massive front door to a large foyer where a table was filled with champagne glasses sitting on a tray. I took one after I saw another guest carry one away. The foyer echoed with voices from the large room next to it, where forty feet of tables filled with food; in two corners were bars, the other two corners had cakes and pastries. One cake was as large as a wedding cake; it was on a table by itself. Everyone was dressed like they were at a wedding. I recognized a few faces, a few customers from the car center.

Petey saw me and waved. He wanted me to meet the man whose shoulder he had his hand on. I slowly approached. The man was tall with black eyes and thick gray/black hair combed straight back. He smiled, and his top teeth were straight and white, but his bottom teeth didn't line up right, and were a darker tint than the uppers. I suspected his top teeth were dentures; I couldn't keep my eyes off them as he talked.

"Sonny, I want you to meet Consigliere Alfred Maretti."

"That name sounds familiar," I said.

"It should be, your boss Jimmy is my son; he said you've done good things and tonight it's official. The cake in that corner is for you — welcome, I can see a good future for you."

I looked to the back wall of the great room; it was a wall of decorative round topped windows with small wooden grills. The entire room was mahogany, with twenty foot ceilings. A crowd of mostly guys stood by the back wall. One of them was Jimmy, and once he saw me he for waved me to come closer. I excused myself and backed away from Alfred and Petey.

I got close to him and saw that the crowd was looking at the Lamborghini parked in the courtyard; it had a big ribbon and bow on it and sparkled like a jewel.

"What do you think of that?" asked Jimmy.

"She's a lucky girl."

"She probably won't even want it. She has a nice Mercedes." He looked at his watch. "You'll meet her soon; she's supposed to be here at 8 o'clock."

"You didn't mention that your dad was going to be here. He's a Consigliere. What's that?"

"He is the family advisor, a lawyer. He advises Don Mancini. He's involved with the inner workings of the family; legal matters and whatever big moves that involve the Don."

"What about Petey? Where's he fit?"

"Petey is a financial advisor. He knows good investment, bad investment. It was his idea to get Sal's artwork and car collection. They call it collateral."

I held my hand up to my forehead, and slowly lowered it as I talked. "So it's Don Mancini at the top, then your dad the advisor, then Pauly." I paused and he finished the order of the family.

"Petey and then me, and Tony and finally you and Johnny, and of course the associates and wannabe's. There's more than one in every spot except for the four men at the top, Petey, Pauly, Alfred, and the Don. That's why you have to show respect to the family." He snapped his fingers and said, "just like that a guy can move up and next thing you know he's your boss. I've passed a lot of guys that have been at the same level their entire life." He put his hand on my shoulder and bowed his head to my eye. "I don't beat people, or sell drugs on the street — that's a soldier's job."

"Johnny seems old to still be a soldier. He told me not to drink tonight."

"He almost moved up a few times but he got drunk and embarrassed himself and the family, so he stays at the bottom. Tony is loud too, but he gets the job done and people fear him, and sometimes that's a good thing. He won't go any higher, but he respects those who do. He's a good man. I could tell that man to cut his own fingers off and he'd start looking for a knife. You need guys like that."

I looked at my fingers and then at him.

I felt a hand on my shoulder, Pauly's. "Don Mancini is waiting to see you."

I took a deep breath. Jimmy leaned close to me and said, "I'm going to grab a tray of champagne and I'll be right behind you."

I followed Pauly down a wide hall, past an open doorway to a big library. Pauly walked by but I looked inside. I saw a small foot at the leg of a long table. It looked like water had been spilled on the floor. There was a small boy; he appeared to be unconscious face down with an empty cup close to his hand. I went inside, knelt down and dragged him by the foot to get him away from the table. "Oh my God, this kid is turning blue," I hollered. "He choked on something!" I tapped his chest, without getting a response and then I yelled, "Get some help!" Pauly heard me and rushed to the doorway. I had spun the kid to face him — his chest against my back.

"His face is blue, my grandson!" Pauly yelled. "Get some help over here, someone get the fuck over here!"

With the music and the distance to the crowd, no one came. I squeezed the kid's chest rapidly. I had seen this move done before, but I didn't know if I was doing it hard enough or quick enough.

"Do something Sonny! He's fucking blue!"

I jerked the kid so hard I felt his spine click and I worried that I'd break his small ribs. I tried once more, and something flew from his mouth. He was still out, so I spun him around and laid him on the table, popped my fist on his chest and started mouth to mouth, and after a few seconds he came to.

He cried and Pauly scooped him up in his arms and kissed his neck. "You're all right, Dominic, you're all right. I want you to point out which guy gave you the drink with ice in it."

The boy kept crying, and Jimmy came to the doorway. "What happened?"

"Some asshole gave Dominic a cup of soda with big chunks of ice — he choked and thank God Sonny saw him and knew what to do. Dominic was dead on the floor. I want whoever gave him the soda to feel my wrath."

Dominic sobbed for a few more seconds and then Pauly patted his hair. "Are you all right Dominic? Are you breathing OK?" said Pauly.

"I'm OK, Grandpa."

"Take my hand and show me who gave you the drink. I'll break a chair over his head, that stupid fuck."

Dominic didn't put his hand in his grandfather's, he looked at the floor. "I took it from the table; Mom won't let me have soda, so I came in here to drink it."

Pauly was madder than a wet hornet. He didn't have anyone to take his frustrations out on.

"I hope you learned your lesson Dominic," Pauly screamed. "You almost died! Now thank Sonny for saving your life. You were lucky this time, but next time there might not be someone there to save you. Did you learn something?" he screamed as he held the little boy's face between his thick hands.

The boy nodded his head. "Thanks Sonny, I won't do it again."

Pauly let go of his face and then hugged him again and kissed his neck. "I don't know what I would have done if I would have lost you. I probably would have killed the entire wait staff."

He let the boy down and Dominic went through the doorway, past a man who moved slightly to let him pass. Jimmy followed him into Don Mancini's chambers. I could hear from the echoing voices as they traveled through the open doorways.

"Don Mancini, Sonny just saved Dominic's life — two seconds more and we'd have lost him," said Pauly.

"I saw, you seem to be at the right place at the right time Sonny." Then he held his hand out and I hesitated, until Jimmy elbowed me. I dropped on one knee and kissed his ring. I kept looking at the floor until he took his hand from mine and turned and walked down the hallway. Pauly grabbed my elbow and helped me up, even though I didn't need help.

"I'm going to need a minute alone with the Don. Jimmy get your father and meet us in the chambers."

Jimmy walked away and I stood in the library doorway and watched them walk by as Jimmy had his father's ear. They entered The Don's chambers and Alfred shut the door. Pauly was already inside and after about five minutes I heard the door open and Jimmy waved for me to follow. Once inside the big room, there were wooden chairs with cushioned backs fastened with small brass tack heads; they were in a crescent in front of a large desk that the Don sat in. Jimmy was sitting and so was his father. Pauly paced the floor and I didn't know if I should stand or sit.

The Don stood and walked to the corner of the mahogany desk. He curled his hand, gesturing for me to come close and then pointed his finger to the floor. I knelt before him.

"Sonny, you know your father had saved my life? He had a small amount of Frenchman in him. Your mom, she's full Sicilian; a good woman and who pledged you to serve the family. You saved Dominic — it's a sign." He paused and took a sip from a small glass of scotch. "I want you to pledge your service to the family, anything or everything at all cost. You take care of the family the family will take care of you. Now under free will — Sonny do you pledge yourself before all other things in this world to the family?"

"Yes Don Mancini."

He took a picture of Saint Francis of Assisi, put it in my hand and lit it on fire. "Hold this as long as you can and repeat after me Sonny: As this card burns, may my soul burn in hell if I betray the oath of Omerta. I enter alive and have to get out dead."

I repeated word for word and held the card until my fingers were burned, and the small corner dropped on the marble floor. They smiled at me.

"Excellent, from this day forward you will use your Sicilian name, and the name Pauly gave you. You will be known to the family only as Sonny DiMambro. Jimmy, Pauly, and Alfred and I have agreed to make you a full sgarrista, a made man. Through your loyal deeds and unchallenged attitude you will skip serving as a Piciotto."

He lowered his hand and I kissed the ring and smiled. I couldn't believe it; I skipped being a foot soldier and started at the same level as Tony. I was boss over the Piciotto and the associates. The Don backed up and I let go of his hand. Jimmy handed each of us a champagne glass and we toasted.

"To you, Sonny DiMambro: You are family," said Don Carmine Mancini.

Chapter Twenty-Eight

Good News Travels Fast

Most family members shook my hand. I feared some might be disgruntled, but soon I learned that no one dared doubt the decisions of Don Mancini. They fell into line quickly; even Tony and Johnny the Bump seemed happy for me. Jimmy had introduced me to almost everyone in the room. I stayed at the party until 11, long enough to show respect. I didn't drink, as Jimmy had advised me not to, and I was polite to the wives and girlfriends but rarely made eye contact with them as a sign of respect.

I drove home wondering if I had been enlisted in the devil's den, if this was my fate. I wanted to blame my mother for being born in the mob and taking her living from them. I was grateful that I skipped a level and wasn't a foot soldier, but I wondered if I would become a target. I knew I wasn't in the Boy Scouts and I knew that more power meant more responsibility, and more involvement with crime and dirty deeds. The kind of involvement that can get a guy in prison; that was my big fear. I was young and never thought I might get killed. I had daydreamed about being in the military and although bullets whizzed by head, I would crawl in the sand and run to safety as my troops got shot, but never me. I always felt death would wait until I was 100 years old, when a cool night with an open window; a wheezing cough and a chill would get me to fall into a deep slumber and never wake. That was the way I had it figured.

I looked at the clock on the dashboard. Alice would be home. I wanted to tell someone the news but I was almost certain that she was not a family member — her last name was Thomas. Then my phone rang. It was Jill.

"Hey, is this Matt?"

She sounded drunk. "Yeah, who's this?" I asked even though I already knew.

"Me and Bonnie are at a party and we were thinking that our bottle of rum is empty and who would be a sweetie and get us some more. She said Matt, but she's in the bathroom so I called you. Can you get us a bottle and bring it over?"

"I'm at home in bed, I can't go out."

"Get up and get us a bottle, you can do it."

"I would but I lent my car to my roommate, and he won't be back for a few hours."

"You can get another car, or call a cab; he can take you Matt — please."

I knew she was wasted and would be passed out by the time I got there, so I went along with her nonsense. "OK, where am I going?"

"It's Chad's house, you know my car?"

"Yeah of course."

"I parked on the corner, you'll see it."

"Perfect I'll see you in fifteen minutes?"

"Thanks Matt you're the best," she said as she hung up.

I turned my phone off in case she called again and then I pulled into the driveway and got out of the car. I saw the blinds move and Alice opened the door for me. I walked in and could smell freshly popped corn. She had a bowl on the couch and she was in her pajamas.

"I'm watching the movie, 'How to Lose a Guy in Ten Days.' Have you seen it?"

"I think so," I said as I took a seat next to her and put my hand into the popcorn bowl. I held my hand to my mouth and funneled the entire handful into it. Only one piece fell on the couch. She looked at me as she popped one at a time into her small mouth.

I reached for another handful. This time I ate one at a time.

"I like this part, when she brings over that stupid dog and he gets stuck with it," I said.

"That dog is cute. I love animals."

I stayed up for a little while and then I went to bed. She watched the rest of the movie. By the time I woke up in the morning she had left for her shift. She left a note, *"I'm doing laundry later and it's no problem if you put your things in a basket, I'll get them done while I do mine. Have a great day."*

I looked around the room. I had a lot of socks and underwear, and a few towels that had been on the floor for a week. I rounded up all that would fit in the basket and pushed it next to her laundry. I knew it was going to suck for her to go to the Laundromat. I always dropped my clothes off and picked them up, folded and clean. I opened the refrigerator and saw there was milk, eggs, and orange juice. I wasn't used to having groceries. I opened a cabinet and saw two boxes of cereal and a box of Pop Tarts. I filled a bowl with cereal and milk, and while it softened I got my phone from the charger and looked at the screen.

I had a text message from Jill: *"Sorry to bother you last night, but we got up early this morning and would like to see you today. I hope you can come to our moving party, # 22 Hessling St. Kissimmee."*

She wasn't giving up. I ate my breakfast and looked at my watch, maybe I could help for a few hours before I had to work the late shift at the rental center. I drove to the address; a moving truck was backed up to the front door. An aluminum ramp spanned from the truck to the steps. Two people were carrying small boxes into the truck. One girl was out front smoking a cigarette. I got closer, and parked across the street behind a few other cars. I walked in the house and the girls were putting dishes in boxes as two guys dragged a mattress across the floor. One young boy and a skinny young girl were standing too close together to get anything done. Jill saw me and elbowed Bonnie.

"Hey glad to see you made it," said Jill, "I sent one of the guys down to get beer, and pizza is on the way too. I hope you're hungry."

I looked around and asked, "What's staying and what's leaving?"

"Everything except the stove and refrigerator."

"What about the washer and dryer?"

"We have to sell them; the new place doesn't have hook-ups. They work fine but we'll be lucky to a get a couple hundred bucks for them since they're not a pair."

"I've got hook-ups at my place. Is that what you want for them? Two hundred for the pair? I'll take them."

"That was $200 each . . . are you trying to take advantage of us girls Matt?"

"No, I thought you said you'd be lucky to get $200 for them."

"You look like the type that takes advantage of nice girls. I'll ask Bonnie if she can stand to part with them."

Bonnie walked in the room carrying a box of towels.

"How much do you want for the washer and dryer?"

"I don't care. I'd give them away if someone can haul them off," she said. "I don't have anywhere to store them. Maybe we should just leave them here and let the landlord throw them out. The dryer takes all day to dry the clothes."

Jill turned to me and said, "I guess we can do three hundred," she said laughing.

"No thanks, I'll just have Sears drop a set off."

I took the box of towels from Bonnie and brought them to the truck. I came back for another load. Then the beer showed up, and another guy, who helped me with the sofa. Jill kidded with him the same way she did with me and she had him interested in the washer and dryer. This time Bonnie kept quiet — he gave her $250 for the pair and we loaded them on his pick-up truck. I felt they would have suckered me if Bonnie would have played along. I helped with the dressers until the kid I was moving it with lost interest — he saw the pizza delivery car pull in and dropped his side of the dresser. I didn't care if I ate or drank so I waited by his truck. The delivery driver carried a stack of pizzas in the house. Jill handed him some cash and they talked and laughed for a few minutes and then when he turned around I recognized him. It was Kenny's friend. He walked past me and I ducked behind the dresser, I was sure he saw me. I didn't want a scene in front of the girls, especially if he was a friend of Jill's. He drove away with his head turned looking back at me. I wanted to give him the finger.

I went back inside the house to get the drawers to the dresser. Jill was bent over the table pulling a slice of pizza from the box. "Do you want a piece?"

"Sure, but don't you think you're being forward?"

"I meant a piece of pizza," she said.

"You were bent over the table, so I figured you got weak."

"Is it because we ordered 'meat lovers?' Did that give you the wrong idea?"

She handed me a slice after she took a bite from it. Hey you bit it."

"It wouldn't be any worse than kissing me, and beside I wanted to try it," she said.

"The pizza, or the kiss," I said as I bit the pizza.

"Just pizza for now. There's too much work to do," Bonnie took a slice of pizza. I wondered if they made a decision on which one was interested in me.

"How do you know the pizza guy?" I asked. "His name is Troy."

"Just from delivering food," Bonnie said. "He always hits on Jill; we get food cheap or free."

"I'd never date him, but he doesn't know that," said Jill. "I don't date bikers."

"He's a biker?"

Jill nodded and Bonnie took a piece of Hawaiian pizza and then she turned to Jill.

"The cars and pick-up truck are loaded with our clothes and dishes. You and I should go to the new apartment and start putting things in the closets," Bonnie said to Jill.

Jill turned to me, "are you going to stay here and help load the things in the cellar?"

"I guess so," I said.

She took some of the beer and two boxes of pizza for the crew that was at her new apartment. Once they were gone I got in my car and left.

Chapter Twenty-Nine

Sing A New Song

I went to work an hour early. I was frustrated with Jill and Bonnie; work seemed like a 'home away from home.' I had money that I felt I couldn't spend, a home that wasn't really a home, and a family that wasn't really a family, a girl but not really a girlfriend. I saw how Jimmy lived — low profile, nothing flashy. I didn't know if he was scared, or his father advised him to be low key. He was obviously going places; his dad was the Don's right hand man. Jimmy was under the radar and I was confident that once it was his time, he would emerge with power and enough money to swim in. I guess I wanted the same but I wondered how to handle it. Jimmy would be at work in an hour and maybe that's why I came in early. I needed guidance, not just with my job or the family, but with life in general. I'm not sure if Jimmy was enough older than me to be the right person to guide me, but we had a lot in common, so I welcomed his words whenever we talked.

Alice was getting forms from a supply company; Darcy the part timer was doing the office work until she got back. I made small talk with her until I saw Alice's car pull in. She popped the trunk, and I walked to the car and started to unload the boxes of supplies.

"You're in early, I see," she said.

"Yeah I was helping a friend move and I didn't want to go all the way home and back to work, so I figured I'll come by and see what's happening around here. I almost bought a washer and dryer, but it was used and I didn't want to put junk in the apartment."

"That would be awesome; if you get a set I'll do all the laundry. I don't mind the Laundromat, but there's nothing like having your own, in the house."

"I was going to call Sears and have them drop off a set. Maybe that's what I should do."

"There's some fliers in the newspaper, let go inside and pick out a set."

She was excited. I liked how simple she was. We went inside and she found the fliers and thumbed through them. She dog-eared the pages of appliance stores and then passed them to me.

She stared at them with her eyebrows down, like she was picking out a new car. She read the specs and pointed to the sales. "My mom had this set ... it works good but the washer is loud."

"We don't want that," I said. "What about this set?"

Before she could answer my phone rang.

"Hello, this is Steve. I tried to call Alice but I got a message — her phone is no longer in service. I figured she might be out of area, or maybe she dropped it in the lake."

"Steve, the karaoke guy, right?"

"That's right, my brother and I are going to be up at the club. I wasn't sure if you would be there with Alice, but I would like to extend an invitation for you both to come up and sing a few songs, have some drinks and appetizers — my treat."

"I'll be sure to let Alice know. What night will you guys be there?"

"Saturday night. See you then if you make it — I understand it's quite a drive. Give Alice my best," he said and hung up. I could see Alice was ready to ask me who called.

"Steve invited us up for drinks and a few songs at the club. Remember Steve the singer?" Then I made my voice low and held my fist near my mouth, *"I've got friends in low places, where the whiskey drowns and the beer chases my blues away."*

"Really? He wants us to go back up there? That was a lot of fun, can we go?"

"You can go."

"I won't go without you."

"Why not?"

"I could never find that place again and besides it won't be fun unless you're there."

"That's a four-hour ride, it's a long way to sing a few songs and eat a plate of nachos."

"Come on — they were nice and besides this time I'll pay, it's my treat. Darcy can work for me and you already have Saturday night off."

"Steve said he'll treat. A minute ago I was buying a wash machine and now I'm going on tour with you and Steve. Isn't there karaoke around here?"

"All the places around here will have Kenny's friends. I can't go out and risk seeing him or them. I need to get out of town until this blows over," she said.

"OK, I understand. I ran into a friend that knows that Troy guy — Ken's friend. She said he's a biker. Is Ken a biker too?"

"He's a wannabe biker — he's not officially in the club; Troy is his spotter, he's a member."

"Why did you get involved with such a loser?"

"It didn't start out that way. He was just a regular guy when I met him and then he met new friends and got caught up in drugs and strippers and you know the story about my mom. It just went to shit all in one year."

I looked back at the flier. "Let's get a washer from Sears. Help me make a decision."

"Why Sears?"

"It's the only credit card I have, so it's Sears."

She looked at the models and picked a heavy duty set. I didn't know anything about them, so I agreed with her. I circled it with a pen and called it in like I was ordering a pizza. They took my card number and it was a done deal. "Delivered on Wednesday, next week," I said.

She looked at the schedule. "Wednesday is good — I'm off until 7 p.m. I'll be home all day."

"OK, it's settled — you stay home and wait for it."

"What about karaoke on Saturday night?" she asked.

"I guess so."

I stood up and walked to the glass door. Jimmy had just pulled in. I walked out and lit a cigarette. He walked close to me. "What's new?" I asked.

"An associate told me that a biker has been asking a lot of questions about you."

"I just found out that Alice's ex is trying to be a biker. I just saw one of them this morning. He was one of the guys in the bar when I gave Ken a beating."

"I think you need to pay them a visit and introduce yourself, before some pledge gives you a beating. I'll send Tony and Johnny the Bump with you."

"When are we going to do that?"

"No time like the present," he said, dialing his phone. He put it on speaker. "Tony, are you busy? I need you to make a house call for me. Sonny needs to make an announcement at the biker clubhouse over on Whittier Street."

"Do you want a few soldiers and some firepower?"

"I was thinking about you and Johnny, and something to make them think, but I don't want bloodshed — they're good paying customers. Come by and get Sonny once it gets dark. I'll send a few strippers over to break the ice, then you can walk in and say your piece. Make sure they don't disrespect Sonny."

"Trust me boss, they won't disrespect me either, or I'll give them a lead salad sandwich," he said.

"Keep it professional Tony, and call me once you're done, let me know what was said."

He hung up and looked at me. "Word travels fast and it's always on the street. We need to nip this in the bud. I don't want some shitbag biker thinking he can cause the family any trouble. They still don't know who you are Sonny, but in a month or so, they'll shake in their shoes when they see you. You don't see anyone giving me any shit, do you?"

"No, never," I said.

"That's because they know if you fuck with me, you fuck with the family, and trust me, even the bikers don't want to be on the bad side of the family."

"What did this guy say about me?"

"He has a picture of you and put it up on the corkboard in the club house. You need to go there and take it down."

"What's with the picture?"

"They get a picture up there and every wannabe looks to beat the shit out of you to get their patches. You could have 20 guys looking for you right now. That's why you're going down there to-night. Tony will know what to do and what to say, just keep cool. He's been a made man for some time and everyone knows he's with Don Mancini. No one will dare say a word that Tony doesn't like."

"How many people are going to be there?"

"Eighty, a hundred — I don't know, but trust me, they'll know your face when you leave and they won't dare give you any shit, ever."

"Three of us are going to walk in on a hundred bikers, in their club house?"

"That's the plan."

Chapter Thirty

You Could Hear A Pin Drop

It seemed like only a few minutes had passed and Tony was pulling into the lot. I was full of anxiety. I hated bikers — I was afraid of them, but now we were going into the devil's den.

Jimmy put his hand on my shoulder. "Go in the office and put on the blazer that's hanging on the back of the chair. You need to look sharp." I did as he told me to and adjusted my collar.

Tony waved me to the passenger seat; I got in and looked to the back seat. It was empty.

"Where's Johnny?"

"We don't need him, but if you want, I'll swing by his house and get him."

"I want him there, don't you?"

"Sure I guess, but those guys know I'm connected. We could walk in and piss in their faces, and no one would lift a finger. Besides, Jimmy sent in some strippers and I have a gift from Pauly, it's for the big cheese."

"The big cheese?"

"Yeah or whatever the fuck they call him, usually a fat tattooed fuck. Unless you want to give him the gift — it'll be a hit, I can tell you that," Tony said laughing.

"You're not going to cause a big scene are you? You're just going to give him his gift and we're getting out of there, right?"

"Sonny, me and you are the same rank, so you can't tell me what to do. If I feel that the situation needs a scene, then trust me, there will be a fucking scene. And another thing, we will leave when I'm good and fucking ready to leave. I'm not running out of there until they're uncomfortable. I don't run off like some fucking chicken shit. These fucking guys are nothing and when I leave they'll feel like nothing. I'm not a nothing and neither are you. Anyone can buy a motorcycle and be a biker. Not everyone is born in the Mafia, so start acting like it. Jimmy has his style and I've got mine, but they want me to take you under my wing and sort of give you a crash course on the proper way to treat others and the way they should treat you. By the way, did you just smell shit?"

"No."

"That's because my shit don't stink. Do you get it? You need to act like your shit don't stink. That's lesson number one."

"Got it," I said.

He pulled up to house in a regular neighborhood. I expected a mansion, but it was just a common home. The neighbors must have thought he was an insurance salesman, or banker — never expecting he's a soldier in the Mafia. Tony flashed the high beams a few times until the curtains moved. The door swung open and Johnny walked out eating a big frosted cupcake — another thing I hadn't expected. He got in the car, and Tony said "don't be spilling all that crumbs and shit all over the car."

Johnny didn't look up; he concentrated on getting the cupcake in his mouth, while holding his big hand under his chin.

"We're going to shoot bikers and this fucking guy is eating a cupcake — go figure."

"We're going to shoot bikers?" I asked.

"No I'm just fucking with you, relax Sonny, it's like a walk in the park. You're learning from the best, ain't that right Johnny?"

"I think so Tony. Are we going to shoot some people? I only have a couple clips," he said as he opened his blazer and two guns were strapped to his chest.

"That's plenty. I brought a couple of noisemakers too, but we won't be using them — this is just going to be a meet and greet. They need to welcome Sonny to the neighborhood. Jimmy said they got the wrong first impression, so we need to reset that."

We drove down a few back roads and I saw the sign for Whittier Street. I took a deep breath and Tony elbowed me. "Relax Sonny; get your game face on. You represent the family now. This is your first coming out as Sonny DiMambro. Matt LePage or whatever your Frenchman name is doesn't exist in the family. Look and act as though you demand respect. Now take this ring box and present it to the big cheese, and let me handle the rest."

I took the small box and slipped it in my blazer pocket. We parked out front like we owned the place. We went up the steps and were greeted by a fat biker.

"We ain't listening to Jehovah Witnesses tonight fellas, you have the wrong house," said the biker.

"Well you got that half right. You're going to listen to a few "Good Fellas," Tony said laughing as he turned to Johnny.

"Good one, Boss," said Johnny.

The biker looked at me and then to Tony. Tony yelled at the fat biker, "tell whoever the fuck is in charge that the party of Don Carmine Mancini is here. Jimmy Maretti sent us. He sent the strippers too, and we're coming in here one way or another."

The biker was confused, but he walked away. His jeans were low on his hips and his fat hairy ass showed a crack as he walked away. Another bum took his spot watching us. Then he returned. "Snake said to let you in."

"Oh you have a guy here named Snake? I have a snake too, it's in my pants," Tony said, laughing loud. The biker waddled when he walked and he didn't laugh.

The entrance opened up to a large room where it looked like they had taken down a few walls. It was run-down and semi-finished. Big TVs hung at the corners and there was a line of kegs and a bunch of bums wherever I looked. On one side of the room there were five leather chairs — the important ranking bikers sat there. The big boss sat in the middle, his chair was higher than the others. The strippers were just getting started. I saw a young biker point to me and then another pointed to the corkboard. The girls had brought their own music and Tony went to their CD player and turned it off.

One biker approached the biker boss and pointed to me and the corkboard.

"Get the fuck lost, punk," Tony said to the biker. "Doesn't this puke have any respect for the Mafia? I'm glad that shitbag pointed to the wall. You have a picture of Sonny DiMambro up there. He don't fucking like it, and you know who else don't like it?" The more Tony talked the madder and louder he got. "I don't like it, Johnny the Bump don't like it, Jimmy Maretti don't like it, and you can be sure that Don Carmine Mancini won't like it. You know those names and what it means to be on the wrong side of the Mancini family, don't you? Now get that fucking thing down, now! Get it down before I take my phone and get a picture of you dumb fucks and send it to the entire Mafia. I was sent to introduce you to Sonny DiMambro. He's got rank and I'm hoping he has mercy. You better spread the word that he better get respect or there will be hell to pay. Jimmy sent the strippers for all of us to enjoy — do you like them?"

Snake nodded his head, and then he motioned for one of the guys to take the picture down. He handed it to Sonny.

Tony motioned me to give the biker boss the small box. I passed it to him, and I noticed he didn't look me in the eye. He knew the power of the mob. It was silent; no one dared talk. Snake opened the box and inside was the pin to a grenade.

Tony turned and yelled to the near silent room. "That, my friend is a gift from Sonny DiMambro. Looks like he showed you mercy. The next time you'll get the other end of the grenade. Do we understand each other?" Tony yelled.

Then he pulled the grenade from his pocket and handed it to Snake. "Put the pin back in it you fucking idiot," Tony said.

Snake was careful to keep the lever squeezed down as he slid the pin back in. Tony had their attention. He held his hand out until Snake gave him the grenade back. Tony put it in his pocket and said. "Put the music back on and get out of them chairs so we can watch the strippers. And get us a cold beer."

The other high-ranking bikers sat until Snake gave up his chair. Tony let me take Snake's seat and he and Johnny sat on either side of me. I felt like the king of the world. A guy brought us each a beer and when he came to me I curled my finger for him to bend down. "Is a guy named Troy here?"

"Yes. He's over by the kegs."

"Send him over here," I said.

"What's going on?" asked Tony.

"One of the biker punks is here. I think he's the one that got my picture. I want to make sure he gets the message."

"Gotcha."

Troy approached and when he got close, Snake and all the others were watching.

Troy nodded his head.

"What the fuck is that? That's disrespectful — Johnny," said Tony. I think no matter what Troy did, Tony would say it's disrespectful.

Johnny stood and with one smooth action he pulled a 9mm pistol and put it on Troy's temple. He frowned when he yelled. Drop to your knees you disrespectful fuck. That's Sonny Fucking DiMambro and you kiss his hand before I blow your fucking brains out."

Troy dropped and kissed my hand. "Get out of my sight you piece of shit," I said as I pulled my hand away from his face.

Troy scurried away and left the building.

Tony drank his beer and laughed at the top of his lungs. He tipped the strippers and then we left. We had stayed for almost an hour. That was the night I learned that a made man can't be killed unless the Don says so. Whoever kills a made man will be murdered and most likely his entire family will be killed. It was a family code and most gangsters knew we were untouchable. Even the cops knew.

Chapter Thirty-One

Clean Cut

Saturday came, Alice was up early and made breakfast; the smell of bacon and coffee woke me from a sound sleep. I kept my eyes closed and took in the aromas. She hummed as she set the table. It brought back memories of when I was young and my mom would cook for the family. I loved the smell of coffee, even before I was old enough to drink it. I associated it with home, warmth, and safety, and somehow it made me think of my mom. I wondered if she heard that I was Mafioso   that I made wise guy.

Alice didn't waste any time packing an overnight bag. She had laid out clothes for me; dress slacks and a button up shirt was my typical attire. She had been looking forward to meeting Steve and Trapper for a night of karaoke. I wanted to be supportive and be a fan in the crowd. I left for a few hours — I needed a haircut and under-arm deodorant. Alice did most of the grocery shopping, but I still needed personal items.

I stopped in Supercuts, but the girl who normally cut my hair was not available. A girl with dark hair, parted on the side, and an arm full of tattoos snapped an apron into the air. She reminded me of the tattoo artist Kat Von D. I looked up from my chair and she tilted her head as she chewed her gum with an open mouth. She was rough, but strangely attractive.

"Are you ready for a haircut?" asked the receptionist.

"I stood and ran my hand through my hair and nodded. She pointed to the young girl and I walked to her seat. She pumped the foot lever until my head lined up with her shoulder.

"What would you like, Sonny?"

"Do we know each other?" I asked.

She talked to my reflection in the big sheet mirror.

"I know who you are. I was at the club house the other night when you and your boys made a scene. You're Sonny DiMambro, right?"

"That's right, what's your name?"

"I'm Tammy. I gotta tell you, I've never seen anything like that before. I wouldn't have guessed it in a hundred years. You guys walked in there like you owned the place, especially that little guy. He was loud and strutted his stuff like he was a pit-bull. I couldn't believe he stood up to Snake. One time I saw Snake punch a guy in the face so hard his nose folded over and then he kicked him until his legs were tired and then another brother took over kicking him — I thought he was dead... I thought for sure he was going to do the same to you guys. There must have been a hundred drunken bikers against you three guys. I couldn't believe it; you have some big balls. I'm kinda nervous about cutting your hair, but I'm excited at the same time. Does that sound weird?"

"Don't worry about it, just give me a trim and clean up my neck. I hate when the hair pokes against my collar."

"You guys are Mafia, huh? Can I say that out loud?

"Why not, you're not a cop are you?"

"Yeah I'm a cop working at Supercuts."

"Are you wearing a wire?"

"Yeah an underwire bra," she said laughing.

"So you're a biker chick?"

"Not really. I've dated a few bikers. I find them to be exciting. It's like they live like they don't have anything to lose. It's life in the fast lane, you know the saying, *wine, women, and song.* There's a party every night and road trip every weekend. It must be the same for you, except you dress nicer, and you guys have money, don't you? The bikers are always broke, except the ones at the top."

I wasn't sure how much I should talk. I knew we had a code of silence.

"You must be high up. I've never seen bikers back down from anyone, not even from the cops."

"I never said I was anything. I'm just a guy that came in for a haircut."

"Gotcha, I don't want to piss you off," she said.

"Let's change the subject," I said.

"Do you have a girlfriend?"

"Not at the moment. The last one couldn't swim very good and she drowned."

"Really?"

"It might have been because she was wearing cement shoes," I said with a straight face.

She put her hand over her open mouth, but she started laughing once I cracked a smile. "You had me going. See I like that, you're a hot ticket Mr. DiMambro."

She guided her fingers along my head and snipped my hairs. I felt her fingers against my ears and neck. I knew how hairdressers worked. They flirt with everyone, male and female. Whatever it took to get a tip. I knew when her hair was down and styled, she was very attractive and some women might not like their guys getting to know her. I knew her game.

We looked at each other in the mirror as she snapped the red button on her small black clippers and worked them up and down my neck. Then she bent down and blew the small hairs away with her breath. She snapped the clippers off. "How's that?"

"Great, but I think you spit on my neck."

She covered her mouth and laughed. "Did I? I didn't mean it. I'm sorry."

"That's a sign of disrespect," I said.

"You're killing me," she said laughing.

"One pair of cement shoes coming up."

"I wear a size 7...I'll make it up to you the next time you come in, next time just a haircut, no spit."

"Damn spitters," I said, laughing.

I stood up and she turned and bent over. I thought it was so I could see her backside, but when she turned around she handed me her card. "If you call ahead I can get you right in. It was a pleasure meeting you Sonny," she said as she extended her hand to shake, but I grabbed it and turned her hand so my knuckles were up. Then I lifted it to her face. "Do you want to kiss the ring?" I said with a straight face.

She laughed and let go of my hand, "you aren't wearing a ring."

I looked at my hand, "What happened to my ring? You stole my ring, didn't you? Next time I see you, size 7 cement shoes."

I took her card and put it in my wallet, and pulled out a $10 tip for her, then I paid the cashier on the way out.

I walked to my car, it was the first time I was embarrassed to drive it. I hoped the girls didn't look outside to see what I drove. I sped off and the more I thought about it the more it bothered me. I was a made man, and making good money. I wanted a new car, so I could feel good about myself. Six months ago, a new car would have been out of the question, but now that I was Mafioso I had an image to uphold and a fifteen year old car wasn't cutting it. I called Jimmy.

"Jimmy, it's me Sonny. My car is on its last leg, what do you think I should do? I don't want car payments, I'm not even sure I can get a car loan, but this shitbox needs to go."

"You should come down here and take a mustang convertible, use it until you stash enough cash away to get a new car, but don't get a loan, don't sign anything."

"That sounds great, I'll be right over."

I knew the car I wanted. There were two; one was dark blue, with small stripes at the bottom of the doors, and a white convertible top. The other one was black with a black top, with chrome wheels, and a standard shift. I wondered if the car Jimmy drove was his own. I suspected that most of the family drove cars that couldn't be traced to them. I was starting to catch on to how things were run. I pulled in the lot and Jimmy had the keys to both cars in his hand. I got out of my car and walked to him.

"Take whatever one you want or take anything on the lot that you like, you don't have to have just one … they're like women, you can have a different one every night if you want to."

"What do I do with my car?

"You can sell it or give it to someone that needs it. You shouldn't have a car in your name — I don't. The business owns mine. I like a big car, but you'd look good in a mustang, or maybe a truck. You're a made man now Sonny, this is one of the many perks."

"Awesome, I guess I'd like the blue one for this weekend and then maybe a Chevy Impala. I like the black one we have."

"Take whatever you want, just let me know," he said.

I couldn't believe my ears. I took the keys and parked my car in the corner of the lot, and then I got in the Mustang. I turned the key and listened to the small v8 rumble against the parking lot. I unlatched the roof and then put the top down. I looked at myself in the small mirror — my fresh haircut and dark sunglasses. I felt pretty good about myself. I pulled around the building and disappeared down the road. I took a small joy ride and I even pulled into the Supercuts and drove slowly through the lot, wondering if the girls saw my new ride.

Chapter Thirty-Two

Stevey Wonder

I pulled into the driveway of the apartment; Alice was sitting on the steps, smoking a cigarette. Her face showed that she didn't recognize me, until I slid my sunglasses down and looked over the top of them.

"What are you doing with that car?"

"Mine shit the bed, so we're taking this one to karaoke."

She went inside and grabbed her overnight bag. I got out and went inside to get a bottled water and that's when I noticed a bag packed for me. She was behind me, "I packed a few things, a nice shirt and another pair of pants and of course underwear and socks."

"What's wrong with the shirt I have on? I can drive home in these pants, it's not like I'm out doing manual labor, I'm just driving in an air-conditioned car."

"What about your socks and underwear, you need to change them, don't you?"

She looked me in the eye until I smiled and said, "of course, what do you think I'm a scumbag, with dirty underpants?"

"I'm beginning to wonder, I did the laundry and there were only four pair of underpants in there, so that means you must go a few days without changing your skivvies."

"No way, not me. Did you check under the bed?"

"No."

"Well that's where they'd be. I didn't know you were the underwear police."

"If that's the case, then go in there and get the ones under the bed."

I didn't move, I just looked at her. We both knew there weren't any under the bed.

"I thought so," she said.

I took the night bag and said, "Let's get on the road. I'll get the underwear later."

We got in the Mustang and her attitude changed. "At least we can ride in style," I said. "Jimmy is letting me use a company car as part of my perks, until I can get on my feet."

"I wish he'd let me use one. This is awesome."

I didn't think she was on to the family business and who she really worked for; I intended to keep it that way.

We drove down a few back roads and then up one of my favorites that hugged the Georgia coast. The Mustang squatted into the corners and with the open warm air hitting our young faces it was impossible not to smile. I pulled into the same hotel that we stayed in on the first visit. Alice asked for the same room, but it was unavailable. She was superstitious and wanted to repeat the first time we were there. I didn't care what we did. Staying busy was the most important thing for me. I didn't like being bored.

We went in the room. I turned on the TV and sat on one of the two chairs. "Karaoke won't start for a few hours, why don't we get something to eat, like a real meal?"

"Don't I make you real meals?"

"You sure do, but this time you don't have to cook and someone will wait on you, wouldn't that be nice?"

"You're right, I just didn't want to get filled up and there's no sense in getting a doggy bag. Do you think we can split a meal?"

I didn't answer right away, so she did, "I'll just get a small salad and maybe a dinner roll. That way you can eat whatever you want."

"Fine," I said, as I stood up and opened the door.

The hotel had a nice restaurant attached to it, and through a large opening I could see the lounge. A few people were starting to get seated and order drinks. We sat and watched the TV until our meals came. I had ordered a steak with a fancy name, but when I tasted it I wasn't impressed. I hated when some chef soaked a nice cut in some salty spicy sauce and renamed it. I renamed it as shit. I was mad since I was in the mood for beef, and that was the one thing Alice didn't seem to cook. She felt beef was for the barbeque and she didn't barbeque. That was how men cooked.

I cut a small piece off my steak, and passed the fork to Alice, "try this thing."

"Thing? Is it that bad?" she said as she took the fork and pulled the meat from it with her teeth. She rolled it from cheek to cheek. "It's a little spicy. I think it's been marinated in bourbon. The problem is that you don't like bourbon."

"Do you?"

"Not really, but I don't usually eat beef, someone must like it or it wouldn't be on the menu," she said.

"Yeah some drunk. Maybe the chef is a drunk and that's why he had a taste for this shit. I wouldn't feed this to my dog."

"Can we get a dog?"

"No," I said as I pushed my fork through the mashed potatoes. I tried some of the zucchini and summer squash. "That shitty sauce leaked all over the vegetables too. I can't eat this shit," I said as I pushed the plate to the center of the table.

"Do you want some of my salad? She said pushing her plate close to my hand.

"No thank you, I should have listened to you and got nachos at the lounge. They do them right."

She nodded her head, and when the waitress came by Alice stopped her and said we were both done.

I paid the check and we went to the lounge. I ordered us drinks and a plate of nachos. We took a seat far away from the stage so we could see well, but still talk. We looked at the music booklet and then Alice looked up and saw Trapper sitting at a table with two women. Alice had her hand on the table and pointed to them with her index finger.

"There's Trapper, and I'm assuming the one sitting close to him is his wife. I don't see Steve."

"What if that girl is Steve's date? I feel like a fool. Do you think he forgot he asked us to come? Maybe he thought it was too far for us to drive. What do we do now?"

"Who cares? We came to have fun and that's what we're doing."

"It's men. I hate them, they're all the same. I'll bet he has back-up, or maybe he thinks I'll be his back-up."

"Hold on there, I'm a man. And besides it looks like you're here with me, so it would be easy for anyone to get the wrong idea. After all we are sharing the same hotel room tonight."

She was quiet for a few seconds. "You're right, let's just have fun, and thanks for driving me up here, that was really sweet."

"I wanted to get your mind off Ken ... now I need to get your mind off Steve."

"You're right, what am I thinking?" she said, laughing.

"Let's pick out a few songs." I looked at the booklet and saw songs that I thought would be right for her, but she was picking out songs that were for two singers. That's when a guy approached the table — it was Trapper.

"Hey it's nice to see you guys. Steve is trying to make it but there was a problem at work. It may be late before he shows."

"Better late than never," I said. "Who are the women at your table?"

I knew Alice was dying to know.

"That's Jean, my wife, and her sister Shelly." They could see us talking about them. I waved and so did they.

"Feel free to join us. My wife is too shy to sing, and it's a damn shame; she has the softest voice, but she only sings in the car. Shelly will be up there all night, once she has a glass of wine."

"Thanks, Trapper, we might be over in a few minutes."

He walked away and I leaned closer to Alice. "Do you want to go sit with them? It might be fun."

"I don't know."

"It looks like we're a couple. Let's cut loose and have a good time. You're having fun tonight whether you like it or not," I said. "Let's go over there with these nachos, I'll buy them a round and we'll be instant friends, guaranteed."

She took a swallow from her drink. "Ok, let's have fun."

I stood and carried the drinks. "You should bring the food, it looks better. I'll look like a drunk and you'll look like a cook."

"Good idea," she said as we walked to their table. I pulled a chair out for Alice and then I sat in one that was close to Shelly. Trapper did the introductions and Alice offered the nachos.

"Who sings what?" I asked.

"I'm going to sing *'The Wind Beneath My Wings'* by Bette Midler, said Sherry.

"I like that song, but I like her other one better: *'The Rose.'* I'd sing it but I don't have the range she has," said Alice.

"Let's sing it together," Sherry said.

Jean pointed to me. "Why don't you and Trapper sing a duet," she said.

"I can't do that," I said.

"Sure you can," she said.

I shook my head and then I saw a song I could handle. "I'll do this song with you," I said, pointing to the booklet. I sang a portion of the song, *"Elvira, Elvira, my heart's on fire, for Elvira... Giddy Up, Oom Poppa Oom Poppa Mow Mow..."* I sang with the lowest voice I had, and Trapper laughed.

"You got it, buddy. It's settled, we're all singing that one," he said.

"I was just kidding, I'll be too embarrassed."

"You too, honey, you can sing 'Elvira,'" he said.

"You promised that you wouldn't pester me all night to sing," his wife said. She tapped her sister's shoulder. "See Sherry, that's why I don't come here with him and Steve. They won't let me be."

Trapper went to the DJ with a request from the girls; a few minutes later Alice, and Sherry took the stage and sang *'The Rose.'* Alice out-sang Sherry; everyone knew it but Sherry.

The song ended and Steve walked in. He walked straight up to the DJ and shook his hand, then found his way to our table. I got up and dragged another chair close to Alice so he could sit down. He ordered a beer and then before he could thumb through the booklet for a song, the DJ announced him. "One of our local favorites with one of his favorites — Steve come on up."

A Willie Nelson song started. "Oh, here we go," said Jean. Steve took a sip from his beer, walked to the stage, and took the microphone.

"Maybe I didn't treat you quite as good as I should
Maybe I didn't love you quite as often as I could
Little things I should've said and done, I never took the time
You were always on my mind
You were always on my mind"

"He's really good," Alice said with dreamy eyes.

"He sings a list of heartbreakers. He blames himself for his wife leaving — he needs to get over it and move on. It's been two years," said Jean.

"That's funny," said Trapper. "He has the voice for the heartbreakers, and look at the crowd, they love him."

"Look at his face — he looks like he's about to cry," said Sherry.

"The DJ made him sing it," said Trapper.

"Why did his wife leave? Did he cheat on her?" asked Alice.

"No, not Steve. She wanted kids and they never had any. I think he's shooting blanks," Jean said with her hand on her cheek, blocking her mouth from Trapper.

He heard her anyway. "You don't know that," Trapper said in an aggravated voice. "Maybe he didn't want kids."

"Then there's the fact that he used to travel a lot for his job and she was insecure," said Sherry.

The DJ announced Trapper next and he sang a John Denver song, *'Take me home country roads.'*

"Almost heaven, West Virginia, Blue Ridge Mountains, Shenandoah River.

Life is old there, older than the trees, younger than the mountains blowing like a breeze."

"These two are so predictable. Trapper sings this song every time he's out here," said Sherry.

"He grew up in West Virginia — he misses the place. So, so what?" said Jean.

"I think we should break the mold and sing something fun," said Sherry. What about this one: *'California Dreaming'*? We can all sing it."

> *"All the leaves are brown, and the sky is gray.*
> *I've been for a walk on winter's day,"*

"You know that one," she said

She turned in the request to the DJ and we got up and sang the Mamas and Papas tune. Most of the crowd knew the song and sang along. Sherry was right, it changed the mood. Before we left, Alice gave Steve her new number. He promised he would call and try to come to Orlando. She seemed happy.

Chapter Thirty-Three

Ride To Work

We spent the night — the next morning we had breakfast, and started the long drive home. I felt confident that Alice wouldn't go back to Ken after she experienced a nice time with normal people. I was hoping he wasn't stupid enough to reach out to her. Steve seemed nice. I wished he lived closer — I didn't have any intention of traveling north for karaoke again. The next move would have to be his.

The morning was cool and I kept the top up as we twisted our way down the coast. We crossed a huge bridge, and in the distance I pointed to an enormous ship unloading its fuel into massive storage tanks. Alice looked but didn't seem interested. Under another bridge was a marina with hundreds of sailboats and yachts tied to mooring balls. The ocean seemed littered with boats of all shapes and sizes. Some early risers were already on their way while others had boats that rarely left the docks. Those people worked the jobs that got them the big boats, but had to stay at work to keep them and were unable to use them. Some were more of a symbol of fun than a reality.

Then Alice spoke, without turning her head from the ocean view of the passenger window.

"What do you think of Steve?"

"Where did that come from? He's all right I guess. All of those guys are all right."

"He sang that song to his ex-wife and Jean said he does it all the time. I thought it was odd."

"She wanted kids and I guess he doesn't, so she left. That's what I got out of it." "Sherry thinks he can't have kids — for some people that's a deal breaker," I said.

"I'm not sure I'd want to have kids, especially with the drugs I've done. The poor kid would be born with two heads."

"I know but you just sang a few songs together, and you live 150 miles apart. Now you're planning a family?"

"Stranger things have happened, and I know I might be clinging to the first guy that smiled at me. I know the whole rebound thing and that's why 150 miles of separation is good right now. Do I want a guy to call me at night and tell me about his day? Sure I do, and do I want a guy that texted me good morning, because he wakes at the crack of dawn and he's on the road hours before I wake? I would like that. I don't need someone at my hip every minute, but I want someone I can trust. This may sound funny but I saw a side to Steve that I really like. I don't want to live in his past — I don't even want to live in my past, but when he sang to a woman that got into his heart it made me feel like he's the type that would let me in. I dreamed I was the woman that he lost and he sang those lonely nights away to my ghost. It was really tender, and I didn't want to discount it by being immature and jealous. He's a genuine sweet guy. I just don't know if I'm good enough for him. I'm used to a mother fucker and I mean that in every way it can be taken — a guy that can't be trusted around my friends and even my mother."

"It takes two to tango."

"I know, she's a selfish person without any loyalty, or boundaries, but I'll never let another guy I care about meet her. As a matter of fact if things work out with me and Steve, I'd relocate to get away from her and Ken and all the losers I know."

I didn't say anything else. I turned the music up and at the stop sign I dropped the top. "Let the good times roll," I said as I held my fist out for her to pound.

The rest of the ride I played music and thought about my own life and wondered if Alice was right to relocate. My mother did. I was in a different position than her or Alice. I took the oath of 'Omerta.' I was Mafioso and good or bad I was in, and like the Don said, the only way out is in a box. I couldn't run away. The only thing I could do was make my problems run away from me.

Once we got back to the apartment I carried the bags in — Alice went in to make us lunch. I offered to get drive through, but she insisted on making something healthy for both of us. I looked at my phone while I sat at the table. It had a message, from Jill, who wanted to ask me for a favor.

I replayed the message on speaker phone, "*Hey Matty this is Jill, I need to ask you a favor, and I wanted to thank you for helping us move. Bonnie says hi.*"

"What do you think of that? This chick only calls when she needs a favor."

"What does she look like? Is she hot, and skinny?"

"Yeah."

"That's why, she thinks she's a hot shit and you'll do whatever she wants. Sounds like you already do. You helped her and Bonnie move. I'll bet she wants a ride to the airport, or something shitty like that."

I dialed Jill's number and left the phone on speaker. "It's Matt, what's up?"

"I'm having a new starter put in my car and I was wondering if you could follow me to the garage and then take me to work. Bonnie would do it but we have different hours. I have someone that can give me a ride home after work, so it's just one way."

"You can say that again," Alice whispered. "Tell her you can't do it."

"I can't do it," I said.

"Why not?" Jill asked.

"By the time I drive there and drop you off and drive back, I'll be late for my own job."

"I called you earlier, but I should have called you last night. OK, well have a nice day," she said and hung up before I could say anything else.

"That chick is a user. Let her boney ass take a cab."

"How do you know she has a boney ass?"

"I don't, but I already hate her," she said laughing.

We finished lunch and got ready for work. Once we were there she went in the office. I went to the garage to check in cars from the last shift. I wasn't there ten minutes before Jimmy came to see me.

"There's a christening for my youngest daughter tomorrow afternoon at Saint Mary's. I want you to come; it's at 2 o'clock. Most of the family will be there, and besides, you should be introduced to Father Paul."

"I'm working tomorrow."

"Work until 1:30 and come over, I'll get someone to cover the schedule."

"OK."

"You need to meet Father Paul and you should get to Mass. Most of the family goes to Mass regularly, you should too."

"Do you go?" I asked.

"Whenever I can."

Chapter Thirty-Four

Jill The Pill

It was 1 o'clock the following day. I spent the morning sending out cars to mostly family members and a few occasional vacationers. Jimmy was in early — I kept a fresh blazer in my car to make sure I would be respectable at the christening. I decided to take a Lincoln to the Church. I felt a Mustang would be out of place.

My phone rang and I instinctively answered.

"Hi Matt, it's me, Jill. I don't want to bother you but I need a favor. I'm in a pinch and I need a ride home. I'm stuck here at work."

"I thought you had your car fixed."

"There was another problem with it and it didn't pass inspection, so I need a ride and I was hoping you could help me out, please."

"I can't, I have a family christening to go to and I can't be late."

"Why don't you pick me up and I can come along? Those things don't take long."

"There will most likely be a big party after. These people are not on welfare, we're not talking beer and pizza."

"I like nice things, I'm dressed right. I work retail and I'm a sharp dresser."

I didn't respond, so she took it as a yes. "It's settled then, pick me up at the mall, I'll be out front by the main entrance."

I wanted to tell her it was out of the way, but it wasn't, "OK I'll be by in fifteen minutes, but be ready. I can't be late for this."

"OK I'll get a card. Thanks Matt."

I thought about what Alice had said and I felt that maybe she was right about Jill. She might be a user and a leach, but she would look good at the party, and she didn't know anything about me to embarrass me. I drove to the mall; she stood by the big entrance and it made her look tiny. She was dressed in black slacks and a ruffled shirt with a small hint of cleavage showing. She had her hair down — the slight breeze lifted it from her shoulders. I pulled up to the curb, and let the window down.

"Nice car," she said as she got in and buckled up the seat belt.

"I like it but it needs a starter and won't pass inspection."

She slapped my elbow.

"If that's true then call me. I'll get you a ride to work tomorrow."

"Really, you'd give me a ride? That's nice."

"Not me, but my mom has tomorrow off, she can take you," she said laughing.

"I should have known, you really wouldn't give me a ride if I was stranded?"

"No, I'm busy; don't make your problem my problem. My mom can do it," she said, laughing.

"You really crack yourself up, don't you?"

"Hey it's part of my charm."

"So, no ride for me? I'll keep that in mind," I said.

"I would if I could, but the truth is I don't have a car."

"You told me you were having it fixed and you were dropping it off for a starter."

"I know that's what I said, but the truth is I lost my license and I can't drive for four more months. I got an OUI."

"You got drunk driving?"

"Yes Matt, they got me. I'm a drinker and that's what can happen. That wasn't Kool-Aid we were having at the beach. I like to drink, and I had one too many and drove home. I accidently took out a few mailboxes on the way. I'm going to need some rides and if everyone chips in and helps out there shouldn't be a problem. They are serving drinks at this party — right?"

"I'm sure they will, but please don't get smashed."

"Matt, I already have a father, and he's an alcoholic. He's not my boss and I don't need one. I can handle it."

I didn't know what to believe with this chick, but I was stuck with her for the ceremony. I'd try to make the best of it.

I pulled into the parking lot and looked up at the magnificent church. The arch topped windows and doors all pointed skyward to the two hundred foot steeple with a cross at the pinnacle. From the louvered section a bell rang into the air.

We walked across the street and into the big church. I saw Tony next to Johnny; they were with their wives. I decided to sit behind them. The ceiling was magnificent, pillars holding the arch top ceiling. Everything was arch topped — the doorways, the stained glass windows and the all plaques. The priest walked out from a back room. He stopped at the pulpit and put his mouth on a microphone and when he spoke his voice echoed off the walls, magnifying what he was saying.

I found it odd that mobsters were in church. I was surprised the roof didn't fall on top of us. I was a believer in the savior, but even I felt like a hypocrite. The place was full of killers, cheats, crooks — then I looked at Jill and thought, drunks and liars. I shook my head.

The ceremony went by quickly; everyone was invited to a reception at Pauly's house. Tony walked out with us. He ignored the women and talked like they weren't there.

"You know how to get to Pauly's from here?"

"Not really," I said.

"Where are you parked?"

I pointed to the big black Lincoln.

"You're parked beside Larry. Follow Larry Windows — you know Larry, don't you?"

"Not really."

A large guy came out of a different door, and Tony put his fingers in his mouth and whistled until he looked. Tony waved his arm for the man to come close. He smiled and greeted Tony in a low smoker's voice.

"Hey, Big Tony, how you doing?"

"Good, Larry, I want you to meet Sonny."

"Hi Sonny — we already met," he said as he shook my hand. "Congratulations on making sgarrista. If you need anything don't hesitate to ask. Who's the fine woman that you're with?" he said as he reached to shake her hand. She didn't wait for me to introduce her.

"I'm Jill the Pill," she said with a smile, and then she reached to shake Tony's hand. "Big Tony, right?"

Tony looked at me with a serious look and then at her.

"I gave her that name — she got an OUI and lost her license," I said.

"Oh I get it, she's a pill popper," and then Tony roared a loud laugh and held his stomach. Sonny you funny bastard, that's not nice. Sonny do you want me to talk with some politicians and get her squared away?"

"I'm not sure yet, we can talk about that later. We better get on our way. I don't want Pauly mad," I said.

"No, you don't want that."

Chapter Thirty-Five

Father Paul

We got in the car; Larry backed out of his space. "Hurry before someone cuts you off," said Jill.

"No one will cut me off, it's disrespectful."

"What's with the funny names? Larry Windows and Big Tony. The guy is five feet tall," she said holding her hand flat, up to her chin, and is your name Sonny or Matt?"

"When I'm with family it's Sonny, and when I'm out with the public most people call me Matt."

"What's with Larry Windows?"

"They nickname each other, there's probably three guys named Larry and four named Tony, so they call one Big Tony and one Little Tony, and so on, get it?"

"Larry must stand by the window a lot then, that's why they call him Larry Windows," she said.

"Either that or he throws people out of windows — probably girls that make fun of his name," I said with a smile.

"Do they call you Sonny, because that's the way you like your eggs? Sunny side up?"

"Pauly said they call me Sonny because I'm so bright. Why do you ask, Jill the Pill?"

She slapped my arm, "thanks for giving me that stupid name, you should have called me Jill the Thrill. I like that better."

"I should have called you Jill the Dill, sour like a pickle," I said, laughing. You better watch what you say at the party or they'll be calling you Jill Landfill."

That's when she caught on.

"Those guys are fucking mobsters aren't they? Are you a mobster, Sonny? Are you bringing me to a mob party?"

I laughed at her, she looked worried. It was fun to see the wisecracking, wannabe model shake in her shoes.

"Why would you say that? You're being silly," I said.

"I've seen mobster movies and all the guys have stupid names like Sonny the Bunny." She covered her mouth and laughed.

I knew she partially believed we were Mafia.

"That's disrespectful; they call me Sonny the Gunny. I used to be Machine Gun Sonny," I said with a straight face. "But it was too long of a name."

"You're bullshitting me right?"

I didn't answer.

"I'm kidding, they call me Sonny," I said as we pulled onto Pauly's property. The yard was full of expensive cars. We got out of the car — she held my elbow as we walked into the house. I noticed she was quiet and more observant as I slowly introduced her to the family members, we were respectful of each other and many congratulated me on making Sgarrista. I knew I'd have to explain it later. Some family members didn't have any problem with people knowing that they were Mafia. I wanted to keep it a private matter if it was possible, but I didn't want to insult those who were proud of it. It would take some time to get used to the power and prestige that came along with being part of the family. I guess I wasn't done being Matt, but I was beginning to understand why they renamed me.

I watched Jimmy and how calmly he handled his position. I hoped I could be as cool as he was. He was the future of the mob, he and his father. I wanted to stay on the good side of them. I saw Alfred; he was holding a drink and talking with an older woman. He nodded at me, and I didn't know if I should come closer or stay away. I decided to get closer. He held his hand out a few feet before I got to him. I smiled and he drew me in for a hand shake and slap on the back.

"Sonny, I want you to meet Theresa. She's Pauly's aunt. Sonny is Jimmy's right-hand man," Alfred said as he smiled at me. "He's has a bright future."

"That's why they call me Sonny," I said with a smile.

They both laughed and Jill shook her head.

"What's your name, young lady?" Theresa asked.

"Jill," she said as she offered her hand to shake.

"What kind of name is Jill? Is it short for something?" asked Theresa.

"It's short for Jillian."

"That's not an Italian name is it?" asked Theresa.

"I think it's Latin, if I'm not mistaken. In Italian it would be Giuliana," said Alfred.

"You should get a flower for your hair, you have such nice hair," said Theresa.

"I see Jimmy in the corner," I said. "I've been waiting to introduce Jillian to him. It was nice seeing you both," I said as I took Jill by the hand and walked away.

"I'm not that smart but I know when an old Italian woman says put a flower in my hair, it means she doesn't like my hair," said Jill.

"Why would you say that?"

"Look around, every one in the room has dark hair, or gray hair. Everyone is Italian aren't they?"

"I don't know, why don't you ask them?" I said.

"Then Theresa asked me if my name was Italian I didn't know what to say. I almost said it was, so I could fit in, but Alfred said it's Latin," she said, raising her voice.

"Hey keep it down; Alfred is at the top of the hierarchy. I told you to keep quiet and have respect. Don't embarrass me."

"Maybe we should leave then."

"I can't be the first to leave, it's disrespectful, and we're staying until the proper time to leave."

"You can't tell one of the guys that I want to leave and you're my ride?" she asked.

"Two things here — one is that an Italian man in this family does not, and will never take orders from a woman. The other thing is I told you I had something to do, and we're staying until it's respectful to leave. I will not offend the family, no matter what."

Then she whispered, "this is Mafia, isn't it? Just tell me."

I turned to her and nodded, "yes."

"If I don't do what you say, you could snap your fingers and someone would kick the shit out of me, huh?"

I turned to her again and nodded, "yes, is that what you need?"

She whispered, "no."

I whispered back, "then be a good girl."

I tapped Jimmy's shoulder and he turned around. His beautiful wife stood beside him, she smiled when Jimmy introduced me, and then paused as I introduced Jill as Jillian. I thought it sounded classy. I tried not to stare at Donna, Jimmy's wife. Her hair was dark with light reddish and brown highlights. She had a pretty face with black eyes, and pure white teeth against her plump red lips. She had big breasts for a small-framed woman. She was thin and I would have never guessed she had two kids. She looked at Jimmy when he spoke like he was the ruler of the world, and laughed on cue. I watched Jill stare at her and Jimmy.

"Jimmy is my boss," I said to Jill.

"He's my boss too," Donna said, laughing.

"Have you met Father Paul?" Jimmy said as he tapped the priest on the elbow, stopping him as he walked by.

"He's Pauly's son," Donna said.

I held my hand out, "I'm Sonny."

"He shook my hand, and then said, "You're the one that saved Dominic, am I right?"

"Yeah, but it was really nothing," I said.

"I heard all about it, let's take a walk. I want to give you a blessing," he said as he pulled on my hand.

I followed him until we were at the hallway. We went in a den and then he turned and said, "I want you to know that things are going to happen in this family. Some you can control, others you can't. There will be times when a good confession can lift the weight of the world from your shoulders. I'm the family priest, and although I'm not in favor of what goes on I still see good from the family and it's my job and life to bring the family members to forgiveness and penance."

He paused for a few seconds and looked me square in the eye. "I want to see you in church, every Sunday. It's the most important thing you can do. It's good for you and it's good for the family. Trust me, it's in your best interest. I want to hear your confessions, as often as you need them, but if I don't hear from you I'll visit you and hear your sins and give you the sacrament. It's important for your soul."

I wanted to talk, but I just nodded my head.

"The family is at war, they're always at war. They do things that are not always ethical, but they deal with others that are on the same level and they have to fight fire with fire. And in war time, sins are committed, people die, rape, steal, and pillage. War is full of druggies and drunks, broken dreams and fallen empires. I can't stop it, but I can help reconcile with the Almighty God. God won't turn his back on you because you took your place in the family, just as I have. I won't turn my back on my family either."

He took a vial of holy oil from his pocket and put a drop on his thumb and made the sign of the cross on my forehead. "Kneel and confess your sins."

I dropped on my knees and closed my eyes, "forgive me Father, for I have sinned, it has been five years since my last confession."

"Go on."

"I joined in with a beating, I filmed a rape."

He stopped me, "you can just say you participated in family business, unless you did unauthorized dirty deeds."

"No."

Did you miss Mass?"

"Yes."

"Did you take the Lord's name in vain?"

"Yes."

He went down each of the Ten Commandments and then we said a prayer together.

"I confess to almighty God that I have sinned through my own fault, in my thoughts and in my words, and what I have done and what I have failed to do, and I asked Blessed Mary, ever Virgin, all the Angels and Saints, and you my brothers and sisters to pray for me to the Lord our God." Amen.

I opened my eyes and Father Paul looked at me and said, "I'm leaving the room and I want you to stay long enough to say ten Hail Marys and five Our Fathers."

"Yes Father, and thanks."

"OK, I'll be looking for you at Mass, don't disappoint me."

He walked out of the room and I said the prayers like he said and I went to rejoin the crowd. Jill was holding a drink and looking at the big buffet table of food. I came up behind her and took a plate.

"Where did you go with that priest?"

"He wanted to bless me and give me absolution. It was a good thing. I feel better."

I began filling the plate; she walked beside me and told me what to take from the buffet.

I could feel someone behind me. I turned and it was Dominic. He was holding a plate with a piece of cake.

"What are you doing with that big piece of cake?" I asked.

"Grandpa told me to bring it to you. I didn't get a chance to thank you for saving me."

"You're welcome and thank you for the cake — tell your grandpa I said thank you too."

"I will, thank you Sonny," he said and then he ran off to get himself a piece of cake.

"See, we couldn't leave without Dominic and his grandfather giving me some cake."

She took her fork and a piece of the cake and put it in her mouth, and then closed her eyes as she slowly chewed it, "Oh my God that's the best cake I ever had."

"It was a gift to me; you better swallow it fast before that kid tells his grandfather you ate my gift."

"Shit," she said as her eyes panned the room, "stop doing that."

"Doing what?"

"Forget it, take your cake, I'll get my own. That was so good."

"It's Italian cake. There's a table of Italian pastries over there."

"What are we doing over here then?"

I finished filling my plate with all the best Italian foods, I dropped my plate at the table and we went to the desert bar, where she picked her favorites and went back to the table to eat.

We stayed until others had left, and it was respectful to go.

Chapter Thirty-Six

Who's Who

We left the party and got in the car, and drove away.

"That was quite a party," she said. "Are all those people your family?"

"Most of them are; one way or the other."

"Was the Godfather there?"

"No, he wasn't."

"There's really is a Godfather?"

"The big boss is called the Don, He's Don Carmine Mancini."

"Does he know who you are?"

"Of course."

"What about Jimmy, he's your boss right?"

"Yup, in more ways than one. His dad is Alfred — he's way up there next to the Don. He's the main advisor."

"What about the short guy — Tony, Big Tony?"

"He's a Sgarrista."

"That's what they called you, what's that?"

"Two levels higher than an associate."

"What about Pauly? The guy with the cake."

"He's the under boss, he's a powerful man."

"He likes you," she said.

I smiled and said, "what's not to like."

"I don't know, I've never hung out with a mobster before."

"It could get dangerous," I said.

"Really," she said, looking out the windows.

"You might want to put your head in my lap so no one sees you," I said with a smile.

"Yeah, nice try Matt, I mean Sonny. I think I liked you better as Matt."

"I like you better as Jillian; she wasn't sassy."

"Well the party's over Matty."

"Do you want me to talk to Tony and get your license back?"

"I didn't really lose my license; I just said that so you would feel bad and give me rides. A girl needs to save money on gas."

"What about the starter?"

"It'll be fixed tomorrow. Do you think you can give me a ride to get it?"

"Depends on what time, I'm supposed to work tomorrow."

"Whatever time that you can, I'm off tomorrow."

I brought her back to her apartment. I noticed that Alice had called and I was tired and wanted to get to bed.

I waited for her to get out of the car, but she turned and asked, how come you haven't been more aggressive with me? I'm used to guys that try a little harder than you."

"First of all, I wasn't sure if you or Bonnie was interested in me, or maybe neither one, and maybe you just needed a sucker to help you move your furniture."

"Good thinking. Bonnie is interested in you but I took the first move to meet you, so I owe her a shot, don't you think? After all we're best friends. And for the record we always need a few suckers."

"That's your call. She seems like a nice girl. I don't push myself on anyone."

"I like that, I don't like desperate men," she said as she gave me a kiss on the cheek. "Thanks for the fun time, and the ride."

I didn't answer. I waited for her to close the door and I drove off. I was consumed with thoughts about the party. I felt that letting Jill into the scene was my first time going public about being a wise guy. I knew she wouldn't sleep. I pictured her and Bonnie up late talking about the Mafia, and wondering if I'm a killer or a drug pusher, and wanted by the cops. I really didn't know my place in the family. I knew I had the right to tell the Button-men what to do and I knew the associates answered to me, but I didn't have any orders to give or deeds to do. Jimmy and Tony were running my staff and I wasn't needed.

I drove home and felt bad that I didn't bring some of the pastry home for Alice. She was a good person and I noticed that she didn't ask questions like she used to. I figured it must have been a nervous tick, or maybe the drugs she had been on had finally worn off — she was normal, more normal than most people I meet.

I pulled up to my apartment and walked up the steps. Alice was curled up on the sofa with a pillow under one side of her head.

"How did the party go?" she asked.

"Great."

"I wonder why Jimmy didn't invite me?"

"He needed someone at the store that knows what's going on," I said.

"Yeah, you're right — I figured that. We didn't have much going on once you left. Steve called me."

"Really? That's good."

"He wants to come down this weekend, but I have to work," she said.

"Trade with someone; you can work the morning shift and we can go out that night. Is his brother coming?"

"I'm not sure. I was hoping all of them would come down and we could go to Universal and finish the night at City Walk. There's dancing and karaoke there."

"Sounds good."

I went to bed and the next morning I slept in. I was glad Alice had the early shift, I needed the sleep. I got up and there was no breakfast, just a pot of coffee that had started to cool. I poured a cup and put it in the microwave until it nearly boiled over. I looked at my phone and saw no sign that Jill had called or texted. No Bonnie either. I figured I might have scared them both away. I didn't really care.

I went through the refrigerator; the leftovers were put away neatly, either in storage bags or little, transparent, plastic containers. I opened the meatloaf and decided a breakfast sandwich would be a treat. I ate the sandwich, took a shower and then decided to see if Jill needed that ride. I called.

"It's me, Matt; I called to see if you want that ride. I have to work in a few hours; I could do it before I go in."

"I called the garage and he says it needs something called a strut or whatever and it's another three hundred bucks. I can't pick that car up until I get paid. I get the feeling he keeps looking for things to fix. I only brought it in for an oil change and he offered a free safety inspection. Then he said the starter and now a strut. This guy is going to cost me a thousand bucks before he's done with me."

"It was probably just the battery" I said, acting like I know cars.

"Oh he put one of those in too, thanks for reminding me, I'm so upset."

"Where is this place?"

"Pond View Garage, on Richmond Street, across from John Deere."

"I know where that is, I'll stop by and see what he's doing. He might be taking advantage since you're a girl."

"I don't mind paying if the car really needs the parts. It was supposed to be a $19 oil change and here it is a thousand later. That's not fair to do that to someone." I just moved and it was the first garage I saw with an oil change deal.

"OK I'll take care of it," I said and then hung up and called Jimmy. I told him the story.

"What do you want to do about it?" he asked.

"I was thinking about sending a few associates down there, or maybe a few soldiers and when I get there they tell the guy who I am and then let him tell me what's wrong with her car. If he squirms I'll know, if not, she owes him some money."

"Good idea. Where do I send the boys?"

"Pond View Garage."

"They'll be there in a half hour."

I got dressed and got in the Lincoln; it was the perfect car for the job. I drove to the garage, I was early — I circled the block until I saw a few cars pull in. I waited across the street until it looked like one guy had opened the hood on his car and waited for the mechanic to check out the problem. The other was at the gas pump. I pulled up and parked in front of the bay door. The mechanic looked from under the hood. He was about forty, with a medium build and muscular forearms; he yelled to me, "hey you have to move, you can't block the bay.

The guy with the open hood turned and I could see his face, it was Larry Windows, standing next to the mechanic. "Hey you can't talk to him like that."

"Why? He's blocking the bay."

"That's Sonny DiMambro, and if Pauly, or Don Mancini hears you've yelled at him, you'll be wearing your tongue as a necktie."

Then the second guy turned and yelled, "Hey Sonny, can I help you with something? Do you need someone to pump your gas?" He walked close to Larry and the mechanic. "Hey Larry what's up?"

"I don't know, I got a call from Jimmy and he said Sonny might need some help over here at the station."

I was ten feet from them — Larry pointed to me and said "See Sonny over there? That's a made man, and if he snaps his fingers this station will go up in flames. That's the power that man has. If I were you, I'll run over there and see what the fuck he wants. And the next time you yell at him will be the last time you yell at anyone. Now run, you lazy fuck." The man didn't move fast enough and Larry lifted his leg and kicked him in the ass.

He ran to me with a confused look on his face, "What can I help you with?"

I wanted to be cool like Jimmy. The cat was out of the bag and he knew we were Mafia… I left the car door open, "I'm Sonny DiMambro, and my friend Jill brought her car in here, she brought it in for an oil change. She was expecting to pay $19 for the oil change, and she said you told her you'd do a free safety inspection for the inspection, like your sign says." The sign had a $19 oil change special. "She called me and said you ran the bill up to a grand. I thought she must have heard you wrong, so I came down to hear myself, and read the sign so I could get the story straight. I brought some of my guys who know cars, and they have good hearing, so why don't you tell us what's going on."

I waved the guys closer; Larry crowded him as the mechanic tried to explain.

"The car started hard, so I put in a new battery, but it still cranked slow. I decided to put in a new starter, it's $300 for the starter. I got it started and when I did the safety inspection I noticed that her McPherson Strut was bad. They run $250 each, that's $500 for the pair and there's no point in changing one. I'll show you the slip," he said as he started to walk off. "I have $75 in the battery. That's $875 in parts and the rest is labor. " He pulled the slip from the pile, $1,085

"Where are the old parts?" asked Larry.

"I threw them in the dumpster."

"Dig them out, I want to look at them," said Larry.

The other guy dialed his phone. "I'm calling an auto parts store to see why a Ford Focus has a $300 starter. What year is that shitbox?"

"The mechanic hesitated before he answered 2004 Ford Focus 4 cylinder."

He passed Larry the phone — Larry continued the call: "4 cylinder Ford Focus, 2004. I need a battery, two front struts, and a starter — what am I looking at?" Larry said as he clicked the phone on speaker. The kid on the other end took a few minutes to look up the parts.

The mechanic took the old struts from the dumpster and he tossed them on the ground. He had his elbows on the dumpster as he listened to the speaker phone.

The starter is $119, the struts are $52 each without springs and $129 each with springs, usually you can use the old springs again. The battery is $59. We refund $15 for the old starter," the kid said. "And $10 for the old battery.

"Do you give a discount for a local garage?"

"Yes we give a trade discount; it's normally 10 to 20 percent. Do you want me to pull the parts for you and having them waiting when you come in?"

"I think I might call around for a lower price."

"We have price match, we'll match it or beat it by 10 percent."

"OK, thanks Kid. It's safe to say all the parts with the exchanges and the discounts — I'm looking at under $250."

"Yes sir, roughly," he said.

Larry hung up and looked at the struts, "I don't see any springs on the old struts, where's the springs?"

"I used them on the car. I tried to save her money," he said.

"And where's the old starter?" I asked, "and where's the battery?"

"I traded in the starter core and the same with the battery."

"I don't know, Sonny," Larry said shaking his head from side to side. "I don't trust this fuck. I'll bet the starter never got changed and it's 50 percent chance he didn't change the battery either. Your numbers are way off and you being a mechanic means you can buy the parts cheaper than me. I come up with a total of about $200 to $225 for the parts — you heard the kid on the phone. Do you see we have a problem with your figure of $875 in parts? You're $600 high. Why don't you put that car up on the lift so we can see if you changed the starter, because if you didn't there's going to be a real problem here."

The mechanic started to back up, he wiped his brow and left some grease on his forehead. "We can work something out. Let me think for a minute," he said.

"Why don't you get in my car and we take a little ride. I think a ride through the everglades might make you think clearly. Someone fucks my family it's like someone is fucking me. I think you tried to fuck me. Do you know in other countries when they catch a crook they cut off his hand? I have a joke for you. How long does it take for a one handed mechanic to change a starter?" asked Larry.

"I don't want any problems with you people, so let's not get hasty. The keys are in the car and you can drive it away and I'll rip up the bill, no charge."

"Do you take orders from this guy, Sonny?" asked Larry. "I know I don't. Let me explain something to you: No one is paying you, period — so you're not giving us shit, and YOU take the keys and drop the car off at the girl's house. We don't want to be inconvenienced, and now Sonny will offer you an insurance policy against having a problem with guys like us. You need protection from people like us — people who will cut your hands off."

He looked at me with his eyes wide open. I pointed my finger in his face touching his nose with every other word as I spoke.

"It's going to cost you a grand a month for our services. Starting on the first of the month Larry will be by to get the cash, preferably in hundreds. You don't want to go unprotected, bad shit happens to the unprotected. I'll call Jill in an hour, you should have time to fill her car with gas and run it through the wash. I better hear good things." I didn't wait for him to answer. I got back in the Lincoln and drove off.

About ten minutes later my phone rang. It was Larry Windows.

"Hey boss, what did you think of that? I figured I drum up some business. Jimmy gave us to you, me and Chuck. I didn't want to introduce him in front of Donny, the mechanic. It wouldn't have looked too good. What's my cut for collecting the monthly fees from our new friend Donny? Is it the usual 10 percent?"

"I think we should start on the right foot and you guys take 20 percent. I'll give the rest to Jimmy and he'll take care of me, but nice work. Tell Chuck nice job too."

"You bet, Boss. If you need anything, we're there in a flash."

Chuck was about thirty; he was just an average built guy about 5-foot-10. He had strong Italian features. His nose and ears looked like they had received a lot of punches. Larry was a little older, he was about four inches taller than Chuck and fifty pounds heavier, his hair was thinning and he wore it long with sideburns, he had crooked teeth and a big nose. He had a habit of pulling at his nostril with his thumb, mostly one side like he had problems with nose hairs. So far this was my crew, and I was catching on — the way to make money started at the bottom, went through me and then straight to the top. I had the feeling that Chuck and Larry knew how to shake the money tree.

Chapter Thirty-Seven

Exaggerations

I went in to work, and an hour later Jimmy came in to check on the staff. I told him what had happened and about the monthly dues that I charged Donny. He was proud and slapped my shoulder.

"Tomorrow night I want you to come to a party. You'll represent the family — it'll be me, you, and Pauly. They like to see the line of command at these things."

"What kind of party? It's not a family party?"

"It's a benefit for the firemen and the cops, the family makes a respectful contribution and most of the cops get the message. It's good for them to see who's who and to know you're fearless in the midst of Johnny Law. Half the cops are on the take; there's a few that play it straight, mostly the rookies, but all in all they just want to go to work and not get shot. It's a cat and mouse game. We declawed the cat and trained him to let the mouse go. We share the cheese, that's the catch. I pass a lot of counterfeit money on cops, and they don't even know."

"This is nuts," I said. "At one time I wanted to be a cop."

"Look at the service you did today, you caught a crook and instead of sending him to prison and embarrassing him in the papers, he only got fined. What you did was a civil service, it's all the same thing," Jimmy said.

"I never thought of it like that."

"Start thinking like that. This family does a lot of good things for the community. This car rental business pays taxes and employs nine people who pay taxes and it all goes back to the government. We buy lots of cars, Detroit builds them, and everyone pays taxes." He held his hand out and pulled on his fingers one by one, "We create jobs here, we create jobs in Detroit, we create jobs in the insurance market, and we create jobs in the print and advertising market, as well as the internet. And that's only running this one store. If I counted the other businesses that we operate, we would be here all day long. We support all the local charities and the religious ones too."

"I had no idea." Jimmy had a way of making me feel like the Mafia was a patriotic part of America.

"If we stopped all the business we have in this country, it would cripple the economy. Look at Alice; she doesn't have a clue who owns this place. Six months ago you didn't either. Two towns up from here we own a big brick building that we lease to the town. Their old building is full of asbestos and they needed a place while the new police station is built. Pauly is tight with the mayor. The mayor put the police department and the city clerk and tax office in there. What do you think of that? The cops are our tenants — who are they going to bust, their landlord?" Jimmy was proud and lit a cigarette, "that's how it works, one hand washes the other."

Then my phone rang, I looked at the screen and then looked at Jimmy — he was becoming my friend. "Take the call," he said.

"It's just Jill, she can wait."

"No it's fine, take it."

I did. "Hey, what's up?" I asked.

"Donny, the mechanic dropped my car off and said there's no charge. I almost fainted. What did you do? What did you say?"

"I just said there was a misunderstanding, that's all. I'm glad he got the message."

"Something happened, didn't it? No one lets me out of a thousand dollars worth of repair bills unless something happened."

"Don't worry about it," I said.

"Bonnie's brother is good friends with Donny and I'll find out why he changed his tune."

"Fine, I've got to go," I said as I hung up the phone. I realized she never thanked me. I'll bet she thanked Donny though.

"Are you serious with that girl Jill?" asked Jimmy.

"No, she's an opportunist."

"She's pretty, but maybe you should see whatever else is out there. Being an opportunist is not a good quality in a woman. My father said that there are two kinds of people, ones that are on the way, and ones that are in the way. I think Jill might get in the way. My wife has sisters and cousins, all beautiful and those girls are Italian, if you know what I mean. They wait for you to make a move and they're on board. Not like some women that make you make the move they want. I mean, you can do what you want but you ain't helping yourself by marrying outside the Italians. You're only where you are because of your Italian blood, don't kid yourself. I know your dad saved Don Mancini's life, and it cost him his."

The Don made good on his word and everyone knew when you came of age you would be spotted in the family. But if you were a stranger and had saved Dominic from choking, Pauly may have given you a new car. But since you are family he's giving you a chance to have a hundred new cars. Another one of Dad's sayings: *If you want to feed a man for a day, then give him a fish; if you want to feed him for the rest of his life then teach him to fish.* Pauly wants you to fish, and I'm going to teach you."

I nodded my head. "You said my dad saved the Don's life, and lost his own. I never knew that, what happened?"

"It was a long time ago, your dad was only a soldier, a Piciotto, and the Don was a sgarrista, one level higher — like you. Your dad used to haul tractor-trailer trucks full of drugs and onions. Carmine decided to go on one of the hauls with him and they crossed a narrow bridge and a tire blew out and your dad lost control. The truck broke the guardrail and flipped over the bridge and into about twenty feet of water. The Don can't swim and the truck sank like a rock, so here's your dad and Carmine knocked out cold, with water flooding into the truck cab. Your dad comes to, and kicks the windshield out of the truck and that's when Carmine woke up and drowned. Your dad was already on the surface and realizes that Carmine didn't get out. He dove down and got Carmine and brought him to the shore and revived him."

"They both lived — what killed my dad?"

"Your dad had internal bleeding — they took him to the hospital, but he died on the way. But Carmine remembered being stuck in that cab, he remembered drowning. He vowed to support your family."

I was silent for a few minutes. The company phone rang, and Jimmy answered and went to write up a customer at the airport. I stood around for a few minutes and then he said, "Take the Taurus to gate 'C' for the Preston family. I'll send another car to pick you up."

I got the keys and the paperwork as soon as they came out of the printer, and then I walked out to the car. I saw Jay washing the wheels on a Cadillac — I sent him in to see Jimmy so he could come get me. I found the Taurus and logged the miles and fuel, and headed to the airport. My phone rang. "It's me again," said Jill. "I found out some stuff about Donny."

"OK."

"He said you went down there and two of your guys pulled out guns, one put it against his temple while you pushed his face against the hood of my car. I hope you didn't dent my hood."

"Really? Is that what happened?"

"That's what I heard, and you took a bullet and pushed it up his nostril and said, *the next one will be coming a lot faster.* Donny didn't know who you were so he called Craig. He's a biker, and normally Craig would get a few friends together and take a baseball bat to whoever had the balls to do that to Donny. Donny said your name and Craig got scared and told him you went in the clubhouse and threw a grenade at Snake, and your guys were wired with dynamite so no one would dare shoot you. They said you're fucking nuts, and so are the guys that work for you."

"Who said that?"

"Never mind — I'm not getting anyone in trouble."

"You just told me that Bonnie's brother has a friend Craig who's a biker."

"I never said who said what, so keep your distance from Bonnie and her brother and..."

"And you too, right?"

"For now anyway, until it cools down. I told you I don't date bikers."

"I'm not a biker."

"Mafia, it's probably the same thing, only worse. See you around, Matt. Or Sonny, or whoever you are."

I hung up and realized she still didn't thank me. I really didn't blame her for not wanting to date me, but she had a good thing going as a manipulating cock tease. I figured she had a string of suckers and it pissed me off that she used me like she did. With the money that I was making it was a drop in the bucket, but she didn't know or care about anyone that she financially drained. She was a vacuum, just like Tony said.

Chapter Thirty-Eight

Amusement

The washer and dryer had arrived at the apartment a week ago, and Alice washed something every time she was home. It was great to have clean clothes to wear, but I wondered if she was consumed with doing laundry, like a hunter who compulsively cleans his gun. If a towel hit the bathroom floor it ended up in the machine and an excuse to run a load. I hated hearing the damn thing running constantly. I liked to listen to music, or watch sports without hearing the dryer drum rolling with zippers, or the washer clunking between gears. I didn't do the wash, but I still hated it.

She sat at the kitchen table and read a shopping flyer like it was a Discover magazine and full of interesting information. I used to throw the flyers away before I even got in the house. I didn't see the point of shopping in four stores to save ten bucks, when it was $9 in gas and all the wasted time, but she loved doing that sort of thing.

"Steve is coming over; he should be here in an hour. Are you still coming with us to Universal?"

"I forgot all about it, but why don't you go on without me?"

"I didn't want to go without you, it'll be too weird. Will you please come?"

"I guess so, but I don't like being the third wheel."

"Come on, don't be like that. I don't know this guy. What if he turns out to be a weirdo?"

"He doesn't seem like he's the type, but it'll be interesting to see him in the light. That club is dimly lit and he might have dark circles under his eyes or pitted skin. I've danced with the hottest girls at dark clubs and the next morning they look like witches."

"Shit, I didn't think of that. What if he sees all my imperfections?" she said as she wiped her hand across her face.

"You look good, but he's ten years older than you, so he might not look so young. That's all I'm saying."

"That's even more reason you should come with me."

"I said I'd go."

"You said you guess so. I need to hear you say you would go."

"I'm going, even if you can't go. I'm going and I'll walk around with him. You happy? I'll get a haircut and be back in an hour," I said as I walked out the door.

I drove the Lincoln and I wondered if I should change it for a Mustang convertible. I stopped at Supercuts and went inside, looked at a few magazines and before I finished my first article it was my turn. I got a heavy girl who wore clothes too tight for her weight and she had a crazy haircut of her own. It looked ridiculous and I wondered how she expected anyone to take her seriously. I was nervous. "Can you just give me a trim?"

"I can use the clippers, is that what you want?"

"I want a trim, can you do a trim?"

"I can do whatever you want sweetheart" she said. I looked at her black lipstick and her blue and pink eyeliner done like a cat. Her hair was three inches on one side of her head and about seven inches on the other, and the back was angled to connect the two different lengths. Oddly, her hair was parted in the middle. I never saw anything like it.

Then the girl who cut my hair the last time came from the back room and was talking to another woman. "That's the girl that did my hair last time, I'd like to have her do it."

"That's too bad, she's off today. She came in to get her check."

Tammy saw me and waved, and I waved her over.

"What's new?" she asked.

"I need a cut I was hoping you were working."

"No, not today, sorry."

"I think I'll wait then," I said as I pulled the apron from my chest and stood up. I took a dollar from my wallet and said, "sorry, I'll wait for another time."

I walked out and Tammy came outside with me. "I wasn't going to let that woman cut my hair," I said. "She has an attitude."

"You should have told her you're the Mafia and see what she said. She doesn't give me any shit, she thinks I'm a biker bitch."

"I had an hour to get a haircut and that chick messed me up."

"Do you live close by?" she asked.

"Yeah."

"I could follow you and cut your hair."

"Really? That would be great."

"You don't care if I know where you live?"

"It's just an apartment that I share with a co-worker and what are you going to do? I know where you work and you know I'm not afraid to walk in the club house with a box of grenades."

"You really get me going when you talk like that. What are you driving? I'll follow you."

"The black Lincoln."

"I should have known."

"Keep up, I'm used to losing a tail."

"You won't lose this tail," she said, laughing.

I stood by the Lincoln and looked both ways, like I was checking for someone watching me. Then I crouched down and acted like I was looking for a bomb under the car. I saw her watch from her car, and then I got in and drove away. She followed and pulled in the driveway behind me. There was a strange truck out front and I assumed it was Steve's. I walked in and held the door for Tammy. Steve was in the doorway of the bathroom, talking to Alice while she straightened her hair.

I pulled a chair from the kitchen and spun it around and Tammy put her case on the table and unzipped it. She was dressed well and her hair looked natural — it wasn't dyed, or over styled. She put the apron on me and Alice looked out from the bathroom.

"What's going on?" she asked as she walked in from the hallway. Steve followed her.

"She's my hairstylist and I'm getting a haircut. This is Tammy, that's Alice and Steve." They waved to each other and Alice went back to the bathroom.

Tammy heard them talking about going to Universal and City Walk.

"I haven't been there in years. Isn't that funny? Most people think if you're from here then you'd spend every weekend in the parks, but I usually work all weekend."

"You can come along with us if you want, it's just us three," I said.

"I just got paid, I'd have to stop by the bank and get a few bucks, but I'd love to go."

"Good, I won't feel like a third wheel," I said.

My haircut was almost finished and Alice already had the vacuum out and was waiting for the last hair to fall before she started the motor.

"I brought a Lincoln — if everyone wants to ride together, there's plenty of room."

Alice's eyes got big, and Steve asked, "Do you want to take my truck and let them ride alone?"

"I'd rather all go together. It's cheaper to park and besides I don't want to be rude," said Alice.

I went in the bathroom and checked my hair and then I pulled out a twenty for the haircut and when I handed it to Tammy she refused to take it. "It's on me this time."

"Then the day is on me. I already stopped by the bank."

"You didn't rob the place did you?"

I didn't answer, I just laughed as we walked out to the car. I popped the trunk. I knew Alice would have something to take along. She put an extra sweatshirt in for both of us and then she turned to Steve, do you have a jacket in case it gets cold later?"

"I like it cold; if it gets too cold I'll buy a sweatshirt."

Tammy sat in the front with me — I drove to the amusement park. Once inside, I wanted to split up but I didn't want things to be awkward, for Alice, or Tammy. We were there as a group of friends. I saw the roller coaster "The Hulk" — one of my favorites. We stood and watched the people scream as it passed under the foot bridge and nearly hit the water.

We took our turn on the big green monster. All screamed as the coaster left the launch. It twisted and looped the track. We got off the ride and went to see our pictures. All of us were caught smiling except for Steve. He had his mouth and eyes closed.

"That was fun, let's go again," said Tammy.

"I can't go again, but you guys go on and I'll get a picture of you when you go under the bridge," said Steve.

"Go on ahead, I'll stay with him," said Alice.

We got back in line and a drunken guy stumbled and cut between a father and his son. He stood next to another drunken guy and they laughed as they watched the coaster roll through the turns. They were loud and disturbing.

Tammy shook her head, "those two are pledges from the club house."

Just as the words left her mouth one of the guys turned around and heard her and said, "what are you looking at, bitch?"

The other one laughed and turned, and when he saw I wasn't smiling he said, "I know that dude, but I can't figure out from where."

They both took a closer look; one tapped the other on the shoulder with the back of his tattooed knuckles. That's the fucking guy with the grenades. The guy that was going to blow up the club house, remember? Because they put his picture on the corkboard. Remember?"

"Oh yeah," he said, bobbing his head.

The father turned and put his hands on his sons' shoulders and pulled them almost out of line. He looked at me and asked. "Do you want cuts, so you can be next to your friends?"

"They're not my friends and they cut you. I think they should go to the end of the line. What do you people think?"

About ten people looked at me, but only the man's son answered. "They cut the line and I think ..."

Before he finished, his father covered his mouth.

"The boy is right," I said. Then I pointed to the two bums and said "get out of line while you still can, go all the way to the end. I'm only going to say it once, because you know if I snap my fingers there's going to be hell to pay. Do you want me back at the club house and you can explain yourself to Snake? You cut my family and they're all over this place. I better not see your face again, and you better apologize on your way out, especially to Tammy, and this brave boy."

The two bikers bowed their heads and said, "sorry" to the boy and "sorry" to Tammy. The boys smiled and I gave my fist to pound. Tammy put an arm around my waist and hugged me. "Thanks, those guys are so embarrassing." I could tell that the surrounding crowd was uneasy when they heard about me and the grenade, but the line kept moving and we rode the coaster again. When we got off we waited to see the pictures and then I said, "Alice doesn't know my business with the family, she only knows me as Matt. I'm sorry that happened and today I'm not here as Sonny, I'm here as Matt."

"I like that you dress respectably and you can be Matt. The bikers wear their vests, and that's their identity, patches and colors. It was awesome to see them back down, especially in their vests."

"They knew better than to cause problems. The Mafia doesn't bluff or make empty threats. I don't need to bark and strut around with a sign on my back. The more people that know me will know the family doesn't like disrespect and as long as they don't ask for a problem, there won't be one. Jimmy the Capo told me that no one gets the wrath that they didn't invite. I think it's a good policy."

"Are there a bunch of mobsters here watching our backs?" she asked as she hugged my elbow with both arms. "I find it exciting."

"Our backs — you're not Mafia," I said with a straight face, and then I laughed.

"I meant your back, but I'm with you so, it's our backs."

"A free haircut only gets you so much protection, you know," I said with a wink.

She looked around the crowd to see if she could pick out mobsters, and then pointed to a few sharply dressed middle aged men who were most likely waiting for their kids to get off a ride. "Those two guys are Mafia, I can tell by the nose on that one and the leather face on the other one," she said.

"Don't point," I said, playing along with her. "The tall one is Billy, they call him Billy Club. He beats people with a club, hence the nickname."

"So I'm right — and the other one?"

"Leather Face Luke — he took acid to the face," I said with a serious look, and then I slid my sunglasses on.

"I can spot them. It takes a few minutes, but they sort of stick out. They have their own look."

I took my sunglasses off, and said "What do you mean? Do I look like a mobster?"

"You do a little, but you look like the boss — probably been protected your whole life. You snap your fingers and someone gets whacked," she said as she snapped her fingers. I grabbed her hand and startled her.

"Don't do that, someone might get whacked."

She laughed, "I'm on to something, ain't I? And that's why they call you Sonny — you're the son of one of the big boys, aren't you?"

"It's Matt, remember? It's just a day with Matt."

Chapter Thirty-Nine

Political Party

We went on rides and ate junk food, and listened to music at Jimmy Buffett's Margaritaville, where Steve and Alice sang along with the music. The warm breeze picked up and pushed away the day's stale air. I enjoyed watching them have fun. A gray squirrel saw I was eating peanuts and came close to my chair. He was used to large crowds and begging from the tourist.

"Throw him a nut," said Tammy.

"No, he'll have to take it from my hand," I said as I popped a peanut from the shell and held it between two fingers. He hesitated and then he put his tiny hands on my thumb and took the nut.

"What would you do if he bit you?" Tammy asked, and then I tipped my head to one side and looked at her. "I know, you'd have him whacked, right?" she said, laughing.

"Didn't you see a little red laser dot on his head?" I said.

"I wouldn't be surprised."

"Surprised at what, the squirrel?" Alice asked.

"He's probably a robot, knowing this place." said Steve

"Pat Benatar is playing here tonight — we should make our way to the stage area," said Alice.

I assumed Alice was having fun, and wanted her date to continue. We saw the concert and stayed until 10:30, and then I drove us back to the apartment. Tammy went home and Steve slept on the sofa. I had an early shift the following day, so I went in my room and watched TV until I fell asleep.

The next morning Alice was up in the kitchen, scrambling eggs. She had a midmorning shift and she liked to get up early. I heard her in the bathroom, preening herself before Steve saw her. I wanted to talk to her but he was there, and I didn't want him to hear. I wanted her opinion on him, and on Tammy.

Jimmy and I had the party for the police and fire departments to go to. It seemed odd, but I was excited to go. I hadn't had a run-in with the law, so I didn't fear cops.

I was busy all day; Jimmy didn't come in until the end of my shift. He pulled a car up to the garage and beeped the horn. I came out and walked to the driver's door.

"Jay's shift starts in an hour, get in the car, I'm taking you shopping."

I didn't ask any questions, I just got in the car and we drove to a men's clothing store. We walked inside, where a few of the workers recognized him. "Hi Jimmy, what can I do for you today?" one said.

"My friend Sonny needs a nice suit — we have a formal party to attend and he has to look sharp. I'm thinking black suit, white shirt, and red tie. Something that shows power."

The man walked to a big rack where jackets lined the wall. "You look like a 44 athletic cut, and a 32 waist, 34 inseam … is that right?"

I looked at my waist, "Yeah, you're right on."

"I have plenty to pick from," he said.

Jimmy wandered to a different section, where he tried on a few jackets and then he picked out a white shirt and black tie with tiny blue diamonds printed on it. He picked a blood red tie, and then a tie clip and cufflinks. I liked to wear a leather coat as a dress coat, but I didn't doubt Jimmy's judgment. I went in the dressing room and tried on the suit. I came out and admired myself in the mirror.

"You look sharp," Jimmy said. "Let's pick out a new pair of shoes."

I followed him to the shoe area; he picked shiny black shoes with decorative cutouts and fancy stitching. It wasn't what I would have picked, but he knew what mobsters wore and, again, I trusted his judgment.

"I'll need size ten," I said to the worker.

He quickly fetched the shoes; I tried both on and walked in front of a full view mirror.

"Perfect," Jimmy said.

We went to the counter and the clothes were rung up to a house account; we walked out with an armful of clothes.

We went back to the rental store. "Go home and get showered and changed, then meet me here at 7 o'clock. We'll ride together, just me, you, and Pauly."

"I'll be here at 6:45."

"Good, that shows respect. You're learning."

I went home, showered, and drank a beer while I changed into the new clothes. I sniffed each bottle of cologne and wondered what a mobster was supposed to smell like. I didn't feel like Brut, or Old Spice was going to be a hit. I had a few drops of cologne my ex-girlfriend had bought me for Christmas, so I trusted her nose and dripped the last of it on my cheeks and neckline. I slid my new shoes on and stood in front of the mirror. I could hear a key in the door. I looked at my watch and thought it might be time to get a Rolex — I needed the rest of the outfit; the watch, gold chain, and a ring.

The door opened and Alice walked in with a bag of groceries hanging from her small hand.

"Are there more in the car?" I asked.

"No, this is it. I wanted to make a nice dinner for us. We haven't eaten together for a few nights, you know, just me and you. You look nice; why are you dressed up?"

"I was invited to a party with Jimmy and it's formal."

"Jimmy must like you; he never invites me to any parties. I'll bet you're getting a promotion. What kind of party is it?"

"A charity for the police and fire department," I said.

"It must be a chamber of commerce type of thing where he wants people to see who the top guy of the company is, and it looks to me that he wants you to rub with the right people. I guess maybe tomorrow night we can have a nice meal, if you're available. I was going to make lamb and asparagus. I hope you like lamb."

"It been a long time since I had lamb, but I like it and I'm sure it will be delicious the way you cook. Now an important question — do you know how to tie a tie? I've tried three times to get this thing even but it is either too high on my stomach or too low."

She came close and I had my collar up and the tie draped on my shoulders. She reached up and grabbed both ends of it and pulled my head down, it almost felt like she was getting ready to kiss me. She looked in my eyes as she made the first few loops and then she watched the tie until she slid the knot up to my neck and then pulled my collar down and tugged at the corners of the shirt that rested on my shoulders. She smoothed the tie out as she pressed it against my chest and stomach. "Looks perfect to me," she said as she backed up and looked at me.

"Thanks," I said as I pulled the tie clip from its piece of plastic and pushed it into the tie and fastened the small chain onto my shirt. It matched my cuff links. I slid the jacket on and Alice pulled at the sleeve to free up the wrinkles.

"I guess I'm ready."

"Have a good time and don't make plans for tomorrow's supper."

"You've got it, Roomie," I said as I backed out the front door.

I got to the store early; I pulled the Lincoln up to the building and listened to the radio while I waited.

Another Lincoln pulled up beside me; the tinted window went down — it was Jimmy. He pointed and yelled, "park your car and ride with us."

I pulled the car forward to the employee spaces. Jimmy followed and I got into the passenger seat and greeted him and Pauly.

Pauly was on the phone and was agreeing with whoever was on the other end. We drove in silence to be polite to Pauly, and once we arrived at the party, Pauly hung up the phone, and I jumped out of my seat to open the back door for him. Jimmy saw me and winked.

We walked into the party; there were mostly guys there, though a few wives were gathered together at a long table with hors d'oeuvres. I was hungry, but people kept coming up to Pauly, and he introduced Jimmy and me so I couldn't leave to get a snack. Everyone was dressed nicely, either in formal uniforms, or dark suits. The city officials were there as well as the big donors from real estate and development companies looking to grease a few palms to get projects to pass. Pauly knew the game. We were there to represent the Mancini family, and let the cops know we're the middle rank, the working faces of the mob, untouchable and powerful. Most of them already knew Pauly from his years of service; he introduced us as the successors of the family.

Some of the police force were young, like us. We needed to get along to do our jobs, so no one gets hurt. Jimmy told me that most cops were in it for the power and the pension. They didn't want to be killed in the line of duty. They were a lot like us — they wanted people to respect them and when they spoke they wanted to be obeyed. They were a fickle type, just like us. Some cops would bend all the rules for a buck, and others couldn't be bought, but most of the old timers were in Pauly's pocket. Jimmy said that after a cop is on the street for a few years they see the light. The closer to the pension, the softer the cop; mentally, morally, and physically — it's the rookies who get people killed. Most local cops were not a problem, it was the state troopers and the Feds that could ruin a good thing, but Pauly had friends in the departments who kept us from having problems. Alfred knew the politicians, people planted with our interest in mind. Corruption had no limits.

We sat at a table of honor and ate alongside of the top ranking civil servants. By the end of the night they knew my name and face.

Chapter Forty

Appetite

The next day I got a surprise; Tammy came by at lunch time.

"I was hoping that you hadn't eaten yet. I picked up a sub and a bag of chips, and I was hoping to have lunch break with you," she said.

"That depends on what kind of sub you brought."

"Your favorite."

"What's that?"

"Italian, and the chips are garden herb — it was the closest to Italian as I could get. Maybe I should have gotten salt and vinegar. Don't you Italians like oil and vinegar?"

"Yeah we love it," I said, smiling. "You didn't bring a cannoli?"

"No, I figured you might have had one for breakfast. Don't you guys keep one of them in your pocket?"

"That's not a cannoli."

"Just eat the sub and stop sexually harassing me," she said, as she handed me the bag.

"Let's sit at that picnic table. You're eating half this sub."

"I'll have a few chips, but the sub is all you."

We sat at the table; Alice had gone outside to smoke a cigarette. She saw us but didn't wave.

I bit into the sub, which was very good. "You need to have a bite of this," I said.

"I can't — I have to go back to work and that sub will stay with me all day. I can't be burping in everyone's face. I'll never get a tip."

"I'll have the same problem."

"Yeah but what do you have to do today? Break a few knee-caps and maybe play a few hands of poker?"

"Is that what you think I do? I'm an important piece of this intricate business. I have to work — I check the cars in and out. It's like being an air traffic controller. It's important shit."

"Right, like an air traffic controller, you're funny."

"I'm serious, I've got stress I said with a grin. "See that car there, the white Malibu? I know for a fact the windshield wiper fluid is low, and if it goes out like that and there is an accident, I'd feel like shit."

"So where's the stress?"

"I have to fill it up without getting fluid on my nice clothes; it's not easy being me."

I opened the bag of chips and she took a few and ate them one by one. She looked at her watch.

"I should get going; I like to set up my station before my shift starts. Am I going to see you again, when you need a haircut?"

"Maybe we can split a cannoli sometime."

"I'd like that."

"Thanks for the lunch. I have to get going to the bank. I have to drive the get-away car, and I don't want to be late," I said.

"Really? You make my temperature rise when you talk like that."

"No, I'm not driving a get-away car."

"I wouldn't be surprised."

"Why?"

"Matt, you're a fucking mobster, a real live Italian Mafia wise guy. Who are you trying to shit with this windshield wiper fluid story? I know who you are. I saw you at the club house. I like the bad boys and you're as bad as they get. It's like the rollercoaster we went on, it scared the shit out of me, but I can't get enough."

"You don't like the safe guys, the ones that work 9 to 5 with a car payment and a mortgage?"

"It's not about what a guy has for possessions; it's what he has for a life. I like excitement. The bikers are always in trouble and fight a lot, but they're kinda bummy and they strive to be that way — dirty and vulgar. They don't turn it on and off well. I didn't realize how different your life seems. You're well dressed and clean cut, more of what I'm attracted to, but you're like a James Bond type of character, where anything can happen. I watched Mafia movies and I love that type. I just never thought I'd meet one."

"It's pretty dangerous hanging out with me. You could get kidnapped."

"Who would kidnap me?"

"You never know."

She smiled and laughed, "I know you're kidding but it excites me. I must be strange; I still haven't told anyone I've been out with you."

"Maybe we could rent a mobster movie and stay in so you'll be safe."

"I have a 'Bronx tale' I can bring over, or you can come by my apartment."

"Sounds good, maybe tomorrow night," I said.

"I get the new schedule today, so I'll call you later," she said as she looked at her watch and walked to her car.

"Thanks for lunch," I said again.

She left and I went to the office for a new chart. Alice was on the phone. She held her finger in the air until the call was finished and then said, "looks like that girl Tammy really likes you."

"She wants to watch a movie with me, and she brought me lunch. I thought it was nice."

"I hope you remembered I'm making lamb tonight."

"I remembered."

"Maybe I should rent a movie. Have you seen 'Rock of Ages,' with Tom Cruise? I love that movie."

"No."

"Good, I own it. I'll pick up a twelve pack of Coronas and a bag of Doritos."

"You bought the meal, let me get the beer and the chips," I said, as I took the chart and walked out to the lot.

A few hours passed and she got off before I did. I went to the store and bought the beer, Doritos, some ice cream, and flowers.

When I got back home, I put the beer on the steps and fumbled with my keys. I could hear music, and smell the lamb cooking before I opened the door. Alice was bent over with her arms in the oven, trying to lift the hot baking pan. The table was set and rolls were in a basket wrapped in cloth to keep them warm. I put the beer in the refrigerator and put two on the counter, and popped the caps.

"Wash your hands, you have perfect timing."

I looked at my hands and went to the sinks; she took asparagus from the pan and into a serving dish and our backsides bumped as I wiped my hands on the dish towel. She handed me the dish and I walked it to the table, and then she carried the beers and the gravy. I sat and rubbed my hands together as she served me and then herself. I held my beer up, she did the same — we touched the bottle necks together as a toast.

She watched me slice the lamb and take a bite. I closed my eyes so she would think it was the best meal I had ever had. Slowly I chewed and then when I looked at her she smiled and took a bite of her own.

"It's so juicy, I was afraid you'd be late and it would be dried out. I'm glad you were on time. I made onion gravy, from the drippings, the same way my grandmother used to do it," she said as she spooned some over her potatoes and lamb. I reached for it when she was done.

"I can squeeze a slice of lime in your beer, it's a recipe my grandfather handed down," I said.

She smiled and took a sip. "How are things going with Tammy?"

"OK I guess, how are things with Steve?"

"Good, he calls when he wants. I try not to call him, but sometimes it gets lonely around here. I don't want him to think I'm desperate and chasing him. Kenny used to tell me not to call him; I'm used to a guy that doesn't want to be bugged. Do you like it when a girl keeps calling you?"

"I haven't had a girlfriend in a while, but if I like her, it's OK. I like to call her when I want — I don't worry if she thinks I call more than she does."

"I think of stuff like that, there's a line when if you call too much, then they think they have you, and they lose interest. That's what I noticed."

"I guess I never really cared. I figure, I'm young and not looking to get married, so if I get along with someone and have fun, then so be it, but if they get an attitude or I feel like they might be sneaky I move on. I can take it or leave it. I don't want a disease and I don't want a baby, or a hard time from a girl. Some girls have a lot of drama, and I don't need that. The guy that used to live here, Brad, his girlfriend works with him, they eat every meal together, she thinks she's pregnant every other month — it's crazy."

"I don't like a clingy guy. I'll be honest, the distance Steve has is good, but he's a little too far away. He thought it was strange that we share a place, and he asked me how long I planned on staying here. I wonder if he might have a problem with it. How does Tammy feel?"

"She didn't ask any questions, and I only went out with her to the parks with you guys. She might think, Steve is my roommate and you are his girl, or maybe the three of us are here."

"I'll bet that either he, or she will eventually have a problem with it," she said.

"Who cares, as long as we're happy. Are you happy?"

She nodded and took a bite of lamb.

Chapter Forty-One

Trim Time

A few weeks passed, I had talked on the phone a few times briefly with Tammy, but we hadn't seen each other since the lunch at the rental center. The night to watch a mobster movie didn't happen; I was a little disappointed.

My schedule was mostly nights lately, and I wasn't going out after work. By the time I got home, Alice was either on her phone, or in her room. She had started taking an online course and needed time to read, but some nights we sat and talked. I admired her for the strength she had after the breakup with Ken, whom she rarely mentioned, and alienating her mother had to be hard. Taking a course and working her hours, cooking, cleaning, and shopping, not to mention doing all the laundry was another feat I admired. I felt like an underachiever, and I wondered how she was ever interested in a guy like Ken.

Then I thought about Tammy, a talented stylist with great looks, nice smile, and nice body. I hadn't met the biker guy she was with, and I wondered why these losers got the hot girls. She didn't seem to be a user like Jill. I rubbed my hand over my head and decided it was time for a trim.

I lay in bed and wondered about my mother and sister, and then my new family. I knew things changed, nothing stays the same. I felt like my future was on a preordained track, like destiny. I knew I couldn't undo the past, I couldn't change it and I felt I didn't have control over the future. Alice seemed like she was taking steps to control her future, but a few night courses and a degree wouldn't have any effect on mine. Mobsters may be clever, cunning, and sly, but most are not overeducated. A degree won't get a guy promoted or more money.

The next day I slept late, took a long shower, and by the time I finished Alice was gone and a note was stuck to the counter. *"Tammy stopped by yesterday at work when you were off. She said she had something to tell you and she wanted it to be in person."*

I couldn't imagine what she wanted, maybe her boyfriend saw us together and forbid her from seeing me — I wouldn't blame him, I wouldn't like it either. Or maybe she had been arrested and had spent a week in jail.

I called Supercuts and asked for her, and then I tried to make an appointment, but I didn't have any luck. A drive down there would be necessary to answer the question of whether she was trying to dodge me or if she got fired.

I pulled into the lot and didn't see her car. Inside I saw the heavy girl with the strange haircut.

"Tammy's not here, do you want a cut?" she asked as she approached the sales counter.

"Do you know when she'll be back?"

The girl's eyes shifted from one side of the room to the back room and then she whispered. "She checked into rehab this morning, she's gone for six weeks."

"Six weeks, huh?"

"Do you want a cut? I just did a guy with your exact hair."

"I guess so, but just a trim."

I sat in her chair and everything the girl did and said annoyed me, right down to her open shoes with a foot tattoo of a mouse eating a wedge of cheese. She saw me look.

"Get it? He's eating foot cheese, you know toe cheese?" she said, laughing enough to make her lowest stomach roll move.

She needed another tattoo of a turd on her tongue; because her breath was so foul I tried to only breathe out. She continued with small talk and sang along with the store radio when I didn't answer.

Finally she trimmed my neckline and took the big apron off. I felt my head and looked in the mirror.

"Is it all good?"

"Yes, it's just right. Nice job there, 'Toe Cheese'."

"Thanks."

I paid and gave a nice tip and once out the door I lit a cigarette and looked at the traffic going by. I wondered what had happened to Tammy. Rehab explained why I hadn't seen her in a few weeks.

I got in my car and drove around a few roads that the tourist never see. I daydreamed; the song on the radio took me away from my troubles. The song was from the band Shinedown, "Second Chance." I joined in with them.

"I just saw Haley's comet, she waved

Said, "Why you always running in place?"
Even the man in the moon disappeared
Somewhere in the Stratosphere

I thought Tammy was running in place and like the man in the moon, she disappeared.

And sometimes goodbye is a second chance. I never had a drug or drinking problem. I'm not sure why others do, but a lot of people ruin their lives for a good time.

Then a sound that was not in the song startled me, the *whoop, whoop* of a police siren. I looked in the rearview mirror and the cop was so close I thought he was going to hit my bumper. I pulled over and one cop got out of the cruiser and adjusted his hat as he walked toward my car, and then he touched his gun. I watched him in the small mirror on my door. He tapped my window with his wedding ring and I let it down. I recognized him from the party. He was one of the rookies; his senior partner was still in the police car. I handed him my license and registration.

He read my name, "Matt, do you know why I pulled you over?"

"No I don't."

"You look familiar; did I arrest you last weekend?"

"No, I'm Sonny DiMambro, from the benefit banquet. I was there with Jimmy Maretti and Pauly."

"Sonny, Sonny … let me think. Let me run this and I'll be right back."

He went to the cruiser and handed the license to the other cop. I saw him nod his head and give it back to the rookie. He came back to my window and I made him wait until I lowered it again.

"What did you find out?"

"My partner Don said he recognized the ID, so I didn't run it. You're set to go, sorry for the inconvenience."

"No problem officer, keep up the good work."

I wondered what he thought when he saw I used a different name than the one on my license. He didn't even question it. I felt important and untouchable.

Chapter Forty-Two

Soldier Down

Another month went by, and I had gone for another haircut. I asked about Tammy and one of the girls told me where she was and that she had gone to see her. Sundays were the only day they allowed visitors. I decided to drive to the center and see her. It was a two-hour ride through orange groves that went on for miles. I saw the building along a narrow stream that fed a pond. The long driveway ended at the side of the building and from the parking lot I watched patients play badminton, while another group was playing croquet. I didn't see Tammy, so I went to the main office and introduced myself as her close friend.

I was led by a young woman to an open patio where a few girls were reading novels and sunning themselves. Tammy looked up from her book and smiled, "what are you doing here?"

The woman walked away and I whispered, "I'm breaking you out."

"Really?" Her face was drawn and without make-up, she had dark circles under her eyes, and her hair was pulled back.

"No, I'm kidding. You need to stay until the professionals say you're cured."

"I've learned a lot since I've been in here and they say you're never healed, never cured. The temptation will always be with me. I'm not going to lie to you; it's going to be tough. Did you know that 80 percent of the people in rehab will fail and have to come back? Three people in my group have been here before, one of them three times."

"What happened?"

"They've been teaching me stop making excuses, so I'm not going to. I tried heroin and I liked it. That's why I haven't seen you. I started a few years ago with opiates, you know — oxys and Percocet's, my boyfriend could get it all."

"The latest thing was heroin and I got away with it for a short while and then one night after shooting-up I dropped on the floor, and if it wasn't for the EMT that gave me a shot of Naloxone I'd be dead. I need all new friends — that's step one, clean friends. My partying years are over; I'm a new girl with a second chance."

"Has your boyfriend been here to see you?"

"Are you kidding, the last place he'd be seen at is a rehab center. He's probably high right now. Besides he wasn't really my boyfriend, he was a guy that couldn't get me, but my habit and cravings turned me into his girlfriend. I lived his life with the bikers and the parties at the club house. Who knows what the fuck I was doing over there? I was out of it for a long time, but you know what? I could still cut hair and I've always been good with people. I'd be high as a kite and bleach someone's hair or do a foil, or perm and it always came out good. That's when you really have a problem, it's when you can function on the shit, and I could. That day with you, at the park; I had a great time, but I was high — I popped a few perks."

"You don't need to do that shit around me," I said.

"I think you are an awesome guy, and I have fun with you. I need a friend right now and nothing more. They cram information at me all day long. I'm being counseled constantly, and, truthfully, I need it. They said no relationships, for at least a year. I could fall in love and then if it ends I'd be right back on heroin. I can't risk it — that's what happened to Cindy over there," she said pointing to a girl smoking by the window. Her hand jittered as she brought the cigarette to her mouth. "See how skinny she is? She's only twenty five; she looks like she's forty. I don't want that to happen to me."

"I don't blame you. I can be your friend, and I'm not looking for a romance right now. I don't drug and I really don't drink often, but I like to go out to eat and see a movie. I can take you out for a meal when you get back. I won't let you order mushrooms, how's that?"

She laughed, "that's not funny — I've done them too."

Then the woman came back and touched my elbow and whispered, "it's time for you to leave. Tammy has class in five minutes," she said, looking at her watch.

Tammy stood and hugged me. I could smell her unwashed hair and nicotine on her clothes. "Thanks for coming, Matt, it means a lot," she said with a tear leaking down her cheek. "I wish you didn't have to see me like this."

I wiped her cheek and said, "what are you crying about? I had to let your co-worker cut my hair — look at this uneven mess! I should be the one crying."

She laughed, waved, and walked away. She was wearing sweatpants and a tee-shirt, but she still looked sexy.

I walked away shaking my head. I wondered if there were any normal girls. Eventually I'd like to meet someone that I could have kids with. I didn't want my kids to be born with something wrong because my wife had a drug-filled summer, or at any minute could fall back into the grips of her addictions. I think I was born in the wrong generation. I wished I had lived in the '50s, with Elvis and the gas guzzling cars. I'd give up my cell phone and laptop in a second to live in that innocent era.

I drove back to town. It wasn't my shift, but it was hard to stay away from work — maybe because work didn't feel like work. The office was empty except for Jimmy. Alice was off, but I didn't feel like being at home. I parked the car and went inside. The phone rang, and Jimmy answered but didn't speak — he just paced the floor. I knew it must have been something to do with the family and he was too smart to discuss those things over the phone.

He hung up and looked me in the eye. "Johnny the Bump is dead. I'll call and see if Alice and Jay can come in and cover our shifts. We should go and see Don Carmine Mancini. He might want us to do something."

"What happened?"

He held his hand up, dialed the phone, and put it to his ear.

"Alice — this is Jimmy — I realize you have the shift off, but I need you to cover for about three hours, can you do that?"

I couldn't hear her answer but I assumed she said yes, because he instantly dialed Jay.

Jay agreed to work too. Jimmy hung up and said, "Let's take my car and find out what's going on."

I didn't know what to say, Jimmy concentrated as he drove. Guys stood on the lawn smoking cigarettes by the Don's driveway; two cars pulled in behind us. It was Tony, with Larry Windows and Pauly, with Petey. Pauly nodded to Jimmy and we walked into the big house. The lower-level soldiers stayed either in the yard or in the hallway. Jimmy put his hand on my shoulder and said, "Stay here with the others, I'll find out what's going on."

I stood with my arms crossed, as more Capos came to see the Don. I counted six, besides Jimmy. The organization was larger than I thought. I couldn't imagine how many soldiers there must be. A servant with a platter of crackers and Italian cold cuts went into the chambers another pushed a cart with bottles of wine and liquors. Then a familiar face appeared. My mother's half-brother, Francis DiMambro, came staggering into the house. I didn't see him much as a child, but I recognized him from pictures that hung on my mom's walls. He was known as the family drinker. He knew who I was.

"Matty, it's me, Uncle Franky; I pulled some strings to get you in with Jimmy. It's been a long time, huh?"

"Thanks," I said as I stood and shook his hand.

"Sucks what happened to Johnny — he got shot in the face."

"Who would do that?"

Franky shrugged his shoulders and said, "that's why we're here. Don Mancini will figure it out and strike back. I'm with Geno's crew and I won't know shit until he gets out of the meeting. We're all on defense until Don Mancini strikes back."

Uncle Franky took a cigar out from his jacket and chewed the end. "I better take this outside," he said. "Come with me, we can catch up."

I walked outside with him; we talked about my mom and sister and a little about his wife and kids.

Meanwhile, inside the Don's chambers, the officers were coming up with a plan. "Someone brief me on what happened to Johnny, why did he get shot?" asked Don Mancini.

"I'm pretty sure the Damato family took him out," said Pauly. "They run the casino; Johnny dumped a lot of funny money on them. That Johnny had some balls."

"The word on the street is that Sal has been asking the Damatos for protection from us," said Geno.

"Don Anthony Damato? I haven't had a problem with him before, but there may have been a change in command. Maybe his son, Little Tony, is Big Tony now. Shooting a wise guy in the face is a hit and not an incident from a circumstance caused by Johnny.

Send a guy to the casino and have him gamble with the funny money, and see what happens. Send another to see Sal and see how he acts. Confront him on what you heard. I want to know if we are going to war with the Damatos or not. It could be a different family, or maybe Johnny was fucking someone's wife," said Don Mancini.

"It could be a hit from Sal's partner's family. He had connections and maybe the family figured out who killed him" said Alfred. "I'll see what the cops know. We have a few that work the club, and there's a few that watch Sal, so if the cops know, then we'll know."

"I want everyone to watch their backs and no one hits the Damato family until they get the word from me, said Don Mancini. "If Sal is hiring protection, then that's a new ballgame."

"What happens if that's the case?" asked Geno.

"Then we kill Sal and most of his family. That way there's no one that will need protection. If he hired the Damatos for protection they won't strike, they'll just flex, but if they hit one of us, then it's war, and there won't be a Damato left to pass on their name when I'm done with them. Make sure that the word gets out, and it comes straight from Don Carmine Mancini."

"If we find out who killed Johnny, do you want him iced?" asked Pauly.

"Not right away. If it's a single guy acting on his own, I want him kidnapped and brought here. I want whoever it is alive. I want him thrown off a building alive," said Don Mancini, and if the sorry bastard survives the fall, throw him off again. Are we clear?"

"Yes sir," they said. They ate the Italian meats and drank wine.

Chapter Forty-Three

The Funeral

Three days had passed, and it was Johnny's funeral. There was no wake, since he was shot in the face. The family was working every angle to find out who took him out. The paper said Johnny was shot in an armed robbery. The casino had pull with the newspapers and didn't want bad publicity. It looked like he had been killed in a nearby park.

I stood by the casket and then knelt to say a prayer. Father Paul consoled the widow, and once he left her side, Tony vowed he would kill the man who did this and shoot his dog too.

There were large displays of flowers. Jimmy came to my side and pointed to one of the largest. "Read the card on that one."

"May our deepest and sincere sympathy be with you and your loved ones on this day, respectfully yours The Damato family."

"What do you make of that?"

"The word got out that they were suspected of killing Johnny and they want it clear that it wasn't a Damato hit," said Jimmy.

"Do you think it could be a trick?"

"No, it was signed by Don Anthony Damato, and he would never do a chicken shit move to send flowers to his enemy. Don Carmine Mancini will call him in a few days to thank him for the gesture and if the Damatos know something they'll tell him, to keep the peace."

"What's going to happen now?"

"Here comes your uncle. It looks like he's shitfaced again."

He stopped in front of Jimmy and shook his hand, and then when he went to shake mine he pulled me in close and hugged me. Jimmy walked away and Franky pulled me aside and said, "I was with Johnny when he got shot."

"You were?"

"I got drunk and passed out," he said. "We were at the casino, gambling and drinking — we drank a lot. Like I said I passed out. I didn't tell Pauly I was with him. I couldn't — he knows I have a drinking problem and I was supposed to have Johnny's back. I let him down; most thugs would have killed us both. I don't understand why I'm still alive."

"Did you see who did it?"

"I have a good idea who did it, but I was out cold and the E.M.T.s woke me when they took Johnny. I thought he had passed out from drinking tequila, I didn't know he had been shot. They left me behind; somehow I got out of there before the cops came. Truthfully, I don't know if the cops ever came. They said it happened in the park, but I don't remember going to no park. I don't know who called the E.M.T. s either. It wasn't me. You have to help me."

"Help you what? What do you want me to do?"

"I need a story. Maybe you can tell Jimmy I was with you, at your mom's house visiting. We went out to dinner, and then played cards or something. Can you do that?"

I didn't answer, I just shrugged my shoulders. He staggered off when he saw a guy from his crew, Billie Bones, a skinny guy who wore a hat like a 1940s gangster. He acted a lot like Tony. He was a lot taller, and every other word he spoke was a swear word. I figured Franky would forget that he asked me to cover for him.

Father Paul waved his hands for us to get closer to the grave as he opened the bible to pages he had marked with small colored ribbons. We bowed our heads. Most of us wore sunglasses, a few chewed gum.

"Today we place our friend John to rest; his life was a testament to three very important qualities in a man. He was a protector, and had the greatest devotion and loyalty to his family as one man could have. But one of his most memorable traits was his word, and if he gave his word it may as well have been etched in stone. If Johnny said he was going to do something it got done, no ifs, no buts — nothing. He was the definition of dependable. He leaves behind his lovely wife of twenty years and his two daughters. He was very proud of both of them. I remember when I came home from college, I needed a car and Johnny was the first one to offer. He never waited to help. The minute I landed at the airport he had a car for me — It wasn't his, but he still came through." The crowd laughed, knowing that Johnny had stolen a car for the priest. "And that's what will be missed the most, his loyalty, dependability, and accountability."

We bowed our heads in a moment of silence; the only noise was that of his youngest daughter crying, her face on her mother's shoulder.

"Let us pray," Father Paul said.

We prayed the *Our Father, The Lord's Prayer, and the Hail Mary.*

I was surprised how many people said the prayers out loud. Slowly the crowd dispersed. There was a large hall rented with fine foods for a family gathering. I rode with Jimmy, Tony, and Geno. They were quiet until we got there.

Once inside the party I got a tap on the shoulder from Pauly. "You should get your uncle out of here. He's shitfaced and saying things he don't need to say."

I put my drink down and grabbed Uncle Franky by the arm. He swung his arm violently until he saw it was me.

"We have to get out of here," I said.

"Why, what did you tell them?" he said in a loud voice.

I shook my head, "Nothing, I didn't say nothing."

"I didn't do it, I swear. I passed out and he was dead, and now he's in a fucking box."

Pauly pointed his finger to three guys and they were on Franky like bees. They dragged him out of the party. I followed behind and so did Jimmy.

"Take him home, find out what the fuck he's talking about, and then get back here," Jimmy said to me.

"What do you mean?"

"Exactly what I said."

The guys dragged Franky until he cooperated. I pointed to where I parked and they escorted us to the car. We got inside and I looked at him as his head nodded and his chin rested on his chest. He slept for a few minutes until I took a sharp corner and he slid against the window. I blasted the air-conditioner and the cool air helped revive him.

"What's going on, where are we?" he asked.

"You're with me, it's Matt. What's going on, Uncle Franky?"

"I'll tell you what's going on. I spotted you a place with the family and now you're higher up than me. What kind of thing is that? What's so great about you? I spotted you, it should be me that moved up. I've been at the bottom for twenty years and you are ahead of me, me and Johnny."

"I saved Dominic from choking, you know that. I didn't plan it."

"I'm at the bottom because I'm a drunk, let's face it. I'm drunk right now. I know, and you know, and you guys can all kiss my ass. You, your mother, and father can go fuck yourselves."

"My dad is dead."

"Oh, sorry I didn't mean to say that. I just meant that you can kiss my ass for judging me. I have a disease, and it got the best of me. Johnny understood. I loved him because he understood what it was like to have a disease. He had the gambling bug, and once it bit him, he was fucked, just like me. I'm fucked," he said as he slid a flask from his jacket and took a swallow.

I shook my head. "Is that why you were at the casino with him, so he could gamble?"

He didn't answer he just nodded his head "yes."

"The boss would give him thousands in funny money and tell him what to play at the dog track. The boss would win and get clean money, but Johnny would lose — sometimes he would win a little, but most of the time he would lose. The other night we went to the dog track. The boss sent his numbers with me and Johnny, and they both won. For once in his life he played the same tips that the boss had and he won. That wasn't good enough for Johnny; he said playing a tip is not gambling. He had to stop at the casino and play his winnings so the gambling bug would be happy. I played a few tables, but with the free drinks — I got drunk."

"So what happened?" I asked.

"He lost all his money, and then he started to play the boss's money. I didn't know what happened, because I passed out at the table. I was watching him, and the next thing I knew he was dragging me outside to put me in the car. I remember telling him we needed to go home before he lost any more money — any more of the boss's money. He got pissed and shoved me on the ground and said find the car myself. I told him he better get in the car or else."

"Or else what? Or else what, Uncle Frank? What the fuck did you do? You shot him didn't you? And that's why you're so fucked up."

"I didn't mean to. I pulled my piece when he threw me down, it was a reflex. I told him or else and he didn't listen. I fired a shot to scare him. I never thought I would hit him. It was an accident, and now I'm fucked."

"An accident is an accident."

"I found the car and crawled inside and spent the night — when I woke up, Johnny's body was gone, someone must have seen him lying dead and called the cops, or an ambulance. I drove away and I'm not sure if it really happened. I was so drunk Matty, you have to believe me, it was an accident."

"Don't worry, things will work out. I'll talk to Pauly; he'll know what to do."

"No, not Pauly, he doesn't like me. Jimmy likes me, but Jimmy likes everyone. I think you should talk to Geno … would you do that and explain it was a mistake?"

"Of course I will Uncle Franky."

"No, not Geno either. I had a problem with Geno. His daughter said I propositioned her and she's a fucking liar, but I was drunk and Geno had me beaten — he might have a grudge. Don't tell him, that might be bad."

"What about Don Mancini?"

"No, fuck no, not the Don. I was the driver, and one day I left him somewhere and I couldn't remember what time to pick him up — he stood around for a long time, he was pissed."

"Did you get beat?"

"He had the boys beat the shit out of me and they pissed on my suit coat.

"How could you forget that?"

"Drinking, again, drinking did this to me."

"Who do you want me to tell? Anthony Damato is going to release the tape from the parking lot to Don Mancini and they'll know it was you."

"Fucking Matt, you fuck," he said through gritted teeth as he shook his head from side to side. "You're fucking right, though; they fucking film everything today, don't they?"

"Yes they do."

"Why haven't the cops got the tape?"

"Don Damato wouldn't turn one of Mancini's family in to the cops, not without Don Mancini seeing the tape first. He must have given the cops a blank tape or said there was a malfunction with the system."

"Mother fucker — you're right again," he said as he slammed his fist on the dashboard. "I'm fucked, I'm so fucked, and it's all because of this fucking flask, and this fucking gun," he said as he pulled the gun from his jacket.

I watched him carefully as he glared into the night. He had one hand on the flask and the other on the gun. He turned the cap off the flask and tilted it three times until it was empty. I knew it was a bad sign when he threw it on the floor, and then in one swift move he opened his mouth and put the gun inside and then the loudest noise I had ever heard echoed inside the car as he pulled the trigger. I slammed on the brakes and pulled over. I didn't know what to do. I knew enough not to use my phone. Jimmy would know what to do. I was in shock, but I had to keep it together long enough to drive back to the party. It was nearly impossible to keep my wits with my ears ringing and my uncle's bleeding head bouncing off his chest as I sped back to the hall.

When I pulled in I beeped the horn until someone came to the car. It was Larry. I lowered my window. "Would you go inside and get Jimmy, tell him I have an emergency on my hands."

Larry didn't ask any questions, he walked into the party and a few minutes later Larry, Jimmy, and Pauly were at the side of the car. They couldn't see inside the tinted windows.

"What's going on, is Franky still in the car? I thought I said take him home," said Jimmy.

"You did, but he shot himself before I got there. He said he accidentally killed Johnny and he was sorry."

"Larry, take the car for a long ride and burn it with him inside — I'll have Billie Bones follow you."

Chapter Forty-Four

Bar-B-Cued Frank

I got out of the car and Pauly put his hand on my shoulder, "Franky did the right thing. He knew he didn't have the right to end Johnny's life, and we would be forced to hit one of our own. It's better this way, and if it makes you feel better he said he wanted to be cremated."

"I hoped you were going to come forward and honor your pledge to the Don. There are no secrets kept from him and holding a secret would be a very bad thing. If you know something and are afraid to tell Don Mancini, then you come to me and I will take it to him. That's what I'm here for. We're family, Sonny, closer than you and Franky. He fucked up and now he's dead."

"It's too bad," I said.

"The Don already knew what happened. I was going to ask you to kill Franky, so it was good he died in your presence. Did you shoot him?"

"No, he shot himself."

"Why wouldn't you shoot him?"

I could tell it was a loaded question, and I was traumatized from Franky's suicide, and my ears were still ringing from the gunshot. "I wouldn't shoot any wise guy, or family member unless I had the OK from the bosses."

"Good answer, Sonny. You're a quick learner."

"Franky said he made a mistake, would you still kill him?" I asked.

"He should have come clean before Don Carmine Mancini. Maybe he would convince Alfred and me — then the Don may have spared his life, but to hide like a coward is not the honorable thing to do. He did the right thing and now it's over. I know you wouldn't want to kill your uncle, but he was poisoning you with his deceitful lies. I see a bright future for you, he saw it too. He was at the bottom and failed at small tasks. It was only a matter of time before he got himself or someone else killed. I'm going to miss Johnny. I need a new man to bet at the track. We're going there tomorrow and I'll show you the ropes and then when I can't go, I'll send you in my place. Do you like the dogs?"

"Sure, I guess."

"Good, I'll pick you up at the rent-a-center noontime tomorrow. I'll have Tony drop you off. Get a good night's sleep and try to forget about your uncle."

He put his hand on my shoulder again. "I know tomorrow seems too soon to do something, but trust me, you need to stay busy and I want you to do this with me. The first time I saw a guy shot in the head it bothered me and I spent a week alone. It didn't do any good. You need to shake it off. You can never stop someone from killing themselves if they really want to. It was a low move on Franky's part to do it in front of you, very disrespectful."

We stopped at a hedge near the driveway. "Wait here while I tell Don Mancini what happened. I'll send Tony out. You shouldn't go inside with blood on your jacket."

I stood next to the hedge, and thought about what had happened. I didn't know my uncle well, but the trauma of seeing anyone, even an enemy; kill himself in front of me left me devastated. I'd never be the same. I've heard my friends say they should kill themselves from depressing times, a breakup, or job loss, but I never thought I'd witness someone acting it out. I hated Uncle Franky for doing it in front of me. Although I had a strong stomach and rarely threw up, I felt nauseous.

Tony came out, "sorry to hear about your uncle, let's get out of here."

I followed him to his car; I didn't want to be alone with him. I got in the car and he drove. We were quiet. It seemed like Tony was uneasy and he couldn't stay silent. "That was a shitty thing that happened to Johnny. We still don't know the whole story. Did Franky tell you what happened before he offed himself?"

I remembered that Pauly said there were to be no secrets. "Franky said he was trying to keep Johnny from gambling all his money away. They were in the parking lot and Franky threatened to shoot him if they didn't leave — he fired a warning shot, but he was drunk and accidently hit Johnny. Right after he told me what happened he shot himself."

"Are you fucking shitting me, that drunk shot Johnny? He's lucky he shot himself, because I'd kill him myself. He was a fuck-up," Tony screamed and pounded the steering wheel with his fist. "I'm glad he finally did something right, no offense, kid. I know he was your uncle but he fucked up everything he touched. I couldn't work with him."

"I didn't know him well but I still feel bad. I still can't believe he did it. What do I tell my mom?"

"Don't tell her shit, she don't need to know."

"She will when they find the car."

"How? He'll be burned to a crisp," Tony said as he lit a cigarette and offered me one. I took it and lit it and blew the smoke against the windshield.

"What about the dental records?"

"Franky had dentures; Larry will get them before he soaks the interior of the car with kerosene. This ain't his first body burn," Tony laughed. "There will be no way to identify the body, he's a missing person, that's all. Problem solved."

"You guys don't worry about anything, do you? You always have the bases covered, or you know the right people that turn a blind eye to whatever is going on."

"Now you're catching on," said Tony.

"Pauly is taking me to the track tomorrow; I'm supposed to take Johnny's place as a gambler."

"That's not a bad gig. You're lucky he picked you. Maybe I can go with you once you get the hang of it."

"What do I have to do? I don't gamble."

"You bet on whatever dog the boss says to bet. He knows what he's doing."

"I'm supposed to bet and win every race? It's fixed isn't it? Somehow it's rigged," I said.

"You use the funny money and if you break even the family wins by coming home with clean dough, get it? And yes, the races are fixed and we win big on a few and lose small on others. There won't be a problem," said Tony.

"What if I get caught with counterfeit money? Isn't that a crime and I'll do prison time?"

"Nah, we have it covered. You won't get caught, there's too much cash that flows through there, and these phony bills are good. I never seen one get rejected yet. Don't worry, you'll be with Pauly, they'd never get him. Besides, another family owns the dog track, a rival family, so it's win, win."

"That's what you do to rival families?"

"Yes sir, they get funny money, cut cocaine, and dirty drugs, and they don't know we're the ones passing it to them. I really don't know if they care. Take the money for instance; you place a bet at the window and walk away, when you win you go to a different window. The window you dropped the funny money passes your bad bills out to some schmuck, 'John Q Public,' and he don't know a bad bill from a hole in his ass," Tony said as he took a drag from his cigarette. He was relaxed with his elbow on the top of door touching the window.

"I get it, the money is circulated instantly."

"Exactly," he said nodding his head, "no risk, nobody gives a fuck."

"Why didn't he have you do it?"

"A lot of people know me; they say I attract a lot of attention. You're a fresh face and you fit in in a crowd. Me, not so good. I don't like a crowd pushing on me."

"Johnny didn't attract attention?"

"He's known as a gambler, he gambled seven days a week. That's why he got the gig, he was there anyways. You need to watch out that the gambling bug doesn't bite you. Johnny would win when the boss picked the numbers, but the boss only picks once a week, and sometimes it's only once a month. He doesn't wreck a good thing, but Johnny would win on a Sunday and gamble all his winnings away by Tuesday and then his paycheck by Thursday — he was awful."

"Franky said Johnny blew his money and was spending the boss's money and that's why he threatened him with a gun."

Then Tony crunched his face up like someone squeezes a sponge — he was angry and pointed one finger at me. "That's bullshit, and a downright dirty lie. Johnny would never do that. Franky, that piece of shit was making that shit up to cover his ass. The reason I know is because they emptied Johnny's pockets at the morgue and you know what they found? They found every red cent that he owed the boss, every fucking penny. So I hope Franky rots in hell for spinning that fucking lie, the piece of shit loser. If he was here I'd kick him in the balls, dead or alive, I don't give a fuck. Telling lies about Johnny really pisses me off. I'd piss on his grave if he had one. No, no, that's not bad enough; I'd take a big shit on his gravestone. Fuck him."

I looked out the window and tried to ignore him, but he cooled down just as fast as he got heated. He tapped my elbow, "hey, I know he's your uncle and I don't want you to think I disrespected you, but you said you weren't close, so I went off."

"That's OK."

"I'm not apologizing, I still hate him, I just don't want bad air between us."

"It's OK, the air is fine."

"I like you, Sonny, and I want you to do good. I've been at this a lot longer than you. You have a chance to move up — me, not so much."

"Why's that?"

"The boss is pretty smart — a good judge of character. It don't take long to get labeled and once you're labeled you only get so far. Let's just leave it as that."

"What do you mean?"

"Franky, was a drunk, Johnny a gambler. Me, I suppose I'm maybe seen as a hot-head that makes quick decisions. It may not be so, but either way that's what I've been told. That's what I mean by being labeled. They don't put guys like that in charge."

"What about Jimmy?"

"Jimmy is another story, he's cool and calculated. His dad is advisor to Don Mancini for crying out loud — he's a golden child. And most likely he'll get Pauly's spot as Underboss once — God forbid — something happens to Don Mancini."

We arrived at the car rental. "I have to pick out another car, any suggestions?"

"I like a car with a nice trunk. You looked good in the Lincoln, maybe a Caddy, but get a black one. There's nothing like a clean black car."

I went to get out of the car, and he grabbed my wrist and stopped me, "for now — me and you are the same level. Pauly asked me to spend a little more time with you, and sort of show you the ropes. I'll come to the track or the casino with you a few times and maybe you can sit in on a poker game and take from the pigeons. Pauly sees good in you."

Chapter Forty-Five

Day With The Dogs

Noontime came and Pauly's car stopped at my apartment. Tony was driving, he beeped the horn. He was different in front of Pauly. He was quiet, and agreed with whatever was said. We arrived at the dog track and once we parked Tony opened the trunk. All three of us went to the back of the car. Pauly opened a briefcase full of money, he grabbed a stack of what I suspected was counterfeit hundred dollar bills and handed it to us to stuff into our pockets. He did the same.

We walked down the long path that led to the racetrack. Pauly took out three programs; each had bets highlighted and which windows we would go to for our wagers to be placed. We found seats in the center of the track, halfway up the stands. I watched the lit board that displayed the odds, and then looked at my sheet. We waited 30 minutes before the first race started and then made our way to the windows — each of us at a different one. My first wager was two thousand dollars on a dog named Meter-maid. Then I walked to a different window and placed another bet for four thousand, the odds were 7 to 1.

I went window to window, bet after bet, until I finished all that were on the sheet. Pauly and Tony did the same. I still had a few hundred dollars left. I saw Tony and went to stand beside him, but Pauly saw me and waved for me to come close to him. "Let's get a chili dog and a beer; we have a few minutes before we collect our money."

We went to the food window, where the guy inside recognized Pauly. He held up three fingers and pointed to the large painted sign of a chili dog. The man ignored the other customers and served us. "Three Michelob beers, Pauly?" he asked.

"You bet," Pauly said, passing a fifty to the guy. "Keep the change."

He smiled and passed a box with the chili dogs and chips, and another with three beers. I took one box and out of nowhere Tony's hand grabbed the second box. Pauly held his hand up and showed the guy five fingers, he nodded and gave Pauly five collapsed food boxes, each about the size of a shoe box. We stood and ate our food and sipped the beers at a shelf that lined the walls. A TV showed the race in progress and I watched Meter-maid win the first race. We finished eating, and Pauly handed us each a box.

"Go to the window on the program — get the money and put it in the box. Once they're full, we can stuff our pockets and count it when we get back to the house."

"Are we going to have enough boxes?" I asked.

"We won't win every race, nothing is a sure thing at the track, but as long as we have a good score it's a good day." said Pauly.

That confirmed it was all funny money. If we left with the same amount we came with then the job of laundering the money was a success, and if we won more it was a plus. Either way the family was a winner. I didn't figure out what he needed from me until I had a big winner and collecting the payout required my tax information. I mentioned it to Pauly and he told me the family would take care of any taxes when the time came.

It was a strange feeling when I won; winning was exciting, but the feeling I had done something wrong was overwhelming, like I was robbing a bank in a secret sting — all that was missing was the mask. I wondered if other mobsters were doing the same thing, or if Pauly and Don Mancini were just brilliant criminals. By the end of the afternoon my box was filled and so was every pocket I had.

As we stood together for the last race, I realized we hadn't placed a bet. "How come we haven't bet?" I asked.

"Tradition. Take a grand and bet on whatever dog you want; if you win, it's yours — Tony, you do the same," said Pauly. "Don't tell what dogs you bet on, I've got my own pick and I don't want to second guess myself. Now go on, this keeps the fun in going to the track."

I didn't have a clue about which dog to bet on, but a thousand was a lot to lose, so I put five hundred in my wallet and then went to the window. "Five hundred on Hot Flash," I said as I hesitantly placed the money on the counter. The ticket printed and I anxiously took it and looked for Pauly and Tony. We got another beer and went to our seats. Having a chance to win did make a difference on how I felt about the races, especially when I saw how much money was in my food box. Other people thought the box was full of chili or a hotdog that I couldn't finish.

Then Pauly touched my elbow and pointed at the final odds — he smiled and pointed to the gate as it snapped open and the dogs sprang forward on their spindly legs. They chased a stuffed rabbit that was attached to the inner rail of the racetrack. The operator kept it just outside the reach of the lead dog. Each determined dog extended their front paws to the maximum to get the largest gain. The crowd cheered as their small feet pulled against the gravel track. "Come on Hot Flash," I yelled into my cupped hands.

They rounded the bend and Tony pointed and yelled for his dog, "get 'em Yellow Fever."

It was a close race, but our dogs didn't win. I watched the photo finish on the big screen. Tony threw his ticket on the floor. I held mine for a few seconds. I looked at Pauly and he laughed like a little kid. "I knew it, who couldn't win with a name like Banana Split?" said Pauly.

The odds flashed on the board, 5 to 1. Pauly pointed, "not bad huh boys, five grand for Pauly."

He got his money and went back to the car, opened the trunk, and put all our boxed money into the briefcase. There was more than what we started with, so I knew it was a good day. Tony got behind the wheel. "Sonny, how did you like a day at the track?"

"I liked it. Beer, chili dogs, and a few bucks to come home with — what's not to like?"

"Money, how'd you come home with money? You bet on Hot Flash? She came in fourth, next to mine," said Tony.

"I only bet five hundred out of the thousand Pauly gave me, so I still have five hundred left."

Pauly smiled and turned his big torso to look at me. "You're a smart kid Sonny, I'm impressed. I was worried the gambling bug might bite you, that's why we only personally gamble on the last race. Johnny had a problem with that," said Pauly. "I'm going to tell Don Mancini about your first day at the track."

"Why didn't he just bet like the family?" I asked.

"The family doesn't always win. We played different dogs on each race; we never all won the same race. The object was to get rid of the money we came with and get back new money. This time we won more than we came with."

"I thought the races might be fixed."

"Some are to help the odds. One guy cut the dog's nails too short before the race, just enough to make the dog sensitive when he digs in on the corners. That's why Banana Split won. He didn't get his nails clipped."

"See that Sonny? Nothing is fair," said Tony. "Some poor schmuck lost his paycheck on the track today, it can happen fast. Me, I can take it or leave it, but Johnny gambled until he didn't have a penny left."

We pulled into the Rent-a-Car center and I got out.

Chapter Forty-Six

Take A Little Off The Top

Months had passed. I had gone to the track with Tony and Pauly once more and I had spent a Saturday night with Tony at a poker game that was interesting but not my idea of a good time. Gangsters smoking cigars and swearing, a few got drunk and loud — I had a couple beers to be social. I left as soon as the first person left — I wanted to leave, but Larry had to leave because he lost all his money.

Alice was taking an online test to get a degree — Steve had come down once, and they stayed in to watch a movie. It was uncomfortable so I went out for the night.

I rubbed my hand over my head and decided to get a haircut. I went to Supercuts and Tammy was working. She didn't see me at first — I sat in the waiting area and read a magazine until the girl working the desk called my name.

The heavy girl that had been cutting my hair saw me and waved, "Hey Matt, I can do your hair once I'm done with Dave," she said as she squirted water on Dave's head and nearly in his eye.

Then Tammy saw me from her mirror. "I'll have Tammy do it, but thanks," I said as I waved to Tammy.

She had finished her customer and I was going to be next anyway. I took my jacket off and hung it on the hooks, as the she rang up her customer. She looked at me and smiled. She had gained a few pounds and looked healthy. I followed her to the chair and she put the apron around my neck and rubbed her hands through my hair and gritted her teeth. "I've been wanting to call you, but my counselor told me to stay away."

"From me, why?"

"From anyone that I am attracted to! I have an addictive personality, and I'm vulnerable. I'm a boring girl now, things have changed — I work every hour that they'll let me. I have to stay busy."

"What about the bikers, and the guy you were seeing?" I asked.

"That was my old life; I can't hang with them anymore. I'm serious about being straight and sober. My health means everything now."

"Health is wealth — my mother says that."

"She's right."

"What do you do for fun, crossword puzzles and checkers?"

"Is that so bad?"

"No, I was just kidding," I said.

"It's not that bad, I still want to have fun. As a matter of fact the girls are going to Typhoon Lagoon tomorrow and I'm going down 'Crush and Gush.' It's going to be awesome, and then maybe I'll sit and drift on the tube rides."

"Sounds like fun. It's going to be hot tomorrow, so you'll have a good day for it."

"If you're not doing anything, you should go," she said.

"You just told me that you're supposed to stay away from me, I'm dangerous."

"I know, but I like danger. I'm an adrenaline freak, and besides, if you show up there and we happen to meet up, then what could my counselor say anyway?"

"Good point, it's a public place. I hope you told her I don't drink or drug, and I barely smoke. I've even been going to church almost every Sunday."

"Right, my little saint Matthew. Or is it Sonny?"

I smiled. "Look, it is what it is. You know the story with me, I'm born into it and that's the bottom line."

"I know, I told my therapist and she thinks the danger you might present is half the attraction I have for you, like with Reggie the biker."

"That bum with the dirty shirt and the holes in his pants, you should have called him Raggie," I said, laughing.

"You might be the only person that could get away with calling him that. He was a mean prick and proud of it."

"Maybe in his biker bum world he's something, but in my world he's nothing, and if he gets in your way I'll squash him like a bug."

"I wouldn't believe it if I hadn't seen you guys in the clubhouse, so I don't doubt you, but like I said, that's my old life and I already told him he has to stay away from me."

"Has he been staying away?"

"Yeah, he called me a few times, but one time was late at night and he was trying to get a piece. I wasn't interested."

My haircut was finished, and she looked at me but her eyes were distant. I knew she thought I wasn't good for her — I wondered if I was good for anyone. I stood up and walked to the register, reached for my wallet and pulled out a twenty, "Fifteen dollars," she said.

"Keep the change."

"Thanks — maybe I'll see you tomorrow at Typhoon Lagoon."

"Maybe."

I left and drove to the apartment. Alice was working and I had the place to myself. I usually took a shower after a haircut — it got rid stray hairs and I liked to comb my hair the way I liked it, not the way the girls styled it. I turned on the radio, set the water temperature and got in the shower. The bathroom filled with steam, so I flipped on the fan when it got hard to breathe. I liked a hot shower almost as much as a hot meal. The water ran cold after twenty minutes and it was time to check out my hair and get dressed. I grabbed a soda from the refrigerator, a bag of chips from the counter, and sat in front of the TV. A half hour passed and then there was a knock on the door. I looked out the shade and saw it was Tony. He had never stopped by before. I wondered if someone was dead. I opened the door and he walked inside and took a seat.

"What's up?" I asked.

"Nothing much, I was going by and saw your car, so I figured I'd have a cup of coffee and chew the fat. You do have coffee don't you?"

"Of course," I said as I went to the kitchen and put on a pot. "I'm not sure if we have sugar, do you like Sweet'n Low?"

"That's how I like my women, sweet and low — I like them short, since I'm not so tall — get it?"

I looked around in the cabinets. "I found some sugar. Alice uses all that aspartame shit."

"It don't matter, I take my coffee black."

"I know, just like your women — right?"

"Who the fuck said that?"

"No one, I was kidding."

"It would have been funny if it was true, but I married a hundred percent Italian woman, straight from Sicily. She's a good woman; old fashioned — stand by your man type. You should get yourself one like her."

"I'm not ready to settle down. People today don't get married like they used to."

"You know, that's true. I like being married, and I know I'm not the best husband, but I love my wife and I truly believe there's not another woman out there for me. To tell you the truth, I don't even know why she loves me."

"Maybe she likes the way you look or your personality," I said.

"I think in the beginning she liked what I represented. You know a powerful family and a certain lifestyle. She knew exactly what she was getting into. Her dad's family is in the same business, only they're over there. It's kind of like when a girl is raised in a military family, they are attracted to that life, and the uniform and such. They want to hang around the base and make friends with all the military wives. Same shit here. She'd never leave me because she likes the life."

"Sometimes I wonder how all this got started, you know, the whole Mafia thing," I said.

"Look, the Italians are the chosen race of God."

"I thought it was the Jews."

"No that's bullshit. It was us, the Italians — the Italians discovered America, Christopher Columbus, and Amerigo Vespucci, both Italians, and we spread the good word of God, and he takes care of his people for doing that."

"I thought they sailed for Spain."

"They might have, but they were still Italians, because it took an Italian with balls, big balls to sail the unknown. Tony pointed his finger at my face even though I was seated ten feet away. "Did you know they thought the Earth was flat? It takes nerves of steel to sail right off the Earth. Maybe at night they thought they would go over the edge. You can't tell me it wouldn't scare the shit right out of a normal man, but not an Italian. That's why we're the chosen ones — the ones to discover and conquer. The Roman Empire baby, and since we got here, America is the new Roman Empire. We found it; it's ours, finder's keepers."

I laughed and went in the kitchen to get the coffee; he had already lit a cigarette and followed me. "It's like when there was pirates, our ancestors were pirates, they had ships and were in business for themselves and if the king, queen, or whoever was in charge didn't pay a fee, then they were robbed and sunk. We do the exact thing to this day. If the businesses in our area don't pay, then we sink them."

"Like Sal?"

"Exactly, he said.

We stood in the kitchen and drank coffee. "Have you eaten yet?" he asked.

"No, I just got out of the shower when you came over."

"There's a Chinese place on the corner — I'm craving Chinese, so let's go grab a bite."

"OK, I can do Chinese. I have an hour before I have to be at work." I said.

I got in his car and we drove a very short distance. We should have walked, but I had the feeling that Tony didn't walk much. We went inside and sat at a booth. Bamboo was shaped like a roof over the tables. A young Asian man came to our table and Tony knew exactly what he wanted, he kept pointing to the menu as he ordered. "Order what you want, but there's going to be plenty."

I ordered fried shrimp, and the guy left the table to get our drinks.

"Hey, you know what his girlfriend says when she sees him?"

"No."

Then he tried to do an Asian accent and said "Are you happy to see me or is that just a piece of rice in your pocket? Ba ha ha."

I laughed, but was afraid someone might hear him.

"Get it? It's supposed to be, are you happy to see me or is that a gun in your pocket, but with him I said is that a piece of rice in your pocket. That's a riot, you know, because he's Asian and they have small dicks."

"I get it. An Italian guy would have a gun and an Asian guy would have a piece of rice."

Tony held his finger up. "I've got another one. Do you like chicken fingers?" he said in an Asian accent.

"Yeah," I said.

"Chicken no have finger — Ba ha ha," he said.

Then the server walked by the table and Tony put his finger on his lips. "Shhh, I don't want him to spit in my soup. The last time I came here he called me a muffler-fucker. I just raffed."

Chapter Forty-Seven

Special Delivery

We finished the meal; Tony paid and gave the young guy a healthy tip. There was a lot of food left over, so I decided to take it to work and see if Alice or the others might want some. The shift went by fairly fast. I stood in the car lot and looked to the sky, hoping to see a shooting star, and wondered if my dad was up there. I wondered if he had gone to church and did Father Paul hear his last confession. Then a car pulled up near me, and the driver's window went down.

A drunken man pointed to me and asked. "Are you Jimmy?"

"No, he's not here right now, is there a problem?"

"You tell Jimmy he better loosen his grip on Sal's balls or there's going to be a big problem."

"Who are you?"

"You never mind who the fuck I am, you just pass the message. He keeps fucking with my family; I'm going to fuck with his."

The man sped off and held his arm out the window with his middle finger in the air.

I wished I had gotten a picture of his face, but I did catch the license plate. I wrote it down and called Jimmy.

"What's up?"

"Some drunk came here and said for you to back off on Sal or he's going to mess with your family."

"Don't worry about it; did you get a good look at his face?"

"Yeah, I have his plate too."

"Good work. I'll have it run and we'll shut him up. Some people are just stupid."

He hung up — I was a little shaken. Jimmy, as usual, was calm. I called Tony. I wasn't sure if I should, but Jimmy didn't say not to tell anyone.

"Tony here," he said.

"Tony, some drunk drove in here and threatened to hurt Jimmy's family if he don't back off of Sal."

"Fuck him, who is this piece of shit?"

"I don't know."

"If he had any balls he would have shot you. Did you get a shot off at him?"

"No, was I supposed to?"

"I would have. I'd cap his ass. I would have run down the street and emptied my gun in his car."

"He was drunk; Jimmy acted like it was not big deal. I got his plate."

"Good work, Sonny. Let me have it and I'll get it run."

I gave the plate number.

"I'll call you back in a little while," he said.

A half hour passed and then my phone rang.

"What did you find out?"

"It's Sal's son, he's 32, lives in Miami, divorced with two kids, and graduated college at Georgia. How's that for detective work? I even had a picture sent to my phone. He's fucked now."

"Are we going to do something?"

"Not until the boss says so. I'm sure Jimmy is talking to his dad, and Alfred ain't no pussy, so the shit will hit the fan soon enough. I'm going to call Jimmy and tell him what I found out and send him the picture," said Tony.

I was edgy all night, and then my shift ended and I went home and tried to sleep. I had to work a half shift the following day. The next morning, I skipped breakfast and was early for work. Jimmy was early too. He stood at the desk and drank his coffee. Alice had a mid-morning shift and she wasn't up when I left. I waited for Jimmy to speak, but he was quiet.

"I talked with Tony last night. He said he would have put a bullet into the drunk that threatened you. Should I have done that?"

"No, you would have started a war, and we don't want that. I already took care of it."

"Did you kill him?"

"No, just taught him a lesson, that's all. I figured he was drunk and he let the liquor talk. I had him checked out — he's no tough guy."

"What did you do?"

"Lenny, and Meatball Marc found him — they gave him a beating and stripped him naked, rolled him up in a piss soaked rug, then dumped him in a ditch on a back road. He woke up this morning sore, and had to fight to break the duct tape to get out of the rug. I figure he might have to walk five miles naked until he finds the first house. He'll be lost, with no chance of being helped."

"That should teach him," I said.

"The next time he runs his mouth he's dead."

I remember Lenny and Marc; they were both six foot four and three hundred pounds. Lenny was bald and had a broken nose that healed crooked, and Marc had thick greasy black hair and jagged yellow teeth. They must have beaten the living shit out of Sal's son.

Then my phone rang, it was Tony. He was laughing and yelling at someone on his end. "Hey Sonny, Pauly wants me to swing by and pick you up. Are you at the car lot?"

"Yeah — what's this about?"

"I'll tell you when I get there," he said and then hung up.

I turned to Jimmy, "Tony said he's coming to get me, what's that about?"

"He's just following orders. Sal's son threatened me and my family. That was a stupid move, threatening my father involves the Don, and he doesn't like threats."

"What do I have to do?"

"Tony will fill you in, he's pulling in now."

Tony beeped the horn twice, the second beep longer than the first. He was moving up and down in his seat like he was excited. I looked at Jimmy. "Don't keep him waiting," he said.

I went outside and got in the car. "What's going on?"

I turned in my seat to look at Lenny, and Meatball Marc in the back of the car. Marc held a shoe box and handed it to me.

"What's this," I asked.

"You were the one that heard the threat, it went from you to the Don — Sal needs to know that — so you need to present this to Sal. Go on, look inside."

"Do I dare?"

"Look inside, don't be a pussy," said Tony.

I opened the box and inside was a man's penis and balls, ball sack and all. Whose is this? Is this his son's?"

"Of course it's his son's. You don't think you can pick one of these up at the butcher shop do you?" said Tony, laughing.

"You cut his cock off?"

"You don't think he gave it up willingly do you? Read the card, Tony wrote it," said Lenny.

"Alfred told me what to write."

I opened the card. *"YOU AND YOUR SON DON'T HAVE THE BALLS TO THREATEN FAMILY MEMBERS OF DON CARMINE MANCINI — SO NOW YOU DO — P.S. SAY HI TO YOUR DAUGHTER FOR ME...Alfred Maretti..."*

Tony was smiling and was nearly hopping up and down while he drove. "Is that a fucking riot or what? See how we strike? It's fast like lightning, from his mouth to Alfred's ears. One day is all he got, one fucking day — his big mouth changed his life."

I put the cover back on the box and handed it to Lenny. I was trying to get my mind wrapped around what I was hearing.

"Are you going to sit there with your mouth hanging open? Say something, Sonny," said Tony.

"You beat the shit out of the guy and you wrapped him in a piss soaked blanket and threw him in a ditch ten miles from town, and that wasn't enough? You had to cut his cock off?"

"It was a piss soaked rug, and Lenny gave him a shot when he was in the van, so he would be out while we cut his dick off."

"I had to cauterize the wound or he might bleed to death," said Lenny. "He was out cold for most of it. I drugged him once we grabbed him, and we dropped him about four or five miles from town — naked, so everyone can see we made him a girl. Who knows, he might like it better."

"I drew a fat pair of red lips on him with lipstick," Marc said, laughing.

"You drugged him and cut his dick off?" I said shaking my head.

"Yeah they just don't unscrew like a light bulb, they're hooked on pretty good," Tony said.

"Pauly said cut out his dick so I did what I was told. Do you have a problem with Pauly?" asked Lenny.

"No, but what am I doing here?"

"I told you, you need to give this to Sal and tell him his son Angelo ran his mouth to you, and this is what happens when you threaten the family. When Sal opens the box, he'll be in shock, but we'll be right behind you with our guns pointed on his head and if he says one fucking word, he's a dead man. He's not our friend and if he fucks up I'll kill him myself," said Tony.

"I don't have a gun ... why don't I have a gun?"

"That's what Alfred wants, you will look powerful and untouch-able — we'll be there," said Tony

"Why me? I'm the same level as you. Why didn't they have you do it? You're more experienced with this type of thing."

"I'm here for you, this is your gig — these two guys are sol-diers, once you make it to capo you send people to do this shit, that's why Jimmy ain't here. We're still 'wise guys,' you need to pay your dues and this is one that you need to do. I like the action, so I come along," said Tony.

"You'll be fine, Sonny, we got your back," said Meatball Marc.

"Take a few minutes and think of something to say. He'll re-member your words for the rest of his life, so come up with some-thing. I'm not good with talking," said Tony.

I thought about the last thing that the drunk said to me in his threats as we pulled into Sal's strip club.

"Let's do this on the front entry way," Tony said.

We walked up the granite steps and into the lobby. A woman was behind a small window selling tickets to enter. Tony walked up and said, "We need to see Sal, we found something of his and he'll want it back."

"I can have one of the bouncers take it and bring it to him, what is it?"

"That ain't going to work, sweetheart, so get on the phone and page him, or do whatever you need to do to get him — we don't have all day."

"Can I tell him who is here to see him?"

"No we want him to be surprised."

"Does he know you?"

"He knows us quite well," said Tony.

I stepped to the window. "We're from the bank that financed this business, and recently there has been a concern that his son has brought to my attention. We need to clear this matter up quickly before it escalates."

"I see," she said as she called him. "There are some representatives from the bank here to see you, and they said it's quite urgent. They're here in the lobby."

She hung up the phone. "He'll be right out."

Sal walked through the big wooden doors. He stopped in his tracks when he saw Tony. He must have recognized him from the film he had made with his fiancé.

"What are you doing here?"

"Hold on," I said. "This is a very serious matter, Sal. I have a gift from Alfred Maretti. You do know who Consigliere Alfred Maretti is, don't you?"

"Yes of course."

"Your son came to me and said if Capo Jimmy Maretti doesn't back off on pressuring your debt that he was going to fuck with Jimmy's family. Maybe your son didn't realize Alfred is Jimmy's father, but needless to say, Jimmy spared your son's life."

Sal began to tremble. "Thank you, tell Jimmy thank you."

"Alfred wanted you to understand how seriously he takes a threat to the family of Don Carmine Mancini, so he sent you this card."

I held my hand out for Lenny to pass me the card and then I handed it to Sal. His mouth moved as he read the card. He looked puzzled.

I turned to Meatball Marc and he passed me the box, which I handed to Sal. His hand shook as he opened the lid. Sal looked at the penis and then at me.

"You parked my car one day and you know what I found in my trunk. I didn't recognize you at first, but you were the valet," he said in a huffy voice. I looked at Tony and that's all it took. The three of them pulled their pistols and pushed them against Sal's head — one on each temple and Tony's in the center of his forehead. The girl ducked down under the counter and the bouncer put his hands in the air.

"Say the word, Sonny, and I'll smoke him right here," said Tony.

"If you don't want to find another head in your trunk you better back off. Tell your son if I see him again, or hear his foolish threats, he's a dead man, or woman, or whatever he wants to call himself. I'll be expecting an apology note sent to Jimmy and his family ASAP."

Sal nodded.

Chapter Forty-Eight

Big Splash

We left just as a cop car was pulling in. We walked past and no one stopped us. When we got in the car, Tony lit a cigarette and passed one to me. "That was beautiful, Sonny — you see, that's why Alfred wanted you to handle it. I would have lost it on Sal. I just can't help it. I had all I could handle not to crack his skull with my gun. I can't help it, but you were smooth and cool. You made him thankful that his son's life was spared as you handed him his penis. That was fucking beautiful. I mean, where the fuck did you come up with that shit? I would have been more like, *Look Sal, your son fucked up. I cut his cock off so he wouldn't make more shitheads like you, so say your last words you fuck..."*

Tony's face looked angry and he held his hand like a gun and spit flew off his teeth as he swore.

"He remembered you Sonny, what did you think of that?" asked Lenny.

"I don't know what to think. He recognized Tony from the porn he made with his woman."

"He must be shitting bricks," said Marc.

"On the bright side, the cops must have found his son by now and he'll be getting a call," I said.

"Good, we claimed the deed before there was any doubt. We're not cowards. He knows if there's a war, we'll bring it to him," said Tony.

I looked at my watch.

"Are you late for something?" asked Tony.

"I was meeting someone at the water park and I was wondering if I should go, or skip it."

"I'll go with you. You should have a few guys around for a while — this could go either way. Sal is a pretty powerful guy, and he might strike back, once he feels he has nothing to lose. You should live your life, but we need to bump up security. You might want to carry a gun."

"Do you guys want to go to Typhoon Lagoon?" I asked.

"Who gives a fuck what they want, they work for us," Tony said. "I haven't been there in years and I could walk around and see the scenery. I like girls in wet bikinis."

Tony pointed to a gift shop, "pull in there, we'll get some swimsuits and make a day of it." I pulled in and we got out and went inside. Tony's phone rang and I assumed it must have been Pauly. Tony told him what had happened and I was surprised at how well he remembered what I had said. Then he handed me the phone.

"Sonny, Tony told me what a good job you did. I'm impressed, and I'll pass it on to Alfred and Don Mancini. You did good representing the family."

"Thanks, Pauly." He hung up and I looked around the store to find the guys. Lenny was holding swim trunks that were obviously too small for him. Marc told him they were too small, and the two argued about who was fatter. It started getting serious, until they both tried on swim suits and it turned out the two men wore the same size. Marc pointed out that Lenny's suit fit tighter and he should get a larger size, but Lenny disagreed and grabbed Marc's love handles.

Tony held up a Speedo. "Where are you supposed to put your pecker? Sonny, try these on," he said as he threw them at me. The store clerk came rushing over.

"Can I help you?"

"Do you have regular swim shorts for regular guys? I have a normal body under this suit."

"Over where your friends are," he said, pointing to where Lenny and Marc were."

"That's big sizes for men built like balloons; do I look like a balloon to you?"

The clerk went to the rack and pulled a few pairs that were Tony's waist size.

"I saw those but the legs are too long. I need a regular size, not ones that come to my knees."

"That's the style," the clerk said.

"Roll them up, Tony," said Lenny.

"Shut the fuck up, I ain't rolling up a pair of swim trunks, I'll look like a fucking moron."

I picked a simple pair, red, with a fine white line on the side, almost like a lifeguard's pair. "Tony, get the blue pair and ask him for a pair of scissors, we can take a little off the legs and they'll be perfect for you. They don't make men's swim suits anymore so we can fix them."

"Yeah?" he said with a raised voice.

"Sure."

"You're right, give me those blue ones, and buddy do you have some scissors?"

"I sure do and people do this all the time," he said as he went back to the counter.

He trimmed the swimsuit and Tony went to try them on, in a few minutes he came out and had them rolled up in his hand, "I'll take 'em, let's get out of here."

We got back in the car and drove to the water park; I was surprised how excited these thugs were. Once at the park we got changed and put our street clothes in lockers. Tony pointed to a slide with a long drop. "Let's do that one first and get it over with."

I was hesitant, but these guys didn't fear anything. We climbed so many stairs that I could see the entire park. It was manmade, but it was beautiful. A river circled the whole place, and people floated along the rocky walls with waterfalls and rapids.

We finally got to the top of the tower, where a small boy hopped into the water tube and shot almost straight down, until he slid horizontal to the waiting pool. Lenny hesitated, and Tony pushed him aside and hopped into the tube — away he went. A young lifeguard watched him drop and once he was out of the way he pointed to Marc. Marc backed up and Lenny moved forward. "You might have to carry these two girls down," he said as he sat on the stream of water and pushed himself off. He screamed all the way down.

I got on the tube; the warm water seemed cold as it soaked the bottom of my suit and my back. I crossed my arms and lay down and instantly I felt myself drop a hundred feet. I felt my back come away from the tube and I thought I was going to tumble. Then the big splash into the warm pool — it was safe to laugh. Tony was by the edge with Lenny. "You should have seen your face. Did you have your eyes closed?" asked Tony.

Then Marc dropped and the water splashed over the water tunnel, he swore all the way down and when he hit the pool, his fat body skimmed across the water. Lenny laughed and pointed.

"Let's go and float around the river," said Marc.

Tony pointed to a slide that dumped into a large bowl that swirled the rider around until he went down a drain, "that one, let's do that one."

We got out of the water and walked to the next ride. This time I went first, and Tony followed. I figured it was good to show that I wasn't afraid. We went on three more slides and then ended up floating down the river that circled the park. The hot sun was beating on my face and forehead, my wet hair and the cool water tricked me into thinking I wasn't burning. We went around the river three times and then got out. Lenny smelled the smoke from a small hotdog shack and he led the way.

"We have to go to the locker to get money," Tony said. "Shit, that's way the fuck over there, and I'm starving," he said like a little kid.

"There must be a hotdog shack over by the lockers," Marc said, as he took a fast stride toward the lockers.

"I ain't that crazy about a hotdog myself," Tony said. "What about you?"

"I don't really care what we eat, but let's follow them."

We went over to the bathrooms and Tony pointed to a girl in a bikini, "Hey look at that one."

It was Tammy, who filled out her bathing suit very well. She looked at me through her big sunglasses. I didn't think she recognized me until she smiled and came closer.

"Matt, I'm glad to see you could make it," she said. She came close and I hugged her.

"Matt? That's Sonny," Tony said.

"Oh yeah right, I forgot. I recognize you, you were the guy that came into the clubhouse and shook down Snake," she said to Tony.

"Oh yeah that fucking guy, Snake," Tony said, laughing. "They should have named him Worm."

"Is it just you two guys here?" she asked.

"No we came with Lenny and Meatball Marc," I said.

"It's just Lenny? Not Lenny the Lefty or something like that?" Tammy said.

"No, he ain't left handed," said Tony.

"Don't they get nicknamed from things they do?" asked Tammy.

I could tell that Tony had picked up that she was fascinated with the mob and he liked being recognized for the scene he made at the clubhouse.

"We could call him Lenny the Luggage Lopper, since he just lopped off a guy's luggage last night," Tony said.

"What? What do you mean?" she asked.

"He cut off a guy's penis," I said quietly.

"He ripped his dick off and gave it to his dad. Well technically Sonny handed the dick to his dad," said Tony. "But it was in a box. I don't want you to think Sonny is gross like that. He didn't actually touch the dick."

She covered her mouth and looked at me. I tilted my head and raised one palm up, "It was in a shoe box, and he threatened us, so the orders came down and that's what happened," I said with a grimace.

"Do you want Sonny to go rip Snake's dick off? He'll do it," Tony said with a straight face.

I looked at him with a raised eyebrow. "You're not helping."

"She's the one that asked what the fuck we do. She knows, she saw us at the clubhouse. Remember I was going to drop a few grenades on those bums? She knows I don't give two shits about them, or that dickless fuck Sal and his son." He paused and looked at the ground and rubbed the back of his head. "We're getting something to eat, you can join us if you want," Tony said.

"I'm here with a few friends, can they join you too?"

I nodded.

Her friends came out of the bathroom and she told them she wanted to take a break and get something to eat with us. They took one look at us and told her they weren't hungry and wanted to float in the river. I couldn't blame them for leaving. Tony sat at a table with Lenny and Marc, I picked a spot for the two of us where we could talk and not be heard by the guys. I got us food and drinks.

"I was hoping that maybe me and you could get a tube for two and ride down the river, what do you think?" she asked

"That sounds like fun, but what about your therapist?"

"It looks like you're the one with the eyes on you," she said.

"They want to protect me, since things are fresh, but I feel safe, don't you?"

"Are they going to follow you around all day?"

"Probably, until Sal writes an apology letter to Jimmy's family. I didn't do anything, other than tell Sal a few words and hand him a box. I don't know why anyone would do anything bad to me, just like I didn't do anything at the clubhouse."

"No but they all know your name."

"Don't worry," I said.

"How do I know you guys aren't going to grab some guy and drown him when no one is looking?"

"I'm not planning on it."

"Yeah but that guy Tony and his hit men might be picking out victims as we speak."

I shrugged my shoulders. "You can go your own way once we've eaten."

"I told you I like the danger, it excites me. I'll hang out with you guys and if someone gets killed I'll look the other way. I have to admit, I'm kind of scared shitless of that Tony guy — he's a character right out of the movies."

"He's a good guy once you get to know him," I said.

I went to buy ice cream while she sat on a big fake rock. There was a long line and she and Tony talked the entire time.

Chapter Forty-Nine

Extra Meat Matt

Tammy stayed with us for a few more hours. She seemed happy, she laughed at whatever Tony said, and I truly believed she had a thing for the "Bad Boys." It seemed she was more attracted to Tony than she was to me, even though he was older and shorter than her. He had a no-nonsense way about him, and he ate, breathed, and shit Mafia. She was right when she said he was a character right out of the movies. He was a short man but he stood ten feet tall, and that's why they called him Big Tony. I was different; I walked and talked like a regular guy. I wasn't wise, or loud. I usually wore a leather jacket when the weather was cool; Tony wore a sport coat and sometimes he had the gangster hat.

Tammy found her friends and I left with Tony and the guys. We had fun for a Saturday afternoon. Pauly sent a guy named Desi to work with me; he was ten years older than me, tall and rugged, with a crooked nose and a scar on his upper lip. I didn't want the details on how it got there — he was one of Tony's guys and was set in his ways. We hung out after work and went to a pool hall. I felt like he was waiting for me to act like Tony or one of the other thugs that he was used to being around. I almost felt like I was letting him down with my meek ways.

I didn't have much luck meeting new women with him around. He was loud and thought a noisy fart in public was nothing to be ashamed of.

The following day I worked until noon. I decided that a nice long ride up the coast was what I needed. I checked out a convertible Mustang and went back to the apartment to get sun block and swim trunks. Just as I was on my way the phone rang — it was Tammy. "I could be wrong but I thought I just saw you drive by. Are you in a silver Mustang convertible?"

"Yes I am, where are you?"

"At the post office — where are you going on such a nice day?"

"I'm taking a ride up the coast. I have an afternoon shift tomorrow and depending on what happens I might be getting in late."

"It looked like you're all alone."

"I am."

"I have tomorrow off and I love the ocean ... do you mind if I tag along?"

"I guess it would be all right."

"Good because I'm right behind you. I can drop my car off at work and we can ride together. I have my bathing suit in the trunk. I have a towel too."

"Good," I said. I hadn't thought about going with anyone, but it would be a nice ride either way. I pulled up to her salon and she ran inside with her bag, when she came out she was in a pair of cutoff jean shorts and a bikini top.

"I might as well get some sun while the top is down," she said.

"Good idea."

Her hair lashed against her face until she pulled it back and twisted it with an elastic. The top down was nice but the car was loud and so was the wind. I turned up the radio and an old song played that she sang along to: *"Baby's got Back"* she laughed, and knew that the people in the car beside us were watching her sing. She pulled the visor down and watched herself in the small mirror. She turned to me — her sunglasses were dark and I couldn't see her eyes. "Sing it, Sonny."

I bobbed my head and sang along with her. She touched my leg and then said, "you should take your shirt off and get a tan."

At the next light she grabbed my sleeve and helped me with my shirt. I was self-conscious about my stomach. I wasn't fat but I didn't want to hold my stomach in while I drove for an hour. She scanned the radio for good songs and it wasn't long before I felt like a young guy with a pretty girl in a convertible. I was hungry and saw a sign for fried clams and hot dogs. I pointed and she nodded her head.

"Do you like seafood?" I asked.

"No, but I like hotdogs."

"I'm getting fried clams."

"I'm getting a hotdog and a chocolate shake, and I'm treating, so you might want to get a shake too."

"I think I will," I said as I went to the window and placed my order. She popped her head beside mine and ordered a hotdog and small fries.

We went to a picnic table and sat while we waited for a scrambled voice to call our numbers over the speakers mounted on the corners of the building.

It didn't take long. I ate a clam on the walk back to the table, and the hot grease burned my tongue. I rolled it from one side of my mouth to the other as it cooled enough to crush it with my teeth.

"How're the clams?"

"Good but hot. I'm surprised you don't like them."

"I don't like sand in my food, and every time I get clams they have sand in them. I hate that."

"Not these, I ordered the sand-less ones. They must have thought you were a tourist and threw a handful of sand in yours. How's that hotdog?"

"Good, no sand," she said as she bit it. "I like the toasted roll."

"True Florida gourmet cooking."

We finished eating and then drove to the beach. I drove onto the sand and parked. We walked along the edge of the water up to our ankles. I didn't like the creatures that lived in the water — jellyfish, crabs, and sharks. Going in any farther didn't interest me. We walked what seemed like miles, holding hands and smiling into the sunset.

"I have fun with you, Matt. I actually had fun with your whole crew, Tony, and the other two guys."

"Tony is a little unpredictable."

"I don't think so. He says what's on his mind. Once you realize he's a mobster, you kinda expect what he does or says. When you went to buy me an ice cream, he asked me if we were having sex yet. He had a serious look on his face like he was asking me if I knew your name. I asked him why they called you Sonny, and why don't you have a nickname. Then I made a mistake and asked him his nickname. He said Big Tony. I didn't dare laugh, and then he said they used to call him *Two Hour Tony* when he was single, and there wasn't a woman around that he couldn't please. I had all I could do to keep a straight face; he's so full of himself."

"I'm just glad he didn't give me a nickname."

"He called you Extra Meat Matt," she said, laughing.

"Extra Meat Matt, why would he call me that?"

"I'm not sure, but did he see you naked or something?"

"No."

"Maybe you ordered extra meat on your sub sandwich or something like that."

I took out my phone, "I'll call him and find out what he meant."

The phone rang and he sounded like he had a few drinks. "Who's this?"

"It's Sonny, I'm with Tammy."

"Hey did I get you laid? I told her your nickname was Extra Meat Matt, what a fucking riot, huh?" he said with a roaring laugh.

I could hear Marc and Lenny laughing in the background.

"I can hear the guys laughing, are they laughing at me? What's so funny?"

"Lenny used the same nickname on Marc, but I told a different story about him and it's funny, that's all."

"What's the story? I'd like to hear it."

"Me and Marc were after the same woman. He's the one that told her his nickname was Extra Meat Marc, like he was hung like a horse. I told her that he was born with two dicks, and his mom had to pick which one to cut off when he was an infant. She didn't know what to do so she did that eeny, meeny, miney, moe rhyme and had the doctor cut off the bigger of his peckers and left him the small one." Then Tony and Lenny roared with laughter.

"You cheap bastard Tony, I'll never forgive you for that," said Marc.

"Imagine the woman thinking Marc had a small dick and a little stub beside it where his other dick used to be." Tony and Lenny laughed again and I couldn't help laughing too.

"I'm glad you didn't use that story on me."

"Shit I wouldn't do that to you, but Marc is a dog and he thinks all the women want him, so fuck him, he deserved it."

I hung up and Tammy was waiting to hear what was so funny, so I told her the story. She laughed and then got serious. "I hope you know that even though Tony thinks he was trying to get you laid that I can't do that for a long time. I have to stay true to what my therapist says. We can hold hands and spend time together, but I can't sleep with anyone for at least a year — no sex for twelve months."

I realized that we were limited about what we could do and where we could go, since Tammy would be tempted to drink if we went to a club or a beach-side bar, so we went to a restaurant, and once we finished eating I decided we might as well drive home.

I dropped her off and went back to the apartment. Alice was home and Steve was there. She had made him a large dinner and he was sitting on the couch watching TV. I felt like I was in the way and went to my room. Alice was almost the same as Tammy, both recovering drug users, both coming from a bad relationship, both seeing me as a big brother. At least Jill had been honest enough to move on. I wondered if there was anyone for me, someone without a drug or drinking problem, or someone who didn't want to use me as entertainment because they weren't healthy enough to have a boyfriend.

Chapter Fifty

Missing In Action

The next morning when I went to work, Jimmy was in his office. I had almost nothing to do so I decided to see what he had been up to. I stood by the door until he was off the phone.

"I talked with Tony and he said you had a date with a hot girl in a bikini," said Jimmy.

"I did, but she has problems and it's not going anywhere."

"Tony said he set it up, so you would get laid. He called you Extra Meat Matt," Jimmy said, laughing.

"You guys are like old women."

"My wife wants to fix you up; she has a sister and a few nice looking cousins. There's a lot of nice-looking Italian women to pick from. You should think about it."

"I can't right now. Alice is living with me and I need to wait until she moves out with her man, or I need to find a new place. I wanted to sit on the couch and watch the big screen, but they were kissing and eating popcorn. I can't bring a girl home to that."

"You need a girl that knows the family and what you do. You need a good woman that will stick with you. You need a woman like Pauly married. He did eight years in the big house and she stayed by his side, she went up there every weekend and she raised the kids and kept his house in line."

"He did eight years?"

"He took the fall for Alfred and Don Mancini, he confessed to a crime he didn't commit."

"Really, why?"

"They promised him he would become 'Under Boss' and when he came out he made it. They protected him in prison, Don Mancini sent a few guys in with him."

"So that's how he made it," I said.

"Yup, he had the family and a good woman behind him, he's all set."

Then the phone rang, and it was Tony. "Lenny is missing. He was supposed to make a run this morning — he didn't show and no one has seen him."

"Come over and get Sonny, check the usual places, and put the word on the street," he said. Then he hung up and looked at me.

"Lenny's missing and when one of ours is missing you just don't go to the cops. It's always something stupid or foul play — let's hope it's just something stupid."

Tony arrived ten minutes later, and came in the store. "Jimmy, I have a bad feeling," he said with his hands out.

"Don't jump to conclusions, maybe Lenny had a few too many and he couldn't find his way home," said Jimmy.

"That's what we thought about Johnny and he turned up dead."

"Yeah, but that was just a stupid accident. This is different, he'll show up."

"What if he got arrested and he's locked up?"

"He's too smart for that — he'd call Alfred, or Pauly, so most likely he didn't," Jimmy said.

"What if the F.B.I. got him? I heard they inject you with that truth serum shit — sodium pentothal — then they ask you all kinds of questions and tape the conversation," said Tony.

"Don't get your piss hot," said Jimmy. "We'll find him, and if the feds have him we'll know in a short while," Jimmy said," you two get going and stop talking nonsense."

We got in Tony's car; he lit a cigarette and shook his head from side to side. "I have a bad feeling, Sonny, and I'm usually right. Jimmy can say what he wants, but when the feds come down on the families they start at the bottom and work their way up. Sometimes they get one of the pigeons, like Sal or his son. They squeal like pigs — turn the family in and enter witness protection. That's how they got Don Carmine Mancini the first time."

"Is that when Pauly took the fall?"

"Yeah, yeah it is — you knew about that?"

"I only knew that Pauly did prison time and when he got out he became Under Boss."

"Yeah, that's right, but it still sucks to do time, especially hard time."

"Do you think Sal will go to the feds?"

"I don't know … what would you do?"

I shrugged my shoulders.

"We're squeezing him hard, we have his club buried in debt, and we took his cars and artwork — we're forcing counterfeit money up his ass and then we killed his partner and cut his son's dick off, so what choice does he fucking have? The next move is he'll end up dead. You're not wearing a wire are you?"

"No, of course not, but I think you're jumping to conclusions, like Jimmy said."

"Jimmy is young, OK? I just came from Pauly's house and I told him just what I thought might be going on, and if Lenny don't show up soon we're going on a full-on mission — me and you. Don't you worry, Don Mancini has a plan and you bet your ass he's not going to prison. You and me — we might go, but not the boss."

We drove to three restaurants that Lenny frequented, but no one had seen him. Then we drove to the dog track. Still no leads. Then we went to the liquor store, the dry cleaner, and the hospital — no sign of Lenny.

Then my phone rang, it was Jimmy, "Any luck?"

"No, not yet," I said.

"I talked to the cops and he's not there."

"We checked the hospital and he's not there either," I said.

"That was a good idea — why don't you try a few more hospitals. He may have been in a car wreck. I'll check the news and see if I can find out anything."

Jimmy hung up and Tony and I did as he asked. Then it got late and we gave up.

Chapter Fifty-One

Infection

The next day I slept until mid-morning. I sat at the table and poured milk over my bowl of cereal. I spun the spoon and pulled the flakes under the milk as I read the paper. I flipped the pages and folded them so I could hold the paper in one hand and eat with the other. In the obituaries I saw Sal's son — he died from an infection. I had to read it twice. Minutes later my phone rang, first Jimmy and then Tony, both with the same message — we were to meet at Don Mancini's in a half hour.

I looked at my watch and with no time for a shower I wet my hair and splashed on after shave, and put on my leather jacket. Once on the road I realized I hadn't brushed my teeth. A roll of breath mints would have to do. Don Mancini's house was a twenty minute ride and I knew I didn't want to be late, he might think it was disrespectful. Passing slow drivers and taking a shortcut through a shopping plaza got me to his driveway with five minutes to spare. I rushed inside and Tony and Jimmy were in the foyer. Pauly walked down the hall that led to Don Mancicni's chambers, and motioned for us to follow.

We took a seat. Don Mancini sat on the corner of his desk with one knee raised. He held his ankle and chewed an unlit cigar. Alfred paced the floor and stopped to look out the window.

"I take it that you have seen the paper — Sal's son is in the obituaries. Lenny is still missing and I suspect foul play. I believe Sal had something to do with his disappearance, and I want Tony and Sonny to pay him a visit. You will go with Pauly."

"What do you want us to tell him?" asked Pauly.

"Tell him I got wind that he dusted Lenny, and I also heard he was talking with the feds, and I don't like what I heard. His partner threatened to go to the feds and he ended up in the trunk. I want you to remind him who he's playing with."

"Offer him the noose or a bottle of sleeping pills — he's coward enough to take the easy way out."

"You don't want us to shoot him in the face?" asked Tony.

"No, I want it to look like suicide, are we clear?"

"Yes, boss," said Pauly.

Then he waved his hand for us to leave. We were quiet until we were outside.

"Sonny, you should drive," said Pauly.

"Where are we going?"

"Tony, call the club and see if Sal is there."

Tony called and he asked the staff if Sal was in. He shook his head.

"He's at his house ... let's go to his house. Get on the turnpike and head north," said Pauly.

We drove for fifteen minutes and then Tony tapped my elbow. "Turn off at this exit, there's a hardware store, and a drug store at the plaza."

"For what?" I asked.

"The rope and a bottle of sleeping pills," said Tony.

"What if Sal didn't have anything to do with Lenny? What if Lenny shows up in a few days?" I asked.

"He better be damn convincing, because Don Mancini thinks different," said Pauly.

"What if he is convincing, what then?"

"Then he can take it up with the Don himself. Until then we have orders," said Pauly.

Tony bought a rope and then we went to the drugstore and got sleeping pills. When we arrived at Sal's house, Tony opened the glove box and took out a pistol and handed it to me. Do you know how to work this thing?"

I was too embarrassed to admit I didn't, so I nodded, "yes."

He flipped a small lever, "here's the safety," and then he slid the barrel back and I saw a bullet enter the chamber. "Point and shoot."

"I thought we were going to let him take sleeping pills. The Don wants it to look like an accident," I said.

"It's unlikely he's in there alone," said Pauly as he pulled a pistol from his jacket and flipped the safety.

We got out of the car and Tony and Pauly hid their guns. I tucked mine in my pants like they did in the movies, and then Tony went up the stairs and rang the doorbell. A woman answered and Tony grabbed her hair and put his gun under her chin. She squealed and didn't resist him. He pulled her head down by the hair until his lips were at her ear.

"Is Sal here? Where is Sal?"

She pointed to a hall and we quietly walked to a door where soft orchestra music was playing.

"Is he alone?" Tony asked.

She shook her head. "No."

Then Tony curled his finger at me and when I came close he handed the woman to me and motioned for me to hold her hostage the same way he had. I put my gun under her chin and held her ponytail.

He listened at Sal's door and then he slowly turned the knob. Pauly followed and I stood in the partially opened doorway as they stormed into the room with drawn pistols. Sal and another man put their hands in the air.

There was a tape recorder on the counter and a pad of paper with the family names written down.

"Norman Braski, F.B.I. Drop your weapons, you guys are in enough trouble."

"I told you they were crazy," said Sal.

"Do you want me to add breaking and entering and interfering with a federal investigation to your list of crimes?" Braski asked.

"No. Please. I'll drop my weapon," Tony said as he fired a bullet into Norman's forehead.

"Now that we have your attention, what do you have to say for yourself?" asked Pauly.

"My son died for no good reason — he was just trying to protect his family and you monsters cut off his prick, and now he's dead. When was it going to stop? I can't live like this. What did expect me to do?"

"Don Carmine Mancini has big ears and sharp eyes — you say something — he hears, you do something — he sees. But he's a fair man and he has options for you," said Pauly.

"What do you want from me? I'll do anything."

"Is this room recorded?" asked Tony.

"No," said Sal.

"Where's the security system? Where's your recorders?" asked Pauly.

"Only the outside has video, the inside has sound alarms at the windows and doors, no video."

"Sonny come in here," said Pauly.

I walked in with the gun to the woman's head and when she saw Sal she cried out loud.

"Who's this woman?"

"She's my niece."

"Do you want to save her life?"

He hesitated, then said "yes of course."

"Like I was saying — Don Carmine Mancini gave you two options — the noose or these sleeping pills." He said as he rattled a bottle in his hand and put them on the desk. "I wanted to cut your cock off like we did to your son; right here in front of your niece, but the Don gave orders. What's it going to be?"

Tony pressed the button on the recorder and played Sal's voice naming several family members and their crimes. Sal nodded, he knew there was no escape from his fate. He opened the bottle and filled a water glass from a pitcher sitting on a table. He lifted the bottle to his mouth and emptied it and then drank the water.

"You will spare my niece?"

"As long as she keeps her mouth shut," said Pauly.

"Do I have your word?"

"You have my word; she will stay alive as long as she can keep her mouth shut. If she opens it I give her ten minutes to meet her maker."

We stayed in the room with Sal until he fell asleep in his big chair. Tony wore gloves and wiped his prints from the gun and placed it in Sal's hand, making sure it was covered with his fingerprints. He lowered his ear to Sal's mouth and said "He ain't breathing, it's official. He killed the cop and himself. What do you want to do with her?"

Pauly looked at her. "Where is the security system? I don't trust Sal and I'll be damned if he has this on tape. We followed her to an office where the cameras were on two TVs, each screen split in four. The cameras showed the outside just as Sal had said. Tony disconnected the system and took it, as well as the tape recorder from the detective.

"You are going to set me free, you promised Sal," the woman said.

"You will be set free, don't worry. But first we have to take you to meet Don Mancini. He might have some questions for you."

Chapter Fifty-Two

Tight Lipped

We drove back to Don Mancini's house. A few of the guys were outside — we greeted each other and one held the door open as we walked inside. Meatball Marc stopped us and he went to the Don's chambers and knocked on the door. The door opened and he whispered through the small opening, and then he signaled us to come inside.

"Leave the girl with Marc," Pauly said.

I let go of her arm and Marc grabbed her and pushed her in a chair. I went in the room, where The Don and Alfred sat at a small table, across from each other with a marble chess board between them.

"How did it go Pauly? I see you're still alive," said The Don.

"He took the coward's way out, just as you said."

"I knew it. He was a pussy, is that the end of things?"

"No Don. Tony had to ice an F.B.I. agent; we walked in on their meeting. I got the house security system and the agent's voice recorder," Pauly said as he pulled the small recorder from his pocket. The Don nodded and Alfred extended his hand. He touched the rewind and then the play button and we waited silently until the recorder played the part where Tony walked into the room, most of what happened was recorded. The Don nodded his head.

"Loose ends, what do we have for loose ends?"

"I have his niece in the foyer," said Pauly.

"I figured you would bring her. You promised you would let her live if she kept her mouth shut."

"I did."

"Take her for a nice ride on the boat about fifty miles off shore and let her swim back in. She will live as long as she can keep her mouth shut. Give her a life vest so it looks like an accident," said Alfred.

The Don nodded as he touched his chin.

"What if she makes it? If she floats for hours, she might get picked up," said Pauly.

"Cut open the life vest and take some of the floatation foam out, just enough so she sinks a little. It's supposed to rain later on and she'll wash up in a week wearing a vest — it'll look like an accident. What else do you have for loose ends? What will the feds think when they see a bullet in the agent's head? Norman Braski — right? He's a nobody," said Don Mancini.

"Tony wiped the gun down and put Sal's prints on it, it'll look like Sal shot the Fed and then took sleeping pills because his life was hopeless," said Pauly.

"Good, I didn't hear anything on the recording to make me worry, so you guys did a good job. Take care of the woman and tell the boys to be available for Sal's funeral, we need to pay respects so it will look good, especially when the niece will show up dead in a few weeks. Take the boys on a nice boat ride, they'll enjoy it."

We walked out and took the woman with us. I had enough killing for one day and I didn't want to go on the boat, but I saw how ruthless Tony and Pauly were so I kept my mouth shut. I couldn't help feeling sorry for the niece and truly I felt sorry for Sal and his son and all that the family had put him through.

It was an hour ride to the marina where the boat was docked. The boat was long and sleek, like the ones I saw in the movies.

The name on the bow was *'Filthy Rich'* and seemed befitting his lifestyle. I saw someone on the deck wave, it was Jimmy. We walked aboard and when the niece got the idea she was going for a ride, she cried and swore.

"The Don has a nice boat," I said to Pauly.

"This is Alfred's boat, Jimmy is the pilot. He grew up on this thing."

"That Jimmy never ceases to amaze me."

"He's a smart guy and the Don loves him like a son."

Two other guys were on the boat and manned the ropes and helped Jimmy with whatever orders he gave to get us out to sea. I felt like I was on an episode of 'Lifestyles of the Rich and Famous.' Tony found a life vest and made a small slit in one side and dug at the floatation filling. I didn't want to think about what came next. We went inside the cabin; it was full sized like being in a restaurant bar, dark wood and brass, and mirrors.

"I know you don't like what you see Sonny, but you didn't do eight years in the big house because of some snitch — I did, so I don't have no mercy for a piece of shit squealer like Sal. Let me tell you something: I don't know how the Don knows what's going to happen, but that man is like a psychic or something. If we would have waited another day, that Fed would have got the recorder back to his office and agents would be up our ass until they found something. Now he's dead, Sal's dead, and that piece of shit son is dead. Once the woman is dead he doesn't have any family left, so fuck them before they fuck you — do you understand? That's the mafia way."

"I guess so."

"You would if you got busted and had to do some hard time, you don't get that time back, you know. There's nothing like sitting in a cell watching your life pass by. I'll never go back inside, I'd rather die."

"I like to stay in the galley when you throw the woman overboard."

"If you would have been caught, she would have turned your ass in, and trust me when I say this, if that had happened and you could go back in time you'd throw her off the boat yourself with a chain on her feet. She can't live, she can't talk, and that's the bottom line. It's her or us— the needs of the many outweigh the needs of the few. Haven't you ever heard that?"

"Yeah, but in different situations."

"It's all the same."

Jimmy drove us miles and miles out in the ocean, he didn't seem like he was in a hurry to dump the woman — instead we ate lobsters and steamed clams, with corn on the cob. She was free to roam the boat and Tony talked her into having a few drinks. I wondered if she was an alcoholic. She ate and drank, and then took a seat at the stern and watched the waves roll off the water and dissipate into the sea. A pod of dolphins hopped over the boat's wake and she pointed to the leader as he came closer to the boat. She stood and admired him.

Then dusk approached and then darkness. Pauly sent me to the galley as he and Tony put the life vest on the drunken woman and tossed her overboard. Jimmy throttled the twin engines and within a few minutes we were miles from where she was dumped. There was no possible way she would get back to shore alive and the life vest was useless. She was dressed in dark clothes and no one would see her in the night. Before we came to shore, the rain began. Jimmy guided the boat into its slip like Cinderella putting on her dancing shoes. All of us got off the boat, except for the two deck hands. They stayed to wipe the boat down and put away whatever we had used.

Chapter Fifty-Three

Murder Suicide

I couldn't sleep that night, I was tempted to take a sleeping pill, but it reminded me of Sal. I wondered if he had started out like I had. Maybe he was innocent at one time, before his family corrupted him. The possibility that my life could end up the same as his made me wonder if I should take a bottle of pills myself. A year ago Sal was living large, with fancy cars, artwork, a few big houses, and a strip club. A younger woman, power, money, and respect — all of it gone.

The next morning I turned on the TV. I looked around for Alice as I got myself a bowl of cereal, but she had left a note on the refrigerator saying that she had gone to see Steve for the weekend and would be back on Sunday evening. I poured my flakes into the bowl and used the last of the milk to wet them. I stood with my back against the counter as I watched the TV and ate. A story flashed across the newscast, *Local business owner committed suicide in a murder-suicide scene at his Orlando home.* I had the volume too low and couldn't hear over my own crunching noises. I put the bowl down and went to the TV and sat in the closest chair to hear the details.

Sal's picture flashed across the screen and so did the F.B.I. agent's. Another agent was interviewed by a newscaster with a serious face. "At least four other people were in the room at the time of agent Braski's death. Exactly what prompted the incident is under investigation, and we are confident that arrests will be made."

I called Jimmy, but his phone was busy. I grabbed a jacket and ran to the car and drove to the Rent-a-Car center. When I arrived Tony was inside with Jimmy, who was still on the phone. He curled his finger for me to come close and when I did he handed me a car key fob and then pointed to the lot. I went out and Tony followed "We're in a world of shit, you know that?" he said.

I walked to the car and unlocked it. I didn't know what he wanted from me, until Tony grabbed the key fob and popped the trunk. It slowly lifted and I saw Lenny inside. Tony quickly closed it.

"That fucking Sal got the last laugh, didn't he?"

"I don't get it, why would he do this?" I said.

"We killed his partner and he evened the score. Someone had this car dropped here and the F.B.I. will most likely be here any minute. How are we going to explain this one?"

"I'm sure Jimmy will have the answer," I said.

"You better pray to sweet Jesus he does."

Then Jimmy walked out with his usual cool manor. "Take the car to this address," he said as he handed me a piece of paper. "Tony, go with him."

"What are we doing with the body? It's Lenny — we can't just dump him," said Tony.

"No, of course not. That's McCoey's home address — he's our family mortician. I just got off the phone with him and he'll take him to the funeral parlor. The garage door will be open, so drive in and wait for him."

Tony got behind the wheel and we left. He talked the entire ride. "I have a bad feeling about this, I knew that son of a bitch Sal killed Lenny, didn't I tell you that when he first turned up missing?"

I just nodded my head. We arrived at the address and once we pulled into the driveway Tony drove into the garage. A man was waiting for us and Tony popped the trunk. I was slow to get out, but Tony got out and lifted the trunk lid. The man pulled at Lenny's arms and Tony took his legs. They set him on the floor. "At least he didn't get shot in the head," McCoey said as he opened Lenny's jacket, exposing a gunshot wound to the heart. "I'll make him look good — nothing to worry about."

Tony helped put Lenny in the back of McCoey's station wagon. We left and drove back to the store. I followed Tony inside, where Jimmy was on the phone again. This time it sounded like he was talking to his father. Once he hung up, Tony tapped him on the elbow and said, "Sal shot him in the heart, so he can have an open casket."

"I just got off the phone with Alfred. He said Don Anthony Damato's Consigliere called him and explained what happened to Lenny."

"What do you mean, explained what happened to Lenny? Sal shot him in the gut, that's what the fuck happened to Lenny. I seen it for myself," said Tony.

"Turns out Sal borrowed money from Don Anthony Damato and he was using it to make payments to us. He said Lenny was shaking down Sal for money on the side. Don Damato's men where there to collect money and it went bad — he said Lenny pulled a gun and they shot him. They said they didn't know he was part of the Mancini family. He said it was a mistake. Bottom line is Lenny shouldn't have been there, it wasn't his job to collect Sal's payments."

"Damato's men dropped him off here so Lenny could get a proper burial. They could have ditched him in the everglades and let the gators get him, and honestly they didn't have to call — we would have thought Sal killed him. The good thing is that Don Damato will surrender the club to Don Mancini — sort of a peace offering. So we are not at war with the Damato family ... Understand?"

"So we're just going to sit back and let them get away with killing one of us?"

"It was a mistake. Don Damato paid for his funeral and he already sent Lenny's widow a cash settlement — I heard it was pretty healthy."

Tony put his hand on his head, "this is fucked."

Chapter Fifty-Four

Another One In The Ground

Lenny's funeral was two days later. Don Anthony Damato was there as well as his second in command. Don Carmine Mancini told everyone to respect them for doing the right thing. I could tell Tony wanted to say something, but he behaved himself. Once the funeral was over I noticed there were six well-dressed men I didn't recognize — F.B.I. agents with warrants for me, Pauly, and Tony. They took us downtown, with the embarrassment of handcuffs. They had the recording from Sal's body — he was wearing a wire and none of us was smart enough to check him. It turned out he didn't trust Braski, the F.B.I. agent, and he was making his own recording. The meeting between them took place at his house — he didn't want to be seen at a police station while he squealed on the Mancini family and the Damato family. Two members of the Damato family were also arrested. Alfred bailed us out.

Months went by and I slowly accepted that we would not get off scot free. Alfred plea bargained and it looked like we would be dismissed from murder charges, but had to serve five years for racketeering and extortion — with parole in two years. The closer the day for sentencing came; the more I wished I had never become a mobster. Shock went through the family as the news spread that Pauly took his own life. He put a gun in his mouth — keeping his vow that he'd never return to prison. Jimmy took his spot as Under Boss, and Tony and I would enter prison as full Capos.